GRASSHOPPER

By the same author

BARBARA VINE

GRASSHOPPER

LONDON   NEW YORK   SYDNEY   TORONTO

This edition published 2000
by BCA
By arrangement with Viking
The Penguin Group

First Reprint 2000

CN 6871

Set in Monotype Bembo
Typeset by Rowland Phototypesetting Ltd, Bury St Edmunds, Suffolk

Printed and bound in Great Britain by
Mackays of Chatham plc, Chatham, Kent

AUTHOR'S NOTE

Although I have done my best to render the appearance, atmosphere and architecture of Maida Vale and its environs in this novel, I have also allowed my imagination some play. Paddington Basin, the canal, the main streets, the churches, parks and gardens are much as they are in reality, but Russia Road does not exist and, though these are typical and characteristic names for the area, there are no such places as Torrington Gardens, Peterborough Avenue or Castlemaine Road.

I

They have sent me here because of what happened on the pylon. Or perhaps so that I don't have to see the pylon every time I go out or even look out of a window.

'We've thought of selling this house and moving,' my father said. 'Don't think it hasn't been in our minds. Still you won't . . .'

He left the sentence unfinished but I knew how he would have ended it. You won't always be here, he'd meant to say. A girl of your age, you won't live at home much longer, you'll be off to college or a job, a home of your own. And out of sight, out of mind, he meant too. Gradually people will stop thinking of us as the parents of *that* girl, they'll stop asking what kind of parents we were to bring up a girl who would do that, and they'll stop staring and pointing us out. Especially if you don't come home very often. Maybe they'll think you're dead. Maybe we'll tell them you are.

That last bit was in my imagination. I'm not saying they wish me dead. They have my welfare at heart, as my mother puts it. Which must be why they were so happy – happier than I've seen them since before the pylon day – when Max made his offer. The best they'd hoped for was a room in whatever accommodation the college had available or for me to be the fourth girl in a shared flat somewhere.

'A whole flat to yourself,' my mother said, 'and in a lovely part of town.'

I had a picture in my mind then of rows and rows of mock-Tudor houses, striped black and white like zebras, with pampas-grass in their front gardens and Audis outside their garages. Daniel and I had seen plenty of them, riding around the ring roads on his old Motoguzzi. Our London was the outer suburbs, Waltham Cross and Barnet, Colindale and Edgware, Uxbridge and Richmond and Purley. We counted the pylons and took photographs of the barbed-wire guards on their legs. We never penetrated as far as Maida Vale and we'd never heard of Little Venice. But still I thought 'a nice part of town' must mean houses like our house. How Max could have a flat in it, I couldn't imagine. Flats were in blocks, there had been plenty of those up along the North Circular Road too, great sprawling flat-roofed buildings painted custard colour with their names in letters of black or silver: Ferndean Court and Summerhill and Brook House. So when I got here this afternoon I wasn't prepared for what I found.

My father had been going to drive me. It's what parents do when their child goes off to college and a new place to live in. I've seen enough of it to know. They pack up the boot of the car and all the back of the car too, with clothes and sports gear and books and radio and CD player and maybe a computer and, of course, a hamper of food. It's a joyful occasion, a turning point in someone's life, and if it's the dad driving and the mother left behind, she's tearful but she's smiling too, calling out 'Good luck' and making the departing one promise to phone as soon as she's settled in and not to forget the cold chicken in the hamper and the homemade cake. My leaving home wasn't like that. I wouldn't have expected it to be and I never had much faith in my father's promise. As it happened, the car went in for service the day before and the garage phoned and said they'd like to keep it for another day to have a look at the electrics. Maybe Dad didn't fix it that way, I expect it was just a piece of luck for him. Anyway, they said it couldn't be helped, I'd just have to manage on the train.

So I left in much the same way as I've lived these past two years, under a cloud. After the pylon my parents had counselling, just as I did, and the counsellor told them they had to be understanding and supportive. It was their responsibility to help me put all that behind me and make a fresh start, not blame myself and feel guilty all the time. But they couldn't. I suppose they couldn't help themselves. I think they really saw me as evil. One of the ways they dealt with it was to tell me they didn't 'know where I got it from', as if every action you performed and every mistake you made had been made by a string of ancestors before you and passed on in a gene of thoughtlessness or daring – or evil. This morning and all through lunch they were giving me those looks that are a mix of wonderment and – well, resignation, I suppose. And I could see something else there too: relief, hope maybe, a fresh start for them as well.

I packed essentials into two suitcases and the rest into a trunk my father had had when he went off to university. My mother said she would send it on to 19 Russia Road, London w9. The whole journey would take less than two hours, with luck. She phoned for a taxi to take me to the station. In case I wouldn't do it, I suppose, if it was left to me. She hovered and I could tell she was wondering whether to kiss me. Neither of them had kissed me or so much as touched me for two years. It was as if I had a contagious disease. My father appeared from the garage where he has a little sanctuary for himself with a TV set and an armchair and said he expected I wanted to be off.

My mother looked at her watch. 'The taxi hasn't come yet.'

'I did try to save him,' I said. 'I held on till I couldn't hold on any more. I wasn't strong enough, that's all.'

'We don't talk about that, Clodagh,' my mother said. 'We've put that behind us.'

My father said, 'We have to get on with our lives.'

The taxi came. The man rang the bell and walked back down the path. Mum kissed the air an inch from my face. Dad laughed in an indulgent kind of way, a how-sweet-look-what-a-happy-family-we-are way, and he snatched up my cases and carried them to the taxi. Before I got into the back I took a last look at the pylon, planted there in the middle of the field, a skeleton with steel bones. My father, watching me, shook his head and went back into the house. We got to Ipswich with ten minutes to spare before the train came in.

Warwick Avenue is the name of the tube stop. I'd been in the underground before but not often, not since I was a child, not since the car wash. The worst thing that ever happened to me was the pylon but the next worst was the car wash. I'll write about that another time, not now. *Now* was the tube. I hated being down there, I clenched my fists and set my teeth, but there were plenty of people and that made it a bit better. A taxi would have taken me from Liverpool Street Station but I couldn't really afford it and besides it was too late now. I was down there, in the tunnels, the roofs pressing down on me, the walls crowding in. I concentrated on my London A–Z all the way from Oxford Circus to Paddington and when I knew I'd know the way without looking at it again, there was just one more mile to go before I could climb up into the light and air.

The first thing I saw when I came up the steps was a strange ugly church, just about as old as me, with a sharp-edged spire like a knife pointing up into the pale grey sky. I leant against its wall, breathing deeply, resolving never to go into that tube again. The church was the only new thing I could see. The houses, rows and rows of them, set at angles and in crescents and avenues and shorter streets, were all old. Victorian, I suppose, tall and pale and rather gracious with porticos over their doors and white pillars thick as tree trunks and steps leading up to them. And there were a great many real trees, tall and old, with yellow- and green- and brown-spotted trunks like the camouflage trousers Daniel used to wear. Max's wife Selina, whom I'd talked to on the phone, said something about a canal, that this was called Little Venice because of a canal, but I couldn't see it, not the direction I was walking in, along Warwick Avenue itself, going northwards.

I was glad I hadn't filled those cases but left most of my stuff to be sent on in Dad's trunk. They were quite heavy enough as it was. There wasn't much traffic, not moving, that is. All the cars were parked in the street, nose to tail, lining the pavements. A few people passed me, all young, and all of them belonging to what newspapers call 'ethnic minorities'. That must be hateful, if you're black or Chinese or one of these beautiful people from East Africa, to be called an ethnic minority. I found Russia Road without any trouble, as it was exactly where the A–Z said it would be, turning out of Castlemaine Road at a right angle.

It dips down a hillside to a roundabout at the bottom with flowers and bushes in the middle of it and mansions like Italian palaces all round. Russia Road itself is about as far from the idea of a suburb I had as that suburb is from a country lane. I don't know why the words came into my head because I'd never thought them before or even know what they really mean, but I said to myself: Gothic London. The buildings on the left side were very tall, almost like towers joined together in a solid red-brick unbroken row. I hadn't known people could build so high all that time ago, I thought it had come in with modern tower blocks. These houses are so tall they must shut out the sun until it gets very high in the sky. The camouflage trees look quite small in front of them.

On the other side, the odd-numbered side, the buildings are nearly as tall, maybe about ten feet shorter. I've never seen anything like them before. They are in three blocks and all the blocks are different.

4

All they have in common is that they are all four storeys high and all have flights of stone steps climbing to their front doors. The first set I passed are painted a pale cream colour and have windows with rounded tops except for the big bays on the ground floor and rounded porticos held up at the ends by lions' faces resting on sharp-clawed paws. After them comes red brick as on the opposite side, with windows set in ivory-coloured stone blocks and around the middle of the houses and the edge of the roof kind of friezes in the same ivory with tops like on a castle – castellated, is it called? Max's house is the first one in the last block (or the last if you're going the other way), No. 19, in a row built of silvery grey bricks and red bricks in a kind of mosaic design. All the paintwork is black and cream on his house and quite new and shiny, but some of the others need painting and some need a complete cleaning.

Instead of going straight up to the front door of 19, I walked along looking at the faces. Above every front door, above the balconies which run round at this level and look like black lace, is a window made of three arched panes, the centre arch being the highest, its pointed top set amid plaster garlands of flowers and leaves, and among them, in a wreath of leaves is a different face. I mean a different face on each house, an old man with a beard and drooping moustache, a young lady with her hair looped back and a mantilla set on it, a young man like a picture I once saw of Lord Byron, another in a turban. Some have been cleaned up and repainted and look fresh and new while others are still grimed with soot which covers the faces like a dark veil.

I dragged my cases back and looked up and up and up. Max's house is very clean, as if someone regularly washes it. One of the teachers at school told me that in Holland the people wash the fronts of their houses but I have never heard of anyone doing it here. The face on his house is a girl's and she wears a kind of cap on her long flowing curls. The leaves around her look like vine leaves and the flowers like lilies. Up above that are another three rows of windows, the first row with arched tops, the other two just ordinary squares. Then I saw what I'd missed before. There are more windows in the bit of roof that comes over the top like a pelmet of grey slates. So the house had five storeys, not four.

Why didn't I notice the basement? Maybe because I always lift up my eyes to the heights. I went up the path, set the cases down and rang the bell. Selina came to the door. I knew who she was, I'd seen her on television, as everyone in the whole country must have, so perhaps she didn't think she needed to say. Anyway, I think she's a woman who never uses people's names, her own or anyone else's, she calls them 'darling'.

'Why didn't you have a taxi, darling?' she said. 'It's much too far to carry cases.'

In spite of that 'darling' she said it as if I'd done something wrong. Or I think she did. The trouble is, as my counsellor told me, I'm paranoid. I see and hear slights, snubs, rebukes. Maybe because I've had so many. Maybe Selina was just concerned for me. She looked behind her, as if she thought someone might appear who would carry the cases. No one did. She picked up one of them, winced at its weight, and left the other to me.

I expected to climb stairs. I even thought they might have a lift. We went down a long passage. There was a door at the end of it and, behind the door, stairs going down. I followed. She put the case down the moment she got to the bottom. I think there were eleven stairs. I'll count them tomorrow. Not that it matters. We were below ground and although it was bright outside and would be for another three hours, we had to put the lights on.

'It's all yours, darling,' Selina said. 'Have a look round. When you've tidied yourself, come up to the first floor and we'll have supper. Max should be back soon.'

'The first floor?' I said.

'One flight above the front door.'

Claustrophobia is what it is, I suppose. Although I'm not sure about that. I'm not afraid of being in small rooms or shut in cupboards or lifts. It's tunnels and underground places I can't stand. I had borne it in the train because that was the only way of getting to Russia Road that I knew, but it had half-killed me. As I looked around the place I was to live in, I vowed to myself that at least I would never go in the tube again, I would take buses or walk, I would never use underpasses, even if it meant going a mile out of my way to avoid them. But I couldn't vow not to live here, I *am* living here, writing this diary here, trying to shrink myself very small and hard and invulnerable, so that the walls don't move in more closely upon me and crush me to death. It isn't that it's small but that it's below ground level . . .

2

I was nineteen when I wrote that.

Ever since I'd learnt to write, I'd kept a diary. Maybe it was because I was an only child and had no one to tell things to or else I'm a natural diarist. Some people are. It hasn't much to do with being a writer or good at it or anything. It's more a need to record what you think worth recording. All my life I have written down things that happened to me when they were really important or just seemed important to me. The ordinary day-to-day stuff never got a mention until I met Silver and after that nothing was ordinary any more.

I took my diaries with me to Max's, then to Silver's, back to Suffolk, then to Beryl's, to the various colleges I went to, to the flat we had in the East End and finally here, to our home. Most of the entries, naturally, were written in the first person. All but one. And that, which chronicles the most terrible thing that had ever happened to me up to that date, I seem to have written in the form of a short story. Why? All these years later I can't remember writing it or what reason I had for writing it. I had no literary ambitions then or at any time. What I do now and what I love doing must be as far from being an author as one can get. I wonder if my counsellor suggested that I write it all down as an exercise in therapy, or if, later on, the psychiatrist I was referred to after my conviction told me to do it and write it as if it'd happened to someone else. I don't know, I don't remember. I'd even forgotten that I'd kept it and it was only seeing Liv again that made me search for it and the papers that were with it.

The call from a Mrs Clarkson had come in the afternoon before. Darren, who works for me, took the message (or one of his girlfriends did) and sent it over by e-mail along with all the other calls for the day. He was tied up, as he put it, with a rewiring job, which brought me a picture of a very handsome lithe black man struggling to escape – like Leviathan, was it? – from coils of cable come alive like snakes.

So Mrs Clarkson and her dimmer switches in Downshire Hill were left to me and I made her my first call.

I live, and have lived since just before I got married six months ago, in the penthouse on top of a block of flats in Highgate. The view over London is stupendous. I can step out of my living room on to my roof garden. The only thing about it I don't much care for is the underground car park. It could be worse, though. There's no part of it from which you can't see between the concrete uprights that support the block to the light and air outside. Besides, I'm a lot better about enclosed spaces now. I've even been in the car wash all by myself and sat there with the soapsuds blinding me and the brushes slurping and the red darkness enclosing me like the belly of a whale.

Hampstead is just at the other end of the Spaniards Road and I was at the house in Downshire Hill in less than ten minutes. By the look of things, builders had been doing some sort of interior conversion. Debris in grey plastic sacks and piles of broken timber filled the front garden, which, fortunately, was mostly paved. A face at the downstairs window, no more than a pale blur, told me an anxious Mrs Clarkson was on the look-out for my arrival. Once she had seen the white van with C. Brown and Co. Ltd, Electrical Engineers, printed on it in red above my logo of the curve of a C with the double loop of a B inside it (logos should always be as simple as possible), she dropped the curtain and went to let me in. I recognized her before I reached the door. Whether she recognized me then I couldn't be sure because, of course, as nearly always happens, she was amazed to see a woman at all.

There still aren't all that many female electricians and there are very few highly qualified ones with their own businesses like me. Because I'm proud of what I do and I know I'm good at it, I'm quite prepared to boast about landing the contract for the electrics for a hotel of the status of the Four Seasons in Knightsbridge, and later for those new houses they're building in Paddington Basin. But most people think it very strange indeed when they call C. Brown and Co. and a woman turns up. Once or twice I've even been told I wasn't wanted, thank you very much, they'd sent for a *real* electrician. Mrs Clarkson gave me just such a doubtful wary look and said (which no one had ever said before), 'Isn't your husband coming?'

I didn't laugh, though I wanted to. Nor did I say my husband was in Africa and knew nothing about electricity anyway. 'You'll have to put up with me,' I said. 'I'm the electrician.'

'All right then, if you think you can do it.'

'Don't know what it is yet,' I said, 'but I'll give it a go.'

That house was astounding inside, open-plan, minimalist and bleak. The living room, marble-floored and islanded with pieces of furniture shaped like bright-coloured grubs or molluscs, was cut off diagonally by a gallery rail and its ceiling ended at the same point and angle. Above was soaring space that terminated as far as I could see in a turret of glass. It might have been warm up there in the turret but it was very cold down here. I looked for candles, once Liv's undisputed accessory, but couldn't see any. Lamps were everywhere, standards that were glass funnels on steel stems apparently growing out of the floor, wall lights like champagne flutes and wall lights like Roman vases, and two great chandeliers, the modern sort that you see in international hotels (I don't stay in them, I rewire them) that look like glaciers or frozen waterfalls. Mr Clarkson must be doing very well for himself.

I wasn't sure at that point whether to enlighten his wife or not. Perhaps 'enlighten' isn't the word, for by now I was sure she knew me just as I knew her. It might be better to do the job, whatever it was, and leave. Get down to Paddington Basin where I had a meeting at midday with the Clerk of Works. She didn't look at me and I realized that she hadn't looked at me after that first amazed stare.

'I don't know if you can do it,' she said, and for the first time I heard the accent that was once so familiar, the sing-song rhythm of the Swede speaking English. Her English was perfect now, but she was nervous. 'I mean, maybe I should have got the original electricians back. But they've disappeared, they're not in the phone book. It's the switches, they don't work – well, they don't do what they're supposed to. I mean, there are supposed to be thirty-two ways of having the lights on in this room, but when you push those buttons you just get a lot of bright light.'

It wasn't for me to ask who the hell would *want* thirty-two light-level variations. The rich are different. They have more money. So no doubt they want as much or as little light as they are prepared to pay for. As that went through my head, I also thought that the way I was going, it might not be too long before I was rich myself.

I went back to the van and got my toolbag. On my way back in I glanced at myself in the enormous mirror with a steel frame and steel stars clustered about in the corners of it which covered one wall of the hall. Who can tell if they look different from how they looked eleven years before? Everyone must do, I suppose. I saw a tall thin woman in the same gear as Darren wears, jeans and T-shirt and leather jacket, with very short black hair, nearly-black eyes and eyebrows that draw together all the time in a way that's already giving her frown lines. The best thing about my face is my cheekbones, which in Silver's words are sharp enough to cut cheese. The frown lines aged me, I supposed, not much caring, as did the crinkles round my eyes that come from enjoying life.

Liv looked older but she also looked better. She looked beautiful. The make-up she had on was the kind you can have done in the cosmetics department of big stores. It takes half an hour to get it right, longer if you do it yourself. Her fair hair, which was always very long, shaggy and tangled before that look was fashionable, was now absolutely straight, cut just to cover her ears with a straight-across fringe, and bleached or dyed the colour of unsalted butter. I'd seen her looking at my hands (rather than my face). All I can say about mine is that at least they're clean. Hers were white as milk and the nails very long, square-trimmed and painted a silvery ultramarine blue. They matched the sapphire in the ring on the third finger of her left hand. What fascinated me most about her was the thing she wore round her neck. I knew what it was, though I could hardly believe my eyes and my memory.

While I was outside she had disappeared. I found a door in the hall that looked as if a cupboard might be inside but in fact opened on to a wall of keypads and plateswitches as well as several fuse boxes, and set to work. The way the 'original electricians' had wired it up was a mess and probably quite dangerous. I would have to turn the power off before I began and from then on it would be a simple job that didn't take much thought. I called out to her that she'd be without electricity for the next half-hour but there was no answer, so I cut the power to the circuit on this floor and maybe to the one below it too, it was hard to tell.

I'd been sorting out the various connections and thinking about Liv and her dizzy ascent to where she now was, twelve years later, wondering of course how she'd done it, when a woman holding the hand of a child on either side of her came down the wide staircase. I'm not good at children's ages but I would think the boy was about four and the girl three. The woman, the girl, was obviously an au pair-cum-nanny. There's a look that identifies them, you can always tell. Invariably they have puzzled, anxious expressions, pink noses, chapped lips, long hair, and they are always dressed the same, in jeans and big sweaters and lace-up boots, as if they're off hill-walking in the Cairngorms rather than taking the kids on a trip to South End Green. I exaggerate, but they often do look like that and this one was more like that than usual. She passed me on her way to the front door and to my 'Good morning' returned a shy smile. So, exactly, had Liv looked when she had just such a job with just such children. Just such a house as this, only no doubt more traditional in its design and its furnishing, and in Maida Vale not Hampstead, had she run away from and joined us in our refuge on top of the world.

It was seeing the au pair-nanny and the children that were undoubtedly Liv's and 'Mr Clarkson's' that decided me. Having found being in her presence a mite awkward, I now wanted her to come back. I switched the power on. I tested the lights, going through the thirty-two permutations I'd achieved. In fact, it was thirty-six, which made me feel quite pleased with myself. Whether she was upstairs or downstairs I'd no idea, but I went to the gallery rail and the widely curving wrought-iron staircase that led into another vast chamber below and called out what I always call out when I don't know the customer's name or, as in this case, don't want to use it.

'Are you there?'

No answer. I called again. She appeared behind me, materializing from some room whose existence I hadn't suspected. 'Liv,' I said.

Again the fear flashed in her well-painted, black-outlined blue eyes. I saw I must be gentle. What was curious and funny to me was a threat to her. I forced myself to take my eyes off that lump of ivory, that *tooth* she wore mounted in gold on a chain round her neck.

'Liv, I knew you at once,' I said. 'Please don't be anxious. You do know me, don't you?'

She shook her head, then nodded. 'Chloe,' she said.

It was just possible she had forgotten my true name. 'Clodagh,' I said, 'Clodagh Brown.'

She whispered, 'C. Brown and Co. Ltd. I found you in the *Yellow Pages*. How was I to know?'

'I've done the job. Do you want to try your lights?'

She didn't move, apart from her hands. She began wringing her hands, the blue nails like frightened beetles wildly scurrying this way and that. Then, incredibly, in a high voice, she said, 'I'm trying to think where we met. It must have been at college. Or when I was Lavinia's PA, I met so many people, it's hard to recall . . .'

I took pity on her. I'd been on the point of saying that it was in Russia Road, on the top of Silver's parents' house, on the roofs, don't you *remember*? Don't you remember what happened? Don't you remember Jonny and *Wim*? I didn't say any of those things. I hadn't the heart to torture her further. Instead I took her through the light sequences. There wasn't a chance she'd remember which switches worked what. Her head would be full of me and of the threat I represented. I wanted to be able to say to her that she need never see me again, never fear me, but I didn't know how to begin. I couldn't find any words to say what in any case would only result in her telling me she didn't know what I meant.

'Right,' I said, 'I'll be on my way.'

'Would you like me to pay you now or will you send in your account?'

'I'll send you the bill,' I said.

She'd closed the door before I'd reached the front gate. And the garden path was only a few yards long. I'd frightened her very badly. My usual procedure, when I've done a job for a new customer, is to call them a couple of days later and check that all is well. It's a good system. In a very few cases all isn't well and they're foaming at the mouth because they've forgotten your name and haven't got the bill yet. On the other hand, when all is well as it mostly is, calling them puts your name back in their minds as well as making them think you're a thoughtful caring person. I decided I'd waive this calling back in Liv's case. It would do more harm than good. She would never call me again anyway. There, as it happens, I was wrong but I didn't know that at the time.

I'd be early for my next appointment but I drove straight down there just the same. I quite often get called out to the Maida Vale area and sometimes to Little Venice, once even to Russia Road, but I'd never been back to Paddington Basin since I was chucked out of the Grand Union Polytechnic and their mixed course in Business Studies and Psychology. Even now I can't think of that place, since renamed the University of Latimer, without shuddering and then laughing at my shudders. But then, the only way I could find of getting there without one way or another descending below ground level was to walk along the canal bank and thus pass *under* the Westway exit road but not *underground*.

You can't drive to the Basin. You have to park your car as best you can (and pay a pound an hour) in Howley Place or Delamere Terrace and walk down through the little garden that overlooks the point at which the canal branches and the island where they say Browning used to sit and write his poetry. They're big on Browning round there. There's even a pub called the Robert Browning. Selina once had an apron with a picture of him and Elizabeth Barrett on it. A path that no one would suspect is there, still less that it leads anywhere of importance, runs down through a kind of shrubbery and brings you out on to the canal bank and the bridge. Above you is the Harrow Road and it's quite a wide bridge but not dark enough under there or shut in enough to upset the claustrophobic. On the other side of the canal are all the houseboats, moored aft to bows, all with their names on their sides in painted wreaths of flowers, *Susannah* and *Water Queen* and *Cicero* and *Garda*, plants in pots on their roofs and plants on the canal bank in the gardens the boat people have made. At this time of the year those gardens are full of tulips and wallflowers in bloom. The boats are doomed, of course. Once building starts down here, and building is scheduled for the whole of the Basin, the boats will go and the gardens, the wild buddleias that push their purple spires out of every cranny and the elder trees with their flat white platelets of bloom and the brambles and nettles and tall milk thistles – and the mess and awful slumminess too.

The clearing on this side has already started so I was able to walk quite a long way down, under the Westway exit and past the point where the underpass comes out. On the other side, on the towpath between the boats and the gardens, was where, twelve years ago, I first saw Wim. He was talking to a man on one of the boats, though who he was I never found out, and the two of them were gazing upwards at the sky and the traffic roaring along the great curved concrete flyover. It was cold that day. The boats were covered in tarpaulins like horses in coats, the flowers had been nipped and browned by the first frosts, and an icy mist hung over the motionless dull green water. I didn't know it was Wim then, I didn't know who he was or where he lived, only that his face was one of the strangest and most beautiful I'd ever seen, away from the cinema or TV screen.

The Clerk of Works is already in residence down there, in a temporary building too grand to be called a hut. He didn't react to my turning out to be a woman, he expected that, we'd talked on the phone. We studied the architect's plans together and went on a tour of the cleared area, trying to form some sort of idea in our minds as to how it would look when rows of tall houses faced each other across the wide lake the Basin becomes at this point. It was after two by then. He was pleased as men are when I did as I always do in this situation and produced from my toolbag a rather carefully thought-out lunch for two. Smoked salmon sandwiches this time, pâté and cheese and Bath Olivers and strawberry tarts I'd stopped off on my way and bought from Raoul's. A man wouldn't think of doing that but when I do it, even if he tends to be sexist, he'll think that there may be more to having a woman electrician on the job than first meets the eye. You see, I can't afford to neglect any move that might improve my career chances or enhance my reputation.

After that I dropped in to see Beryl, for a chat and a cup of tea. I had one more call to make that day. It was on my way home, a town house in Tufnell Park, and I'd more or less guessed what it was before I got there. You'd be surprised how many householders can't mend a fuse. And not only can't mend it but don't even know it needs mending and that that's what the trouble is. I charge £40 as a minimum for any call-out and it does puzzle me how anyone would rather pay that amount of money for a job that takes five minutes than get someone like me to show them how to perform this simple operation. That would cost them £40 too but at least it would be a one-off. I've tried, I've offered, but they either refuse point-blank or ask me why I think they've sent for me. One woman even said she wouldn't keep a dog and bark herself.

I was ignorant about electricity myself once, criminally ignorant, you might say, and it cost me dear, me and Daniel, especially Daniel. If I'm out of my glass house now and can therefore throw stones, I'll never forget being inside it, I'll never forget messing with the mystery and the way it struck back.

Tufnell Park to home on North Hill took me ten minutes. It'd be less than five when the traffic is light. The block I live in is ten floors high and so far, unlike in Beryl's tower on the Harrow Road, the lift has always been in working order. My flats are called Cityscape Court but you can see far more than the city from my roof garden: the river like a silver string, Greenwich and the Observatory and the green hills beyond, a segment of the Millennium Dome if you know where to look for it, a hundred church spires and towers, the Royal Festival Hall and the National Theatre, and on this side the Palace of Westminster with the sun shining on its bright pinnacles and the face of Big Ben. I did what I always do at this hour, if I'm home in good time, that is, and if it's warm enough, take my drink out on to the roof garden, sit in one of my very comfortable loungers at my cane and glass table and gaze and gaze at the great panorama that lies below and around me. Earth hath not anything to show more fair, as the only poem I ever remember learning at school puts it. But no, not the only one, there was another, and that too is part of this story that I'm writing. Having kept a diary as I went along, not every day or even every week but just from time to time, is going to help me do that.

In winter I sit just inside the window or glass wall, rather, that forms the whole garden side of my flat. In summer or on warm spring evenings or in autumn before the air gets damp and the chill settles in, I'm outside. There's only one person I really want and he's 3,000 miles away. So, apart from that, being alone at this time suits me fine. Besides, I'm not alone, I've got Mabel. She always comes out from whichever bed she's been on to greet me when I get home and always accompanies me outside.

I don't want to be disturbed, I want to sit and gaze and stroke Mabel on my lap and think about my day and drink my drink. Always gin and tonic or vodka and soda, by the way. In my opinion, unless you're a wine drinker, you're either a white-spirit person or a brown-spirit person and I'm the former. I'm sociable enough, I like to see my friends – I'd rather see my husband but that can't be, not yet – I like it a lot if Darren drops in as he sometimes does on his way to Junilla's or Campaspe's, or if other friends come, but not before eight, please.

By eight I've had my drink and thought my thoughts and gazed my fill and I'm ready to eat.

That evening, not unnaturally, those thoughts were of twelve years ago. Along with my gin and tonic I'd brought outside those diary extracts and that curious story I'd written at maybe a therapist's behest. Strange, but I nearly said 'she' there instead of 'I', yet I know quite well it was me to whom all those things happened, not another. Whatever some people say, and I think Liv may be one of them, we were not once 'someone else', we didn't live in 'another life' or a 'different world', that's just a cop-out, a way of defending our actions because since then, of course, we've changed out of all knowledge, we're not 'the same person'. But we are. The girl who climbed pylons and the girl who scaled the roofs is me, and without her and the things she did and the crimes, if you like, she committed, I wouldn't be the woman I am today. And for better, for worse, she's all I have.

One thing, for the story I wrote the evening I got to Max's house, I underplayed the feelings I had about the underground. I made it look as if being in it, its passages, its escalators and above all its trains, wasn't so bad, just a bit unpleasant but something I could control. In fact, it was very different from that. I went down into it without knowing what it was, having had no experience of it since I was a small child, and found the very heart of terror. If you've ever read Orwell's *Nineteen Eighty-four*, you'll remember the torture of Winston Smith with the things he fears more than any others, the objects of his phobia. In his case it was white rats, in mine it would be tunnels. I have never been in the underground since that afternoon. I shall never forget it.

These days I can manage below ground level. I've had to, I've had to work in basements and cellars, and I don't like it, but it was either that or pick another trade. Airline pilot? Steeplejack? Bungee-jumping instructor? I've dealt with my problem by telling myself it was the only obstacle I had to surmount once I had begun on the one thing I really wanted to do. The course itself wasn't difficult, perhaps because I loved it, the maths wasn't a problem for long, and when I started on the practical work I was in my element. All right, a pun *was* intended there. So I disciplined myself when I had to work underground and I did it by concentrating on the work and the work only, doing my

16

best not to look around me, not to see the walls, the lack of windows, not to feel the ceiling dipping down to crush me. Sometimes I could even teach myself to imagine different surroundings while I was down there, a high-up airy glass roof (rather like Liv's), wide-open doors, and through them all the bright blue and white sky. But mostly I applied myself to the microcosm of the cables in front of me, the new point I was putting in, the small immediate area of intricate but precise wiring. Guy Wharton once told me that in the sweatshops of the East End women employees were preferred for the french polishing because their fingers were smaller and more delicate than men's. And that's one of the reasons women make good electricians. I think I perfected the technique of using my small (I don't know about delicate) fingers accurately and fast down in those subterranean places because I seldom looked elsewhere but at what those fingers were doing, and never paused or got up to stretch or to smoke a cigarette until the job was done and I was out of there.

But that evening in September when I first came to Russia Road and Max's house, I was as bad a claustrophobic as you can be. It had all started when Dad took me with him to wash the car. I was about ten. Our local garage had had a car wash put in, the latest thing, I suppose it was, in Suffolk in the seventies. Dad was thrilled, he'd never used one, and he hated cleaning the car. And, to do him justice, he thought I'd be thrilled too. It was to be a treat.

You had to put coins into a slot machine in those days, it was before punching in a code came in. Dad put in the coins, checked all the windows were shut, and moved the car forward until the light went red. I didn't know what to expect and I don't suppose he did. I probably thought it would be a bit like a bigger and more powerful shower and I had no idea it would start so quickly. The roar it made was like a threat. And the big red brushes coming so fast, covering the whole car in a swirling mass which shut out all light and air, which seemed to be swallowing the car in its gulping crimson throat, that was what started me screaming. Dad was angry, he thought I was fooling around, pretending to be frightened, and he was rough with me. I put my hand over my mouth to stop the sounds coming and then the worst thing happened. The whole roof came down, a metal bar moving towards the windscreen. It was going to smash the glass, pass right through the glass and crash into my face, it was going to chop my head off. I tried to get out, of course I did. I opened the door and water came into the car, I was screaming all the time. That the bar wasn't going to cut my head off or smash my brains to a pulp – well, that was evident by then but I was still screaming. When they say someone is beside herself, that describes how I was. Dad didn't know what to do, I can see that now, but I didn't then. The car was filling with water inside. He had to get the door shut before the metal frame part of the car wash ripped it off and he had to calm me down, which he did by slapping my face. I suppose he was nearly as frightened as I was. I was afraid of being swallowed up by the car wash but he was afraid his daughter had gone mad.

That was the beginning of it. I had never done anything about it and no one had ever shown much interest. All Dad wanted to do was forget and when I told Mum she thought I was exaggerating. But really, what could they have done? Did they even know I had a phobia about enclosed spaces? For one thing, the Suffolk countryside is probably one of the best places on earth to *be* a claustrophobic, except for the Sahara Desert. It's all wide open spaces, huge fields, enormous skies, flat land, level horizons. Apart from seaside resorts, there must be more bungalows in Suffolk than anywhere in the British Isles, and you seldom find an ordinary house more than two storeys high. There may be underpasses beneath a few big roads but I'd never seen them. I'd never seen caves either or houses with cellars. Our house was all on two floors with big picture windows and my school was a modern building mostly made of glass. The world there was a claustrophobic's paradise. And suddenly I was in Russia Road, having arrived after a terrible journey through tunnels, to find myself doomed to live for three years, a lifetime when you're nineteen, in a place where very little light ever came and no window's top reached even as far as street level.

Max's grandmother had lived down there. He told me so while we had supper. As soon as he could afford it, he bought the house and moved her into the basement from the place she lived in near Paddington Station, a Victorian cottage which was damp and subsiding and due to be demolished. After his father had left home and his mother died, she had brought him up in that house and made many sacrifices for him so that he could have his chance of a good education. Here Max, being Max, couldn't resist saying that of course he won scholarships and that helped. His grandmother was very old when he brought her to Russia Road and past ninety when she died.

'She didn't actually die downstairs, if that's what you're thinking, darling,' Selina said. 'She doesn't haunt the place.'

I hadn't supposed she did. That would have been the least of my worries. Max looked pained, as if suggesting that coming back as a ghost was an insult to old Mrs Fisherton's memory, as perhaps it was.

'All the furniture was hers,' he said fondly. 'I've kept it just as she left it.'

His face wore that dreamy sorrowful look it often did when he spoke of the past. Twelve years ago he must have been about sixty. He's dead now but he was my mother's first cousin, her father's brother's son, that brother being the man who had deserted his family when his child was just two. Max was a professor of Modern History at London university. By the sound of it he had spent all his twenties getting one degree after another, he had more of them than anyone I've ever come across. All that time, my mother used to say, old Mrs Fisherton went out office cleaning and flat cleaning to give him an allowance over and above whatever it was the scholarships paid. He was a very tall, very thin man for his age, a condition of fitness he put down to jogging round Regent's Park three mornings a week. I never saw him dressed otherwise than casually, in tracksuits most of the time, through the round necklines of which his long scaly neck emerged like a turtle's. For work he wore a tweed jacket over one of those tracksuit tops and a pair of baggy trousers. His face was not so much boyish as babyish, though of course an elderly baby's. His smooth forehead bulged and so did his cheeks, his eyes were round and his nose turned up. What hair he had left he grew long at the back, to compensate perhaps for the lack of much at the front. It was white and fluffy and covered his ears.

Strangely enough, for Selina was thought of as good-looking, he and she were rather alike. You could have taken her for his much younger sister. She was — is, I suppose — a small woman but no one would have called her short, for that word implies stockiness and solidity. Selina is slight and dainty, a Barbie doll or a fairy on a Christmas tree. Her legs are shapely and beautifully carved, as if made of some pale shiny wood such as sycamore and turned on a lathe. Her face is shaped like a plump heart and her eyes bulge a little, her nose is delicately tip-tilted, her mouth another heart. Round cheeks repeat themselves in her alarmingly large, gravity-defying breasts which pout and bounce, the nipples showing themselves like fingertips pointing through her clothes whenever she is animated.

I never saw her in trousers or sweaters. She was as formal in her dress as he was casual, favouring little suits with short flared skirts and nipped waist jackets or dresses with belts and big padded shoulders. Lots of jewellery, lots of heavy make-up, her nails always painted, her mouth outlined in dark red and filled in with rose-pink to make it look even juicier and plumper. I've met a lot of actresses over the past few years, seeing to the electrics in their flats and houses, some of them very famous, and off-set or off-stage they've always looked – well, like me, jeans and T-shirts, no make-up, and as if they've never seen the inside of a hairdresser's. Perhaps Selina hadn't been in the business long enough to get into actressy ways. After years spent 'resting' or taking jobs not much better than an extra's, she'd auditioned for the part of Annabel, the licensee of the Crown and Anchor in *Streetwise*, never expecting to get it or if she did that the serial would run and run, be still running after fourteen years, and its four stars become more famous than actors who had been on the stage for a lifetime.

He and she seemed as unsuited to each other as any couple I've ever known. He was dry, academic, censorious, short-tempered with anything he called ignorance, an intellectual snob; she was almost uneducated, frivolous and flashy. She loved parties, going to them and giving them, the kind where people never sit down but stand around, talking media gossip, and no one knows anyone else better than as a party acquaintance. But in spite of the 'darlings', the word she used with everyone from Max to the man who came to mend the dishwasher, she was as cold and wary, judgemental, impatient as he.

So perhaps they did have things in common. He met her when his university gave her an honorary degree. Not a doctorate, they were too mean for that and she, after all, was only the star of a sitcom. They gave her an M.Litt. (Drama). I expect they made it up for the occasion. Max was at the degree congregation and afterwards the Vice-Chancellor asked him to sit next to her at tea. He hadn't wanted to, he'd tried to get out of it, but after they'd eaten their sandwiches and their meringues he was in love for the first time in his life and a lost man. At least, according to Selina's often repeated account of this meeting, he was. I heard it for the first time that first evening, Max sitting by, picking at his microwaved prefrozen lasagne and defrosted *petits pois*, saying nothing but sometimes giving little tight smiles, not sympathizing or approving or even remembering, but as if he knew some secret that Selina and I didn't. Perhaps it was only his own intellectual superiority to almost everyone.

We had a Sara Lee chocolate cake for the next course and then Nescafé with Longlife cream. My mother was a good cook and I wasn't used to this sort of food. I sound ungrateful, I *was* ungrateful, but although I didn't know it then, it was not only the first but, with the exception of a birthday lunch, the last meal I was ever to be given by Selina and Max. When it was over, the moment we got up from the table, she dismissed me below stairs, with the words, 'You'll want to settle in, darling, so we'll say good night.'

There were five minutes to go before half past eight, and what I also didn't know then but soon learnt was that on every weekday evening she was at home she watched herself in *Streetwise*. If not at home, she was bound not to be far from a television set, and her hosts at whatever gathering she was at would be obliged to suffer half an hour of banality in Floral Grove, sw12. I really shouldn't take this superior line, it's wrong of me, for I watched it myself evening after evening for a long time, having nothing better to do than sit close up to old Mrs Fisherton's black and white set, staring at the screen rather than at the encroaching walls and descending ceiling.

Selina said that she supposed I hadn't brought anything with me for my breakfast. There were shops not far away that stayed open 'till all hours'. I wouldn't want to go 'out there at this hour', she said in a doubtful interrogatory tone. Perhaps she expected me to say there was nothing I'd like better than foraging for food in the sinister twilit streets of Maida Vale, but I didn't, I didn't know what to say. All my life breakfast had just appeared, to be eaten or rejected as it took my fancy. I was spoilt, wasn't I? I took too much for granted. Selina began one of those conversations with herself that were quite common with her and the only times she didn't call the person she was talking to 'darling'. How would I manage for breakfast? She could let me have something. Yes, but what? They never had cooked breakfasts, did they? She had to watch her figure for professional reasons. Perhaps cornflakes could be managed. What about bread? I would need butter and milk, there was no end to it. Still, it was only the once and after that, when I had settled in ...

Max took absolutely no notice of any of this. He had got up, found himself a book and come back to the table where he sat reading with total concentration. I just stood there, aware of the light in this dining room and realizing that the big triple-paned arched window was the one where the girl's face was among the lilies and the vine leaves. I realized too, though it may not have been at that precise time, that once I had got used to the concept of a flat *in a house*, I simply took it for granted that it would be in the top of that house, would in fact be the top floor.

I took the tray of food Selina gave me, two slices from a sliced loaf, a pat of butter, a teabag and about a quarter of a pint of milk in a small water glass, a bowl of cornflakes and a plate with a spoonful of marmalade on the edge of it. Also on the tray was a key.

'You've got your own door into the area, darling.'

What was an area, apart from being a piece of land or a part of a town? I didn't like to ask. No doubt I would find out.

'Good night, then,' Selina said. She tapped the spine of Max's book with a long orchid-pink fingernail. 'Say good night, darling.'

'Good night,' said Max, without looking up.

The *Streetwise* signature tune followed me downstairs. I put the hall light on before taking the plunge to the subterranean. It was rather like diving into a pool of dark water whose depth you've no idea of but you know it's many fathoms and it may drown you. I didn't really plunge, though, I walked down carefully, carrying my tray, and fumbled about on the wall till I found the switch. The lamps at old Mrs Fisherton's (which was what I came to call the place) were all of very low wattage. Forty watts, I suppose now. Then, though I know in saying this that I'm presenting myself as just as feeble as those lamps – sorry, that's an electrician's word, lightbulbs to you – I thought it was the way things were and there was nothing I could do about it.

You can always tell an old lady's place from anyone else's. It doesn't seem to matter at what period they were young, the thirties, the twenties, the teens of the century or even its first decade, or what was the style in furnishings when they first grew up. In the here and now they always have the same sort of decor. Chairs done in grey velvet with a little pattern of red flowers and black leaves, chintz sofas with extra covers for the arms, in case, I suppose, people with dirty hands sit in them; tables with piecrust edges and curly legs, glass-fronted bookcases full of books by authors whose names are long forgotten, grey and pink rugs on top of bigger red and black rugs on top of green and beige carpets, umbrella stands and standard lamps with parchment shades and workbaskets full of cotton reels, vases of fluted glass shading from emerald through jade green to white, stained brown inside from chrysanthemums left standing too long in stale water, landscapes in gilt frames, their shiny surfaces darkened to invisibility by time and neglect, innumerable tiny white china pots and urns and vases bearing the name and crest in red and black and gold of the seaside town where they were bought a lifetime before. And, of course, the framed photographs, depressing to the visitor because their subjects are nearly always lumpish and awkward, miserable while trying to look happy, or posed in unnatural or fake surroundings.

In old Mrs Fisherton's there was one of these of Max, in academic gown and mortarboard, apparently seated in a library. I could just about tell it was Max from the protuberant round eyes which hadn't changed and the long, then smooth and unwrinkled, neck. The other people in the pictures might have been Max's grandfather, his father, his mother, aunts, uncles. The mystery was why anyone would want to keep them down here after their original owner was long dead.

I walked about the flat from room to room, examining everything. Claustrophobics are better when they're on the move. One good thing about the place was that the rooms were big and the ceilings quite high, though lower than on the upper floors. The bedroom was the least subterranean and the top few inches of its window were above the top of the wall that divided the back area from the garden. I was thankful for that because there I was to sleep, and in this old lady's high bed with wooden headboard carved with ridges and shelves and designed apparently to stop you sitting up in bed, still less reading, and panelled wooden footboard on which to stub your toes. The clothes cupboard, which I didn't know then should be called a wardrobe, was the kind nervous children imagine things will come out of in the night. I was too old for that but still I didn't like this wardrobe, its blackness, its panels with carvings on the bits in between, its clawed feet like the paws of a very old arthritic lion; and I very much disliked the kind of crest thing that surmounted its front and which looked to me in the dim half-light, and many times later after I knew what it really was, like snakes and scorpions engaged in some dreadful struggle, inextricably interwined.

I unpacked my cases. A great many wire hangers, the kind they put your clothes on at the dry-cleaner's, were on the rail inside the wardrobe. They jangled with a ringing noise like discordant bells, not only when you opened the doors but if you so much as touched the wardrobe when you passed it. I hung up my clothes, I put my sponge bag in the bathroom (claw-footed bath, the tub iron-stained, no shower, overhead toilet flush with a chain). There was linoleum on the floor, something else I didn't know the name of until Beryl enlightened me, probably at the same time as she told me the wardrobe was a wardrobe and that I could buy lightbulbs 'fit for a human person not wanting to lose her eyesight' round the corner at the supermarket.

The black and white television held my attention for about half an hour. Sitting down for longer than that became unpleasant, so I walked about, looking into the two rooms I was never to use, a spare bedroom and a dining room with no window at all, only a string you pulled to set a fan going. That dim and shadowy cavern with prints on the walls of ancient manor houses and ships in storms at sea, a large square table and eight bow-legged chairs, a sideboard and an old metal trolley stacked with apparently an entire green and gold porcelain dinner service, I resolved never in any circumstances to enter again. Things might have been very different if I'd kept to that resolution and not hidden Liv's money in the sideboard drawer. I should have locked the door and thrown away the key, only there was no key. I was breathing rather quickly and shallowly when I came out, catching my breath and very nearly sobbing. That evening – and it was probably the very worst of all the evenings – I asked myself what I was going to do, how was I going to handle things, how was I going to stand it?

When we get older one of the things we learn is that things change. Hardly anything stays the same. If old Mrs Fisherton's didn't change, I would and my circumstances would, but I was only nineteen and a very young nineteen, in spite of the life-transforming experience I'd had. Max and Selina shouldn't have treated me the way they did but, on the other hand, they'd let me have a large flat rent-free in a highly sought-after part of London and quite near the college I was going to. The flat had been got ready, was clean and had clean sheets on the bed and towels in the bathroom. I see it that way now but I didn't then. I don't mean I thought they had treated me badly, I didn't, but I felt ill-used by some disembodied fate and I felt afraid.

Fortunately, I suppose, I was so ignorant of any sort of household management that when I went into the kitchen I didn't notice there was no fridge and no machines for washing clothes or dishes. My eyes focused fearfully on the gas oven and the electric ring with an old blackened kettle standing on it. I had never in my life cooked anything, I had never made a cup of tea, though I had – and to this accomplishment I clung as to a lifeline – poured boiling water on to a spoonful of powdered coffee in a mug.

Like most teenagers I was a late retirer, never in bed before midnight. But that night I went to bed early, I didn't know what else to do. Before going to bed I did one more thing. I took the key Selina had put on my tray, unlocked the door at the end of the passage that led to the outdoors and found myself on a stone-flagged floor, seemingly at the bottom of a tank with mossy walls over which trailed long-stemmed ivy-leaved plants. But the sky was up there and the open air at the top of the iron staircase. I went up it and into the front garden, marvelling that I'd noticed nothing of the 'area' when I arrived.

It was a mild night and windless. I'd been used to darkness and starry skies. No stars were visible here in the smoky purplish redness above me. Street-lamps were on, amber-coloured cubes like fruit gums. The huge pale glimmering façade of the houses opposite was punctured by squares of light. I looked up, of course, I always do look up to top floors and gables and peaks and chimneys, and saw that on the fourth floor, on the very top, there were as many lights, all shining from windows tucked under those dizzyingly high roofs. Who lived up there? Who had the luck to live there? In those days, I don't believe I ever considered that for those who fear depths and enclosed spaces there are just as many who are afraid of heights, who would die rather than go to the top of a tower or look over the edge of a precipice.

I never thought of it but went indoors again and crept, struggling for breath as if the place were full of gas, towards the bearable place, the bedroom.

3

I'm not as self-indulgent as I used to be. I don't suppose you want to know the details of the trapped-in-an-underground-cell dream I had early the next morning and from which I woke up screaming, so I won't go into it. In fact, one very seldom actually screams in those circumstances. What comes out is a feeble squeak. I didn't make enough noise for Max and Selina to hear me, even if by that time they were down on their ground floor. It was late for anyone but teenagers, past nine. I had slept for eleven hours and if anything had come out of the wardrobe, I'd missed it.

By then there was enough natural light in the bedroom, almost enough, to read by. It showed me the scorpions and snakes on top of the wardrobe for what they were: ivy tendrils and oak branches. I looked out of the window, I mean by this that I pressed my head against the glass and craned my neck to look upwards, saw a brick wall with urns and stone animals on it, a segment of lawn, clusters of spindly tree trunks and far, far up above, a pale blue sky criss-crossed with the white plumes of plane trails. Whether it was that morning or some other that the tortoiseshell cat came and stood on the wall and looked down at me with hopeful yellow eyes, I can't remember. I know that I had only been a short time at old Mrs Fisherton's when she came. I went to get my breakfast, creeping warily again into the twilight zone, and found that Selina's milk had gone sour. But among the ancient kitchen equipment was a toaster that worked. I experimented with it and after two attempts produced a burnt slice.

It was Saturday and on the following Tuesday the autumn term, the college year, was due to start. That was what I was doing there, that was why I had come, to begin and if possible (I doubted then if it was possible and I was right) see through to the bitter end the course I had been accepted for. I knew nothing of psychology but at least I could summon up a glimmer of interest in it. Business was another matter. Not only was I ignorant of business, I scarcely knew what was meant by the word, but I knew very decidedly that I wanted nothing to do with it. So why was I embarking on it? It's easy to ask that now. The answer is weak and defeatist, I know. I had to do something, I had to train for something, I couldn't be a recluse living with my parents in the country until they died and I got old, which was their way of putting it, and what at times I'd have liked to do. Brooding about Daniel's death and my part in it, which they didn't say but I thought, hiding myself, knowing no one, or best of all but impractical, going back in time and dying myself in Daniel's place.

I had been seventeen when it happened and my A-levels were a year in the future. But after the pylon I was ill for months. One thinks of people falling ill as the result of a shock or a traumatic event as something confined to characters in Victorian novels, but it really happens. I was in the hospital for four weeks and then in bed at home, feeling, I suppose, the way you do with a really bad flu, lethargic and hopeless and unable to do anything, scarcely able to move. More than that, though I had cried and cried, I felt the pressure of unshed tears, as if my head was full of salt water. I wanted to tell Daniel about it, tell him how I felt. Strange, wasn't it, longing to tell the dead person you're grieving for how sad you are?

The counsellor used to come to me because I couldn't go to her, and when she was done with me, bringing about no change in my condition, the tutor came to coach me for my A-levels. In spite of that, I made a mess of them. Except in one subject I got poor results, and that exception was an A in Physics. I only got that A because science was easy for me, logical and plain and undeniable, as I saw it, and I didn't have to work at it. Considering the circumstances, eleven months after the pylon, in which I did those A-levels, it's not surprising I got Ds in English Literature and History. The three grades were quite good enough for the Grand Union Polytechnic, I may well have been the one student they had who had an A at A-level in anything, and my only difficulty was choosing between Psychology and Business Studies and the other option, Management and Social Sciences. I chose the former because at least I knew what one of the words meant.

When I left old Mrs Fisherton's by way of the area and the iron staircase that Saturday morning, I intended to find a route to the polytechnic. It had to be an itinerary that didn't involve going in the underground or, to put it more precisely, going in the *tube*. If you've a phobia, you become very aware, not quite all the time but for part of every day, of the possible encounters you may have with whatever it is that threatens you. In the previous week I had found out, from an old street plan of my father's and a book he had about London Transport, that a line runs from Baker Street via Paddington to Ladbroke Grove and Latimer Road and for none of its route does it pass underground. All I had to do was get to Paddington which, according to the map, was a short walk away. If I had then had the A–Z I'd have seen there was a catch in it, but I had only bought the A–Z the day before.

It was a lovely morning, very warm for late September, and there were a lot of people about. That was when I first saw the au pairs doing their best to be nannies, Liv-lookalikes, one of them may even have been Liv, pushing buggies with one or two children in them and holding another by the hand. By the canal, then as now, the tourists congregated, walking very slowly, pointing out to their companions a particular house or a boat. One of the boats had vases shaped like swans all along its roof and green plants growing out of the swans' backs. One of the houses had a vine with bunches of green grapes hanging against the white plaster façade. This is the smart bit of the canal, the part that lies between Blomfield Road to the north and Maida Avenue to the south. I stood on the bridge along with the tourists and looked along the canal's shining course to where it disappears under the low arch into the Maida Hill tunnel. Outside the café above the tunnel mouth, people were sitting at tables having morning coffee or drinks, and I thought how I'd like to have been there myself, maybe with one dear friend, only the one dear friend I had had was dead.

The boat that plies between Jason's Wharf and Camden Lock came smoothly out from the under the bridge below me and I felt the same sort of envy of the girl who steered it, she looked so free and yet so responsible. But she took the boat and all its passengers under the café and into the tunnel mouth and I no longer wanted to be her because I knew how it would be for me, the low, slimy, moss-covered tunnel walls, the rocking boat on the black water and the darkness but for a pinpoint of light ahead. Claustrophobics need not experience a place to know how it will be. Their imaginations do that and more.

I walked along Warwick Avenue, looking at, and by now hearing, the traffic rushing across the concrete flyover that scars the blue sky, the green spaces and the pretty houses. The Westway. It was on the A–Z but not on my father's old map. I stood on the Harrow Road and saw that I hadn't a hope of getting across it. There were barriers on the pavement to stop anyone crossing. To go to Paddington, or even as I later learnt, to get to the southern bit of the Edgware Road, you had to go *under* it. The underpasses were marked in my A–Z. I even found one of them, its entrance close to St Mary's Church and Paddington Green, but rather than go inside, I'd have risked my life dodging the cars tearing along the Westway at seventy miles an hour.

Standing there, I could see that there might be one way. There might be one route to Paddington that avoided the subterranean: the canal. An arm of it branched off here, its waters must have been under my feet. That was how I came to retrace my steps and after several failed attempts to make the descent, went into the little garden and down the winding shrubbery path to the canal bank. Even so, I still had to pass under the bridge, under the road I had been on minutes before, but it wasn't dark or enclosed, I was soon out on the other side where the boats were and the gardens and a boat-owner's dog sitting on a red-painted roof above the nameplate that said *Cicero*.

It seemed very unlike the London I had known from my rare visits, a backwater (literally) of floating homes and flowers and trees in tubs, chairs and tables on the canal bank, someone even had a barbecue, brambles and stinging nettles and buddleia and builders' rubbish, dumps of rubble and tin cans, plastic bags and bits of timber drifting on the green shining surface. And a backdrop of old and new buildings in the Edgware Road. Was the Stakis Hotel there then? The white tower was, the huge one with the scarlet piping on its top, so that it looks like a piece of equipment for a giant's kitchen, a freezer maybe or a hi-tech cabinet. Dull, dark, ancient buildings were there too, all their windows broken and all their doors padlocked, and in the distance, though I knew nothing of this then, the old engine sheds and mar-shalling yards of Paddington Station. I walked along beside the trees, under the second bridge, and came to a path and a ramp and there, on the left, was the exit from the underpass whose entrance made me shudder when I looked at it from the other side. I didn't have to go in, I turned my back on it, and went up in the open air and the sunlight to the Harrow Road roundabout and over Bishop's Bridge to Paddington. It was easy, I could do it every day.

It's an odd thing how success in a venture like that can trans-
form, if temporarily, not just the problem that's worrying you, but
your whole outlook on existence. Suddenly I was happy. I had
found a tunnel-free way to GUP and because of that become
capable of shopping for food, even possibly cooking food in a basic
way, of adjusting to life at old Mrs Fisherton's and somehow putting
up with windows that looked out on to brick walls and an iron staircase.

I did find the shops and the food, though the things I bought in
the beginning, a piece of ham I didn't understand had to be boiled,
various things that could only be cooked by microwaving, and beans
I didn't know how to slice, were a mistake. But the pizzas and the
Dundee cake weren't a bad choice. I lived on pizza and fruitcake,
washed down with milk, for a week. The ham I gave to the little
tortoiseshell cat, not knowing then what a vet later told me, that cats
can't digest pig meat. It seemed to do her no harm.

It was a long time before I went back to Russia Road that day. I
found a park with green lawns and trees and a single flowerbed, sat
down on the grass and ate my lunch of biscuits washed down with
milk. Most of the afternoon I slept. My counsellor had told me that
the sleeping I did, all night and half the day sometimes, was a way of
avoiding facing my problems and perhaps she was right, though I
seemed to face them all the time I was awake. I was very lucky no
one stole my shopping bags while I slept. Maida Vale and Little Venice
and Paddington, not to mention Kilburn, are a den of thieves, as I
was soon to find out through personal experience. You only have to
put something you want to be rid of, any kind of rubbish, a broken
teapot, a carpet cut-off, a heel-less shoe, out on the pavement for
someone to take it. But no one stole my shopping that afternoon, nor
my purse, which was sticking out of my jacket pocket, nor my watch
that I had taken off and laid on the grass because the buckle on the
strap was sticking into my arm. It was still there and it told me the
time was nearly half past six.

Max and Selina were having a party, a garden party, though I don't
suppose they called it that. I heard the voices of their guests before I
saw them. I climbed up on the chest of drawers under the bedroom
window but even then all I could see was legs, legs in trousers, male
and female, a woman's long elegant legs in high-heeled shoes whose

skirt I couldn't even see, it was so short, and a man in shorts. I knew it was a man only because the legs were so hairy.

Someone gave a little cough behind me and I nearly fell off the chest of drawers. It was Selina, very smartly dressed in a stiff and shiny red silk suit with pink pearls round her neck and pink-pearl nail varnish to match. She hadn't knocked at the door at the top of the stairs but even if she had I wouldn't have heard her down here.

'I've been looking for you, darling,' she said reproachfully, 'ever since ten this morning. An enormous trunk has come and your mother's been on the phone, she's frantic, and I don't wonder. She says you promised faithfully to phone her last night.'

I'd forgotten. 'There isn't a phone,' I said.

'Not down here, naturally.' She said it in a highly indignant tone. Who would ever have needed or expected to find a phone at old Mrs Fisherton's? She could only have looked more affronted if I had pointed out the absence of a jacuzzi. 'Surely you knew you could use our phone in an emergency?'

Phoning my mother to tell her I had successfully made a journey of seventy miles was an emergency? 'You'd better do it now, hadn't you? Yes, I really think so.' She had begun one of those arguments with herself. 'I mean, I can show you where the phone is now, it may not be possible later. We shan't want a lot of disturbance later, shall we?'

I said I could do it whenever she liked and followed her up the stairs, one flight, then another and another. The backs of her stockings had seams and tiny red roses printed on them from the heel to halfway up the calves. Their drawing room – as both of them called it – was a magnificent place, its windows, two facing the front and two the garden, were dressed, for you couldn't say 'curtained', in streams of golden brown velvet, overhung with swathes of yellow satin. The chairs were covered in yellow satin and the sofas, of which there were three, in some sort of brown and yellow and emerald striped material. Huge gilt-framed mirrors faced each other across an expanse of emerald carpet. Max told me one day, much later, that the vases were *famille jaune*, and I was impressed without having the faintest idea what he meant.

The phone was between the windows that overlooked the garden. While I spoke to my mother and suffered in silence her reproaches, I watched the company on the lawn. There were about fifteen people out there, drinking champagne. The man in shorts with the hairy legs was smoking a cigarette, which made me think that I'd like one, that I'd start smoking again, my parents having made me stop while I was so ill. As soon as Mum had finished admonishing me and giving me all sorts of advice over the phone, not to speak to men, what to eat and what to drink and to remember never to be late for anything, I'd go out and buy a pack of cigarettes, Marlboros.

Selina stood there, listening. I suppose she was listening. At one point she too looked out of the window and, when I'd rung off, she said, 'Jack Silverman is smoking, it's too bad of him when he knows how Max hates it.' She turned to me. There is a rule in Latin about questions expecting the answer 'yes' or the answer 'no'. Daniel, who was doing classics, told me that, and though I have forgotten the Latin words and everything else about it, I could tell Selina was asking me a question expecting the answer 'no' about as strongly as could be. 'I don't for a moment suppose you'd want to come to the party, would you, darling?'

At least she had asked. 'No, thanks,' I said. 'I'm going out again.'

She shook her head. For some reason she disliked that. She escorted me from the room and shut the door behind us. Perhaps she thought that if she left me there on my own for five minutes I'd wreck it. 'By the way,' she said at the head of old Mrs Fisherton's stairs, 'Max would like to see you.' There was a kind of relish in the way she said it. 'In his room.'

I didn't ask why, though I wanted to. 'When?'

'Whenever it suits you before Tuesday, darling. That's what he said, "whenever it suits her". Of course it will have to be when he's not writing his book, when he's finished for the day, that is. He never finishes before five.' She put one finger to lips that matched the red silk. 'That's why we all have to be very, very quiet all day.'

'All right,' I said. 'Tomorrow at six-thirty.'

She couldn't leave it quite like that. She tripped off towards, I suppose, the garden door, turned back and said, 'You'll remember about the being very, very quiet, won't you, darling?'

I went out to buy my Marlboros, opened the packet and lit one as soon as I was outside the shop. It was the first I had had for two years and the first draw made me feel a bit faint and dizzy, though not sick, and smoking again was such a relief, such a bringer of contentment, that I wondered why on earth I had held off for so long. I walked back slowly, the way known to me now, the neighbourhood not yet familiar but no longer strange and frightening. Broad daylight still and the sun not yet reddening, the sky a misty blue.

That evening began my love affair with the architecture of Maida Vale and Little Venice. I knew nothing about architecture then (I don't know much now), only a few terms like 'Palladian' and 'pediment' and 'architrave', but I was keenly alive to its beauties, favouring, like most people *except* architects, the Georgian and the Early Victorian. But what attracted me most about those single villas, those pairs of houses and long, long rows of houses, was their height. It's natural that it did, I love heights just as I hate depths. The psalmist who wrote about lifting up his eyes to the hills might have been writing for me, only I'd substitute 'sky' or 'rooftops' for 'hills'.

There were buildings in those streets six and seven storeys high, the tower blocks of the nineteenth century. Later on I was to learn from Wim, who mountaineered on their roofs, that one red-brick fortress of a block called Clive Court was eight and nine storeys high. That evening, as I strolled slowly along one of the broad avenues, smoking my cigarette, I gazed up to the top floors of terraces with gables on the ends of mansard roofs or eyelid dormers peeping under eaves, to classical pediments of moulded acanthus leaves and bucraniums (you can look that one up), to chimney stacks, long disused, with their sprouting row of pots, forming high walls that divided one pair of houses from the next. The sky had a look of evening that comes without a loss of light. By then the sun was low and its rays a dull yellow, the old trees that lined every street casting long spidery shadows. For a while I had a feeling of hope, of optimism, but it was the last I was to have for a long time.

In Russia Road the party guests were going home. I recognized the man Selina called Jack Silverman. He was on the doorstep of No. 15, inserting his key into the front-door lock to let himself and his wife in. That was my first sight of Silver's parents and glimpse of the interior of their house, the darkish carpeted hall, the phone on the table between two tall candlesticks, a painting on the wall. The front door closed behind them. In the plasterwork above the big triptych window the head in its wreath of flowers was a man's in a turban. Another couple came out of 19 as I opened the gate. They took no notice of me. I went down the iron staircase, the trailing ivies brushing my face, and into old Mrs Fisherton's.

Max's room was at the top of the house, on the fourth floor not counting the basement. Going to see him in this way, toiling up all those stairs at a precise fixed time, was very like being sent for by the headteacher. I think he and Selina knew this and it brought them satisfaction, it and subsequent summonses were their reward for letting me live in their flat. My mother was a stickler for certain kinds of etiquette, though she had never had to use it much and some of it was of the kind to seem absurd to a rational person in the present-day world. One of the things that had rubbed off on me, for I can't say she *taught* me any of it, was that no one knocks on doors in a private house. The time was right, exactly half past six, so I opened Max's door and went in.

He was sitting with his back to me at a big computer linked to a huge printer, both of them old-fashioned even then. He wasn't using them but writing in a notebook with a fountain pen. The room was a wild jumble of books and papers, books face-downwards on the desk, the various small tables, the floor. Sheets of manuscript, of newspaper and magazine cuttings, of photocopies, some flat, some screwed up, covered every surface, balanced on top of stacks of books or tucked into bookshelves on top of book spines. Everything was dusty. Beryl told me she was never allowed in there, it was a sacred place, only for the elect. A wastepaper basket as big as a dustbin overflowed with paper. The green velvet curtains at the window Max faced had been flung back, presumably when he came up here in the morning. One of them was looped over the edge of his desk, the other caught on the back of a book-laden chair. The place smelt of dust and newsprint and old books.

Like an actor playing a headmaster in a film about nineteenth-century school life, he went on writing for about two minutes after I came in. Two minutes is a long time in those circumstances. He neither looked round nor said anything. At last he put down his pen, looked over what he had written and turned it face-downwards on to a blotting pad. Rather slowly he swung his swivel chair round and regarded me with pursed lips. His eyes protruded like a King Charles spaniel's and his wild white fluffy hair seemed to be standing on end. Perhaps he had washed it that morning.

'Sit down, Clodagh.'

There were three other chairs in the room but all were repositories for books and papers, folders and box files. I took hold of the smallest pile and put it on the floor.

'Be careful, please. Watch what you're doing. I have a method, it's fragile and it's easily disrupted.'

He made it sound like an ecosystem in some endangered wetland. I thought he might be joking but not the faintest hint of a smile touched the deep gravity of his face. He looked grimmer and sadder than ever. Selina told me some time after this that he felt unfairly treated because he had never received any honour, not only no peerage or knighthood but not even an MBE. That was why, she said, he kept writing all those books about the First World War and the decade before it, hoping that at last his worth and expertise would be recognized.

'So you begin at this polytechnic of yours tomorrow?'

It was a question that seemed to require no more answer than a nod. I nodded.

'I don't know very much about that sort of establishment. I have never had occasion to be associated with any of those places. They are rather outside my ken.' Max might have been speaking of a strip club instead of what was, after all, a perfectly respectable centre of higher education. 'From what your parents have told me, it looks as if you personally, indeed wantonly, destroyed your chances of a real education by your criminal behaviour and its inevitable consequence.'

I had expected a lecture but not this. When I was young – I mean a schoolgirl – and Max used sometimes to come and stay for a weekend before he was married, he had helped me with my history homework. He had seemed kind enough. I even quite liked him. When he said those things, I took my eyes from him and looked down into my lap.

'But now you are committed to this mixed course at this polytechnic –' I could hear the inverted commas sticking out round the key words – 'you must put all possible effort into doing well. You must redeem yourself. You must make your parents feel, and Selina and me feel, that our efforts on your behalf have not been in vain, and then gradually you will be able to mount once more in the world's esteem.' He changed the subject, sniffing suspiciously. 'Have you been smoking, Clodagh?'

'I sometimes have a cigarette,' I said.

'Yes, I can smell it. You smokers believe you don't smell of your habit but there you are wrong. It's one thing in a man, quite bad enough, but repulsive in a woman. And you are a woman now, you know. You must give it up. It's expensive and bad for your health. I am sure I don't have to tell you that in no circumstances whatsoever are you to smoke in Grandmother Mabel's flat.'

So that was what she had been called, Mabel. A strange old-fashioned name. I rather liked it and I'm afraid that to me the most important detail in Max's homily was the disclosure of old Mrs Fisherton's first name. Never mind the smoking, the wantonness, the blowing of my chances, I had found out what she was called. I smiled at Max.

His features relaxed. Not quite into a smile, not that, but there was a softening. 'What do you want to do when you have your, er, degree, Clodagh? Have you any ideas for a future career?'

I hadn't, I had never thought about it. Something to do with business and psychology seemed indicated. I wasn't going to say that. I needed to say something that would make him angry. No doubt, in some ways, I had been the prototype rebellious teenager, and now that I had left my own parents, I was projecting parenthood on to Max and Selina. Perhaps I learnt that was possible and even common from the few months I stayed the psychology course. This was what I'd have said to Dad if he'd asked me that question.

'I'd like to be a steeplejack.'

His face hard again and his eyes bulging, Max shook his head this way and that. 'I was serious, Clodagh, as you well know. Don't you think I deserve a serious answer and not a rude, frivolous one?'

'I don't know,' I said. 'To both, I mean. I don't know.' I got up and asked, like someone half my age as I well knew, 'Can I go now?'

He shook his head again, then nodded. I went downstairs, feeling a bit hollow inside, as if I had done something appalling. Would they throw me out? And if they did, where was I to go? Once inside old Mrs Fisherton's, old *Mabel* Fisherton's, I broke Max's rule and lit a cigarette. I thought about the answer I had given to his question ('What are you going to do when you grow up?') and what I had meant by it. Of course it had been frivolous and not considered at all,

I might as well have said I wanted to be a plumber or a bus driver. On the other hand, had it? Had it been so frivolous? Ever since the pylon – well, not ever since but lately – I had been thinking, as part of my continual facing what I had done, that I needed to atone and not only to atone but get something positive out of the experience as well. I had failed and Daniel had died because I, who had instigated the whole thing and badgered him into it, knew nothing about the pylon. When I said to Max 'I want to be a steeplejack', maybe in my unconscious was a feeling that I ought to be, that I ought to make a career of climbing up tall buildings and repairing them, for working constructively on heights was what I owed the world and Daniel's memory and myself.

After a while I unpacked my trunk. Then I looked in the drawer where I had put the stuff out of my suitcases and found the photograph I had of Daniel. It's quite a big photograph, a portrait his mother had had taken on his sixteenth birthday. I hunted among old Mrs Fisherton's framed photographs, found one of anonymous people, two men and two women dressed in the fashion of I don't know when, maybe the twenties, but in a good silver frame. I took the four unknown people out and put Daniel in. He looked nice, very young and handsome, surrounded by chased and fluted silver. I did something I had never done before and have never done since I left Russia Road, I brought the portrait to my lips and kissed the glass where Daniel's mouth was. The unshed tears were still there, still behind my eyes, and I wondered when I'd find someone I could tell about my grief.

It was coincidence that when I went out into the area to climb the staircase and pollute the nice fresh air with another cigarette, I saw Silver's parents packing up their car in preparation for going back to the country. They had been in London for a rare weekend, though I knew nothing about their country place then, or that London weekends were a rarity. Jack Silverman's legs covered in dense fair hair, almost fur, were the first thing I had noticed about him. Now those legs were covered up in jeans and I'm afraid I thought him too old to wear them. Silver's mother was in jeans too, the designer kind, I expect, and she had a very smart tweed jacket on as well and a Hermès scarf (I think), the sort that have a pattern of ropes and knots all over them. She was as dark as he was fair and looked Jewish with her handsome aquiline nose and full lips, though he was as much so as she.

He went back into the house and came out again with two more suitcases which he put into the boot before closing the lid. It was Beryl who told me they had a country house in Hertfordshire they had bought when his business moved out to St Albans. Erica Silverman liked being there far more than in Russia Road and they spent as little time in London as possible. As I watched, she got into the passenger seat and he into the driver's seat and they drove away towards Sutherland Avenue and the Edgware Road.

I came out into the front garden (two flowering currant bushes, a Christmas rose and a couple of thistles) and looked up at the house they'd left, I don't know why. Foresight perhaps? I had no such feelings at the time. I fancied I saw a light in a window on the very top floor, in a dormer on the mansard, but it was only where a slanting ray from the setting sun had touched the glass. As far as I knew, the Silvermans had left behind them an empty house.

So where does the coincidence come into all this? I'll tell you. I'd been wishing for someone to tell my story to and he was up there all the time. He was up there with a story of his own.

4

Kissing faces through glass is no longer my style. But I still have that photograph of Daniel, still in its silver frame. I took it with me when I left old Mrs Fisherton's, stole it, I suppose. After all, I had stolen the photograph in the first place. It and a lot of copies of it were on the table when I went to see Mrs Fleetwood after the hospital discharged me. I should really say when she summoned me to tell me what she thought of someone who'd sent a boy of sixteen, her only son, to his death. She went out of the room because she was crying so much and while she was away I took one of the photographs, rolled it up and put it inside my jacket. Poor thing, she'd have torn up those prints rather than give me one.

That portrait stands in our living room now, along with one of Mum and Dad. There ought to be one of my husband but the only time he ever had his photograph taken was when we got married. Our wedding photograph has pride of place. But Daniel is there too and the one man who might be jealous doesn't mind. When people ask me who the boy with the keen eyes and the cheerful grin is, I don't tell them, I say in the words of Emmylou Harris's song that it's just someone I used to know.

The days, the weeks, after that interview with Max have jumbled in my memory. The diary was abandoned for a long while. All sorts of things happened; it's the order I can't recall. I started at GUP in a daze, confused by everything, but at least my journey there was underground- and underpass-free, and I discovered buses for days when I didn't feel like walking to Paddington Station. As for the place itself, the college, I was so deeply uninterested in what I was supposed to be doing and so unable to find my way around that I passed whole weeks in a trance-like state. Because the buildings were on opposite sides of a fairly important road, many rooms were reached by means of an overhead walkway and yes, of course, an underpass. I never used the underpass but toiled upstairs to the walkway, was late for lectures or sometimes hopelessly lost. I spoke to scarcely anyone and after a time people stopped making overtures to me. As early as that first term I was missing lectures, skiving off or not bothering to go in. Most people have bad dreams that are specifically about that sort of thing, dreams in which they find themselves back at school or college with tests or exams or finals looming, they have attended no classes, done no work, made no notes, and, barely knowing the basics of their subject, either retreat from the scene or fly into a panic. But it's a dream and you wake up from it. For me it was real life.

I told nobody. Max might have helped me but he was the last person I'd have told. On my way to phone my mother one Sunday I encountered him coming out of the drawing room. He stopped and asked me how I was progressing at my polytechnic in the tone some people use when asking children how they are getting on at school. I said everything was fine and he didn't pursue it, only pursing his lips and frowning in the way that made him look like a cross pekinese.

I was desperately lonely. That was when I started talking to old Mrs Fisherton. I don't mean I believe in ghosts or ever did, I never really thought she was there, but we do talk to people in our heads, usually people we love, and we no more get answers from them than I did from her. I told her about GUP and how awful it was and sometimes I asked her what would become of me if I did no work, got no qualification, so that there was nothing for it in the end but to go back to Suffolk and my parents. I couldn't talk to Daniel in his silver frame, he seemed in a strange way more dead than she was, perhaps because of my ever-present guilt.

One morning when I should have been attending a lecture and demonstration on marketing but was lying in bed instead, looking at the segment of pale sky above the wall, something set the wire hangers in the wardrobe jangling and when I turned round I saw a small old woman standing in the doorway. I didn't scream, I was paralysed with fright. A prior belief in ghosts isn't necessary when you see a ghost. A ghostly manifestation would be a miracle and the laws of nature overturned. I thought, I've brought her back by talking to her. Like a medium might, I've conjured her up.

'Sorry to intrude, love,' she said, 'but it's my morning for cleaning down here.'

Of course there were no ghosts and of course old Mrs Fisherton was dead and gone. I got up, I said to give me five minutes and I'd be dressed. I'd be ready and I'd make her a cup of tea. Her first name was Beryl and I never knew her by any other, though of course I found out later, when she gave me a home and looked after me, that she was called Mrs Collett. She is still one of my best friends.

Old Mrs Fisherton was past ninety when she died but Beryl wasn't really old, though she seemed so to me then. I suppose she was still under sixty. She wore trousers that she called slacks and bright-coloured jumpers. Her face was old and her hair thin and grey but her figure was like a young girl's, which I later learnt she attributed to never having put on weight and never having lost any. Food she thought one of life's nuisances and she ate little, she ate to live. She showed no surprise at my being there and being still in bed at ten-thirty. It was what she expected from 'the young', of whom she had several of her own.

'Nice smell,' she said while we had our tea. 'I like a place to smell of cigarettes, it reminds me of my late husband. I don't smoke myself and nor do the two still at home. I've tried taking it up, mind, but it didn't agree with me.' She sniffed appreciatively. 'Don't you let the Professor catch you.' She always called Max 'the Professor'. Presumably he had asked her to, or Selina had. 'He's a raving fanatic when it comes to smoking.'

'I know,' I said. 'He said I wasn't to smoke in here.'

'Girls will be girls is what I always say.'

It may have been that time or on her next visit that she remarked on the dim lighting. 'Not very cheerful down here, is it, love? You'll ruin your eyes, reading your college books.'

I seldom did read them, but I wasn't going to say so. I asked her what I could do about the light and she looked warily at me, the way you look at a person in the street who's gesticulating or talking to himself. 'You need stronger bulbs, don't you? Like hundreds, not forties. It'll be an outlay but worth it, I reckon.'

I could get them round the corner, she said, at a store which had some fancy name but which everyone called 'Superglue' – a title instigated originally by Beryl, I expect – and that same day I did. She showed me how to put them in the lamp sockets. A couple of months ago I showed my gratitude (for that and a thousand other things) by rewiring the flat she has recently bought from the council. The

41

100-watt bulbs made a great difference to old Mrs Fisherton's and if I still felt enclosed and oppressed, the breathlessness and the sensation of the ceiling sinking and crushing me were less bad.

Beryl lived in a tower block on the Harrow Road and a son and a daughter lived with her. Neither of them could be induced to take up cigarette smoking, for as with their mother it didn't agree with them. Her son was an electrician and her daughter sold cosmetics in one of the Oxford Street stores. Beryl had made a corner for herself in Russia Road, cleaning for Max and Selina and the people at Nos 13, 15 and 17.

'Those Silvermans,' she said, 'they only come up for a weekend and not many weekends in a year. The place is like a palace, never a fingermark, I don't know why they keep it on, really.'

I asked her where they lived in the country and she told me. Did she mean No. 15 was empty most of the time?

'Barring the top flat, love. Their son's up there, him and I don't know who else, half a dozen of them if you ask me. He gets rid of them or maybe he hides them under the beds when his mum and dad come but that's only once in a blue moon.'

The people at 17 and 13 were less interesting, an elderly doctor and his wife next door to us while 13 was divided into two flats whose occupants Beryl hardly ever saw, they were out all day and she had keys. One couple she called, with a fine disregard for political correctness, 'Indians and very dark'. The others had virtually no furniture but mattresses on the floor and steel chairs. It may have been minimalist (not Beryl's word) or perhaps they could afford nothing better.

The next time I went out, which was probably that afternoon, I stood on the other side of the road and looked up beyond the floral mouldings and the turbanned man to the top floor of 15. Three casement windows in hood-like dormers were tucked in the mansard just as they were in all the other houses in the terrace. It was November and all the windows were shut but the middle one had been closed carelessly, catching up a corner of a net curtain between casement and window frame. It flapped in the breeze, a thin greyish rag. This was the window that had caught the light from the setting sun that evening I had watched Jack and Erica Silverman leave in their car. I wondered what Beryl had meant by saying 'half a dozen' people lived up in that top flat but when I asked her she said, as she often did in answer to my questions, 'I don't know, love. I've told you everything I know and now you know as much as I do.'

Some days, instead of going to GUP, I went for long walks. I specially did this when even the new lighting seemed unable to dispel that oppressive ceiling-coming-down-on-my-head feeling and I had to get out for a while. I walked Maida Vale up to Kilburn and stared in wonder at St Augustine's Church, big as a cathedral, its tall spire visible for miles. How I would have liked to climb that spire! I walked St John's Wood and Primrose Hill and Camden Town, always lifting up my eyes to the rooftops, and I walked the canal, from Camden Lock to the Portobello Road, being obliged, of course, and not at all unwillingly, to come up briefly on to the street at the Maida Hill tunnel. I admired the tall Gothic church of the Holy Catholic Apostolics in Maida Avenue and St Mary Magdalene in Woodchester Square with another high climbable spire and soaring tower blocks all round it. Eventually, I suppose, I'd have climbed one of those spires if I hadn't met Silver.

I walked in daylight but as winter came on and evening started earlier and earlier, I was often out after dark. Lighted streets and glowing lamps in warm depths behind windows make one long for companionship, for someone to sit with in those rooms, those restaurants and pubs and cafés. Clubbing as a way of life for the young was only just coming in then, but there are always places where teenagers and people in their twenties congregate.

Young people were at GUP. In fact, apart from a few mature students doing a degree in mid-career, everyone was young. But I had got into the habit of going in for a lecture or a seminar and, immediately it was over, setting off for a walk. I had never been to a tutorial. We were expected to take part in group marketing sessions but no one ever asked me to answer a questionnaire or write an essay. I went there less and less and when the term ended I barely noticed. It had been two weeks since GUP had seen me.

Days went by when I talked to no one. I looked forward to the days when Beryl came just for the sound of a human voice talking to me, not to someone else. As winter closed in I walked about less. It was always raining and it was cold outside. The flat, like the whole of 19

Russia Road, was very warm. It was dark long into the mornings and dark most of the afternoon. I talked to old Mrs Fisherton, I asked her how she had borne it, living down here for years on end. She never replied, I'd have known I was going mad if she had, but I answered for her. I answered that she was old and tired, walking wasn't easy and nor was climbing stairs, she liked the warmth and the quiet, the cosiness of it. Besides, her beloved Max used to come down and talk to her, sit with her in the evenings sometimes and maybe they watched *Streetwise* together on the black and white television.

Weeks passed without my seeing him or Selina. When it wasn't actually raining, and sometimes when it was, he would set off for his run round Regent's Park at eight in the morning. I was hardly ever up but I was by the time he got back and once or twice, carrying my rubbish bag up the iron staircase, I'd catch a glimpse of him jogging down Russia Road and turning in at our gate. When Selina went off to a shoot, a hired car would come for her even earlier, so I only saw her on Sunday evenings when I went upstairs to phone my parents, and not always then. She'd smile her little tight smile at me, her mouth quickly returning to its heart-shaped pout, and say, 'You won't be too long on the phone, will you, darling?'

If I had done what I was supposed to be doing and concentrated on my studies and my course, made friends among my fellow students, I might have seen 19 Russia Road for what it was, a lodging, and Max and Selina my landlords. So it was all my own fault, but knowing that did nothing to help the loneliness. There was one person and only one who made contact with me and whom I sometimes saw. His name was Guy Wharton, he was a neighbour of ours in Suffolk. At any rate, he lived in a house just across the river from us, or his parents did, and when he wasn't there he was in London in a flat he had in South Kensington. I had been at old Mrs Fisherton's for about two months when he wrote to me. Anyone who wanted to get in touch with me had to write since phoning was impossible.

It wasn't the first letter I had ever had from him. He wrote to me when I was in hospital after the pylon and again when I was back home and going through that long miserable depression. And of course he came to see me. Guy was the only person who didn't blame me for what happened or lecture me about it or ask why, why, why? He never talked about it at all unless I raised the subject. When I did, he managed to suggest that this adventure which went so disastrously wrong was just an unfortunate episode in my life I was lucky enough to have come out of physically unhurt, and that Daniel's death was nothing to do with me but his own fault.

Somehow I never dared agree with that. If I didn't take responsibility for it, I had a strange superstitious feeling that he'd die all over again, and die reproaching me. But it was a comfort to hear Guy say it, the only one who did. And it was good too to have one friend who treated me as a normal ordinary human being and not a monster.

The letter I got in November was asking me questions like, was I settling in, getting on all right, enjoying the course? Guy was older than me, about the age I am now, and he had got beyond that time of life when people don't ask others how they are or tell them they're looking well or, come to that, ask them if they're settling in. He was grown up. The letter didn't ask me out anywhere, I had never been out with him, but it said I knew where he was if I wanted him and please to give him a ring sometime. Could he have my phone number? It would be nice to meet before Christmas.

My mother was fond of Guy. She had that peculiar respect for him women in her situation – suburban-type house outside a country village, professional but underpaid husband, no career of her own, no status in the country – have for a young man whom they've known since he was a child and who is educated, well-off and the heir to landed property. Guy was all those things. He was also the man who, if he hadn't been able to save Daniel's life, had tried to do so and could tell himself he had saved mine. At any rate, I don't know if I'd have acted as I did if he hadn't come up the field from the river at that crucial time.

If he had come ten minutes earlier, as he almost did, I wouldn't be writing this story at all.

5

The first thing I ever climbed was a tree. Elms are the best for climbing, an old man in our village told me, they have footholds, branches and twigs growing out of their trunks at intervals from the bole all the way up. But the elms began dying before I was born and Dutch elm disease had killed them all by the time I was ten. The first tree I climbed was an oak, and after that horse chestnuts and limes and more oaks. Ash trees are hard to climb because they are at the other extreme from the elm and have no small branches or twigs growing out of their trunks. Much the same goes for beeches and planes, which I called camouflage trees when I first came to London.

I was about twelve when I first climbed a pylon.

I didn't go far up, only as high as the first crossbar that time. The guard on the uprights a little way above daunted me. That was in the days before I carried wire cutters as a matter of course. I stood on the bar and read the small yellow rectangular notice on which was printed in black: *Danger of Death. Keep Off.* When you're twelve you don't believe there's such a thing as death or you believe it's for old people, not for you and your friends.

It occurs to me that though you've seen pylons, you may not have looked at them too closely. You may find them an eyesore. Most people do, and quite a lot are adept at 'not seeing' them, in other words pretending they're not there. So I'll describe a typical one and give you, if you'll bear with me, a bit of pylon history. And I'll try not to be too technical. But, after all, I am an electrician.

Pylons first appeared in this country during the construction of the National Grid in the late twenties and early thirties, but those used for the 132,000-volt network at the time were much smaller than the kind we have now. I expect they were like the ones Spender describes in the other piece of poetry I know, we had to learn it at school:

Now over these small hills, they have built the concrete
That trails black wire;
Pylons, those pillars
Bare like nude, giant girls that have no secret.

Our modern pylons don't look like naked girls, I doubt if any ever
did really. They look like insects, not just any insects but the cicada
or cricket type.

'An insect has six legs,' Daniel said, 'and so does a pylon. It's a
grasshopper hopping across the fields.'

Strictly speaking, pylons have six *arms* with dangling insulators on
the ends of them for carrying the conductors and they stand upright
as if about to take huge leaps. The hanging insulators resemble the
creature's claws and the pylon's small head is insect-like too. Ugly to
some but not to me. I loved pylons. I loved them more than trees or
church steeples or any other tall things, loved the strength of them,
the power of them and the danger.

The foundations of a pylon can extend ten feet underground, and
though they're made of concrete, the pylons themselves are of steel,
a latticework of steel bars, widely spaced at the foot and tapering to a
point, the shape of the Eiffel Tower, and the big ones that carry
400,000 volts are more than 150 feet high. The line of them that
marches across the field next to our house was put up in the late fifties
to carry the power from the nuclear power station at Sizewell on the
east coast – just visible, as I later discovered for myself, from the
Silvermans' country house – into Essex and Hertfordshire. These are
the big ones, bearing the maximum voltage. The National Grid paid
the owner of the field quite a lot of money to put up the pylons and
the story goes that he used it to leave his wife and set up house with
a man he had been in love with for years.

The electricity is carried along the wires or conductors strung
underneath the pylon in 'quad' or 'twin' formation – that is, two or
four wires are suspended from each arm, being held apart along the
span between the pylons by spacers at regular intervals. The stack of
porcelain or glass discs hanging from the arms are the insulators which
prevent the current flowing through the rest of the pylon and to earth.
I know all this now, I didn't then. When I was about fourteen I read
a book about training electricians to work on live wires. It looked

easy, it looked as if you just had to be fairly careful. There was an anecdote in the book about a man who pioneered work on live transmission lines and was raised to the line in a steel-mesh cage. That's the point, that cage, as you'll later see. He leant out and lit his cigar from the current. If he could do it, I could do it. The trouble was, I joked with myself, that I didn't smoke. I started smoking the following year.

Nearly all pylons have guards on them at about head height from the ground to prevent people climbing up. Some are like a raft of interwoven barbed wire and others are more of a frill round each of the uprights. Daniel said they were barbed-wire garters on the pylon's legs and that that proved it was a girl like in the poem, but where he had seen real garters I don't know. The guards wouldn't stop anyone who really meant to climb up.

On most big pylons there are four crossbars with struts criss-crossed in between them. Above that it's all latticework to the top, which is a triangular shape or pentahedron. The six arms start about halfway up the latticework and end just below the top. By the time I met Daniel I had climbed all the pylons in the field up to the lowest arms, either cutting the barbed wire with wire cutters or, later on, when I was more proficient, climbing up inside the guard. Several times I saw the National Grid engineers come in their white van and mend the guards I'd damaged. Mum and Dad said they couldn't understand such vandalism, what sort of a person would want to destroy a pylon guard, it was mindless wanton destruction by some idiot taking revenge on society. No one ever knew it was me, no one saw me on the pylons as far as I know. The fact is that a lot of people don't *see* pylons, they've unconsciously trained themselves not to see them because to most of us they're as ugly as Spender said they were, a blot on the landscape, a violation of the countryside. So it seemed that when I was on them I became as invisible as the steel tower I climbed.

Daniel was at school with me, the Upper School, a kind of comprehensive I had attended since I was eleven. He came at thirteen when his parents moved from where they had been living, somewhere in Norfolk. He was younger than me, but not the vast amount people made out after he was dead. I had become seventeen in the February and he would have had his seventeenth birthday in November if he had lived. It was October when we went up the pylon.

It's legal to ride a motorbike in this country when you're sixteen. Daniel and I went all over the outskirts of London and the Home Counties on his Motoguzzi. Our elders disliked that motorbike. Mr and Mrs Fleetwood kept saying they wished they had forbidden it from the start, now he had got it, it was too late, and every time I went out on it my parents said that was the last time, Dad was going to put his foot down, it had to stop. They all said, and said repeatedly, that we'd be killed on that motorbike, it was one thing when *they* were young but the traffic was too heavy now and there were too many container lorries on the roads to make a motorbike safe. We'd be killed and it wasn't fair on them, giving them all that worry. Ironical, wasn't it? We never had a spill on the bike, we never had any sort of accident, not even a near-miss. It was on the pylon that we came to grief.

That summer we made love in the fields. Sometimes we were lucky enough to have a bed when both his parents were out or both mine were. Such chances happened very seldom. I knew a girl whose parents let her have her boyfriend to stay, to sleep in the same room as her, in the same bed. I talked about it at home, I told Mum and she told Dad. Some part of me knew that would never be allowed in my home, but just the same it would do no harm to let them know, pave the way, prepare the ground. It wasn't that I expected them to acknowledge that we were lovers now, but in the time to come, in a year or two maybe . . . I thought, of course, that there would be a time to come.

That girl's behaviour shocked them very much, the one whose parents let her and her boyfriend share a bed. Mum and Dad had been young in the sixties and we were always being told that those were the days, that was the time of licence and promiscuity, the sexual revolution. If it was, it had passed them by. Or they had put it behind them and forgotten. Also I've noticed that behaviour which was all right for a parent in his or her youth won't be permitted in their children. What's sauce for the goose and gander isn't sauce for the gosling. When I did tell them about Daniel and me, that we had loved each other and been lovers, it was after he was dead and I don't think they believed me. They thought it was all right to disbelieve everything I said because I was an irresponsible person. But we did love each other. We were as much in love as they had been when first they married. They said our love wouldn't have lasted and probably it

49

wouldn't have. Had theirs lasted? I saw no sign of it. But what do I know except that I sent him to his death?

I did. It's not much use saying I didn't mean to. I could read those black words printed on that yellow notice: *Danger of Death*. I'd climbed every pylon in that field – and stopped before I reached the lowest arm that carried the conductors. So why did I? Because I loved him. Because he loved me and wanted me to admire him even more than I did. Spiderwoman, he called me. When he watched me climb he'd call out, 'I love you a lot, Spiderwoman.'

This is how I began that piece I wrote about it:

Marching across the field in which Daniel and Clodagh lay, striding in couples, the pylon line carried its heavy burden of black cables. It crossed the bright green and dun-coloured land, the little river with its double fringe of alders, mounted the other side where a cluster of white houses nestled and a white road wound and disappeared over the brow of the hill . . .

It won't do, will it? There is too much of the promising sixth-form essay about it. Maybe it was good enough for a therapist but it's not good enough for me now and it's not good enough for you. I suppose I was hiding what I really felt, my pain and remorse, under those descriptions of green meadows and nestling houses. Reality was different. Here goes, then.

He wanted to go up the pylon. I didn't dare him to climb it or ask him to prove something by climbing it or tell him, as I suppose some girls would, that I'd know he really loved me if he'd go up there to the top. But I did tell him about the man lighting his cigar from the live wire and once he had heard that story he was wild to try it himself, only in his case it would be a cigarette he was lighting.

'I might light my cigarette from the conductor halfway up,' he said, 'and smoke it at the top.'

'I'll come up behind you.'

That brought him a faint chill, I wrote. *It wasn't only that he would have preferred her to wait down here, stand down here looking up and see him light his cigarette from the conductor, but that he felt for the first time responsible for her. She had said she loved him and that, strangely, put him in charge of her and made him her guardian.*

Did it? Or was I just passing the buck?

The sun had barely gone. He thought he had never seen such a red sky,

50

the clouds purple now, the great clear spaces that had been blue changed to flame and gold.

'Better start, then, before the light goes,' he said.

He set his right hand to one of the steel diagonals. It was the first time he had ever touched a pylon. He expected it to be hot or at least warm but it was cool. Again he looked up.

'There are footholds.'

The steps. They jut at right angles from one of the four uprights and, spaced a few inches apart, they can have no other purpose than to make ascent of the pylon possible. Whether Daniel really said that about footholds and starting before the light goes I can't remember, but I know he said, at this point, 'People do go up, you see. They go up using the footholds, like climbing a ladder.'

I should have said, for I knew it perfectly well, that when they went up the power was off. I didn't say it. I didn't remind him that the man in the anecdote was in a cage, not standing on the pylon. The pylons stand there in the fields, steady, strong, clean, they look harmless. You tell yourself, if you think about it at all, that they wouldn't be allowed to be there, governments wouldn't allow it, if they could really hurt people. Daniel and I would be quite safe if we were careful. When we came down we'd have proved they were safe and the people who had put up the notices just overcautious. I handed him the wire cutters.

'Got your cigarettes?' I said.

'In my pocket.'

I won't quote any more from that piece I wrote. It attributes thoughts and feelings to Daniel I don't in the least know that he had. For instance, I've no idea if by climbing the pylon he thought he was proving his love for me or even proving to himself that he was not afraid. Perhaps and perhaps not. But I knew then as I know now that he wanted to do it. Nor was he under some kind of malign influence exerted by me, for I've never been what Guy (referring to someone else) calls a *femme fatale*. But I could have stopped him and I didn't.

The guards on this pylon were the sort that Daniel had defined as the garter type, shelves or frills of barbed wire encircling each upright just below the second crosspiece. Because the steps only started higher up Daniel had to swing himself on to the lowest crossbar, get a purchase with his feet and pull himself upright. The pylon shone that afternoon, that early evening, every bar and strut gleamed in the slanting sunbeams.

Pylons sing in wet weather, the damp rustling and humming through the wires, but that day ours was dry and shining. Daniel stood on the crossbar and began cutting the wire. He did it more methodically than I ever had, snipping each separate strand and bending it away from him against the upright. I climbed up beside him and let him go ahead once he'd made it easy to pass the guard. I read the *Danger of Death* notice as I went by and so did he but he didn't say anything about it. As I passed that notice the sun was setting. I watched it drop and vanish beneath the horizon or, as anyone who honours Galileo and is a humble sort of scientist should say, I watched the earth turn away from the sun towards darkness.

Even from as low down the pylon as this, we had a good view of things, the fields and woods, the river valley and the slope of the hills on the other side. The long shadows had gone as soon as the sun went, there was a duskiness lying over the land and in the west the sky was a dull red striped with thin black clouds. The only house to be seen was our house. A light had come on in the living room and one of the bedrooms. The pylon would be nearly invisible to my parents by now but it and its fellows generally were, even in broad daylight. They were among those who 'didn't see' the pylons, somehow managing to envisage the field as it was when Constable painted it nearly 200 years before, a deep meadow, low between thick lush hedges and overhung by shaggy trees.

Daniel climbed the ladder of steps and I followed, passing the third of the horizontals where the pylon became markedly narrower. I wrote in that piece that the sky had become violet and a single bright star had appeared, *a clear white pinpoint high above the distant hill*. It sounds like 'fine writing' to me now, I don't know if it was so, I can't remember. I saw Daniel pass the fourth crossbar, climbing on the steps, holding on to the latticework. I swung up on the lattice, ignoring the steps. We were both high up now, at least 100 feet up. I could see more houses in the distance or see their lights, and a church whose floodlighting brought to it an unearthly greenish glow. I said something to Daniel about climbing that church tower. Would he like to? One night when it wasn't floodlit?

A man was walking up the field from the river bridge. I recognized him as Guy Wharton, someone I'd met once or twice. He lived on the other side of the river, and was quite young, though older than us, and he owned all this land. It was his grandfather who had spent the pylon compensation on running away with his lover, but his father who had made the Whartons' money.

'Has he seen us?' Daniel said.

'I don't know.'

'Better be quick, then.'

Daniel was now under the first of the pylon's arms. I expected him to light his cigarette from that position, reaching out to take a light from the lowest line suspended from the arm by its string of glass insulators. He didn't. He went on. I should have told him not to, I *thought* of telling him not to. Something stopped me, his obvious enjoyment, I think. He laughed, he called out, 'It's great up here, Spiderwoman.'

'I know,' I said. 'I told you.'

'Come up a bit and when I've lit my cigarette I'll pass it to you.'

'I'm coming.'

'We'll go to the top and share it.'

He did what I doubt I'd have dared do. He climbed across the struts, pulled himself up and stood on the first arm, the horizontal bar from which two lines are carried, one on each side. With his left hand he held on to the upright and reached up with his right, the right hand with the cigarette between his fingers. 'Now!' he said, 'Now!' or 'Wow!', I never knew which. But I saw him clearly enough and shall for ever see him as he was at that moment, in the twilight, against the dusky red sky, a tall thin boy with long legs in blue jeans, feet apart, standing on the pylon arm, his dark hair blown by the wind. He was laughing, exhilarated, up in the sky, on top of the world. Then he reached up towards the second arm, the dangling insulator and the conductor.

I couldn't have described this when I wrote that piece for whoever it was. In any case, I didn't have the knowledge. I didn't know what had happened but I do now. Four hundred thousand volts leaping from an overhead line to someone standing on the pylon cause an explosion. A small explosion, perhaps, but loud enough and bright enough to terrify. It seems as if the climber the line has struck has been engulfed in a ball of fire. To be a bit technical, just for this once, it's not the voltage that flows through you but the current. The automatic protection equipment at the substation at each end of the line detects the change in flow and trips out the circuit. Although it does this within a fraction of a second, 20,000 amps can still flow through the human body.

Daniel's body. The flash was blinding and the noise like a bomb going off. I don't think he cried out. The force of the electricity flung him off the pylon but instead of falling, he was caught in the struts. He hung in a diamond-shaped frame of steel, one knee hooked over a strut, the other dangling. I made a grab for him. I held him by the belt of his jeans and he hung there, half-seated in the latticework, his back to me, his head hanging, his arms limp and swaying.

I began to shout and scream for help, I shouted at the top of my lungs. I screamed, 'Help me, help me.' I don't know how long I was screaming before Guy came running up the field. It was Guy, but I hardly knew him then. He saw us, called out, 'Hold on. I'll get help,' and ran to his car up on the road. Not many people had phones in their cars then but he did. I talked to Daniel, I said he'd be all right, I said help was coming, an ambulance would come and we'd get him down. I said, 'I'm sorry, I'm sorry.' Even then I said that. I so desperately wanted him to speak. I didn't know then that he was past speech, that he would never speak again.

It was just as well for me that I didn't find out for a while what happens when that number of amps flows through someone. He effectively cooks from the inside out with deep and widespread burns, often to the bone. Nasty, isn't it? Not something one wants to dwell on. An insensitive doctor, visiting me in hospital, hating me and blaming me, I suppose, compared it to what happens to meat in a microwave.

It was some small consolation that the victim of the pylon would very likely feel nothing. The shock would be massive and the nerve endings destroyed. He'd probably die in hospital from secondary infection or organ failure. Weight will be much reduced due to fluid loss caused by the burns. A few have survived such a shock but they have always been disabled for life.

Daniel didn't survive. I thought he might be already dead when I held on to him by the belt of his jeans on the pylon. He felt heavy and inert. I could feel the warmth of his body through my knuckles. If he were dead, would he still feel warm? How did I know? I knew nothing. Then I heard him give a harsh whimpering groan. That sound I was to hear for years to come, I still hear it in my quiet moments, in my dreams. My husband has held me in the night when I've cried and shivered. I make the noise Daniel made, keening softly for a moment until a bubbling in his throat silenced him. I think it was the life going out of him.

It was very nearly dark. Lights were on in houses on the hillsides around. I imagined the people in those houses who knew nothing of us, of what had happened, of how we hung there, people who were having an ordinary evening of food, television, talk. Mum and Dad were at home in the nearest house, unknowing, but not long to be in ignorance. The cars, ambulance, police cars, Super Grid cars, would all have their headlights on and they'd see them come up the road from the village.

Time passed – how much time? I don't know, I've never asked and no one told me. It may have been only minutes, perhaps half an hour. My hold on Daniel was growing weaker, he was sliding ever so gradually over the angle, his body collapsing, all its strength lost. He dragged me with him, pulling me down. Being tormented on the rack must feel the way I felt then, when the torturer screws more tightly. My arms were stretched to the uttermost, straining till they felt tugged from their sockets. His leg slid off the steel bar, and I could do nothing to stop it. He hung then like a sack, like a carcass on a hook. But my hands were the hook and I could stand no more. The pain of it was huge, shooting from my shoulders down my back in great shuddering thrusts and burning in my brain. My own body was bent half over, my head pressing against his back, and he was slipping. I knew I'd have to let go. Balanced with a bar supporting each underarm lest I fall myself, I opened my hands. I had to, I couldn't hold on any longer.

He fell, plunging to the ground cleanly, clear of the pylon, down and down, twisting a little, his arms like wings. The grass down there received him silently and he lay spreadeagled, as the lights of the cars appeared round the curve in the road. Thank God he made no sound. He was dead.

6

I was sitting on my roof terrace with Mabel on my lap and my gin and tonic at my elbow, trying to guess the identity of a castellated building I could just see on the South Bank, when Darren called round. He often does at this sort of time, he's usually on his way to Junilla, who lives in Crouch End, or Campaspe, who lives in Stroud Green. I asked him if he'd like a drink but he refused.

'I'm driving and, besides, I don't like Callum smelling liquor on my breath.'

'So it's Junilla tonight, is it?'

My tone annoyed him. He hung over the roof garden wall, muttering that he wanted to check on what someone had told him, that you could see Harrow-on-the-Hill from here. Darren has a son by one of his girlfriends and a daughter by the other. He knows I don't approve, though my disapproval mainly takes the form of laughing at his domestic arrangements. In spite of having a flat of his own in Hendon, he spends almost every night with one or other of the girlfriends. To see his children, he says. 'No nonsense', with those girls, Afro-trash, as he calls them. I don't believe a word of it but he insists sex is in the past, all over and a mistake at the time but too late now. He's a good father, attentive and anxious, and he supports Callum and Olympia heroically. The refusal of a drink lest his son detect it on his breath was typical.

'I wouldn't say no to an orange juice,' he said.

I fetched it, with lots of ice. The day had been very warm. I don't expect him to have a reason for calling but he always has one. This time it was to talk about the Paddington Basin project, we'd have to take on extra help. I wasn't kidding myself he and I could do it on our own, was I? How about our regular customers? Or suppose there was an emergency? Darren strolled about the roof garden, lifting his hands, opening them, nodding and shaking his head. He's never much of a one for sitting down. Very tall, slim, with that peculiar feline grace that belongs only to the black man, a lazy, laid-back carriage, he's one of the most beautiful people I've ever seen. Silver wasn't in the same league. Darren is very dark, his skin is matt ebony and his hair coal-black tight curls that he wears very short and like a crown on top of his head, the sides and nape being closely shaved. His two gold earrings he has discarded since Olympia told him dads don't wear them.

'What do you suggest?' I said, knowing he'd have some relative or friend up his sleeve.

'Campaspe's brother. He's a good bloke and a good workman.'

'All right. Have him round and we'll give him the once-over.'

'I'll have another orange juice if that's OK and then I'll be on my way.'

'Help yourself. It's in the fridge.'

Mabel slipped off my lap and followed him in. I heard him saying, 'Kitty, kitty, kitty . . .' and hoped he wasn't giving her milk, which she loves but is bad for her. Darren had never been into the flat that way before, until a week before it hadn't been warm enough to sit outside, and when he came out again with his orange juice he said, 'Who's the young guy in the silver frame?'

I realized when he said that how young Daniel looked in that photograph and that he would stay young for ever as I grew older. People would soon start asking me if he was my nephew or my godson.

'Just someone I used to spend some time with,' I said.

'OK, Emmylou, I won't probe.'

I nearly told him then about the pylon. I would have if he hadn't looked at his watch and said he wanted to get to Junilla's before Callum's bedtime. After he had gone I thought how I don't tell people, I've told no one but Silver since I came to London, perhaps because while I was still living at home with my parents everyone knew, I used to think the whole of Suffolk knew. In London, however little I was aware of it at the time, I was making a new start.

Max and Selina were in the secret, of course. I overheard my mother talking to Max about it on the phone.

'She doesn't have to know, does she?' I said, meaning Selina.

'Of course she does. She's his *wife*.'

They told a lot of people. Those friends and neighbours who came to the party, I expect. I'm sure they told Beryl. They told her in the

Christmas holidays, I think, because the next time I saw her on my return she was tender with me, very considerate and thoughtful. I needed cheering up, she said, as she polished old Mrs Fisherton's furniture and dusted the photograph frames, a young girl like me shouldn't be depressed.

To cheer me up she chatted away. She told me about the neighbours, the people next door and those next door to them, all the ones she worked for. That a cleaner with a key to her employers' homes might have a duty of discretion never seemed to occur to her. She took it for granted that in allowing her the freedom of their houses they also gave her permission to broadcast what she saw, learnt, picked up and read while there.

The Ahmeds she disliked, largely, I think, because they failed to give her a 'Christmas box'. They were mean, cheese-paring. On the days she was there they locked up the drinks cupboard and took away the key. It was her belief they emptied the place of food too because the last time she was in their flat there was nothing in the fridge but half a lemon and a bottle of Highland Spring. The minimalists at 13 she never saw, had never seen. Mrs Clark, the doctor's wife at 17, had recommended her and they had taken her on without interviewing her or even speaking to her on the phone. The key was given to her by Mrs Clark. Her money was always there waiting for her in 'a nice clean envelope with nothing written on it', which meant she could use it again. The interior of 13B fascinated her. Although the floors were covered in bright blue carpet, the furniture was sparse and in 'weird shapes'. She couldn't imagine sitting in those chairs. A picture that took up half a wall of a nude woman lying on a table among pieces of fruit put her off her lunch. The owners of the flat were called Michael Harding and Susan Potter and they were not married, a fact worthy of Beryl's comment, though not particularly of her disapproval.

'You know as much as I do now, love. I've told you everything I know.'

She had a far more extensive knowledge of the Silverman family. Silverman, she said, was a Jewish name. The girl was as pretty as a picture, the living image of Princess Diana, but she didn't live there any more, she lived with some bloke somewhere, the way the young all did these days. The older boy was dark but the younger boy was so fair, with hair so blond it was white, that you'd have taken him for an albino till you saw his eyes. His eyes were grey, not a very dark grey but grey enough, not pink like someone she'd been at school with in Queen's Park in the thirties.

'I don't reckon they let it happen these days,' she said. 'They do something about it. In the womb.'

Mr Silverman had a business, he had a factory near St Albans 'or somewhere up there', making glue. Well, not exactly glue, but what was the word? Adhesives? That was it, adhesives, stick-on labels and sticky tape and whatever. He and Mrs lived in a big house out in the country like the ones you saw in TV dramas. They only came to London once in a blue moon. The place never got dirty, she only gave it the once-over every couple of weeks, but they sent her her cheque as if she spring-cleaned the place every couple of days. They'd let the son, the very fair one, have the top flat to live in while he was studying at some college. His first name was something ordinary, she couldn't remember what, but everyone called him Silver. On account of him being so fair and being called Silverman. Even his parents called him Silver.

'I don't reckon Mr Silverman and Mrs know how many he's got living up there. They come and go, but last time I was in there, there was the chap and the girl and the other chap as you might call permanent fixtures as well as that Silver and two others I'd never set eyes on before. Mind you, he don't let me in there. I've offered but he always says he likes it the way it is, he don't like it *clean*.'

I asked her how she knew all those people were there if she never went in.

'There's a front door to that top flat and it's got, like, a glass panel in it.' She said this without a trace of shame. 'I have a squint through that after I've done the top bedrooms. Seven he had up in there with him on Monday.'

'Do the permanent fixtures live there all the time?'

'They sleep there, I do know that. The one that looks like Yul Brynner and the girl and the little dark one.'

'Yul Brynner?' I said.

'You're young,' said Beryl, 'but you must know who he is. Didn't you never see *The King and I* on TV?'

It had been shown the week before. It usually is around Christmas and the New Year. I was still at my parents, who had a huge colour television. *The King and I* requires colour, it wouldn't have come over very well on old Mrs Fisherton's black and white set. The strange thing was that a few days later I *saw* him, 'the one that looks like Yul Brynner', I mean. I identified him from Beryl's description, there could be no doubt. It was my first day back at GUP and I was walking along the canal at Paddington Basin, my invariable route to avoid the underground, when I saw him on the opposite bank, talking to someone on the roof of a houseboat. I mean that the other person was on the roof of the houseboat. He was on the towpath. It could have been the King of Siam standing there, tall and thin with that same high-cheekboned pale brown Mongolian face, his head shaven. It was a cold morning in January and though he may have been wearing an embroidered satin jacket – I later discovered that he did, in fact, wear clothes like that – he had a huge and very dirty ankle-length sheepskin coat on top. While he talked he was eating, and offering the other man, squares he broke off a bar of chocolate.

Often, when I look forward to things, I've found I'm disappointed, and when I dread something it turns out to be not so bad. That didn't apply to my return to GUP, which I had really dreaded and which in the event was even worse than I had expected. That term, as part of the psychology course, we had groups scheduled and someone told me that meant group therapy, ten or twelve of us sitting round and telling the rest what went on in our heads. We'd be expected to talk about our childhoods and our relationships with our parents and, worst of all, traumatic events in our lives.

I missed the first session. It was on one of the days that I simply failed to go. There were a lot of those days by the time my twentieth birthday came in February. I didn't plan them, I'd simply wake up in the morning, look at the clock and decide I wasn't going in. I'd get up late and, instead of hanging about indoors battling against claustrophobia, wander round Maida Vale and Paddington, looking at buildings, especially the tops of buildings, following the course of the canal and dropping into cafés for a coffee or a milk shake and a sandwich. Once I ventured all alone into a pub and asked for a glass of white wine. No one stared, no one thought it odd, and after that I'd often have a drink in a pub with a roll or a hot pie for my lunch.

We sometimes have a sunny week in February. We did that year, it was warm and bright for five days. GUP didn't see me on any of them. I treated myself to a half-term holiday. I opened old Mrs Fisherton's bedroom window as wide as the sash would go and the bright fresh air rushed in. Another welcome visitor who rushed in was the tortoiseshell cat. I don't know if she belonged to someone or if her owner had moved and she had come back to her old home as cats do or if she was just a stray. But she seemed well-fed and when I found her curled up on my bed and stroked her she felt sleek and plump. By that time I had taken great strides in household management and was able to cook myself elaborate dishes like beans on toast and boiled eggs and pasta out of a packet. That evening I was going to have sardines but I gave them to the cat and had tinned spaghetti myself. Those sardines did the trick and she was mine. She went out every day and sometimes stayed out a long while but I left the window open for her, even when it got bitterly cold again, and she always came back. I called her Mabel after my ghostly hostess.

By then I had broken two rules of living at old Mrs Fisherton's, the no-smoking rule and the no-pets one. Nobody had told me pets weren't allowed. It was something you took for granted with Max and Selina, just as you assumed there'd be a no-leaving-windows-open rule, no sub-letting, no lovers and no one visiting after ten p.m. On my birthday Selina invited me to lunch. Or, rather, she invited me for a birthday lunch two days later, on the Saturday. She and Max naturally believed I had my nose to the grindstone at GUP on weekdays.

I had none of the sort of clothes you wear for parties. I wore jeans all the time, I still do, though they're designer jeans now and washed each time they're worn. My husband doesn't notice what I wear. He once said he no longer noticed what I looked like and I took it for a compliment. Washing had been a problem at old Mrs Fisherton's. I didn't know about launderettes, you don't if you live in the country. It was Beryl who told me there was one in Clifton Road and another in the Harrow Road. But that useful tip was in the future and I was still washing things by hand and hanging them over the kitchen sink or the bath. So the jeans I wore to have lunch with Max and Selina had been worn at least four times since I last washed them and my sweatshirt (red with GUP on it in black letters) was clean but creased.

Old Mrs Fisherton's iron flashed and fizzled when I tried to use it and I didn't know about electricity in those days.

That there would just be the three of us was what I had expected. Instead I found a full-scale luncheon party with drinks first in the yellow and emerald drawing room. Selina looked me up and down reflectively but said nothing. She was wearing a very short pink dress with a little flared skirt, pink shoes and the pearls. In the drawing room there was champagne already poured into the right sort of glasses on a tray and fizzy water or orange juice for those who preferred it and a great deal of the sort of food I've always disliked, bits of things on little squares of bread or toast or pastry. As I took a glass of champagne I tried to understand why they were doing all this for me, I had scarcely seen them since before Christmas, and now suddenly they were putting on a full-blown party for my birthday. Later on I got used to this pattern of behaviour, a kind of hard-soft technique, hot-cold or hawks and doves, and now I think the explanation is simple. They didn't want me, they didn't much like me and perhaps they regretted their generosity in letting me have the flat. Those were their hawkish times. And then their consciences would trouble them, they became doveish and 'made it up' to me in disproportionate gestures like this party.

I knew no one there, though I recognized the Silvermans. He wasn't wearing shorts this time but a thick tweed suit. When Selina introduced me I thought about what Beryl had said and wondered if the boy called Silver had hastily got rid of his friends for the weekend. Mrs Silverman looked at me the way I've noticed parents of the young look at other young. It's a wary look, an assessing look, distrustful and expecting the worst. If you met their young, would you have a bad influence on them, making them even worse than they already are? Maybe you're dealing drugs. Maybe you drink, do cocaine, drop out, vandalize phone boxes, write on walls, live in even worse squalor than they do. Make up your mind, they seem to be saying to themselves, to keep them away from yours at all costs. All that was in Mrs Silverman's look and her smile. Her handshake wasn't very enthusiastic either.

Her husband was nice. He wished me a happy birthday and even said he hoped I'd meet their son. I ought to meet some young people, not all this lot, he said, waving his hand at a man Selina said was a television producer, *her* producer, and a Wanda Something who had a restaurant in the King's Road. The producer was all smiles and jollity. A life-and-soul-of-the-party man. Like the rest of them, once he had kissed Selina, he started telling her how wonderful she had been in recent episodes of *Streetwise*, she was more famous than a film star. Selina simpered and smiled and said it was marvellous for an artist to be appreciated, it made everything worthwhile.

'I daresay the dosh isn't bad either,' said Jack Silverman.

'You said your son was coming,' replied Selina, showing her claws, 'but I suppose one word from you and he does as he likes.'

'We haven't seen him.' Erica Silverman sounded unhappy about it. 'The place was deserted when we got here on Friday night and the top flat an absolute tip. I sometimes wonder what we pay Beryl for.'

This, I felt, was most unfair. Beryl had often told me how willing she was to clean the top flat. It was 'the son', the missing Silver, who wouldn't let her in. Selina drew me away and introduced me to a woman who said she was 'just a housewife', an actor who'd been a 'guest star' on some of the *Streetwise* episodes, and a woman who designed and made cushions. I didn't catch their names. These last were more my sort of age, she said, lamenting the non-arrival of 'the Silverman boy'. The actor referred to Selina as my aunt and went on doing it after I had corrected him. The cushion designer wanted to know if I had 'ambitions to follow in her footsteps'. I said I hadn't. I was going to be a steeplejack. It was a stupid thing to say, I should have known better, but these people induced a rebelliousness in me and I became reckless.

'Oh, you must be the girl Selina told me about who climbed an electricity pylon with a boy and the boy got killed.'

I was disproportionately upset. Well, perhaps it wasn't all that disproportionate. I think it was the idle, the thoughtless, way she said it, as if it was something that might happen to anyone, all in the day's work, just one of those things. That upset me and knowing for sure that Max and Selina talked unfeelingly about me to their friends upset me too. At lunch I was seated not next to Max, which the cushion designer whispered to me would have been 'the proper thing' as the party was for me, but between the actor and a man I hadn't yet spoken to who turned out to be an accountant. Whether he was Max's accountant or just a friend who happened to belong to that profession,

I never discovered. After telling me his name, which I quickly forgot, and what he did, he never spoke to me again. We had ricotta cheese wrapped up in smoked salmon, followed by pasta, a potato dish with salad and a lemon cheesecake. The actor said that it would be fine if only one or two of one's friends served a whole lunch or dinner from the Marble Arch Marks & Spencer but the trouble was that everyone did it, so you found yourself eating the same things wherever you went. Then he said, 'Oh dear, I keep forgetting she's your aunt.'

I smiled. I'd managed to secrete one of the smoked salmon and cheese parcels into my pocket, wrapped up in my (paper) napkin. Mabel would enjoy it for supper. The food might be routine for some but it was a novelty to me after all those tins of things on toast and I ate greedily. Just as well, for no one addressed another word to me. I didn't mind that. I listened.

A lot of the conversation was about Selina, her rise to fame, her star status. The producer began it, as he began every new subject, laughing at his own wit and shooting questions at everyone. Wasn't Selina brilliant? Would anyone dream of being out of the house at eight-thirty unless they had set the video? Max said nothing but looked – I was going to say 'sulky' except that that's not a word to apply to anyone as august as he was. When the compliments became too fulsome he pursed his lips and looked down at his plate. A change of subject brought him relief and he smiled.

It was at that lunch that I first heard of the couple called Andrew Lane and Alison Barrie. I've only known one person of the age I was then who buys a newspaper and that was Silver. Sometimes I watched television and sometimes I listened to the radio but not to news programmes. So I had never heard of the Lanes (they were married, but Alison didn't use her husband's name) till that birthday lunch when we were all eating our cheesecake. I can't remember which of the company first mentioned them, I suppose it was the television producer, but I remember the question.

'What do we think about those Lanes, then?'

'Who?' Selina said.

'Don't you read your daily paper, Selina? They're the couple who have run away with the child the pernicious social services won't allow them to adopt.'

I wasn't very interested. I only listened because I was trapped.

Everyone began to talk at once. All had their views. The adoption process in this country was draconian and cruel. Social services departments said they put the interests of the child first but in practice that was the last thing they did. Political correctness was ruining people's lives. How about this stupid rule that children of mixed race had to be adopted by mixed-race parents?

I said everyone began to talk at once but Wanda the restaurateur didn't talk. She left her cheesecake half-eaten and, waving her glass, said abruptly to Max, who wasn't generous with the Chablis, 'Can I have some more wine?'

Someone realized then and they stopped awkwardly. The cushion woman told me while we were having coffee in the drawing room that Wanda, now divorced, had tried for years to adopt a child but had been turned down on the grounds of being too rich and upper class. The television producer must have known, everyone there knew, but people were so thoughtless, didn't I think?

'Sorry, I keep forgetting Selina's your aunt.'

I left the party as soon as I could. Max encouraged my departure with an approving, 'An essay to write,' but Selina, catching up with me at the head of the stairs, said that I couldn't be expected to know, doubtless I'd never been taught, but it really wasn't done to leave a party given in one's honour until everyone else had left. Now why hadn't my etiquette-conscious mother taught me that?

I went down the stairs, put the smoked salmon parcel on Mabel's plate and gave the wardrobe a push to set the hangers ringing. I was getting to like their music, the sound of jangling chimes.

7

I saw little of Max or Selina for a long time after that party. Living below ground, you see no comings and goings of the occupants of upper floors. The taxi that comes for them, the postman with a parcel they open the door to, their departure on foot, the van bringing the wine or food delivery, all this is as hidden from you as if it were happening a mile away. They may have forgotten my existence, for I made no noise. Something was wrong with the volume control on the television set and I could never make voices rise above a whisper. I had no friends arriving in the evening and leaving late at night. I had no friends. Instead of going upstairs to the yellow drawing room, I began making my weekly phone call to my mother from a call box. After some initial grumbling, she let me reverse the charges.

Days passed when I spoke to no one but Mabel and old Mrs Fisherton. No one came and no one phoned. Well, they couldn't, I had no phone. I'm not being self-pitying. I know it was my own fault. It was just an extension of the way I had been since Daniel died, reclusive, shut in, hiding away from everything and everyone. In those long months there had only been one person who tried hard enough to reach me and persisted in breaking through the barriers I had put up, Guy Wharton. I had never answered his letter. I had called my mother from a call box but I had never called him. Most women would have said I was crazy. Mum certainly would have. Guy was rich, good-looking if you like that stocky dark type, clever and with the kind of job mothers of girls love, something important in a merchant bank. While I was at home for Christmas, he too was at home on the other side of the river. He phoned and asked if he could come over to see me. I didn't want to talk to him but Mum refused to lie for me, so I took the receiver from her with very bad grace and said I had a bad cold, I couldn't see anyone.

Beryl brought his second letter down to me. It looked as if it had been steamed open and sealed up again but that was something I could

66

never have proved even if I had cared. He was writing to ask if he could take me out to dinner the following week.

'I haven't anything to wear,' I said to Beryl. 'Would jeans do?'

'Are you asking me, love? I was never took out for dinner in me life. I'll tell you what, you can have a lend of my girl's long black skirt, she's about your size. She says forget about the little black dress, it's a long black skirt'll take you anywhere so long as you put something bright on the top.' This was a version of Beryl's own habitual gear, on that particular day black leggings and a jumper in the shade Silver called 'hairdresser pink'. 'And talking of long skirts,' she said, 'I've found out what the Indian woman's name is. Nasreen. Well, I've heard of Irene and Doreen but I ask you, Nasreen.'

'What about the people with the futons on the floor?' I said. 'And what's happening to the Silvermans?'

'Well, dear, they've got so many houseplants it's like a rain forest in there. I half expect to see a tiger come prowling out but they haven't got no pets.'

'The Silvermans?'

'No, love, not them. The other lot. Mr Silverman and Mrs, they've only been up to London once since Christmas. Funny having Christmas in London when you've got a country place, isn't it? Still, it takes all sorts. They was all up here then, the girl and what she calls her partner and the one called Julian and the boy. Silver, I mean. He had to give his pals the go-by for the festive season. It's no good asking me any more because I've told you all I know.'

Beryl brought the black skirt and I wore it when Guy took me to dinner at the first really good restaurant I had ever eaten in, a place in Knightsbridge. I asked him something that had hardly been mentioned between us before. When he came up the field and saw us on the pylon, heard me screaming and came running, where had he been before, and why had he once said if only he had been ten minutes earlier, as he might easily have been?

He looked across the table at me in silence, making a rueful face. I thought it was a nice face, squarish, with good firm features, a strong jaw, a wide forehead, a straight nose. His eyes were dark brown, an eye colour I've never found attractive, but his were clear and honest. He'd raised his eyebrows and half-smiled.

'Are you really sure you want to know?'

'Why?' I said. 'Is it something awful?'

He laughed. 'Not at all awful. Banal. I asked because it occurred to me you might think it a trivial thing to make such a difference.'

'Tell me.'

'My parents were away. They'd gone on holiday to France. I was home on my own for the weekend and I'd arranged to meet a friend of mine, a chap I was at school with, for a drink. We were to meet at the White Rose.'

First of all he thought he'd take his car, but that would very much restrict what he drank and he hadn't seen the friend for a long time. Walk, why not? A mile and a half there and a mile and a half back if he went across the fields. In the event, of course, he never got to the pub. But he had set off about the time Daniel and I were looking at the pylon and thinking of climbing it, about the time Daniel said, 'People do go up, you see. They go up using the footholds, like climbing a ladder.'

Guy had got as far as the bridge. Then he had one of those second thoughts or fears we all have sometimes, you don't have to be an obsessive-compulsive to have them. He thought he had forgotten to lock the front door. The house was old and the front door one of those with a doorknob that don't automatically lock when you close them. There had been burglaries in the neighbourhood recently. Those days were gone, he remembered from his childhood, when you could go out and leave your house doors and car doors unlocked. He turned round and went back.

'And the door *was* locked,' he said. 'I needn't have gone back. That going back meant a delay of ten minutes even though I took the car with me that second time.'

'If you'd got there ten minutes earlier, you could have shouted at us and warned us.' I said it almost sorrowfully, hating retrospective hope. 'If you'd told us we were earthed and the current would go through us, maybe we'd have listened.'

After that I talked to Guy as I never had before. I told him about playing truant from GUP – it was happening more and more often as March came in – and about living below ground. He was sympathetic.

'Do a secretarial course instead,' he said, 'and I'll find you a job in my dad's firm. Then you could get a mortgage and buy yourself a flat on top of a high rise.'

He thought it was a joke, as it would be to most people. Anyway, I decided being a secretary might be worse than a psychological business person. I thanked him for the dinner, which was very good, and he said he'd phone me at Max's. That would be a bit of fun for Selina, I thought.

The dream in which exams loom but you have done no work, not only have failed to prepare for them but scarcely know what the subjects mean or the answers to the kind of questions likely to be put to you, was becoming my reality. In June we would be assessed on our year's work and that assessment would be taken into account when degrees were awarded. The more I thought of it, the more I avoided setting foot on campus – or, to put it more accurately, the wasteland between the canal and Wormwood Scrubs. I never dreamed of GUP. I dreamed of Daniel, the sounds he made while he hung in the latticework of the pylon and I held him till I could hold him no longer.

When parents take their children on holidays abroad in term time, they make the excuse that the children learn more in those few days in the Maldives or Costa Rica than they ever would in school. I acquired more knowledge in Maida Vale that spring than GUP could have taught me. The trouble was that it wasn't the sort of knowledge I was here for and it wouldn't help me to pass exams. I didn't much care, I blocked GUP off and tried to close my mind to it. I looked at buildings, I looked at churches. I even went to church on Sunday mornings to see what these buildings were like inside, to see what Street had done for the interior of St Mary Magdalene, its clerestories and its walls of striped brick and stone, and Comper for St Cyprian's, Glentworth Street, white and gold with angels on the altar. The Irvingites at the Holy Catholic Apostolic in Maida Avenue were unwelcoming, didn't throw me out but made me cover my head with a rather nasty chiffon scarf they produced from a collection kept for that purpose. I joined the library and read books on architecture. I read Ruskin in a spirit of amazement and doubt. 'Architecture is the art which so disposes and adorns the edifices raised by man, for whatever uses, that the sight of them may contribute to his mental health, power and pleasure.' That was all right, I agreed entirely. But as for some of the rest of it, did he really mean all this? 'There is nothing magical about a salvia leaf'? Was he mad? Or was it all a colossal send-up?

When it was Easter I went home and Guy came round to ask me out on the Saturday night. But I was back in London by then. At ten-thirty on Easter Day I was in St Augustine's, Kilburn Park, for Sung Eucharist, aware of the cold splash of holy water and the sound of hymns I had never heard before, but almost entirely rapt in contemplation of the size of the place, the narrow aisles, the buttresses, the gallery and its Gothic reredos and the profusion of sculpture in the chancel. This was a rough area of London, or so Beryl said, muggingsland, Heroinville. Her eldest son refused to drive down Kilburn High Road and made a detour along Carlton Vale. Yet in the midst of it, in a green oasis of lawns and tall trees, stood this cruciform church, vast and gracious, its spire visible for miles. That spire was half as high again as a pylon, a tapering needle more than 240 feet tall.

The wisest thing I could have done at this point would have been to go to Max, tell him how much I disliked the Psychology and Business Studies course and ask him how I could change and do Architecture instead. I nearly did. I went upstairs one Sunday evening (St Mary's, Paddington Green, that morning, the eighteenth-century church restored with compensation for building the Westway which takes its noisy and brutal route past its windows) and, forgetting my mother's rules, knocked on one door after another until Selina came.

'Haven't seen you since for ever, darling.'

I had nothing to say to this.

'I suppose you've been frantically busy. Like me. We're shooting the seventh series and you know what that means, a six a.m. start for little me.'

She was alone in the sitting room at the back of the house, a pretty place done in pink and grey with french windows opening on to a balcony. The drawing room was too grand for daily use. I later found out from Beryl that both rooms had been dismal when Max and Selina first met, furnished much like old Mrs Fisherton's. Beryl told me that Selina had spent a fortune on doing them up, all the money she got from series one and two of *Streetwise*. She patted the pink velvet chair next to hers, motioning me to sit down, as if I were a regular visitor. Although they didn't seem to have had any company that day and it was a Sunday evening, she was dressed in a smart green suit with ruffle-necked blouse pinned with a cameo brooch.

'I was wondering,' I said, having rehearsed this, 'if I could have a word with Max.'

Did I mean now? She could hardly have looked more aghast if I had asked to bring fifteen friends round to supper.

'Well, now,' I said, 'or soon.'

'He's working on his book, darling. It's more than my life's worth to disturb him. He's got a deadline of May 1st.'

'Would you ask him? Would you ask him if I could see him tomorrow or Tuesday?'

Selina said she could try. She didn't know if I could be made to understand this but Max was peculiar about this sort of thing. He liked to arrange his own appointments. In other words, he didn't care for people wanting to see him. It was for him to want to see *them*.

'I'm sure he'll see you. In his own time. I mean, only the other day he was saying he must have a talk with Clodagh, wasn't he?' She had begun one of those dialogues with herself. 'I must have another chat with Clodagh, he said. Those were his words. Something like that, anyway. I must get Clodagh up here and see how she's getting on. So he'll be sure to send for you. I'll be amazed if he doesn't after what he said. It's just a matter of time.'

All right, I said, but would she ask him just the same? It was important. I really needed to see him. Downstairs again, I played the wardrobe bells. After a lot of practice I'd learnt how to make different music according to which parts of the doors or sides I slammed my hand against. Mabel came in through the window. I picked her up and cuddled her and told her I didn't think Max would send for me, or not for weeks. Selina's passing on my request would very likely annoy him and he'd keep me waiting. I was right. I heard no further word about a meeting with Max.

Since then I've often thought about how different my life might have been − like Guy, I'm something of a 'might have been' and 'If only' person − if he had agreed to see me, if he had sent me a note or a verbal message via Selina. I'd have gone up those stairs to the top but, this time, I'd have knocked on the door. Max would have said, 'Come!' He was the kind of person who talked like that. When I went in he'd have been sitting at his desk, he wouldn't have looked up but kept me waiting for, say, two minutes, while I contemplated the quantities of paper in which, by then, the room might have been ankle-deep. I imagined him turning round at last, sniffing the air and asking if I'd been smoking, and perhaps saying, like a doctor, 'What seems to be the trouble?'

Then, of course, when I confessed, he would have been angry. But I think he'd have been gratified too. I should never have gone to a polytechnic in the first place, as he had often said. His anger would have been for my idleness and indecision, his gratification because I had found out my error in time. Architecture, of course, wasn't academic enough for his taste but it was a lot more academic than Psychology and Business Studies. He'd have to make inquiries. A course for me would be found at a 'proper university'. I could start in October. Max would have been in his element researching this, it might even have distracted him from his book. And meanwhile? Surely I'd have been sent home to Suffolk for six months, there would have been no point in my remaining in London with nothing to do but get into mischief. After all, the architecture course would probably not even have been in London, I might first have to take another A-level. He'd have been full of plans, not the least of them very likely being legitimately to evict me from old Mrs Fisherton's. I'm sure he and Selina regretted ever letting me into the place.

I would have got into a course somewhere or other, maybe in Scotland or the north of England, and eventually got an architecture degree. And, who knows, perhaps it would have been me and not Richard Rogers designing the Millennium Dome. What is certain is that I'd never have met the people who lived at Silver's and I'd never have climbed the roofs of Maida Vale. I'd never have met my husband.

But Max didn't see me. He was too busy with his book and, in the event, according to Selina, did meet its deadline of May 1st. Was there anyone else I could consult? My parents would simply urge me to keep on with Psychology and Business Studies. So, probably, would my supervisor at GUP. If I asked her, Caroline Bodmer would certainly ask *me* why she had scarcely seen me this past term, and then, hopeful of seeing the back of me, advise me to change to Social Anthropology or Media Studies. The first day of the new term was a Tuesday. I made an appointment to meet my supervisor and 'talk about my future' on the Thursday afternoon at two.

Wednesday was a lovely day. I spent it walking Maida Vale from Carlton Hill to Park Place Villas, discovering for the first time streets or insertions into streets of houses apparently built in the twenties, and gathered in enclaves behind the towering Victorian terraces. Why were they there? What had been there before them? Some large villa standing in acres of grounds? Or simply fields? I went back to my old haunt, Paddington Recreation Ground, sat on a seat and ate my lunch and read a history of London in maps, which told me those houses owed their existence to First World War bombing. Zeppelins dropped a 660-pound bomb on Warrington Crescent in March 1918. It pulverized four houses and damaged a thousand others. I had had no idea. If I had ever thought about it, I had assumed aerial bombing was invented in 1939, before my parents were born. It amazed me to read that there were fifty-seven air raids on London between 1914 and 1918.

I read that and then I got down to *The Seven Lamps of Architecture*. That was my trouble, I'd read Ruskin and then a library book on domestic building, then Cherry and Pevsner's *London North-West;* I'd alternate a Peter Ackroyd novel with Kent's *The Lost Treasures of London* and then go straight into something about Pugin and the Palace of Westminster. There was no plan to it and, of course, no guidance, which is why my knowledge of architecture today is a muddle, a catalogue of terms like 'crocket' and 'squinch' and 'cantilever', useless anecdotes and an abiding love of London houses. That's one of the advantages of being an electrician, you get to go inside a lot of them.

Walking back to old Mrs Fisherton's I studied all those pathetic little posters people put up on lamp-posts asking if you've seen their cat Gismo or Benjy or Tara, a Blue Persian or an Abyssinian or a Silverpoint Siamese, who's been missing for a day or a week or a fortnight. There were always several and I always looked at them and the sad little photographs on them. I was expecting to see a portrait and description of Mabel but there never was one and by then I was pretty sure there never would be. I was at the top of the iron staircase when a taxi pulled up and Selina got out of it. She came tripping up the path in her kitten-heel white shoes, her short white pleated skirt just brushing her knees, and looking as if about to take part in a women's doubles match.

'Just back from your college, darling?'

I smiled.

'One of those red-brick places wants to give Max an honorary degree. What do you think of that?'

'It's an honour, isn't it?' I said.

'He's turned it down, darling. Naturally. One must maintain one's standards, he says. Polytechnics will be giving those things next.'

I still remember in fine detail that day and the one that followed it, just as I remember pylon day and a certain day walking by the canal in August. Whether other people's memories work like that I don't know, but I have always been able to recall all the circumstances and conversations and the feelings I had on momentous or terrible days, as if these things were written on tablets of stone for me to reread at will or in spite of myself. I don't always need my diaries. So it was on that August day and that Thursday. Thursday was when I met Silver.

Beryl came in in the morning. Her knowledge of honorary degrees was as sketchy as mine but she merited a first-class degree herself in listening at doors and overhearing private conversations. 'The Professor', she said, had written to a newspaper. *The Times*, she thought it was, one of those big papers, anyway, not the kind 'normal people' read, and told them this place had offered him whatever it was and he had turned it down. He was furious because they had neither printed his letter nor written anything about it in their pages. And *she*, Mrs that is, had said maybe they'd only write about it if it was Oxford or Cambridge and the Professor said not to be more stupid than she could help, if it had been Oxford or Cambridge he'd have accepted it. That was my first intimation that for Max and Selina, marriage might not be all sweetness and light.

Beryl was wearing black leggings again, loose on her stick-like legs, and a bright lime-green jumper. She'd covered her hair with a turban which made her look like a 1940s factory worker I had seen pictured in one of my London books. She told me I wasn't to worry about Mabel. She knew for a fact her owners had lived in Sutherland Avenue, moved out and left her with their old neighbours who had never really wanted her. I'd be doing everyone a kindness if I kept her. As to the Professor and Mrs, they were going to have their dining room done up, turquoise and black and white, very nice if you fancied cans of baked beans. The decorators would be in and out for months, leaving dirty footmarks. Beryl sniffed the air appreciatively. I had been smoking like a chimney, she could tell, ruining my young lungs, but it made a lovely perfume.

She left at one and soon after I set off for GUP and my interview with my supervisor. To face the music but also to get advice. I went, as always, down the steps into the little garden in Warwick Avenue, through the shrubbery and out on to the canal bank. That something was wrong I could tell before I had gone under the bridge. On the other side of it, blocking the path, were a barrier strung with blue and white police crime tape and a policeman and a man in plain clothes who might have been another, standing in front of it. I stopped, looked at them and beyond. Up ahead, just behind where the flyover passes, at the point where I normally left the canal bank, were more policemen and something lying on the towpath. I couldn't see any part of it but it was obviously a body. Someone had covered it with a big scarlet cloth. The policemen standing beside it were laughing about something and that shocked me, though not as much as the prospect before me.

'Use the underpass, will you, love,' the plain-clothes man said. 'Just up there and cross the road.'

I said I knew where it was, considered asking him if he'd let me through, saying I wouldn't tell anyone and I wouldn't linger, but I knew it would be hopeless. So I went back the way I had come and crossed Warwick Avenue. It was one-fifteen and my appointment with Caroline Bodmer was for two. If it hadn't been for that and the hoped-for resolution of all my difficulties, I'd have gone back home. I wouldn't have considered the underground route. Even so, I sat on a wall and thought about it. I sat there for a couple of minutes and told myself that I had made great strides towards conquering my claustrophobia at old Mrs Fisherton's. I slept well, in spite of being in bed in a more or less subterranean room. I hardly ever felt the walls were closing in and crushing me. Panic no longer drove me to run up the iron staircase or lean out of the window and stare at the sky. I disliked the place but I was living in it, it was bearable. I got up, crossed Howley Place and went down the ramp to the underpass.

There's a Victorian pub on the way there. I passed it the other day and it's being decorated, smartened up with cream paint. Everything else is that depressing sort of sixties modernity, big blocks of sand-coloured flats. The footpath dips down and just before the opening into the underpass is one of those barriers only pedestrians can pass through. A sign on it says: *Cyclists Dismount*. Up above is a three-tier rack of throughways, the exit road and the twin decks, one above the other, of the Westway. When I went down there at twenty-five past one on that Thursday it was the quietest time of the day for traffic but still the passing vehicles travelling at high speed made a continuous roar and throb. I saw someone come out of the tunnel mouth and turn up towards St Mary's churchyard. Cautiously, I passed through the barrier.

If you see a woman looking warily about her before going into an underpass, you know she's nervous of encountering someone down there who'll mug her or rape her. Those perils never crossed my mind. There was no one, anyway, to see me enter the tunnel and stand on the threshold, close by the wall.

An enormous relief came. The underpass was much shorter than I'd expected, surely no more than sixty feet long. I could see a brick wall facing me at the end and daylight. The passage is lined with tiles, whitish, ribbed, dirty. I made my way along it, my hands on the tiled wall, telling myself that six months before, when I had come here in the tube, I had been underground in the tube for half an hour, and survived without weeping or screaming. Compared to the tube this was nothing, this was a pussycat. Yet all my relief had gone. I still don't understand why this airy, quite light, spacious passage frightened me so much, why it crippled me so that I could scarcely walk. I crept along, each instance of setting one foot an inch before the other a victory. The tiles felt cold and, worse, seemed to move a little, to wobble under my hands as if made of jelly, the walls and ceiling swelling and shrinking, and the floor like shifting sands.

But the brick wall was just ahead, and the fresh air. I reached it, gasping, still pressed against that undulating, slightly sticky wall, and found myself in a roofless circular space, open to the sky. An amphitheatre without seats, it was also without windows, was interrupted only by the tunnel exit from which I had come – and a second opening leading to the rest of the underpass. I hadn't reached the end, I was halfway through.

I can't account for my terror. It wasn't dark or airless in there, I could even see natural light at the end of this second passage. It was no greater in length than the one I had just made my way through. But I was terribly afraid. Of what, I don't know. The claustrophobic's worst experiences are those where the fear has no name and no definition. It's a dread of some unidentifiable nemesis. Trying to analyse it afterwards leaves you confused and angry and knowing it will be just the same next time.

There, in the brickwork cylinder, pushing myself hard against the curve of the wall as if, like a secret panel, it might at the right kind of pressure open and let me out into sunlight and air, I clung, knowing I could neither go on nor go back. I leant against the wall, my back to it, my fingers holding the shallow ridges of mortar while I gazed up at the blue sky, my heart beating heavily, rhythmically, with blows that hurt my ribs.

There was, of course, no longer any hope of getting to GUP by two, there was no hope of getting there at all, of getting anywhere. This was the end of the world. I was there for ever. I sank down slowly to the concrete floor, wrapping my arms round my knees and bowing my head against them. If his footfalls made any sound, it failed to reach me. He came through from the Paddington Station end, treading softly and cat-like in thick-soled trainers. I sensed someone was there and I lifted my head. Saying I knew who it was sounds impossible, but I did. It was his extreme fairness, so accurately described by Beryl, which identified him. I saw a face that was lightly tanned, with just a little colouring on its high forehead, regular features and short nose. His shapely mouth wasn't full enough for a girl but was just right for a man. He had rainwater grey eyes and his hair was cut short and trim, white-blond as crystal. A tall, slim, wiry person of about my own age in blue jeans and a blue and green checked shirt with the sleeves rolled up.

'Is something wrong?'

He said it gently, almost tenderly. It was a peculiarity of our generation, I believe, that, largely indifferent to the fate of the middle-aged and elderly, we cared about the very old and we cared about our contemporaries. When Max was twenty or when my father was, I don't think they'd have stopped and asked what was troubling a girl they had found hunched up on the floor of an underpass. They'd have been too inhibited, too callous and probably too busy. It wasn't, after all, as if I was an attractive sight, with tears running down my face, tunnel-wall dirt all over my hands and streaked down my cheeks.

I saw no point in pretence. 'I get claustrophobia. I'm frightened of being underground.'

The young Max and my father (if they had got this far) would have told me to pull myself together, to have a bit of spirit. Silver put out his hands to take my dirty ones and said, 'Come on, then. I'll get you out. Which way do you want to go?'

'That way.' I pointed behind me. 'I'd have gone along the canal but there's a dead person on the towpath.'

'What an interesting life you lead. Do you mean you found a dead body?'

'I found the policemen beside the body,' I said. 'They were *laughing*.'

'The world's a wicked place.' He said it with deep seriousness, then, 'Does it help to keep your eyes shut? Pretend you're blind and I'm getting you across the street. Trust me.'

'I trust you,' I said, and then, as I closed my eyes, 'You're Silver. You live at 15 Russia Road.'

He didn't seem surprised. 'Everyone knows me.'

Instead of putting his arm round me, he took my arm the way people don't seem to any more but just as he might have supported an old blind woman. 'Right, we're crossing the street now. Are you OK? There's a bus coming so we'll wait for it to go by, it's a 16 going to Victoria, I like dodging in and out of traffic, don't you, the driver's shouting at me and sticking up two fingers, not very polite, and here comes a fire engine, it's turned its siren on, wee-ha-wee-ha-wee-ha-wow-wow-wow-wow, and another one, make way for the fire engines, folks, oh my goodness, there's a truck reversed smack bang into a Volvo, what a mess, and the poor lady driver in tears, her old man's going to kill her when he sees that fender, but never mind, it's not our business and we're across the road in one piece. How's that?'

I was laughing by then, I who had been certain I'd never laugh again. At the same time, opening my eyes on the grey ramp, the pub and a cyclist dismounting at the barrier, I thought how little I had laughed these past six months. It was a wonder I remembered how to do it. Silver was looking at me with his head on one side.

'D'you live in Russia Road, then?'

'At 19,' I said, 'in the basement flat.'

'That must be a bundle of laughs for a claustrophobic.'

'I'm sort of getting used to it.'

He nodded, not so much in agreement but as if he was beginning to gather the information he wanted. 'The old fellow with the fluffy white hair who's a teacher and the woman who's a barmaid in *Coronation Street*.'

'*Streetwise*.'

'They're not your parents, are they?'

'He's a sort of cousin.'

We had gone through the footpath into Howley Place and were walking towards St Mary's Gardens. Silver asked me if I was going home. It couldn't be very attractive, he expected I'd be out a lot.

'I'm a student at a place called the Grand Union Polytechnic,' I said. 'What I mean is, I *was* a student there, but I think I've blown it,' and I told him about hardly ever going there and the missed appointment with Dr Bodmer. 'I suppose that what it amounts to is I've dropped out. I'll have to make decisions now. I'll have to tell Max.'

'Who's Max?'

'The old fellow with the fluffy white hair who's a teacher.' I started laughing again.

'I'll tell you what. Why not come home with me and I'll show you my place. It's on the top, not at all claustrophobic.' He took my arm again and this time we crossed a real instead of a pretend road. 'You don't want to rush into decisions,' he said confidingly. 'I never do. Things have a way of deciding themselves for you if you leave them alone. It's like messages left on the answerphone or letters people send you. If you don't reply, nothing dreadful happens. If I were you, I'd forget about it and enjoy myself. I mean yourself. That's the way to get through life, I find. Enjoy yourself. Have fun. And above all, don't worry. I never do.'

I learnt many good things from Michael Silverman but the most valuable was not to worry needlessly. If I had been the age I am now, it would have been too late, but twenty is young enough for a radical alteration to take place in the character. By example, Silver taught me not to fret about things I couldn't change and he taught me to be patient, to 'wait and see'. Hardly anyone enjoyed life, he said, but when you came to think of it, now no one believed in heaven any more, enjoyment of life was what everything we did aimed at. Doing

79

the work we liked and were trained for, keeping healthy, making money, loving others, having children, eating and drinking, all this was designed to make us happy but it seldom did because people forgot what its purpose was. Silver said he had decided to be happy first, to get into the habit of happiness, and let the rest follow if it would.

One day we were in a train, he and I, not a tube, of course, but the above-ground Hammersmith line that runs from Paddington. A beggar was working the passengers, carrying his tin for contributions in one hand and a card with *Homeless and Hungry* on it in the other. There were some who gave him their loose change but most people ignored him, taking a sudden passionate interest in their newspapers or staring with concentration at the advertisements. Silver beckoned him over and patted the seat next to him. The beggar thought he was going to get a fiver, I suppose, but Silver took the card from him and asked if he'd like something a bit more dynamic written on it, something that would appeal to people's sympathy. The beggar said he would, mate, you bet. *Homeless and Hungry* wasn't getting him very far. Silver turned the card over and wrote on it in big print with the thick felt-tip he always carried, *Would I be doing this if I could do anything else?*

It worked. We followed him into the next carriage and watched him collect, notes as well as coins. Morna told me Silver had done this sort of thing before. They were walking down Queensway together, it was a fine day in early April, and a blind man sitting on the pavement asked them for money. He hadn't a card at all, only his dog and his white stick. Silver bought a card in a newsagent's, wrote on it *It's spring and I'm blind* and propped it up against his begging tin. It drew a crowd, Morna said. He told Silver he ought to be an advertising copywriter and Silver said maybe he would one day, he was too busy with other things at present. I don't know if those two examples illustrate Silver's faculty of happiness, perhaps they don't, perhaps they're irrelevant, but they're typical of the way he was.

That Thursday afternoon in April, when he rescued me from the underpass, we walked back to Russia Road arm in arm. Anyone seeing us might have supposed us old friends who had been together for years. He talked to me about things no young person usually knows anything about. The gardens of Maida Vale, for instance. Had I looked at the gardens? The flowers? A house in Warrington Crescent had a mimosa in a pot in the basement, its leaves and yellow flowers reaching up to the first-floor window. It was in flower in December. Another had a tree fern. Look at that wisteria, he said, look at the garrya and its green catkins. Did I know why the gardens of Maida Vale were full of rare and beautiful plants? It was because of the nursery in Clifton Villas, he said, the best and oldest in London, 100 years old, and it only stocked special plants. Everyone went to it to stock their gardens. Suppose, in its stead, a typical garden centre had been there, selling pampas grass and kanzans and privet. The whole place would look quite different.

He let us into 15 Russia Road. The hall I'd caught a glimpse of before was just like Max and Selina's, same beige carpet, same console table, same, or very nearly the same, but a chandelier instead of a lantern, and instead of the country-house prints a strange dark painting of Dutch people playing cards. On the wall facing the picture hung two glass cases of butterflies, their beautiful corpses with spread wings pinned to a black background, Painted Ladies, Red Admirals, a Purple Emperor.

'You're not bothered by heights, are you?' he asked.

'Not a bit. I like heights.'

'Yes. Silly question. I ought to know that someone who doesn't like tunnels is going to love being high up.'

Four flights of stairs. At the top the arrangement of rooms was quite different from Max's. Facing me, beyond a small square landing, was the door with the glass panel in it that afforded Beryl those tantalizing views of what went on inside. But there was no view that day. Someone had pinned a sheet of paper over the glass on the inside. Silver unlocked the door and we went in. Again I expected something like Max's top floor but it was quite different. It was as if someone had made all the little rooms into an open-plan arrangement and then attempted to turn them back again with makeshift plaster-board walls and a couple of Victorian tapestry screens. I later got to know that there were three bedrooms up there and a living room.

The main room overlooked the back. It was quite big still, the acceptable bit of the open plan. It was very untidy, very 'lived in', and I expect it was dirty but you don't notice dust and fingermarks when you're twenty. There were three of those dormers in the room, just as there were at the front, casements with arched tops, and all of them were wide open, grey net curtains blowing and tangling themselves on the window catches. On a once handsome leather sofa, now scratched and stained with ink or paint, lay a girl of about my own age fast asleep.

'That's Liv,' Silver said. 'She's Swedish. She ran away from some children.'

'*Her* children, d'you mean?'

'They were monsters, she says. She was their nanny.'

Was she his girlfriend? I felt my euphoria waver. 'Why here?' I said.

'People of our sort of age run away a lot, don't you find? They're always running away from something or other and they mostly seem to come here. Word gets round, I suppose. There's a guy called Jonny, he's sort of her boyfriend, I mean he is *now*, he ran away from prison.'

'Prison?'

'An open prison. One of those places where you can walk round the grounds if you want, so naturally he walked round them and walked out. They got him back, it was a while ago. You look puzzled. You mustn't worry, you'll get it sorted after a time. I know it's confusing to start with.'

So there was going to be 'a time'. And this Liv was someone else's girlfriend, not Silver's. Her face was childlike in sleep, a child who had been up a chimney, black mascara smudged on her high cheekbones. The kind of fair hair that comes in stripes, yellow, pale blonde, straw and mouse brown, lay spread out on a cushion in a torn red cover. I went to one of the windows and looked out. The sky was blue and clear, my eyes were on a level with the topmost branches of a tree from which a pigeon with pink breast feathers looked back at me. I could see over the rears of the houses in the next street to a white stucco turret beyond and, distantly, the knife-shaped spire of St Saviour's church. The air was fresh yet warm and I inhaled it gratefully.

'Let's have a cup of tea,' said Silver. 'She'll wake up when she hears the clink of spoons, she always does. And the others will come soon.'

'The others?'

'Wim and Jonny. We're quite slack at the moment.' He spoke as if he ran a boarding house, which in a way, I suppose, he did. I followed him into the kitchen. No one seemed to have washed any dishes for days. Crumbs on the floor were mixed with what I thought might be mouse droppings. Silver filled the kettle and switched it on. It was one of those jug kettles and had once been white but was now encrusted with a thick uneven brownish-grey film. 'You're right about the mice,' he said, though I hadn't expressed my thoughts aloud. 'Liv likes them, she's mouse-crazy. It's a sure way to get them to come out at night, put a heap of crumbs in the middle of the floor.'

We took our tea back into the living room. In spite of what Silver had said, Liv didn't wake. I didn't hear a sound, not a creak or footfall, and when Silver said in his tranquil easy tone, 'Ah, here comes Wim, I think,' I looked towards the hall and the front door. Silver was laughing.

A pair of long legs had appeared at the window on the extreme right. They slid through the open casement, feet in black trainers dropping to the floor. The man I had seen on the canal bank had come in through the window, come from nowhere, out of the sky, for all I knew. He stood there, his eyebrows up, looking at me and smoothing away from his face with long brown hands his non-existent hair.

8

The most difficult kinds of roof to walk on are those on buildings put up in the past 100 years. These roofs are usually tiled, either with peg tiles or pantiles, and they slope steeply. It is as if architects like Lutyens and Mackintosh and Voysey only realized in the twentieth century that it rains a lot here and steep slopes on roofs provide better drainage. The best kinds are shallow and made of slates, preferably with a stone coping or a low wall at the edge, designed to hide from view the fact that the roof slopes at all. The more ornamentation on a roof the better, the more gables, belvederes, single chimney stacks and mansarding, the easier it is to climb. Single detached houses are useless to the serious climber. Standing alone as they do, no matter how shallow their roofs, no matter how many footholds the tops of their dormer windows, their pediments and parapet rails provide, they remain islands. The open air, the gap between them and the house next door, which may be several or many feet, is the sea which divides them from the continent. Climbers need terraces, each house joined to the one next door and preferably not divided from it at roof level by a stack that is a barrier to their progress, a high wall spanning the breadth of the roof and carrying a dozen closely set chimney pots or cowls.

The experienced climber despises television aerials and dishes as aids to balance keeping. He treads fast and light-footed on tile and coping and window ledge. He understands that the first big mistake the climber makes is to dislodge a slate and set it clattering down to ricochet off the coping and crash on the ground. He holds on only to that which is firm and steady, avoiding 100-year-old chimney pots, drainpipes and flimsy plaster mouldings. The best climbers are light in weight and supple.

Most roof sounds pass unheard by the householder who *knows* it's impossible anyone is walking in the sky up above her head. What she hears must be the wind, the rustling and rasping of tree branches. Or a cat may be up there. She has seen a cat on these roofs. At the veterinary practice in St John's Wood they tell her that most of the cats they treat are brought in with broken legs. The cat on the roof or balcony sees a butterfly and leaps in pursuit of it into the shining void.

We were like cats but we saw no butterflies. Mostly we went on the roofs after dark. In daylight you had the view, north London laid out below you, Hampstead Heath and Highgate Wood, the heights of Mill Hill, the canal coming out of its tunnels and entering Regent's Park, but by day you might be seen. Not everyone is in her car or stares at the ground when she walks. Once or twice we were seen but nothing came of it. What would you think if you saw three people in blue jeans and dark sweaters up on the roof of mansion flats? That they were workmen putting up an aerial, of course, or doing repairs to the guttering.

By night the lights were strung out and spread and scattered below us. No unpolluted sky was ever so starry. But up where we were, above the lights, the darkness was like thin smoke, the clouds and clear spaces above us stained plum-coloured. When I first began I carried a torch and Liv had the inevitable candle until Wim stopped her. We must learn to see in the dark, he said, as he did. He was our teacher, as it might be a ski instructor with a class of novices on the slopes.

At my school, on the last day of term, the fourth form traditionally played a game called 'round and round the room'. You had to circle the gym from the main entrance and back without once touching the floor, and you did it by means of wall bars, a horse, a climbing frame and, of course, ropes. People who inadvertently tapped the floor with a toe were disqualified. The winner was the girl or boy to do it in the shortest time. I won it easily in my fourth-form year and got the prize, a tiny silver (silver plate) cat, but unfortunately, you can't take A-levels in negotiating gyms. The roofs of Maida Vale became my gym and a lot of other things besides. For a little while.

People would think you mad, or at least very eccentric, if you told them you climbed on roofs. Of course, you seldom do tell anyone because you know what the reaction will be. They don't understand. They want to know why. But you might as well ask why some shoot up heroin or drink brandy or go dancing or climb mountains or do white-water rafting. They like it or they thought they would like it when they began.

It takes a certain kind of person. No one who was afraid of heights would attempt it. No one unfit or unsure on their feet *should* attempt it. It takes a kind of lawlessness, an unconventional spirit. Claustrophobics are good at it. Some, a very few, are geniuses at it. Wim was, we weren't. Liv wasn't, and Jonny, though good, wasn't in Wim's class. For us, it was the freedom we could find nowhere else, but once we had pushed ourselves to the limits of what we could do and experienced it to the full, we wanted it no longer.

This morning I interviewed Lysander Taylor and took him on. He'll start tomorrow. He can do some of the jobs Darren says are not for me, they're 'beneath me'. Apparently I should be into administration, sitting in our little Camden Town office, managing and directing. When we started on the Paddington Basin contract I should avoid these tin-pot jobs, putting batteries in clocks and replacing fuses.

'I've never once been called out to put a battery in a clock,' I protested.

'You know what I mean. You're an inverted snob, you are, poking about in these crummy council flats and hobnobbing with riff-raff. For instance, this call that's come in from that Mrs Clarkson, my sort of brother-in-law can do that. Let her wait. He can do it tomorrow.'

'Mrs Clarkson?' I said. 'Did she ask for me?'

'Of course she did, Clo. You're the only one of us she knows by name. But that's no reason for you to come running.'

'Ah, but I used to know her,' I said, ignoring his cast-up eyes. 'She's a figure from my past. Tell something, Darren. If Lysander's your sort of brother-in-law, do you have two sort of wives and does that make you a sort of polygamist?'

He gave me a sidelong glance. 'She never said what she wanted, just would you drop in when you've a moment. Maybe she only wants a chat about old times. Never mind your time's precious, you've got to work for your living.' The look became suspicious, the kind of probing stare you get from the doctor when he thinks you may have jaundice or measles. 'What d'you mean, a figure from your past? And don't, for God's sake, say "just someone I used to know".'

'OK, I'll say it's none of your business, if you like that better.'

So Liv wanted to see me. I was intrigued. I asked Clare who's our part-time receptionist and phone-answerer to give her a ring and say I'd be along at midday. Whatever she wanted to see me about, it wasn't two-gang dimmer switches this time.

Liv came from Kiruna in the north of Sweden. It's not far from the Arctic Circle, in the wintertime there's no daylight and in summer no darkness. The hotels have black blinds at their windows so that in June and July guests can sleep. Kiruna's mountain of iron is what once made Sweden rich. A curious feature of the place is the Iceland poppies that grow wild there, pushing up their papery orange and pink and red blossoms through cracks in the paving stones and out of the thin green grass. I went there three years ago to see the midnight sun.

Liv was eighteen and just out of school when she came to London. She was the only child of respectable hard-working total abstainers, her father a mining engineer, her mother a dental nurse. They wanted her to go to the University of Uppsala, which is the Oxford of Sweden – they had ideas much like my parents' – but, like mine, her school exam results didn't reach the required level. Her job as an au pair was properly arranged through a reputable agency with headquarters in Stockholm and a branch in London. She was to be paid the statutory rate, do light housework and occasionally fetch a child, aged seven, from school. There would be babysitting too but she would have three evenings off a week and time in the day to attend her English classes. All Swedes learn English at school and most speak it well but Liv didn't. Part of her reason for coming here was to acquire good idiomatic English, at least as good as her father's.

I've mentioned the post-war houses, of which there are enclaves in Maida Vale, as if bits of suburbia had intruded to remind visitors that the suburbs proper would start a mile or so up the Edgware Road. It was in one of these houses, two-storeyed, detached, half-timbered, with a steep red-tiled roof, that Liv's employers or 'hosts', as they called themselves, lived.

'As if I was a guest and didn't work for them,' she said.

Their name was Hinde, Claudia and James, and they had three children, not one. The youngest was a baby of nine months. Both parents worked full-time. Claudia – Liv was told to call them by their first names, not that she often got the chance as they were seldom at home – was, like Guy, something important in a merchant bank, maybe the *same* merchant bank, and James was on the Stock Exchange. Liv described them as 'rich' with a dizzy lifestyle. The only time of the day when she had help with the children was at breakfast before the parents left for work. With the phone receiver in one hand and a feeding bottle in the other, Claudia fed the baby while James cut toast 'soldiers' for the four-year-old Marcus, his eyes on his electronic organizer. Liv said it was as if, knowing they would have nothing more to do with their children that day but conscious of having some duty towards them, they 'got it over with' first thing in the morning when they were fresh. They were always out of the house by eight-thirty when she was due to take Cyrus, the eldest, to school, and necessarily take Marcus and the baby with her.

Supplies arrived at the house twice a week from a food delivery company but she still had to shop. She was expected to drive the Range Rover, a much larger vehicle than any of which she had previous experience. It was on one of these shopping expeditions that she met Jonny, the attendant at the car park she used, sitting in his glass booth taking payment and raising the exit barrier. But that was quite a long time ahead. She hadn't been in the house more than a couple of days before she realized she was expected to be a nanny, not an au pair. She told Silver she didn't even like children. With no brothers and sisters of her own, she had no experience of children, yet there she was with a baby to feed and with nappies to change, a four-year-old to look after and amuse and a bad-tempered, truculent, very big boy of seven to control.

The 'light housework' never, in fact, came into it as a woman came in to clean and put the washing in the machine. Liv would much have preferred housework to childcare. This woman must have been rather like Beryl, cheerful, chatty, hard-working and herself the mother of a family, and she had been coming in three times a week since before Cyrus was born. Liv said, though not quite in these words, that this woman was the only permanency in the children's lives, the only human being they could be sure of regularly seeing. It was she who hugged them and talked to them and called them 'darling'. If their parents ever did these things, it must have been in the night and Liv had neither the time nor the inclination. She came to hate them and this made her feel guilty and ashamed. But she had so much to do.

The school run was a recurring nightmare, especially as she was afraid of the Range Rover and never in perfect control of it. Both the baby and Marcus had to be strapped into child seats in the back and unstrapped and lifted out to accompany her if she needed to shop. Once Marcus lay on the supermarket floor, screaming and kicking. He often did this at home, he seems to have been a deeply disturbed child, and there she tried to ignore him, for she was afraid that otherwise she would strike him and do him a serious injury. Another time, while Cyrus was at school, she left Marcus and the baby strapped into their seats while she went to buy milk, bread and baby cereal. When she came back to the locked car a crowd of angry people were round it, some of them shouting at the children not to be afraid, it was all right, and where was their mummy. Both were screaming and Marcus was beating on the door with his fists. The terrible thing was, Liv said, that while she was in the shop she had half-hoped someone would come and abduct them.

Why didn't she make a fuss, say this wasn't what she was engaged for? She seldom saw Claudia or James, even at the weekends they were mostly out, saying they needed 'space', they needed 'a break'. But of course she sometimes saw them and then she did complain. She said it was too much for her, she wasn't qualified to be a nanny and had no experience.

They were incredulous. But surely there wasn't all that much to do, no cleaning, for instance, no washing, no cooking, she had her three evenings off a week and her nights were never disturbed. That last part at least was true, but rather through her own determination than from any edict of theirs. She had decided from her fourth day there, her evening beginning only when James came home at nine, that no matter what happened she wouldn't be summoned by Marcus or baby Georgia in the night, and she never had been. But in spite of her dislike of children, she suffered pangs of conscience and shame when she heard Marcus screaming at two in the morning and the baby left crying piteously. If she'd gone to them, she'd have been useless the next day, which was also perhaps Claudia's own excuse for turning over in bed and going back to sleep.

Sometimes she told herself she was making a fuss. It was true what Claudia said, many of the jobs she had thought would fall to her lot were done by the cleaning woman. She usually got her evenings off unless the Hindes asked her to babysit because they had 'an absolutely unbreakable engagement writ in stone' and then they paid her for the extra hours she put in. Money was no object, money flowed. She told James at breakfast she needed to buy milk and a packet of baby porridge and he gave her a £20 note, next morning shrugging at the change she held out to him, pushing her hand away and saying, 'Keep it for next time,' but next time, no matter how she protested, another £20 or £40 or £50 was handed over. She began keeping this money.

She put it in a tin. The food delivery van brought meat and fish and fruit and vegetables and innumerable tins of fancy biscuits, cookies, crackers, wafers, cheese straws, chocolates. One of these, a small round dragée tin, she took to use as a money box. She kept it in her bedroom, on the floor of the clothes cupboard. Her stash of money quickly grew. If anyone had told her when she was a good dutiful schoolgirl in Kiruna that in a year's time she would be stealing from her employers, she'd have laughed at them.

It was this accumulating of money that didn't belong to her which stopped her getting in touch with the London branch of the agency. If she complained they'd find out. They might also find out how often she screamed at Cyrus and how, more than once, she had hit Marcus. Her own parents she did tell of her plight, but not about the money, making frequent phone calls to Kiruna at James and Claudia's expense, though she knew that if she told them they'd have waved away her offers to pay for the calls and said she was welcome. Her mother said she should try it a little longer, that was no way to start out in life, giving up as soon as something was more arduous than you had bargained for. What she was making so much fuss about, her father said, he didn't know. Looking after children came naturally to women. She had no chores to do. He was deeply impressed when she let slip that Georgia's disposable napkins were delivered to the door.

In the night, when the children's screaming woke her, she would get out of bed, light the candle she preferred to a bed-lamp, find the dragée tin at the bottom of the cupboard and count the money. Sometimes she took the tin back to bed with her and held it, as a child might hold a teddy bear, until she fell asleep. It comforted her, it was like a hot water bottle. Before she came to London she had never thought much about money. At home they lived comfortably but not luxuriously – her father constantly complained of Sweden's high taxes

– she had her small allowance and supposed that one day she would earn for herself. The Hindes corrupted her. They taught her the ugly side of money. They earned it and spent it, wallowed in it and threw it about with a feckless disregard for what happened to it, for more would come. Yet they weren't entirely profligate. Once, at a rare moment on a weekend when both Hindes were at home, she heard Claudia shouting angrily down the phone at some dress-shop manager who had overcharged her by £25. She'd noticed only when she got her credit card account. Liv's English was getting better and she had no difficulty in understanding Claudia's abusive language, that the woman was a disgrace to the famous shop she worked for, that she was a thief and a perpetrator of fraud.

Liv learnt then what Claudia's anger sounded like, what power she had and that she knew all about the processes of litigation. She learnt too that the Hindes were not so careless in money matters as she had supposed. Until then she would never have imagined either of them scrutinizing a credit card statement or checking items on it against a bill. The thought came to her that she would be wise to hand the contents of the tin to James and say to him that this was what had accumulated out of the notes he had handed to her. She couldn't do it. The money in the tin was her reason for living, for being there at all. Adding to it was what made the agony of looking after these children worthwhile. And it was the only interest she had, a kind of hobby, the sole distraction – unless you counted Jonny.

Jonny 'chatted her up', to use one of Silver's old-fashioned phrases. She was leaving the car park one afternoon with Cyrus beside her and Marcus and Georgia in the back, strapped into their child seats, and she'd handed him the £50 note Claudia had given her that morning.

'Didn't your old man give you anything smaller, sweetheart? You'll clean me out of change, you will.'

'Old man?' said Liv, unfamiliar with idioms used neither by the cleaning woman nor James and Claudia.

'Husband, partner, feller.' Jonny stuck his thumb out in the direction of the back seat where by this time Marcus was screaming and kicking and Georgia was whimpering. 'Looks like he's been busy.'

Fortunately, or not as the case may be, Liv understood very little of this, but she knew what 'husband' meant. 'I have no husband, I am nanny.' By then she had stopped describing herself as the au pair. If she was going to kill herself for these children, she might as well have the dignity of the title. 'Wait and I am looking for money.'

She found the pound coin and the 20p piece, or whatever was needed. Jonny took it from her, holding her fingers at the same time.

'If you're a free woman with free evenings maybe, how about coming out for a drink with yours truly one of these fine nights?'

Marcus continued to scream. The baby sobbed. Cyrus turned round and made a hideous face. 'Shut the fuck up.'

'Language,' said Jonny, who habitually used such expressions himself. 'Needs his mouth washed out with Dettol.'

'Yours truly?' said Liv.

'Me.'

'I don't know. Perhaps. What fine night?'

'When are you off? No time like the present. I tell you what. I'll meet you at nine in the Robert Browning – you know where that is?'

'I know.'

She hadn't exactly said yes. For one thing, she was unsure whether Claudia would come home at eleven or at eight. She drove off to the accompaniment of screams and sobs, Cyrus letting loose a stream of abuse she suspected was foul but which had no particular effect on her and none at all on Marcus and Georgia.

When she was getting them all out of the car Cyrus said, 'He's been in the slammer, that car park guy. My friend Craig's father told him and he told me.'

But Liv had no idea what a slammer was.

I drove up to Hampstead and Downshire Hill. The bags of debris had been removed from the Clarksons' front garden. In the circular flowerbed in the middle of the paving someone had planted a Japanese cherry, the petals of its pink papery flowers already shed, and in tubs on either side of the front door cone-shaped bay trees. I thought of Silver and the mimosa and the nursery in Clifton Villas. Its goodies hadn't reached this far. The bay trees might have looked less distressed if someone watered them. I rang the bell and the nanny came. Was she as harassed and put upon as her employer had once been? She looked far from serene. Mrs Clarkson was on the phone, she said, but if I would like to come into the 'lounge' and take a seat, she would soon be with me. I sat on a kind of padded bench the shape and colour of an aubergine and the nanny handed me a pile of magazines like the shampoo girl in a hairdresser's.

I heard her run upstairs. The children had been left alone up there, spoiling things, very likely damaging things and themselves. Was she a 'real' nanny or just an au pair elevated against her will? History repeats itself and it may be that just as received wisdom has it that people who have been abused in childhood abuse their own children, so women leading the lives of overworked beasts of burden condemn others to the same fate when they get the chance. Liv had been so tired in the evenings that all she really wanted once Claudia or James returned was sleep. But that evening Claudia got home at twenty to nine and that gave her just enough time to get to the Robert Browning and meet Jonny.

I used to believe that whereas men only go about with women they want to go about with, that they can choose, women often take up with men they don't even like much, just for the sake of having someone and being seen with someone. Since then I've revised this opinion and now I doubt if even the first part is true. People take what they can get, not what they want, and often not much choosing comes into it. Liv didn't much like Jonny or fancy him but still she let him make love to her (if you don't mind I will omit the cruder version) in a dark passage off Shirland Road that smelt of cats and tandoori takeaway. Up against the wall it was, what Silver called a 'knee-trembler'. She neither liked nor desired Jonny but she needed him. He was someone to talk to, someone outside the James–Claudia– children ménage. She saw him too as her means of getting away, without knowing what kind of escape she meant.

Instead of reading the magazines I thought about her, what she'd told me and what Silver had, the things she'd told me about Jonny and what at last made her ask him for asylum. Jonny lived at Silver's from time to time. They had met on a roof. Silver had been on the roof and Jonny emerging on to a balcony from a fourth-floor window with a backpack full of someone's jewellery. When he knew Silver wasn't going to shop him he went back to 15 Russia Road with him and in through the window I had seen Wim enter by that first time I was there. Silver said afterwards that if the jewellery Jonny had taken had been a lifetime's accumulation of treasured pieces, a wedding and engagement ring, for instance, a cameo handed down from a grandmother – he claimed he would have been able to tell – it would not have been in his power to make Jonny put them back, but nor would he have made Jonny welcome and offered him sanctuary and a bed for the night. The house Jonny had raided was well-known to Silver, as were a lot of houses in Maida Vale. He was quite aware that it wasn't divided into flats, that one wealthy couple lived in the whole of it. He examined Jonny's haul carefully, said it would certainly be insured, and Jonny was to give 'a tithe' to the poor, by which presumably he meant underpass dossers. (Well, no, I've never seen them but I know they're there.)

I don't know whether Jonny ever did so. Probably not. But he must have made a promise because he soon became a permanent if irregular resident of Silver's place. And it was there that he took Liv when she escaped and needed sanctuary.

She was on the phone a very long time. I was beginning to think she had forgotten about me when she walked into the room, smiling brightly. Never in the past had we shaken hands but we did now, Liv assuring me how delighted she was to see me and calling me by my Christian name at the end of almost every sentence. Again she looked as if she'd spent hours on her appearance. She was wearing a very short almond-green knitted dress and jacket and almond-green suede shoes, not the sort of clothes to put on when you're going to cuddle an infant but perhaps she never did, as Claudia had not. Her hair looked like a wig, it was so blonde, dense, shiny and symmetrical, its natural stripiness all gone, and her face like beautifully painted china.

She sat down opposite me, showing knees that were smooth and rounded yet with that sharp angle at the patella that defines perfect legs. I realized, amused, that I'd seldom seen her legs before, not counting the night they were splashed all over with blood. In those days they were almost always covered up in jeans. She twisted her diamond engagement ring nervously. Rubbing against the wedding ring, it made a small metallic scraping sound.

'I wanted to tell you, Clodagh, how happy we are with the lights. You really can get thirty-six different versions of lighting in this room, it's amazing.'

I said gravely, 'I'm so glad.' Had she fetched me all the way over here to tell me that? Surely not. 'It's a beautiful house.'

'Yes.' She made a conscious effort to leave the ring alone. 'We had to do a great deal to it, of course.' It would have taken a good ear to detect that London was not her birthplace nor English her cradle tongue, so rarely did the lilt return. When she was tired or even more anxious than she was now the difficulty with her '*W*s' might come back. In the Russia Road days it had been her biggest problem with English. It used to make Jonny laugh when she said 've' for 'we' and 'ven' for 'when', he who would have been incredulous had anyone suggested he learn a foreign language. 'What made you become an electrician, Clodagh?' she asked.

'I fancied it and I thought I'd be good at it.'

'And you are, as I very well know,' she said ingratiatingly.

I could think of many things to say next but they would have been unkind. It was evident she disliked any reminder of Russia Road or Jonny, the roofs or the borderline and worse of criminal activity. Even less would she care to be reminded of Wim. Yet it must have been to touch on these subjects at least that she had summoned me here. What else did we, who were so different and who had grown even further apart in the intervening years, have to discuss? What else did we have in common? Did she, I wondered, expect me to begin it? And if she did, how?

I was about to make some mild reference to W9, a simple inane remark perhaps about the chaos caused by the new traffic lights at Maida Hill, when she said very quickly, 'I want to ask you a favour, Clodagh. Will you do me a great favour?'

The classic answer is the one I gave. 'That depends on what it is.'

'It's easy. It's not at all difficult. It's just that . . . Oh, I do find it very hard to say.'

'That's OK,' I said. 'Take your time.'

The sing-song lilt was back. For a moment she was the old Liv again. 'Those days,' she said, 'when we were all together in that place, me and that boy – what was he called, not the very fair one?'

'You mean Jonny?'

'Right. Jonny. Oh, Clodagh, I've practised saying this to you, I've – what's the word? – rehearsed it, but I'm still getting in an awful mess. Clodagh, my husband, Angus that is, Angus, he knows nothing about any of that, what we did and those boys and that other boy, the one who was crazy about the – the roofs, he knows nothing about any of it. He's rather – well, he's rather –'

'Prudish? Stuffy? Idealistic? Puts you on a pedestal?'

'Something like that, yes. All those, Clodagh. If he knew those things, he'd never feel the same again about me. He wouldn't – love me so much. I'm sure he wouldn't.' She said 'vouldn't' and her coral-pink lower lip trembled.

'I don't know him,' I said. 'I've never spoken to him and I doubt if I ever will. Why should I tell him?'

She got up and went across to a very brightly polished steel table with a circular top of black glass. On it lay a small green suede handbag, the same colour as her shoes. I thought – I really thought – she was fetching from it some proof of Angus Clarkson's love, a letter maybe or just a photograph of the two of them together. She sat down again, opened the bag and began taking out £20 and £50 notes. The bag was stuffed full of money, probably several thousand pounds. She held out a fistful to me. I stared at the money, then at her, saying nothing, beginning to understand.

'Please take it. I want you to have it, Clodagh. Just think of it as a present to someone who I'm sure is in need of it from someone who – well, won't notice the difference.'

I said slowly, 'Why do you think I'm in need, Liv?' But I knew. My job, or what she thought was my job, was plebeian. My clothes, my hair that's in need of cutting, my trainers and my ringless hands, all those things were a sign to her of my poverty. She could hardly know I'm always forgetting my wedding ring and leaving it behind on the bathroom sink. 'Liv,' I said, 'I'm not a blackmailer. Did you think I was?'

She shook her head vigorously. 'You mustn't think of it like that. Think of it as a present and then – and then – well, we can say goodbye to each other for ever!'

'Suppose the dimmer switch goes wrong again?'

She looked so crestfallen, still holding out the money, that I began to laugh. I suppose I hoped that she'd join in, that she too would see what a fool she was being, but she didn't. She got up, the bag fell on the floor and notes went everywhere. It reminded me of another time, only then it was the wind that blew money across the roofs and down into the street far below.

'Oh, dear. Oh, God. Clodagh, I was going to offer you a drink. At least a cup of coffee. Please stay. I can explain exactly what I mean if you'll only give me a chance.'

'No, sorry, I've got to go,' I said. 'Don't worry –' Silver's frequent words – 'don't worry, I won't say a word to Mr Clarkson.' Unable to resist it, I put my hand through that helmet of hair and ruffled it, saying as she flinched, 'He's a lucky chap.'

It wasn't the first time I'd been offered a bribe. A householder in Pimlico once wanted me to take £100 over the odds to put two socket outlets into his bathroom in contravention of the IEE Wiring Regulations. But he made no suggestion that I was capable of black-mailing him afterwards. Very likely Liv had given little thought to what she was doing. The habit of flinging money about she may have caught from James and Claudia just as she apparently treated her children the way they treated theirs. Money, she had seen, really does silence people, keeps them sweet, and may instil fear into them. For hadn't it been so with her? Of the notes given to her to buy a pint of milk or a loaf of bread, she had habitually kept three-quarters, hoarding up a nest egg that was as much a menace as a blessing. She was unable to resist doing it, saving it brought her the only happiness and satisfaction she had at that time. But it frightened her too. It kept her, more or less uncomplaining, the slave to James and Claudia and their children.

She was always expecting them to ask for it back. It was incredible to her, coming as she did from a prudent family of savers, a household where her parents had a strict plan of domestic finances, her mother keeping a careful account of her weekly expenses to the nearest krona, that they didn't remember what they'd given her. Claudia and James must *know*, one or both of them must be keeping a secret tally. Sooner or later she would be asked for it, an account would be submitted to her, a reckoning take place. The screaming of abuse would begin, the threats. She would be in the position of the woman in the dress shop. At night, in her room, she counted her hoard by candlelight, then lay in bed worrying about being found out. She held the tin up against her chest but it was no longer the comforting teddy bear. She thought about Claudia coming into her bedroom or the cleaning woman coming in and opening the cupboard and finding the tin with its contents.

The cleaner, of course, did go in there. One night, in the autumn, while some half-mile away I was trying to adjust to living below ground and jangling the hangers in old Mrs Fisherton's wardrobe, Liv decided to leave her stash unattended no longer. She'd find some way of taking it with her wherever she went. They would be unable to detect it was their money if it wasn't in their house. Unless they had written down the numbers on the notes before they gave them to her. It's some measure of the state she was in even by then that she seriously considered this possibility.

The two bigger ones nagging at her and whining, the baby in her arms, she went to a bank in St John's Wood and changed the money into £50 notes. Round the corner, in the High Street, she bought a money belt. The tin went into the rubbish bin along with all the food that was daily thrown away. From that time forward – while worrying that the bank might tell Claudia and James about the note-changing – she wore the money belt. Not that there was much time forward.

She was still seeing Jonny, going about with him, as they say, running around with him. There was very little going about or running around. Mostly, it was sex and drinking. Jonny believed that women dislike sex but engage in it from other aims than love or pleasure: gain, advancement, keeping men quiet, avoiding violence. This was certainly true in Liv's case. You might say that all these motives were hers. She let Jonny make love to her because she sensed that she might one day need him. Their encounters followed a set pattern: drinking in one or other of Maida Vale's pubs or the rougher pubs of Kilburn, much preferred by him, followed by a sexual encounter in the open air or the back of the van he had recently bought. He wasn't anxious to spend more money on her than was strictly necessary but he thought the alcohol essential to keeping her compliant. Jonny disliked spending money, though he was making quite a lot of it.

He had a scam going at the car park. In an expansive moment, he told Silver about it. It consisted in somehow – I have never known quite how – fixing the machine that stamped the time on customers' tickets to print two hours on the ticket but register one hour. The customer would pay for the two hours' parking he or she had had and Jonny pocket half of what he was paid. He was subtle about this, careful not to overdo it, and of course there were many occasions, most occasions probably, when a car was only parked for one hour.

But it was a nice little earner, as he put it, and he held on to that job until he got the sack for harassment and habitual use of obscene language to female car-park users.

What Silver saw in him I never could understand. But Silver was that rarity who simply likes other people, *all* other people. Jonny was amoral, and more than that, to use one of Silver's words, now outdated in its meaning, he was wicked. His eye was for the main chance, he was the complete solipsist, others being there merely for his use and comfort. 'Love' was to him a meaningless word. Jealousy, on the other hand, was within his understanding, as we all came to see. It might better be called possessiveness.

A kind of semi-prohibition exists in Sweden. You must, for instance, buy your alcoholic drink from a state liquor store, *System Bolaget*, and it's very expensive. Draconian penalties exist for driving with more than a tiny amount of alcohol in the blood. So while some go overboard on alcohol and shopping malls are full of winos, many Swedes are abstemious, especially in remote places, and would scarcely think of keeping liquor in the house. That was how it had been at Liv's home. It would be an exaggeration to say she had never tasted beer or wine before she came to London but she had never touched spirits. In Jonny's company she learnt. And her evening drinking gave her ideas. Claudia and James were no more watchful of their drinks cabinet than they were of their cash. It was always replenished, the Victoria Wine company delivered weekly, and no one noticed if levels went down. In their attitude they were the reverse of those nineteenth-century householders who kept drink in a locked tantalus to protect it from the servants.

Liv found that a stiff gin or whisky at six helped a lot in getting through the horrors of bathing Georgia, wheedling the boys into the shower and all of them to bed. On the day of the accident she projected her drinking time forward and at three in the afternoon, when the baby had thrown her bottle at the wall and Marcus been sick in an armchair, she helped herself to two or three half-tumblerfuls of neat vodka, more likely three.

The two of them strapped into the back of the Range Rover, she set off on her unsteady progress to the small private school in St John's Wood Cyrus attended. Cyrus sniffed at her breath, called her an 'alkie' and said the car 'stank of booze'. He hoped she had bought it with her own money but anyway he was going to tell his father she was driving with more than the permitted level of alcohol in her blood. Georgia began to cry and Cyrus leant over the back of his seat to slap her across the legs, while Marcus began to laugh demoniacally. With all this going on, the baby now screaming wildly, Liv set off for home. It was her nineteenth birthday.

She told the story of her accident and escape to every newcomer to 15 Russia Road. I heard it several times from her and once from Silver. It was dramatic enough to bear repetition. She said she thought she was losing her mind. She no longer cared what happened and the idea came to her of crashing the car and killing all of them. That three of its occupants were small children touched her not at all in those moments. Helpless and innocent they might be, but so what? Nor did she care that they were unruly and intractable because of neglect and the instability of their home life. She hated them. But still, when the time came, the accident was not due to any deliberate act of hers. On that she insisted. As she drove down Marlborough Place and turned into Hamilton Terrace she was already calmer, getting a grip on herself. She realized that what the precocious Cyrus had said was true. She was too drunk to drive. She must shut her ears to the boys' squabbling, the baby's cries, and concentrate hard on what she was doing, so that she could get back safely.

At the first set of lights she waited, then took the right turn carefully into Hall Road. The lights ahead of her at the Edgware Road were green but when she was halfway along the stretch they changed to amber. Believing she had time to get across the road before they changed to red – she was desperate to get into the comparative peace and quiet of Sutherland Avenue – she accelerated, but the driver of the Peugeot in front of her didn't. The Range Rover went into the back of it with a crash as loud as a bomb going off.

The windscreen split into a frosting like a bathroom window. All the children screamed, for once in unison. Cyrus, though still in his seat belt, turned and began punching her, shouting that he'd kill her, his father would kill her. Liv didn't pause to think. She unbuckled her seat belt, jumped out of the car and slammed the door just as the driver of the Peugeot was getting out of his. She was shaking all over but she could run, and run she did, up the hill and up Hamilton

Terrace as fast as she could go, not once looking back, running as if for a race or as if pursuers were after her.

Perhaps she was pursued, but she thought not. Few people in her situation, after all, would run away in those circumstances, leaving three crying children in a smashed-up car. She knew that. It would hardly occur to bystanders and the driver of the Peugeot that this was precisely what she had done. They would assume she had gone for help. So what exactly was in her mind when she abandoned the Range Rover and the children? There was nothing else to be done, she said. The alternative, facing the music, being breathalysed, recounting events to Claudia and James or listening to some policeman do so, somehow *dealing* with those hysterical children, was impossible. Staring at her listeners, red in the face from the intensity of her feeling, she said she'd have killed herself first, thrown herself in front of one of those container lorries that pound down the Edgware Road.

It was to Jonny that she went. He was at the car park, sitting in his glass booth, working his scam. His shift ended at five and it was nearly four-thirty by the time Liv got there. Between customers handing over their tickets and paying their fee, she told him what had happened. By the sound of it, he'd have done nothing for her if her story had not also been about the money in the belt round her waist, almost £2,000 by then. Grudgingly (I'm reading between Liv's lines), he said he knew a place where he could take her.

Jonny had a room of his own. It was in Chichele Road, Cricklewood. None of the people I got to know at Silver's had ever been there. Jonny kept it on for some private purposes of his own, probably criminal, for all I know he may have sub-let it, but mostly he slept at 15 Russia Road. He might have let Liv have that room, he might have lived there with her, the kind of arrangement most young men in his position would have welcomed. For some reason he didn't. When he came off his shift he took her to Silver's. Neither he nor Silver suspected that once in there she wouldn't go down into the street again for nearly six months.

Perhaps he thought it would be cheaper at Silver's. For him, that is. And he would have unlimited access to Liv. I mean, of course, sexual access. And he wouldn't have to be alone with her except when they were in bed, for Jonny disliked women, enjoyed the company of Silver and Wim and whoever else turned up at the flat at the top of the house, and of course he liked what he could never have found in Chichele Road, an easy way out on to the roofs.

Apparently Silver was pleased to see her. There was something deeply old-fashioned about Silver, though in the nicest possible way. He had no interest in the toys of a modern lifestyle, television, video recorders, movie cameras, any cameras, mobile phones, computers and computer games. A radio he had, what he called a 'wireless', and which looked as if it dated back to the nineteen-forties but perhaps was new works in an old cabinet. He read books, something that couldn't be said for the rest of us. Like a character from some pre-printing era of history, ancient or medieval times, he loved to listen to a tale unfolded. I know very little about Homer but I should think his audience was made up of people like Silver. He welcomed Liv, fed her, doctored her hangover with coffee, and sat (literally) at her feet to listen to her story.

9

Not everyone who came to Silver's had been rescued as I had and as Liv had, but everyone had a story to tell. Even Wim. Yet of his own past he said nothing for a long while. But that evening in April when I saw him come through the window I knew none of this. I was all wonder and excitement and near-disbelief. He walked across the room easily and with grace, as if he had come in by way of the door like anyone else.

Silver, old-fashioned in his politeness as well as in other ways, introduced me. 'This is Clodagh. Clodagh, this is Wim.'

Wim looked at me and nodded. His eye turned to the sleeping Liv. He poked her with his toe but she didn't wake.

I can be overawed but I've never been shy. 'What were you doing out there?' I said.

'Climbing,' he said. Just the single word.

Silver elaborated. 'Some of us,' he said carefully, 'go out on the roofs and climb. You can get quite a long way when you know how. Some roofs are better for climbing than others, of course, but it's specially good along here and round into Torrington.' He gave Wim a look of deep warm affection, which his friend had done nothing to merit as far as I could see, wearing as he did the expression of the King of Siam being defied by Deborah Kerr. 'Wim's the best of us. He's a genius at climbing. He could go from here to South Kensington on the roofs.'

'Say Notting Hill,' Wim said, his frown slightly smoothed.

If I had asked, as many would have, 'What for?', I don't think I'd have been received back there again. That would have been the last I'd have seen of Silver or any of them. It didn't cross my mind to ask. I knew immediately what it was for and why anyone would want to do it. Like Everest, like Annapurna and K2, the roofs were *there* and that was enough. They seemed to me as legitimate a place to be, to walk on, to explore, as any street or high road or country village. And in that moment, in the silence that followed Silver's words, I wondered why roofs should be closed to us, forbidden ground, empty, neglected but lovely spaces.

'I'd like to go out there,' I said and, crossing to that open window, I looked out and up. To get up on to the roof would be easy for any reasonably athletic young person, certainly for the one Daniel had called Spiderwoman. 'When can we?'

'Tomorrow,' Silver said, and he laughed, but from delight, not at me.

Wim said nothing. He fetched himself a mug of tea and one for Liv when she woke, as she did within a minute or two. Silver performed more introductions. Liv said, 'Hi,' looking at me warily. The truth is that I didn't see her expression as wary at the time. It's hindsight which tells me it was. She was already painfully conscious that any girl who came to 15 Russia Road might attract Wim's eye, might be *the* one for whom his defences would go down, the girl he might love. That one, of course, must be herself, and she seemed to feel that if she could somehow convince him of this, show him that she was the woman for him, she would anchor him and the peril of possible rivals be lessened. What she failed to understand, could hardly have been expected to understand, what none of us understood then, was that Wim had only one passion, obsessed man that he was, and that had nothing to do with women or love.

At this time she had been at Silver's for no more than three weeks. She was Jonny's. Beyond prodding her with his foot to wake her – she slept for long hours – Wim had never touched her, perhaps never thought of touching her, though her yearning gaze so often levelled at him gave her away to the rest of us. At Silver's instigation, she told her story to me that evening, and that wasn't to be the only time. The two men had heard it before but they listened without protest, Silver with enthusiasm and Wim with no sign of impatience. Perhaps his thoughts were elsewhere.

The silence, the peace, the lack of any sort of disturbance which had followed the accident to the Range Rover mystified Liv. No one could have had the least idea of where she had gone, James and Claudia knew nothing of Jonny's existence, but still for a whole week after her arrival there she had expected the police to come pounding on the front door of 15 Russia Road. She anticipated stories in the papers, news on Silver's radio or on the television set in Jonny's room that only he ever watched. There was nothing. But she disbelieved what Silver said, that Claudia and James might simply be relieved to see the back of her, their children unharmed, their Range Rover covered by insurance. Incessantly she worried, principally about the money she had stolen.

'They won't even know,' Silver said. 'They think a loaf of bread costs £20.'

'But they *can't*. No one can be so silly.' Liv's English had apparently improved enormously in the short time she had been at Silver's.

He, who was always reasonable, always sane and clear-headed, who could always be relied on to put forward the sensible and worry-free viewpoint, asked how she thought they could prove it. Had she considered that? 'Did they write it down in an account book? Did you give them receipts you got from shops? No to both, so don't worry.'

'You think I just keep it and everything is all right?'

'Give a tithe to the poor,' said Silver.

He prepared an evening meal, something he by no means always did but when he felt, in his words, in the 'cooking vein'. It was pasta with carbonara sauce out of a jar, halva and oranges to follow and several bottles of Bulgarian red wine. Everyone smoked, though only tobacco that evening, and Liv lit candles which she set about the room. Silver took me home quite early, about ten. There was no need to escort me, I only had to go down the stairs and out into the street for thirty seconds, but he insisted on coming with me and, after planting a brotherly kind of kiss on my cheek, watched me go into 19 from his front gate and reach the safety of the iron staircase.

'See you tomorrow,' he said, and added in a whisper in case a concealed Max or Selina might be listening, 'We'll go on the roofs.'

The street was empty, the air cool and the sky overcast, the dull pink of faded overwashed clothes, with a segment of moon showing between the ragged edges of the clouds. Is there any time of life when the society of one's contemporaries is so yearned for as in youth? I know that I need it less and less now. My companions may be older or younger than I am and my own company is increasingly pleasant to me. Anyway, I'm married and highly content with that condition. But then, a dozen years ago, I had hungered without knowing it for people of my own age to talk to and be with. My fellow students at GUP might have served the purpose if only I had gone there often enough and been there long enough to get to know more of them. Now I had friends. Next day I was to climb on the roofs. I slept deeply that night without dreaming, Mabel lying on my pillow, her sleek furry face nuzzling my neck.

The next morning I awoke to a sense of doom impending and recalled, for the first time since Silver rescued me from the underpass, what I ought to have been doing on the previous afternoon and had failed to do. Caroline Bodmer had expected me at two but waited for me in vain. Of course, I knew the sensible, the mature, thing to do next: go upstairs, ask Selina's permission to use the phone in the yellow drawing room, phone my supervisor and either speak to her or leave a message on her answering machine. After that, make my way to GUP, attend the 'marketing workshop' that happened every other Friday, check that my message had been received . . .

But at this point my imagination faltered. I knew I would do none of it, so why speculate? Why, as Silver might say, fret? I already had a very good idea of the things Silver might say. And how could I get to GUP when the canal bank was closed and my only access to Paddington Station was by way of an underpass I would never dare enter again?

Eventually, of course, GUP would throw me out and I'd lose my grant. But very likely not before the end of June. Deciding not to think about it till the following Monday, I got up, opened a can of pilchards for Mabel and, peering upwards at the bedroom window, saw over the top of the wall that it was a lovely morning. Mabel ate her breakfast and went out. Craning out of the open window as far as I could, I watched her scale the sheer face of brickwork, stroll across the lawn and, poised quivering at the foot of the wall between us and 17, leap for the top of it, making the ascent with the greatest of ease. She sat there, evidently pleased with herself, surveying from her eminence the spread-out world below. I smiled at her and waved. I understood.

All that time is very sharp in my memory. The details are etched in stone. And that is as well because I either noted nothing down in my diary or the relevant notebook is lost. But I remember. I even remember what I wore. I put on my black jeans and a black T-shirt with a big red apple on the front of it. It was warm enough to go out without a jacket. I put my washing in a black plastic bag and took it to the launderette. Then, while my clothes were going round in the machine, I did something I had never done before. I bought a newspaper.

The day was one of those on which, according to the table of contents on the front page, the paper carried its 'situations vacant' advertisements. It had occurred to me as I was walking along, carrying my bag, that when my grant ceased I'd need a job. Whether I would still be able to live at old Mrs Fisherton's if I was no longer in academe or on its fringes was something I'd decided to think about later. Did I, after all, want to go on living there? On the other hand, I had nowhere else to go. I took my newspaper to one of the tables outside the café opposite and bought myself a cappuccino.

The café had a notice in its window advertising for kitchen staff. I turned to the paper. But if jobs existed for the unskilled there was nothing like that in the 'situations vacant'. Those in demand were all required to have qualifications or experience. I thought of going into the café and asking if I'd do, but did I really want a job at this moment? Did I want it yet? And if I worked at this popular café, where Max and Selina quite often dropped in on Saturday mornings, I'd soon be found out. So instead of offering myself as a washer of dishes or mopper of floors, I turned back idly to the front page.

The story that dominated it I at first ignored because I'd noticed a paragraph at the foot of the page. It was only a few lines but it told me that the body of an unknown woman had been found on the canal bank at Paddington Basin the day before. The police were treating the case as murder. So it seemed that I had seen, or almost seen under its scarlet blanket, a murder victim. It made me feel a bit queasy. Somehow this was worse than if the woman had killed herself or accidentally drowned. That uncompromising black print repelled me, so I looked at the top of the page instead.

It was two years since I had read a newspaper. After the pylon and Daniel's death I was in newspapers myself, first of all in the basic account of what had happened, my name, my age (given inaccurately as eighteen to Daniel's sixteen) and my status as his 'schoolfellow', not his girlfriend. Then, in the days which followed, I was the subject of those articles feature writers produce on the moral or political aspect of things, that could all be summed up under the collective heading, 'What is the World Coming to?' In some of these features, I appeared as typical of eighties adolescents, amoral, feckless, so bored with the routine of life as to need perpetually to court danger, beset by a death wish. In others I was little short of a murderer, thoughtlessly taking the life of a weaker and younger friend. One speculated as to whether I might have been abused as a child, another if what I'd done had been 'a cry for help', and a third portrayed me as a victim of the drugs culture. My parents made a little collection of cuttings to give me when I came out of hospital and show me the error of my ways. After that I never read another newspaper until that sunny morning sitting outside the café, drinking my cappuccino.

I've mentioned Andrew Lane and Alison Barrie before. They were the subject of discussion for the guests at the lunch party Max and Selina gave for my birthday. I had been uninterested then but now I read the story because the photograph of these people and the child they were trying to adopt attracted my attention. It was bound to. Andrew Lane looked the way Guy Wharton might have if he was ten years older and had a beard. His was a solid square face but bright and lively with intelligent dark eyes. Beards cover up a lot, they are as disguising as a mask, so it would have been hard to say what his mouth was like or how big or small his chin. Andrew Lane had thick dark hair that was just frosted with grey but grew in the same shape as Guy's with a peak in the middle of his broad forehead.

The woman he had been married to for the past seven years photographed less well. Perhaps it was only a case of the camera loving him and not her. Alison Barrie was fair-haired, anaemic-looking, her face lined. Her age was given as thirty-nine. She looked harassed, stressed, anxious. The little boy was eight, a handsome child of mixed race, his skin a dusky cream, his black eyes enormous. His name was Jason. The story described him as having come into the care of the local authority before he was a year old, his single mother being unable to care for him. His father had disappeared.

Lane and Barrie couldn't have children. He was sterile as a result of treatment for testicular cancer, of which he was cured; her fallopian tubes were blocked when she had had a bungled abortion in her late teens. All this was in the paper. Five years before this they had tried to adopt a Mexican infant but its mother had changed her mind and decided to keep it herself. This had been particularly saddening for them as Maria's mother was only sixteen, living in the *barrio* of Guadalajara, and had given up her previous child for adoption. They believed that they could have given Maria a happy life while, left where she was, she faced a miserable existence and perhaps an early death.

There had later been an attempt to secure a Romanian baby but the result of the home study carried out on their lifestyle and domestic arrangements was that Lane and Barrie were too well-off, their house was too big and their lives too busy to be suitable. However, social workers for the authority where they had moved to, somewhere in the north, had eventually considered them fit to become adoptive parents. They began by fostering Jason Patel, who lived with them for six months. There was apparently no doubt that in that time he became happier, better behaved and less hyperactive than since he was a baby. He loved Lane and Barrie and they adored him. But he had an Asian mother and a white father, while they were both Anglo-Saxons.

Then, in a surprise move, out of the blue, the social services department decreed that Jason must go to a mixed-race family. That was their policy. Fourteen days from the imparting of their decision to the foster parents was set as the date for removing Jason from their care. Lane and Barrie ran away, taking him with them. They gave up their lucrative jobs, drew all the money they jointly possessed out of the bank, and fled. Their car they left behind in the garage. To their cleaner they gave six months' money in advance, asking her to go in twice a week, pick up the post from the doormat, water the houseplants and, occasionally, mow the lawn. This was in February. Since then they hadn't been seen. In spite of appeals to the public, resulting in many false alarms – a couple with a little 'coloured' boy had been seen boarding the Harwich ferry, they had been seen at Disneyland in France, queueing for admittance to Madame Tussaud's – there was no sign of them. As the story put it, they had 'vanished into thin air'.

Whenever I read that I always think it would be far easier to vanish into thick air, as into a fog. But 'thin air' it always is. The paper had an interview with the cleaner and another with Alison Barrie's half-sister, who swore she had no idea where they had gone and had heard nothing from them since early February when Alison had told her in great distress of the social services' ruling. Jason loved them, you could be certain of that. This was no one-sided affair, the two of them fond of him and he simply acquiescing. He'd have begged to stay with them and gone with them wherever they chose to take him.

Sitting there, reading about it in the warm spring sunshine, I tried to imagine what it would be like so desperately to want a child that you'd give up everything to keep him, your home, your prospects, your family, your friends and your financial future. Of course, I could easily imagine giving up those things, for none of them meant much to me at twenty, I barely knew what I wanted or where I was going, but to abandon them for a little boy you had only known for six months? I understand now, I didn't then. I thought only that it was very unfair. Why should these good people be compelled to give up the child they loved and who loved them? I was yearning after goodness by then, you see, as if association with it would somehow save me. I had already caught the infection from Silver.

I had bought the paper in the first place to find a job but by then I could see that this was something I should think about before rushing into it. I spent very little money. Food was almost my only expense. I'd never have dreamt of buying clothes or going to a hairdresser. The architecture of Maida Vale was my entertainment. Transport costs should have taken a slice of my income but since I so seldom went to college I hardly ever bought a train or bus ticket. I told myself how lucky it was, all things considered, that I hadn't invested in a student's pass. That would have been a real waste of money.

I'm aware that I'm giving a picture of myself as a feckless, selfish, ungrateful and idle young person, one who showed not a trace of gratitude to her anxious parents, blew her chance of a reasonable education, seemed not to realize her good fortune at having a whole self-contained apartment to live in nor understand the generosity of the kindly couple who made this possible. Did I ever ask myself who paid the bills for the electricity I used? The gas and the water? I never thought about it. For all I knew, those benefits might have been freely given, poured out of some invisible infrastructure, and instituted by a supernatural power simply to make people like me happy and comfortable. And the only explanation I had for my behaviour was that two years before I had escaped with my life while 40,000 volts passed through my dear friend's body and killed him. Not the attitude likely to win the sympathy of responsible people.

Still, it's the only excuse I have. And even that was wearing a bit thin as time went by and my life was filled with other things, with, for instance, the way of life on the top floor of 15 Russia Road. So I had no excuse. The trouble is that if I were twenty now – an age I've no wish to be – I'd do it all over again. Well, not quite all, there is one act of folly I'd avoid if I could.

These days the newspapers I take daily are stacked and saved until the end of the week when they go in the bin provided and are put out for recycling. I'm not a hoarder and I've never kept papers and magazines lying about when their useful life is over. But for some reason I kept the paper that printed the long account of Andrew Lane and Alison Barrie's disappearance with Jason. Perhaps I intended it for some purpose now forgotten. I'm sure at the time I had no particular interest in those two people and the little boy.

They receded from my mind as the afternoon came on and I was out once more in the sunshine, this time walking towards the lawns and slopes of Westbourne Green, taking with me something to read from old Mrs Fisherton's bookcase. I remember very well what it was because it was almost the only book on her shelves that, in my opinion then and now, any reasonable person would want to read. I still have it. At the risk of damning myself still further in the disapproving reader's eyes, I may as well add that *The Complete Short Stories of Guy de Maupassant* was another item I stole from Max and Selina along with the silver frame.

In one of the stories I came upon this passage in which Maupassant describes the Eiffel Tower, though he might as well have been giving his idea of a pylon if they had been invented then: *This tall skinny pyramid of iron ladders, this giant and disgraceful skeleton with a base that seems made to support a formidable monument of Cyclops, and which aborts into the thin, ridiculous profile of a factory chimney.* If you don't like pylons, you can't say fairer than that.

I rang the bell at 15 on the dot of seven. It was early but I couldn't wait any longer. There was only one bell for the whole house. I wondered what I'd say if by chance Jack or Erica Silverman was at home and one of them came to the door, but no one came. I rang again, harder in case it couldn't be heard upstairs, and while I was pressing my forefinger on the bellpush I heard a clear musical whistle from high above me. It sounded like a blackbird. I stepped backwards, out of the porch and down the steps, and looked up. Silver was on the roof, lying prone on the horizontal part of the mansard between the curves of two dormers and looking down at me. The slanting rays of the sun burnished his hair to bright white gold.

'I'll come down and let you in,' he said. 'Give me a minute to climb back through the window.'

He was very quick. He looked approvingly at my clothes, jeans, T-shirt and trainers, though these were my invariable get-up.

'It may be cold up there later. No, don't go back. You can have a sweater of mine.'

We ran up the four flights of stairs. He got to the top without flagging or gasping. I both flagged and gasped but not until after the third floor. Liv was in the flat with Jonny, the boyfriend I was still to meet, and a girl called Morna Silver knew from university. He introduced me. Jonny said, 'Pleased to meet you,' and looked me up and down the way someone might a piece of furniture he considers buying. He wouldn't have bought me, I could tell that. He was a small neatly made man, older than the rest of us by maybe five or six years, dark but with very light blue ice-cold eyes, his features blunt with an unfinished look. There was no feeling in his face and no animation. Like us, he wore jeans and trainers but a collarless white shirt instead of a T-shirt and over it the jacket of a dark pin-striped suit.

'Let's have a drink,' he said. 'Celebrate.' His voice was a grating metallic cockney. 'What you done with the bottles I fetched in, Liv?' He pronounced her name as in 'live and let live'.

'I won't drink, thanks, Jonny,' Silver said, 'not before going on the roofs.' He saw me shaking my head. 'And Clodagh won't. What about you, Morna?'

She had been up there only once before. The experience she had found exhilarating but it had frightened her too. 'It's scary. I should have gone up again the next day but I didn't. It's a bit like crashing a car. If you don't drive again straight away, you never will.'

This, of course, was the cue for Liv to tell her story all over again. Morna had never heard it. Jonny cast up his eyes and went off in search of drink. In a whisper, respectful of Liv as raconteur, Silver said we'd eat first, he had got soup and a Tuscan bean stew. Wim ought to be along in a minute. That sounded fine except that I was longing to climb out of the window and get on to the upper slope of the mansard. Liv reached the bit where she'd run away to Jonny and he had brought her here, and then she added something I didn't know.

'Since it is happening I haven't been outside this apartment. Not down there in the street, I mean. I have been on the roofs.' She laughed. 'No one can catch me on the roofs.'

'No, you can just fall off,' said Morna. She was a big dark girl, dramatically good-looking, with large brown Irish eyes. 'Do you think they're looking for you?'

'Claudia and James? The police? I don't know. Maybe. I expect they are, they must.'

Jonny came back with a whisky bottle in one hand and a half-full glass in the other. 'Of course they're not looking for you, you silly cow. What a load of crap. Waste time looking for a stupid bint they can't even prove was pissed at the time?' I listened with interest. I'd never heard someone being called a 'bint' before. 'Now if you was talking about those two as kidnapped the coloured kid, I'd say that's a different story.'

'They didn't kidnap him,' I said. 'They were his foster parents.'

Jonny looked at me. 'It can speak,' he said. 'I thought the cat had got its tongue.'

Silver's voice had become steely and cold. 'I've told you before, you don't speak to my friends like that. Clodagh's a woman, not an object, she's not an "it".'

'Sorry, I'm sure,' said Jonny. 'No offence, sweetheart. What I meant before I was so rudely interrupted – sorry, sorry, come back all I said – what I meant was, they've done wrong, those two, they've no right to remove the kid, he's not theirs, they're just caring for him and a right mess they've made of it.'

I might have said a lot but I didn't want to give Silver the occasion again to reprimand Jonny. So instead I offered to help him with getting the meal. Gently, and with a sickly sweetness, there drifted through the doorway the scent of cannabis being smoked. Silver wrinkled his nose.

'I wouldn't have any of that either,' he said to me. 'I can't think of anything much worse on the roofs than a feeling of nothing much matters and there's no tomorrow anyway.' He looked speculatively at me. 'Perhaps being a country girl you've not much experience of these things.'

That made me smile. I told him the police called the Suffolk town where my school was 'the controlled-substances capital of East Anglia'. I was eleven when first offered amphetamines and amyl nitrate at the school gates.

'Just an ignorant townee, that's me,' said Silver. He passed a spoonful of beans to me. 'Taste that. What d'you think? Not bad?'

'Not bad at all.'

'I cook beans and pasta and lentils and stuff because they're cheap.' He smiled. 'I've got a bit of money of my own. Not a huge lot but not bad. My grandmother left it me.'

'You're lucky.'

'It's a mixed blessing,' he said but without elaborating.

We carried the dishes in, soup plates and dinner plates. They were all different, odds and ends from reject shops by the look of them, some willow pattern, a couple of orange and yellow Clarice Cliff, a Denmark, a green Doulton with the white spindrift pattern, a Wedg-wood with a gold band round the rim. I know, not because I remember from that day but because I have some of those very plates with me here. For sentimental reasons? Yes and no. For one thing, I've never been able to understand why people who wouldn't dream of hanging copies of the same picture all over their walls or fill all their photograph frames with the same family group would want to eat off matching crockery. Plates and cup and saucers in different patterns are more fun.

At Silver's we never ate at the table, always on our laps. I was handing round the soup bowl, Morna and Liv and Jonny's shared joint crushed out but still scenting the room, when Wim came in.

He was such an extraordinary-looking man that I think some further description of him is warranted. His King of Siam facial characteristics I've already told you about, his shaven head and the unrelieved waxen sallowness of his skin. But perhaps I should add how uniform that pale brownish yellow was, so that his hands and his long thin fingers, his arms and his neck, and his legs too for all I knew, were the same parchment shade. You wondered, looking at him, if when that skin was cut or grazed what came from the wound would be more like honey than blood. It wasn't, as we all had reason later to find out. He was tall, thin and muscular, giving an impression of great strength. That evening he wore a Mao tunic, frogged instead of buttoned, in wine red embroidered with peacocks and flowers and butterflies. He astonished me by going up to Silver, who hadn't yet sat down, and hugging him in his arms. Jonny gave a low wolf whistle, of which neither Silver nor Wim took the least notice.

Nor did Wim, emerging from the embrace, seem conscious of anyone else's presence beyond giving us all a company-including nod. I could see Liv didn't want to look at him, or rather didn't want Jonny to see her looking at him, but she couldn't help herself. The expression 'fastened her eyes' always sounds as if the eyes themselves were taken out and pinned to the object in question, but hers were so fixed on Wim as to make the description credible. Wim took no particular notice of her. He poured himself some orange juice from the carton he had brought with him and held it up to the rest of us in the gesture that denotes an invitation to partake. No one wanted any. Liv looked longingly at an unopened vodka bottle of Jonny's. She wasn't much to look at in those days, no more than prettyish. It was her slender big-breasted figure that was her chief attraction. She is one of those women who are entirely transformed by a good haircut and the right make-up and clothes, not to mention an expensive orthodontist. Unpainted, her face was pale but not with Wim's pallor, being pinkish and blotchy, her teeth as well as her fingers were stained brown from incessant smoking and her long, fair but thinnish hair lank from insufficient washing. She told me later that she was torn between not bothering with her appearance in order to keep away Jonny's attentions and trying to improve it to attract Wim's. There was no evidence of the improvement attempts that evening.

We all smoked too much. The atmosphere in the room would have been insufferable if the windows had been closed. But they were wide open, the net curtains fluttering in the light breeze which sprang up at sunset. Silver and Wim discussed whether Morna should accompany us on to the roofs, Morna herself being in considerable doubt. She felt 'woozy', she shouldn't have shared in that joint, and, anyway, wasn't it a crazy thing to do? Why do it?

'We do it because we like doing it,' said Silver.

Wim said nothing. Something seemed to burn inside his clear yellowish eyes. I wondered what colour his hair would be. Light brown? Blond? *Black?*

'But it's not what people our age do. We ought to go clubbing or to the cinema or to a pub or something.'

'If you don't do it at our age,' said Wim in his rather high, slightly accented, voice, 'you'll never do it.' Something came into his face then, a sadness and a fear. 'You're wiped out at thirty.' He spoke as it was some competitive sport he was talking about, running or the long jump.

'Before we get on to "time's winged chariot",' said Silver, and I think he said it to distract Wim from some threat or dread, 'I'm going to tell Morna not to come. Not this time. We don't take risks, remember? Come on, Morna, there's a dear, home time. I'll see you out.'

It was his custom to escort visitors out, especially women. I doubt if I ever left there without his accompanying me to the front door and down the path. But then, of course, I was different. He came back, running up the stairs two at a time, we could hear him, light on his feet as he was. It was twilight then and the sky was the dusky red of Wim's tunic. One by one we climbed out of the window on to the roof.

Liv and I were empty-handed but Wim and Silver each carried a coiled rope and Wim hooks as well, and Jonny had his backpack. Later on I learnt that Jonny took no pleasure from the roofs but saw climbing on them only as a means to an end. Climbing out of the casement was easy, the only tricky bit being hauling oneself up into the ellipse of the dormer, and after that it was a matter only of scrambling up a few feet. Silver did it with practised expertise, Wim with a wonderful elegance.

We crossed the roof to the front and squatted on the flat shelf of the mansard, on its smooth grey slates, and looked at what we could see, Russia Road, car-lined but empty of moving traffic and empty of people, still, silent and deserted. The street lights were on but their lit lamps were far below us. Above was half-dark, the night-time twilight of London, and beneath all was shiny, golden and criss-crossed with leaf shadows that trembled in the breeze. The roof where we were was a shallow slope, almost flat. We walked across it, Silver taking my hand. I was afraid of dislodging slates but I quickly learnt the technique of avoiding this. Roof walking demands lightness and precision, it's not for your stolid plodder. We sat down and surveyed the panorama from the back where there was no immediate, correspondingly high, rampart of houses to impede the view.

We were looking across the backs of houses, the fronts of houses, streets between, the dark tops of leafy trees and their gold-lit trunks, gardens of gloomy evergreens and pale shrubs, the faces of flowers white and shimmering, stone walls and stone tubs and urns, statuary and in one small enclave a dark shining pool in which golden fish darted, Georgian pillars and Victorian porches, slate roofs gleaming like pewter and tiled roofs matt and mottled. There were wells of darkness whose depths were hidden, cobbled lanes running into mews like uncoiling snakes. The spire of St Mark's in Hamilton Terrace stretched to the purple sky like a finger and the spire of St Augustine's like a needle. Nearer to us, companionably near as we approached its level, was the long shaft of St Saviour's, ugly by day and beautiful by night. The trees amazed me, thousands of them, avenues of them, inky bouquets of foliage lining the streets. And everywhere were dabs and splashes of gold where the limited light caught metal and glass, not fierce and blazing as in sunshine, but tiny stars of brightness and hollow cups of it, balustrades painted with a sheen of light and window-panes glowing fruit-coloured.

London rolled away below us, to the Heath and Highgate, the towers of Somers Town and Euston, the ribbon streets of Edgware, and, like a low pyramid, Harrow-on-the-Hill. Regent's Park lay like pastoral acres of countryside or the royal hunting ground it once was, its lake a broken piece of mirror. I recognized very little of all that then, I looked it up afterwards on the map, identifying remembered domes and spires, high rise and palace, dark peaceful open space, streets on which the cars were lined up like shiny oval counters. The course of the canal was plain to see, black as oil and as gleaming, passing from the Portobello Lock into Paddington and Little Venice, a wide still stream hidden for a little while by the Maida Hill tunnel, entering the park like a river. We could see the zoo. We lay on the edge of the roof telling each other of each animal we saw, those that weren't penned by night, a wolf, a bison, two camels. Liv claimed to have spotted a white peacock, its tail spread into a fan, but the rest of us decided it was in her imagination.

As we began to walk again our group broke up. Jonny went off on his own devices, his climbing clumsy. He loped along as a monkey might if finding itself on an unaccustomed perilous walkway, even to the extent of proceeding on all fours. His progress was quite swift, though, as he crossed the roof of 11 Russia Road and dropped down over its distant rim. The last we saw of him was his surly face. He didn't wave. Wim remained with us, strolling rather than walking, never looking down at his feet. The obvious comparison is with a cat and Wim on the roofs moved with the same casual elegance, the same to-the-manner-born negligence and unthinking ease, as Mabel on the tightrope edge of a balcony rail. The only concession he had made to discretion – after all, we none of us had any business to be up there on other people's property – was to change his embroidered coat for a plain dark sweatshirt. His coil of rope he had slung over his shoulder the way a woman carries a bag with a long strap.

When we reached the end of the Russia Road roofs, the point where Jonny had disappeared, I saw that here was a change of configuration. Russia Road met Torrington Gardens at an acute angle. The streets themselves parted in a hairpin bend or triangle shape, the apex of which was a large house, a mansion I had often looked at from below. It had perhaps been built twenty years before the terraces it linked, it was Palladian to their late-Victorian, its roof joined to theirs but some six feet lower on the Russia Road side and more like ten feet on Torrington Gardens. It was quite dark but still I could see that on the wall which was the end of the Torrington Gardens terrace a thoughtful builder had provided bands of stone on the brickwork, four of them, carved in a nailhead design and each about two feet apart, though no doubt for artistic reasons rather than for use as steps. This side presented no problem. There were two drainpipes on the wall, their snaky branches hung with ivy.

'It's all flats, that house,' Silver explained. 'Someone lives in the top flat. They're probably out, they go out a lot in the evenings, but we'd better not take the risk. So don't jump down.' How did he know about the people who lived there? He seemed to know everything about who lived where and their habits and routines. 'We don't really want them telling the police they keep hearing things that go bump in the night.'

Wim laughed. He had a strange staccato laugh, like an engine firing but failing to start. I knew without asking that scaling those walls would be easy for him, the mountaineer who has climbed the Eiger confronted by Ben Nevis. All in the day's work, no more arduous than going up a ladder. He squatted on the coping, placed his hands on the stone to the right of him without recourse to pipes or ivy, and sprang down, light as a dancer. Anyone in the rooms beneath would have heard a soft thud and thought nothing heavier than a squirrel had landed on the tiles. He ran across the roof, which was almost flat. The night wasn't dark. Inner London is never quite dark. But when he reached the other side his figure had become indistinct. It was a silhouette we saw climb the gable end, but 'climb' is not the word for what Wim did. We were climbers, Silver a very good one. Wim walked up walls, danced up them, *ran* up them, negligently waltzed across gambrels and sprang without fear or even thought across pitched roofs.

He vanished from our sight. Silver laughed, said to me, 'One day I'll tell you some of the things he has done.' He took my hand and Liv's. Her face was all woe because Wim had gone. 'Now what we'll do is *drop* down there. Liv's done it before. The coping gives you a good handhold.'

I went first, holding the smooth cold surface of the pipe, choosing footholds in the ivy forks to drop, noiselessly as I hoped, on to the roof. It was a slab construction, with a television aerial, a big insulated tank of some kind, and a chimney containing three flues. I walked as lightly as I could but failed to rival Wim. Liv came next, hesitating a bit like an apprehensive swimmer on a diving board, then Silver. We climbed the gable end, finding the nailhead projections, little shallow pyramids, helpful as hand- and footholds, the next best thing to steps. It was a wide gable, the roof of Torrington Gardens was low-pitched, though steeper than that of Russia Road, and made of similar grey slates. How many slate quarries were there in the world, I wondered. Were there any left or had we plundered them all to cover and insulate and protect in warmth and comfort Maida Vale?

The roofs, divided only by low chimney stacks or chimney shafts, rather in the way groins separate sections of a beach from one another, stretched away into the distance, straight as a Roman road. In the half-dark, under the clear purple sky, it seemed to lengthen to infinity, its end lost in the misty gloom. I went up on the roofs many times after that but remember no other occasion to match the awe I felt that first time, the wonder and the fear. Not fear of falling or of discovery but of the strangeness of it, of seeing what few others had seen or would ever see, that long slate road, segmented by the faintly gleaming pale walls of the stacks, shadowless, dim and quiet. Quiet but not silent for the traffic in Edgware Road was always present, a muted roar and one that always sounded to me when I was high up above it like the sea, like tides breaking on an empty shore.

Wim was nowhere to be seen. He had disappeared over some edge, aided by his rope or perhaps only by his genius.

'Do you think he flies in his dreams?' I asked Silver, whispering so as not to interrupt the quiet.

'I hope not. It would be too frustrating when he wakes up. What do you dream about, Clodagh?'

I'll tell him, I thought. But not now, not yet. 'This and that. My dreams are much like everyone's, I expect.'

Liv said she was cold. She hunched her shoulders and hugged herself as she walked. When I think of her as she then was, not as she now is, I see her in that pose, arms crossed over her chest, hands clutching her shoulders, giving fearful sidelong looks to the world. Or curled up in a corner, head buried, arms embracing knees, the child yearning to return to the womb.

'It's usually cold here at night,' Silver said. 'I bet it's cold at night in Sweden, isn't it?'

'Only in the wintertime,' said Liv and she gave a great sob.

We sat down with our backs to a chimney stack. Silver gave us cigarettes and put his arm round Liv to comfort her. 'Tell us about life in the far north among the reindeer.'

But she could only talk about the car crash and James and Claudia and running away. She talked about hiding too and watching. She had taken to spending large parts of every day watching the street from one of the front windows. Both the living room and Silver's bedroom overlooked the front. In her au-pair days she had often walked along Russia Road on her way to the shops in Formosa Street, the baby in the buggy, Marcus unwillingly holding her hand. Whoever looked after them now would also pass that way. Or James or Claudia might at a weekend. We reassured her or tried to. We told her the

Hindes had forgotten her by now and she had nothing to worry about. Then we went to the end of the roof road, the whole length of Torrington Gardens, and looked over the rim of the gable end at a garden lying deep down below, a mysterious place of tall cypresses and dusky ilexes and in the depths the occasional pale shimmering face of a narcissus. The stucco wall on the other side of this chasm rose to a shaped gable, its peak an ogee arch, its flat surface windowless and with multi-curved sides of red sandstone. Silver, seeing my disappointed face in the near-dark, said, 'There'll be a scaffolding going up there in a week or two. That'll be an enormous help.' After that we went back the way we'd come, down the nailhead steps this time and up the other side, using the drainpipes and the ivy. 'Did you notice,' he said, 'how many top-floor windows were open?'

I, who pride myself on being observant, hadn't noticed.

'A good thing for Jonny,' said Liv in a bitter voice.

'People think they're safe from burglars if they're on the fourth or fifth floor,' Silver said, 'so they leave their windows open and don't put bars on them.'

We went through our own open window. Neither Wim nor Jonny had returned. Liv drifted off to Jonny's room where she put the television on. I sat on the broken leather sofa with Silver, filled with peace and joy, and he kissed me, very softly and gently but not like that first time at the gate, not like that at all. I had to go, I said, I had to go home to old Mrs Fisherton's.

'Don't go,' he said. 'Stay the night. Stay with me.'

Leaving windows open on the top floor is all very well. To do so in a basement is unwise. But I had left my bedroom window open and it was as well I had: Mabel had come in during the night and was asleep on my bed. She woke up when breakfast was put down for her and I told her how I'd been on the roofs. Maybe I'd meet her up there one night but I cautioned her to be careful. I, after all, would be unlikely to leap off a mansard in pursuit of a butterfly.

I'm not going to say much about the night, my first with Silver, except that it was lovely and I was happy. I was happy for the first time since Daniel died on the pylon. I told him a bit about Daniel, just that I had been in love with someone who had died, and he told me about his ideas of life. He'd been at Queen Mary College in the University of London but he had dropped out, it wasn't for him. Unlike me and my shilly-shallying, he had left correctly, informing the authorities that he had had enough and was going. At the age of sixteen Silver had inherited enough from his grandmother to provide him with an income. He had refused to apply for a grant but had paid his own way, just as he gave his parents rent for the flat. Jack and Erica Silverman despaired of him. Their daughter and their other son were so conventional, so *normal*. Erica sometimes wondered, while saying she knew this was absurd, if something had happened to him, during that lost weekend I was yet to hear about, that had left a trauma which would affect him always.

Silver and I became lovers and were what Jonny called an 'item'. At that time each of us believed that there could be no one else for us, it was almost laughable to think of some intervening third. He had a poem he used to quote, something about your face in mine eye, mine in yours appears, I don't suppose I've got it right, but that's how it was for us. And the funny thing was, considering I was just twenty and he was due to become twenty in a month's time, that ours was a mature love, the kind that middle-aged people long to achieve after a lifetime of mistakes and painful break-ups. Or so we thought and told each other. Pompous, weren't we? Proud of being in love. Starry-eyed, sitting entwined on the rooftops, we solemnly declared to one another how each had fallen in love at first sight. I could do even better, for I had loved him *before* we'd met.

If I was grown up in my love, I can hardly say I was in other aspects of my life. The following week trouble began at GUP. It was naive of me to suppose that I was hidden and anonymous at 19 Russia Road. When I had registered, back in the previous October, I had given this address, if not this phone number. The admissions officer also had my parents' address. Max's number was obtained from them and on two successive days my supervisor phoned three times. I had no idea Caroline Bodmer was such a persistent strong-minded woman. She had given me a very different impression of a vague preoccupied creature. Selina had searched for me – I, of course, being up at Silver's or on the roofs – but the third call came at nine in the morning and, entering as she invariably did without knocking, she found me coming out of the bathroom wrapped in towels. It was difficult ever to get into the bathroom at Silver's, there were always too many people competing for it. Fortunately Mabel had eaten her breakfast and gone out five minutes before.

'She's holding on, darling. She sounded rather – well, cross.' Selina shook her head at my appearance, a gesture of Max's she had caught. She herself was immaculate in a yellow linen dress. 'You can't go up like that. Max might see you. Oh dear, now what shall I do? Shall I tell her you'll be just two minutes or maybe you could call her back? Yes, I'll say you'll call her back, darling, but you must do it. You must *promise*. Or she'll blame me, won't she?' This was exactly the sort of pointless fretfulness Silver deplored. 'Or I could say you'll see her at the college. Had I better do that?'

'I'll call her back.' Just give me five minutes to invent something to say, I thought. 'Oh, and thanks, Selina.'

'You're welcome, darling, only the woman has phoned three times and the other two times Max had to answer the phone himself. You know he does find answering the phone very trying. Still, he had the opportunity to have a long talk with her. When you come upstairs you'll remember he's starting work *now*, won't you? He's doing his index and that's fearfully demanding, so you must be as quiet as a mouse.'

'I won't make a noise.'

'One more thing, darling. I don't suppose you ever go down on the canal bank, do you? No, of course you don't, but if ever you were tempted, remember that poor creature who was murdered there last week or whenever. She was beaten to death with a lump of wood. It's all in today's paper, it came out at the inquest. It used to be so *safe* round here.'

How did she know? Before she married Max she had had a flat in Baron's Court. I got dressed and went upstairs. The yellow drawing room was full of flowers. I suppose Selina had carefully chosen them to match the furnishings, for they were exclusively yellow and reddish-brown with emerald leaves and ferns, and arranged them herself in two big vases and an urn. The urn stood on something that I think is called a jardinière, a big iron construction, all scrolls and spirals. The whole effect was less of a room designed to be lived in than a set piece constructed to be photographed for a glamorous interiors magazine. It smelt strongly, not of the flowers but of one of those sprays whose scent is not that of the fresh meadows it claims to simulate but of cheap aftershave. I tiptoed in, looking uneasily about me. I wonder if I've ever been anywhere that made me feel more uncomfortable, with the exception, of course, of tunnels and underpasses.

In the five minutes' grace I had been given I had thought mostly about Max. It was Max who had answered the phone on those two previous occasions. I disliked the sound of that long talk Caroline Bodmer had had with him. Had she asked him where I was? Was I ill? This took some thinking over. Max, even at that moment, up in his disordered eyrie, might be less preoccupied with his index than with retribution and venting his anger on ungrateful me. The form that would take was pretty obvious. However, at least five minutes had gone by, nearer seven minutes. I dialled the number.

I spoke to her. If I hadn't met Silver and become his lover, if I hadn't wanted to stay with Silver and go back on the roofs and discover more roofs, if I hadn't wanted to keep my hold on old Mrs Fisherton's because if I lost the flat I'd either have to go home or do what Liv had done, if all those things weren't true, I would have told her I had changed my mind about the course and was dropping out. Instead I said I had had shingles.

'You're very young to have shingles.'

'I know,' I said. 'My GP told me he'd never come across it before.' I don't know if what I said next is true but I dredged it up from some half-remembered village talk. 'At my age he'd have expected it to come out as chicken pox.'

If you lie, always supply circumstantial details. They convince. She expressed sympathy. When would I be back? Next week, I said. Yes, well, that would do. Did I realize I had missed several lectures, the social science seminar and the management placement? I'd do my best to catch up, I said.

'You do realize, Chloe, that student performance is under review, don't you, and at the end of the year, which is not far off, not at all far off, you could simply – well, not to mince matters, be asked not to come back in October?'

I had a picture, not a very pleasant one, of matters being minced, of a long strip of flesh, maybe a fillet of pork, pushed through a food processor. Nothing was going to take me back to GUP for a second year, but October was a long way off, all kinds of things could happen before October. All kinds of things did, though not what I meant when I vaguely considered the future that morning in Selina's yellow drawing room. Mostly, though, I thought how a whole week would pass before I need go back.

I half-expected a summons from Max and one came, brought of course by Selina, just as I was off to meet Silver in the café on the bridge at Maida Hill. Instead of his study Max was in the dining room, where that first evening I had had dinner with them. Since then, as Beryl had foretold, it had been redecorated. Below ground I had scarcely noticed the comings and goings of builders. But they had been there and done the room in the colours, as Beryl put it, of a can of Heinz baked beans, wallpaper in bright peacock blue and black, dazzling white paintwork. The old black carpet looked deeper and darker than before. Still seated at the table, from which all the lunch things but the small coffee cup in front of him had been cleared away, Max looked at me over the top of the gold-rimmed glasses which had slid down his nose, chin tucked in, round jowls prominent. When he had made sure it was me and not some intruder, ghost or hallucination, he pushed the glasses back to the bridge of his nose with both hands and held them there while he stared, lips pursed. He was wearing one of his tracksuits, pants in a pale shade of cocoa, top in cocoa and bitter chocolate stripes.

It's a successful technique with those weaker or younger or more vulnerable than yourself whom you seek to control: look at them for some seconds without speaking while wearing a expression of deep disapproval, delaying as long as is reasonable what there is to say. I had experienced a lot of it in my short life and usually I had sat there under the censorious scrutiny, taking it mutinously but in silence. But we change fast at twenty and I had changed since coming to Russia Road. I said as firmly as I could, 'Please don't look at me like that, Max. I know you're angry with me and I'm sorry, but would you just come out and say it?'

He might have responded by asking me how I dared speak to him like that or even telling me to come back when I was in a more tractable frame of mind, but he didn't. Standing up to bullies is supposed to work and sometimes it does. I swallowed hard but invisibly, I think. He turned his head to the window as if he had found something very interesting in the garden (Mabel tightrope-walking the trellis, maybe) and said, 'Why haven't you been to that polytechnic of yours?'

I couldn't tell him I had had shingles. I opted for the truth or half the truth. 'I don't like the course. It's not what I want. I didn't know that before I started. I'm not interested in business.'

The head-shaking began. Actress she might be, but Selina would never learn to do it as well as he did. It was such a tiny subtle movement, perhaps through no more than twenty degrees of the circle, the merest tremble, but perfectly controlled, of vertebra on vertebra. It signified far more than disapproval: wonder at folly as well, ruefulness for my misspent past, amazement at the youth of the day.

'I ask myself if you realize, Clodagh, how fortunate you are to be one of those who have the opportunity to enjoy higher – I should say, further – education totally free of charge. It may not always be so, no doubt the time will come when students will once more pay their own tuition fees as I had to, as my poor grandmother whose last home you currently occupy had to on my behalf, working her fingers to the bone.' Max censured a cliché on the lips of others but never minded using one himself. 'No, that time will come under some future government, but it hasn't come yet. Students arrive from all over the world to benefit from our free education – did you know that?

Do you think they abandon a course just because the discipline is temporarily not to their taste? Do you think they fail to understand that in this life the rough has to be taken with the smooth?'

I wasn't sure whether Max meant 'discipline' in the sense of control or in the sense of a mode of instruction. It didn't much matter. 'I don't want to work in an office,' I said, 'and I don't want to be a social worker working in an office.'

'No, you want to be a steeplejack. I've never forgotten that ambition of yours, Clodagh, and I don't think I ever shall.' Max looked at his cup, picked it up and, thinking better of finishing the coffee in it, set it down again. 'Needless to say, I took it less than seriously. That being so, what do you propose to do now?'

I'd been thinking quickly. 'Go back to the Grand Union Polytechnic and ask Dr Bodmer to let me change my course.'

'They have PhDs on the faculty, do they? I am surprised. Change to what?'

'I don't know,' I said. 'I'll let you know. I'll –' I sought for a term and came up with the worst I could have – 'keep you in the picture.'

'A young woman who uses stale metaphors of that sort might be best suited to – Journalism and Media Studies, do they call it?'

'In the picture' was no worse, as far as I could see, than 'working one's fingers to the bone'. Max, his head oscillating in that controlled tremor, said I could go, called me back when I got to the door to say that he hoped I had discussed all this with my parents. Next time I phoned home he'd like a word with my father. I escaped. Silver was waiting for me in the café, drinking black coffee and eating croissants. He had found a shop where they sold diamanté cat collars and he presented me with a green velvet one, sparkling with brilliants, for Mabel.

'Suppose Max throws me out at the end of term,' I said.

We were holding hands across the table top. Can you imagine very pale water-grey eyes nevertheless being warm and full of love?

'There's no problem. You can come and live with me.'

We made plans. I'd abandon GUP and find somewhere else, a place where I could learn something I really wanted to learn. If Max turned me out, I'd go to Silver's and take my cat with me. To that end I went back to 19, fetched Mabel and put the new collar on her. I introduced her to Silver's place and to Wim who was lying on the sofa. Although he seemed indifferent to her, she took an immediate fancy to him and weaved in and out between his feet, rubbing her face against his legs. We'd been there no more than five minutes when Liv came out of Jonny's room. I can't be certain, it was just instinct, but I think she and Wim had been making love and I think it was the first time. At any rate, she had been making love and not with Jonny. Jonny was at his work in the car park. She looked at Wim as she came into the room, giving him a diffident smile. We might not have been there, for all the notice she took of us. Wim beckoned to her. When she came up to him, standing in front of him with a look of adoration on her face that was so naked and intense it was embarrassing, he bent over and kissed her on the mouth. He was smiling. I swear he was smiling throughout that kiss. He touched her shoulder lightly, opened one of the windows and climbed out. A moment later his face appeared at the closed casement, upside-down, to say he'd see us later. When I think of Wim that's how my mind's eye sometimes sees him, the shaven head, then the cool yellow eyes, mouth at the top.

Mabel, who'd been 'marking' everything in the room with her soft cheek, approached the window and jumped on to the sill. I suppose there's never been a cat since the world began, or since windows were invented, who, seeing an open casement, has failed to use it as a door and gone to see what's outside. Mabel was on the mansard before we could stop her.

'Curiosity kills cats, as we know,' Silver said.

He climbed out, caught up with her as she reached the chimney stack and brought her back in his arms. He rubbed his mouth on the top of her sleek head.

'It seems strange,' I said, 'that it's safer for us up there than it is for her, yet she's much the best climber.'

'She doesn't know what we know,' Silver said, 'and she can't know. That's the difference.'

'I'll have to take her to my parents' once Max evicts me. My mother loves cats. It would be nice and safe for her in the fields. She could go hunting something more exciting than squirrels.'

Liv, who hadn't spoken, who had thrown herself face-downwards on the sofa, suddenly sat up and said, 'Are you meaning the apartment at No. 19 will be for rent?'

Simultaneously Silver and I knew what was in her mind. We found that out when we compared notes afterwards. While she was at Silver's she was with Jonny, had to be with Jonny. If she lived down the road, she'd be free to be Wim's girlfriend. I could as easily imagine Max and Selina allowing Liv to rent old Mrs Fisherton's as I could picture them letting it to a homeless family. I said nothing of this, Liv looked so hopeful and pathetic, but I did explain that they only let me have the place because I was a sort of relation. Liv shrugged.

'What am I to do?'

'Stay here and sort yourself out, I should think,' said Silver. He added in a kindly tone, 'You don't have to share that room with Jonny. Not if you don't want to. You can still be here, we'll find a corner for you. There's nothing to worry about.'

'You are always saying that,' Liv said hotly. 'Naturally, I wish to be with Jonny. He is my lover.' She eyed Mabel. Having made sure she would know every piece of furniture again and every square inch of the ragged bit of carpet, Mabel had curled herself up on a patchwork velvet cushion someone had dropped or thrown on the floor. 'Is this cat to live here?'

'You heard me say she can't,' I said. 'She'd fall off the roof.'

'Cats never fall.' Liv could be dismissive and dogmatic at the same time. 'A cat can jump fifty metres and not be harmed. I have seen this.'

'I'd rather not take the risk.'

'Good. You say she is hunter. She will be hunting my mice.'

She was the only woman I've ever known who actually liked mice. I once asked her if there were a lot of them running round Kiruna but she said she had never seen a mouse before she came here. I promised to remove Mabel. Although I much prefer cats to mice, I could see Liv's point and, for some reason – surely not because she was a mouse-fancier? – I started liking her from then on. I've said she was rather unattractive in those days. I've often noticed, and I'm sorry it's there for me to notice, I don't much like it, that women who are with a man they don't care for, a man they've a duty to or simply don't know how to escape from, soon start looking plain and drab. When they get a new man or they take on another, not instead of but as well as, they blossom out and become pretty, even beautiful in some cases. Love conquers all, I suppose. Well, I know it does, I have reason to know.

Silver, who knows the Bible and likes phrases from it, used to say Liv was like Leah, the first wife of Jacob, she was 'sore-eyed and tender', and that describes her very well, the pinkishness round her eyes and on the lids and the chapped look of her face. Her hair always wanted washing. If she didn't bite her nails, she tore at the cuticles and picked the skin on her lips. But once she had Wim, or thought she had Wim, at any rate had slept with him and meant to do so again, her skin cleared and her hair shone and she grew some of the longest pointed fingernails I've seen on a woman's hand. She stopped slouching and cuticle-chewing, stood upright and started washing her clothes. Whether Wim noticed any of this I don't know. I know so little about him except for his passion for the roofs of tall buildings.

'Now if Liv were only a tower block,' Silver said that evening when we were alone on the roofs, 'Wim would be on top of her all the time.'

As Silver had predicted, the scaffolding had gone up, its vertical poles planted in the garden between the end of the Torrington Gardens terrace and the first house in Peterborough Avenue. There was very little difference in height, each was five storeys high, not counting the basement. We crossed the scaffolding easily and pulled ourselves up on to the leads. The long row of small squat pillars, each one moulded in a chair-leg shape, cast a strange ladder-like shadow on to the paleish roof surface.

A brilliant moon seemed to hang directly above us. Its clear greenish light showed us the world above that hardly anyone ever saw, the roof cluttered with aerials and dishes and tanks and cowled pipes, the chimney stacks here narrow columns, each bearing only two pots. The towers of Westminster's estates on the canal to the west, which seemed so tall at ground level were from here reduced to mere apartment blocks. The moonlight painted their pagoda roofs the silvery white of frost. For some reason the canal remained black, its water so calm it scarcely glittered. Browning's island lay dark-treed and peaceful on the wide stretch above Paddington Basin.

Liv and Jonny went off together, she with a bad grace but accepting the inevitable once Wim had disappeared into the distance and she had no hope of keeping pace with him. He dressed in black at night, we all wore dark colours up on the roofs, but that evening, in the bright radiance, paler colours might have been a wiser choice. Any observant passer-by, looking upwards, might have seen us. But few people are observant, they seldom look roofwards and, in any case, the streets were deserted. Fear emptied them, though I never found out what exactly people were afraid of. Muggers? Men like Jonny? From up there you could always see a hundred television screens, glowing moonlight-white through uncurtained windows in every row and terrace.

Jonny was making for the mansion block which was the last in Peterborough Avenue, five storeys in red and white dressings with wrought-iron railings on all but the top one. These balconies made access to the flats easy and most of the occupants had put bars on their windows. But the top-floor windows weren't barred, Silver told me. From where he and I sat on the parapet we could see the copper domes of the mansions and the cupola with its tower of the winds that grew grandiosely from the centre front of its roof.

I suppose I was naive if not innocent, but it wasn't until then that I realized what Jonny was doing.

'He's quite rich, you know,' Silver said, 'and all of it from dealing and stealing.'

The dealing didn't much surprise me. Silver's place was often redolent of cannabis and I'd seen Jonny and Liv do a line of cocaine. But stealing?

'I told you people who live in top flats leave their windows open. Especially in summer. He'll go in through an open window. He won't take her. Not because he doesn't want to involve her; she'd be too much of a risk.'

'Don't you *mind?*'

Silver put his arm round me and we sat with our legs dangling no more than an inch or two above the lintel of the windows below. 'Shall I sling him out?'

'I don't know. It's your place.' I sought for an answer. 'Are you trying to make him better? Are you trying to – well, *redeem* him?'

Silver laughed. His laughter rang round that bare moonlit rooftop. The people in the top flat just below us must have heard him. Perhaps they thought it was an angel laughing or, more likely, sound from next-door's television. 'I'm not a redeemer, Clo. I suppose I like him. I've never met anyone else who does.'

'He doesn't pay you rent?'

'No one pays me rent. I tell myself I'm not – well, harbouring him, giving shelter to a thief, I mean. He's got a room of his own in Cricklewood.'

But he has access to the roofs because he lives in your place. I didn't say this aloud. I didn't have to.

'I know what you're thinking,' Silver said.

'You always do.'

'I've been into one or two flats myself. From the roofs, I mean. I couldn't resist it, just to look.'

'But you didn't steal anything.'

'No. It was curiosity. Like your Mabel. Come on, let's go on.'

We went as far as the second dome that night. All the blocks in Peterborough Avenue were the same height but each about three feet from the next one, making two chasms to cross. We jumped. I don't believe I could do it today, I'd no longer have the nerve. I shudder when I think of the two of us springing across a canyon forty feet deep, its depths lost in shadow, nothing beneath to save us if we fell, not even a twig on a branch, not a wire or narrow pipe. Silver went first, his hands stretched out to catch me as I followed. If I was afraid at the time, I don't remember fear. The achievement was all, the successful leap, and to make it as soundlessly as possible. We giggled at the thought of people below us listening and attributing the thud of our footfalls to a bird landing heavily. I once saw a heron from Regent's Park on a roof in Russia Road. Such a big bird would make a resounding thump as it landed on slates. We clung to each other and laughed in triumph, in the mild night and the soft moonlight sinking to our knees, and embraced, kissing feverishly, as happy as could be.

'Not here,' said Silver, laughing. 'There are limits.'

'I bet Wim would do it on a roof.'

'I bet Wim *has*.'

So just beyond the tower of the winds we turned back, leaving the others to whatever their pleasure might be, and returned to ours.

II

We all went on the roofs, the five of us and sometimes others too, Morna and a girl called Lucy and her boyfriend Tom, Morna's friend Judy and an older man (too old, we thought him) called Owen. But we five were the real roof people, the Famous Five, Lucy called us. The others, in varying degrees, were afraid when they were up there. Basically, to enjoy the roofs, you had to be someone who loved heights, who was what Silver had a name for: 'acrophiliac'. Morna and the rest weren't among their number. Judy was almost the reverse, a girl who had problems with looking out of top-floor windows but who came on to the roofs once or twice in the hope of testing herself, of conquering a phobia by exposing herself to it. It didn't work. The second time she went through Silver's window and out on to the roof of No. 15, she squatted there, hugging herself Liv-fashion, her eyes tightly shut. Silver had to bring her down. She was tiny, not five feet tall and thin with it. Silver carried her down, first in his arms, then in a fireman's lift. And I, who was never afraid while up there, was terrified he might fall and I lose another lover to the heights.

The rest of them walked gingerly on the slates, trying to tiptoe or slide. The chasms between blocks made them draw back as from some awful sight of blood or ruin. Owen was unable to face climbing the gable façade with its nailhead bands, even though a fall would only have brought him down on to the roof of the detached house. Morna was the best of them, adventurous enough once she was up there, though complaining all the while of our ideas of entertainment when pubbing or clubbing would have been so much more to her taste.

We five all had different reasons for going on the roofs. When she was up there Liv felt free and safe. That seems a contradiction in terms, for the rest of us were all aware, however much we loved it, of an element of danger. Liv felt safe on the roofs while she'd have been in peril in the street. On the roofs no one could find her, seize her, bring her to justice.

Paranoia gripped her and, with time, strengthened its hold. The money she had brought with her she kept hidden in a secret place in the flat. No one knew where, not even Jonny. Because she hadn't been out she had spent nothing in all that time. She had never asked one of us to buy her anything. She used Silver's soap and toothpaste and shampoo and washing powder. It never occurred to her to dip into her hoard and recompense him.

One day she told me she was keeping the money intact for when Claudia and James or the police found her and wanted it back. This, she believed, was bound to happen. She was convinced they were searching for her with as much zeal and determination as for Andrew Lane and Alison Barrie and the little boy. I said that if she really felt like that she could send the money back, make a package of it and one of us would take it to the post office in Formosa Street.

She shook her head. 'I can't do that.'

'If you're never going to spend it and you're so sure you'll have to give it back sometime, why not give it back now?'

'I couldn't do it, Clodagh. I could not, I don't know if this is the word, *physically* do it. My hands would not work for me.'

There was nothing more to be said. I thought she was becoming sick in her mind and I told Silver so, but all he said was, 'Don't worry about her. As time goes on she'll come to see no one's after her and she'll go out and then she'll be fine.'

In those months she had never been in touch with her parents in Kiruna. Weren't they likely to be anxious? And how about the agency who had found her the job with Claudia and James? I thought it likely she had been reported missing and I wondered why there hadn't been a hunt for her. When I considered what I read in the papers, saw on television and heard on the 'wireless', how a young girl had only to fail to go home immediately after an evening out or be absent from where she lived for more than a couple of hours for a police search to begin, it seemed strange that there was no hue and cry for Liv.

'It's not strange,' Silver said. 'Her circumstances were different. She got drunk and crashed a car and ran away. They know that. I expect they think she's gone back to Sweden. That daft pair didn't notice Liv was stashing their money away, they're feckless about money, so they don't know she's got their two grand. They'd probably like to see her in court for driving over the permitted limit but, as for the money, they'd be incredulous if they knew she was sweating over them finding her.'

It was the sensible attitude to take but still I wasn't convinced. Kiruna was part of the civilized world, even though it might be at the end of the earth. Liv's parents would have made inquiries, been in touch with the agency, with Claudia and James, with their own police, surely, and with ours. So, if she really didn't want to be found, she was wise to prefer the streets above to the streets below. Sometimes, when I came out from No. 19 to go to No. 15, I'd look up all those floors and see her white face at Silver's window, looking for Claudia and James or their new au pair with the children to pass that way. If only she could have accompanied Wim on his journeyings, if he'd have taken her with him, she'd have been entirely happy. Instead she was stuck with Jonny, who used her as the cat burglar's mate.

His attitude to the roofs was simple. There was no enjoyment in it. If anything, he found the climbing a nuisance, the use of ropes and occasionally a ladder burdensome. They were no more than a means to an end. The views of London spread out in a great relief map below left him cold. He found it literally cold up there and swore long and loudly if it was raining on a night when he'd planned a 'job'.

When Silver first met him, leaning over a parapet to see Jonny come out of a window on to a fourth-floor balcony, he was already practised in gaining access to the inside of houses. But he always depended on scaffolding to help him, branched drainpipes, the trunks of climbing plants, their roots in the earth of a basement area, their tops often reaching twenty or thirty feet up, porch roofs, balconies. The easy means the top-floor windows of 15 Russia Road afforded him of carrying on his trade were a boon.

Silver was the only one of us Jonny talked to – I mean in the sense of confiding in. He wouldn't have dreamt of talking to Liv beyond issuing instructions to her to cook something for him or wash his clothes or come to bed. Wim's was not a receptive ear and as for me, most of the time Jonny seemed not to notice my existence. So occasionally, when he had had a few drinks, he talked to Silver and told him about his horrible childhood. His mother had died of a heroin overdose when he was two. His father had abused him from the age of four and later on passed him around among his friends. In order to secure his compliance without beating him – his father did that too –

he dosed him with brandy, or in hard times with methylated spirits, so that the boy was insensible when the abuse went on. Jonny wasn't much more than five feet tall and he blamed his small stature, with or without reason I don't know, on the quantities of alcohol he was made to consume as a child. His mother had been tall, he said, and his father was tall, so what other reason could there be for him being what he called a 'midget'? All this somehow made worse his habit of quoting lines from nursery rhymes. Although highly numerate and speedily able to do the kind of mental arithmetic others needed a calculator to do for them, he was unable to write more than his own name, and while he claimed to read a newspaper, I think it was no more than the headlines that he meant. So it was not the printed word he quoted but from memory of the spoken word. In the context of what he had suffered as a child, I found this gruesome.

In his own way he was as obsessive as Wim. His ambition was to be a millionaire. 'That's a load of crap that money don't bring happiness,' he often said. 'Money *is* happiness. It's life. If you haven't money, you may as well be dead.'

Stealing was the obvious way to get it. If he had been a tall heavy man, he'd very likely have chosen some other form of theft than that which was the result of climbing drainpipes. But Jonny was made to be a cat burglar. He climbed like a monkey and looked like one, especially when loping across the roofs in a dark close-fitting tracksuit. Of course, he had his car-park scam as well, but the revenues from that and his wages were nothing to what he made from selling the jewellery he stole and his drug dealing.

Rather than the result of stealing or dealing, his prison sentence was for something approaching attempted murder. I think the charge must have been causing actual bodily harm. If he confided the horrors of his childhood only to Silver, he spoke freely to everyone about his time in prison and what led up to it. It was an episode he enjoyed describing. Liv was told by him to shut up when she began recounting for what he called the 'umpteenth' time the tale of James and Claudia and their children and the crashed Range Rover; his own story he repeated as often as he felt like it. I think he believed it demonstrated his courage and his resourcefulness, that he was a force to be reckoned with.

'I don't let him mess with me' was a phrase he often used.

★

He was nineteen and working as a porter in a hotel in Bayswater. The hotel's address was Bayswater but it was more like Paddington, not far from the station. It wasn't a private house conversion but had been a hotel for decades, probably since the beginning of the twentieth century, and apart from the narrow winding staircase, the only way to get to the upper floors was by means of one small lift. The hotel management in 1906 or whenever had very likely been immensely proud of this contraption. It was capable of carrying four people or up to a weight of forty-five stone, had an inner sliding door of metal mesh that closed with a clang and an outer wooden door. In other words, the lift was a moving box in a shaft to which there was a door of scratched and scuffed mahogany on each one of the five floors.

Jonny had been there no more than a few hours when he discovered the flaw in the lift system. He said he hadn't bothered to read the notices pinned to the mahogany door in the reception area. What he meant was that he had been unable to read them. It sounded as if they were in several languages. If they'd been in a hundred, all would have been equally useless to Jonny. After he had had experience of the lift, someone told him what the notices said: *Please close the inner door on leaving the lift.*

Of course, around half the people who used it forgot to close the inner door. If you left it open, the lift couldn't be summoned from another floor and the mahogany door remained locked. Say, for example, you were in the reception area and wanted to go to a higher floor, pressing the button would be useless if someone on the third floor had forgotten to shut the inner door when leaving the lift and going to his room. The only way to make the bugger (Jonny's word) work again was by going up to the third floor by the stairs and closing the inner door. That was just an example, it might as well be the fourth floor or the fifth.

Jonny soon found that his duties humping guests' luggage were as nothing to the nuisance of that lift door. It was almost always he who had to go up those stairs and close it. He counted the stairs. To the top there were sixty-seven of them. A guest might arrive with two heavy suitcases and be allotted Room 52. Jonny's task was to take him and his luggage up in the lift. But nothing happened when he pressed the button. The guest couldn't be expected to use the stairs, so Jonny would run up them, checking on each landing to see if the lift was there with its door open, and finally perhaps find it on the fourth floor. He would go down in the lift himself, take the guest and his luggage up, come out of the room and find the lift had gone. So down the stairs he would go to find the receptionist taking an angry call from a guest on the second floor who hadn't been able to summon the lift. Jonny would go up again and find it stuck on the third floor with its inner door open.

He began to understand why he had got the job so easily, not to mention why no porter they had ever had before had stayed more than a month. One day he climbed those stairs forty-seven times in the eight hours he was there and twenty-two of them to the top. But all that was more or less bearable. People forgot to close the door, it was in most cases a simple failure to remember. One guest left that door open deliberately.

He was an American. What a businessman from Chicago who wore a Rolex watch and carried (or rather, Jonny carried) calfskin suitcases was doing in a dump like the Gilmore Hotel, I don't pretend to know and Jonny certainly didn't. His name was Tudorlap, Clarence Tudorlap. It's strange enough to have stuck in my memory, for I noted nothing of Jonny's story in my diary. In the public places of the hotel he was loud and vociferous in his condemnation of all things British. The United Kingdom was inefficient, old-fashioned, indeed stuck in a time warp, dirty and cold, and it was always raining. The heating didn't work, the trains didn't run on time, shop 'clerks' were rude and officials ignorant.

Jonny, who I'd never thought of as especially patriotic and probably hadn't thought of himself like that, suddenly couldn't stand any more. He'd just run up stairs for the tenth time that day and come down to hear Tudorlap telling the receptionist that the best thing that could happen to this country would be for the United States to 'nuke' it accidentally so that it 'sank without trace'.

'You shut your fucking mouth,' said Jonny.

There were quite a lot of people standing about listening and a couple of them laughed in a shocked sort of way. A very good-looking girl Jonny described as 'lovely, a real lady' said, 'I couldn't agree more. I don't know why you people come here. We don't want you.'

For some reason, none of this reached the ears of the management. The receptionist appears to have told no one and nor did Tudorlap.

He took his own private revenge. His room was No. 54. Every time he went up there, and he went up far more often than he need have done, he left the inner door of the lift open. Jonny had to run up the stairs to the top and close that door. He was sure Tudorlap watched him through the spyhole in his door and when he and the lift had gone, summoned it again. Not to use it but for the simple pleasure of leaving that door open.

It was one of the receptionists who suggested notices with the lettering in larger print should be supplied and affixed to the mahogany doors. Jonny had very little faith in this. He was certain it would make no difference to Tudorlap who, he was sure by this time, was doing it purposely and from a fiendish motive of revenge. And another four days remained before the man was due to leave and go back to Chicago. However, Jonny took the newly prepared notices he could barely read and hung them on the doors himself. He was due to take the notice for the fifth floor up to the top and he tried to summon the lift. Of course, it failed to come. Tudorlap had gone up five minutes before and left the inner door open. Jonny climbed the stairs, carrying the notice, a paper bag containing tacks and a small hammer.

He fixed the notice to the door. Instead of going all the way down in the lift he descended only one level, got out, shut the inner door and, using the stairs, returned to the fifth floor where he concealed himself behind the half-open door of a bathroom. Tudorlap came out of his bedroom, tiptoed across the landing floor and summoned the lift, unable to keep a smile from spreading across his face. The lift came, he opened the mahogany door and then the inner door. He was turning away, was facing the bathroom, when Jonny came out of it, hammer in hand.

If Jonny had been a few inches taller, he'd probably have killed Tudorlap. As it was, he managed one blow to the side of the American's head (rendering him permanently deaf in one ear) and two to his chest, breaking sternum and collarbone, before a man came bursting out of Room 52 and pulled him off. Blood was all over the place and Tudorlap was lying on the floor, groaning and vomiting. The police came and took Jonny away, the irony being that when they tried to get him downstairs in the lift they couldn't summon it because someone had left the inner door open on the floor below.

Jonny got three years and served the whole sentence. It took him a while to get work with his record but eventually he did, washing cars in a very upmarket garage in Hampstead where customers liked their Jaguars cleaned and polished by hand and the chrome worked over with a toothbrush. After that came the car park job, the thieving and the connection with the drug syndicate that seems to have operated from an antique shop in a street off the Edgware Road. He began to dream of making money.

His expenses were small. He had his car, of course, and he was a heavy smoker. Well, we all were. Being exposed to alcohol in that particular way hadn't put him off it for life, as you might expect, and most days when he arrived he brought in a bottle of whisky or vodka. But he bought nothing else as far as I could see. However, he had one expense only Silver knew about.

One day he was going to kill his father. The old man – he had been nearly fifty when Jonny was born – was still very much alive. Jonny never saw him, he hadn't seen him since he was fifteen, and at the time I'm writing of he was twenty-six. But he had had a watch kept on him. For years he'd been paying a down-and-out to keep tabs on George Rathbone, so that he knew exactly where the old man was, the kind of life he led and who his companions were. When the time was ripe, and he'd know when that time came, he would go to him, tell him he was going to kill him and how, and he'd do it. If he hadn't quite killed Tudorlap, he had had practice at attempting to kill. It would be easier, and he'd be better at it, the second time. Even Silver didn't know what form this murder would take. He didn't even believe in it, he said it was hot air.

But for some reason Jonny needed to be a rich man before he could do it. Hence the burglaries and the ranging across the roofs of Maida Vale. He was enormously proud of a newspaper cutting he had, a piece from the *Ham and High*, when they carried a story about him, calling him the Vale Villain and giving an entirely imaginary description of him as tall and bearded. According to their account he had carried out more than fifty burglaries in Maida Vale and Little Venice.

'I wish,' said Jonny.

I'd like to be able to tell you what Silver and I so much loved about roof-climbing, but I can't. I'd no more want to climb out of windows on to roofs now than I'd want to imagine myself Heidi in Johanna

Spyri's books and the gently undulating Suffolk landscape the Swiss Alps, as I did when I was seven. Or to climb pylons as I did when I was in my teens. I no longer understand my motivation or my enjoyment. All I can say is that it became a compulsion and I did enjoy it tremendously. Whatever impelled me impelled Silver also. And, eventually, we lost interest at the same time too.

Sitting up there in the warm nights of that long hot glorious summer or walking on the leads or daring new feats of climbing and abseiling and ascending ropes, we learnt to love each other. So much of the time we were alone, talking, kissing, laughing, or silent and close in the quiet of the heights. Sometimes we picnicked, our backs against a parapet, eating chicken wings and Boursin cheese and the ciabatta which was new in the shops, drinking milk or coke, but never wine. Below us the fourth- or fifth-floor flat-dwellers were retiring to bed and we saw the pale vaporous gleam of their lights fade from the black air as one after another they were switched off.

Up there no one bought or sold anything or advertised anything. There were no notices telling you to do this and not to do that, no phones to ring, no television screens – only the aerials that made those screens function – no background music, no rules and, in a strange way, no time. Silver took his watch off before going on the roofs and, following his example, I began to do the same. One night in early July we slept up there, Silver and I. We chose the flat roof of one of the terraces in Torrington Gardens, took sleeping bags and a futon, two cushions from the leather sofa and a blanket from old Mrs Fisherton's. The evening was dark, though there was a thin lemon-peel moon, and above lamp-standard level the air had that reddish smoky look and feel so characteristic of London nights. We had no means of knowing at what time dawn came, but we saw it come. We saw a round red sun rise over the City, paint the glassy towers with phosphorescence and, as it brightened and lost its shape, sprinkle across the sky feathers of pink and lilac. It was cold in the early morning, sharp as December. We wrapped ourselves in the sleeping bags and drank the hot milky coffee from the flask we had brought with us. The sun climbed the sky and grew warm and down there in the streets the traffic began and the people started hurrying to the tube at Warwick Avenue. A dog appeared in Torrington Gardens and stood on the pavement barking at something invisible to us behind a window-pane.

The garden of the house we had slept above was full of roses, climbers and standards and tea roses, and we told each other we could smell them in the clean morning sunshine.

I said I couldn't tell you why we loved the roofs, but I see that I was wrong and I have told you. 'We could get hooked on this,' Silver said, his arms round me, 'and then we'd never want to go down.'

Wim was hooked. He had no reason for going on the roofs but the roofs themselves, to conquer them, to own them, to *be* them. At that time I had no idea what he had been before he came to Silver's, or where he had been or what he had done or anything about his background. Wim is a Dutch name but he insisted his surname was Smith, or, laughing, Van de Smith when people asked about the Dutch connection.

'I can be Smith if Clodagh can be Brown,' he once said.

Silver told me he had a job but he didn't know exactly what it was, something menial, he thought, in the catering trade. I was going to write that he was an educated person and intelligent. Later on I found out that this was true but I didn't know it then. When someone is mostly silent, secretive, contained, you *don't* know. The obstacle to understanding was that normal people don't want to spend their lives, every free moment they have, ranging the roofs of buildings. You start thinking they are mad. Perhaps Wim was. When he told Silver he could have travelled from Maida Vale to Notting Hill on the roofs he very likely wasn't exaggerating, for he used ropes like a mountaineer, and all the rest of the equipment of Alpinism. What little money he spent went on that and on the dark tracksuits he wore for the roofs and the special trainers. Once or twice I saw him do a line of cocaine but he never used any other drug and he never drank.

Good as we were at our strange exercise, we couldn't keep up with Wim, and he never took any of us with him. If she hoped to accompany him, if she hoped he might come to *love* her, Liv was only storing up unhappiness for herself. He loved no one and nothing but the roofs, with the possible exception of Silver, the only one of us to whom he showed any feeling, embracing him in a rigid, sexless, almost detached way whenever he arrived at the flat. Of those embroidered silk tunics he had several, the red one and a white and a yellow, but a closer look showed them to be old and worn, the cuffs frayed and the embroidery stitches scuffed. Sometimes he slept at Silver's in a sleeping bag under a big rosewood table, turning it into a kind of four-poster bed. I once accidentally entered the bathroom while he was in there and found him shaving his head with an electric razor. He turned and gave me a strange look, not indignant or surprised but puzzled, rather, as if he had never seen me before and wondered who I was.

He wanted nothing but to scale the roofs of London and to do so for ever. One thing only troubled him, Silver said, and that was no small thing. He was twenty-eight. Like any sportsman he would begin to lose his skills, his impeccable sense of balance, his bodily control and, above all those, his stamina. Thirty or perhaps thirty-five would be the watershed. His nightmare, a real nightmare, a genuine recurring bad dream, was not of falling but of failing to perform some strenuous move with rope or hook that had once been child's play to him, his strength ebbing and his energy there no longer.

'If I can't go on the roofs,' he said to Silver, 'I shall die.'

He said it calmly, even conversationally, as someone else might say that if he failed to find the item he wanted at a certain shop, he would try another. One evening, going into Silver's kitchen for a glass of water, I came upon him sitting on the floor feeding Liv's tribe of mice chocolate biscuits. He looked up at me and smiled.

12

This morning Darren and Lysander and I started work on three adjoining houses in Sussex Gardens. They have been gutted and are in the process of being turned into one of those small luxury hotels that have become fashionable. The interesting thing for me is that the middle one is the hotel where Jonny was driven mad by the lift and where he half-killed Tudorlap.

If I had only relied on Jonny's account and not on my own later experience, I'd never have recognized it. By the time we got there today the lift was long gone, as was the sign telling guests that this was the Gilmore Hotel. We were contracted to do a complete wiring job to the twelve suites, twenty-six bedrooms, lounges, restaurants and kitchens. This is what we call the 'first fix', the carcassing, that's carried out before the plastering. Bare walls confronted us, newly boarded floors, large rooms where formerly there were two or three small rooms. Lounges and dining areas were all to have chandeliers and the installations for these, of course, had to be fitted from above. The window curtains in the suites were to be electronically operated and by remote control, but that would be part of the 'second fix', when we put in the switch plates. There would be closed-circuit TV as well. It was a big job and extremely lucrative, just what I needed to occupy the time before work began at Paddington Basin.

'I've been here before,' I said. 'I took a room for the evening,' knowing how Darren would take it. He didn't disappoint me.

'A short time with Mr Mystery, I suppose,' he said. 'Him of the sparkling eyes you used to run around with.'

Lysander sniggered. I grinned at him. 'You're wrong. It was someone else. And we didn't need a room for what's on your mind, we'd got one of our own.' I considered the whole truth and dismissed it. 'We were exploring.'

Darren said he had never heard it called that before, Lysander capped that with some more innuendo, and then we got down to work. If you're a woman electrician who works with men, you must expect that sort of thing. Anyway, hadn't I courted it? Of course it was Silver I had gone with to the Gilmore and in a way we had been exploring. Given a rope and the rest of his simple equipment, Wim could have climbed almost anything, but we needed help in the shape of other windows to climb out of. The houses in Sussex Gardens aren't very tall and there's nothing particularly wonderful about their roofs. The attraction of the Gilmore lay in its being a hotel and therefore with rooms to hire, and in its lift.

It was also cheap. Silver and I booked a room for one night by phone and went along at about six. It was early June. Silver said he wanted to pay in advance as we wouldn't be staying all night and the man in reception was quite unfazed. I suppose he was used to this sort of thing, though I'd have thought that by the late eighties people had got beyond using houses of call. As I soon discovered, I was being naive.

Our room was a single, on the fifth floor and at the back. The receptionist obviously thought we'd taken a single room with a single bed because that was all we could afford, while the truth was that we'd no need for a bed at all. We didn't intend to sleep in it or make love in it. Being at the back made it less likely anyone would see us climbing out of the window. If the Gilmore had let us, we'd have taken a cupboard so long as it had access to the roof.

I suppose Jonny's story about the lift wasn't really funny, wasn't at *all* funny, but laughter is often less about amusement than about astonishment, and we started laughing when we summoned the lift and it didn't come. There seemed not to be a porter about. Silver whispered to me that probably no one would take the job after Jonny's assault on Tudorlap. We pressed the button again. The receptionist got wearily off his stool and went upstairs. He didn't say anything but we knew where he had gone.

The lift came so quickly with the receptionist in it that he must have found it on the first floor.

'Shut the inner gate when you leave the lift, will you?' he said.

It was amazing they hadn't renewed it after what had happened. But perhaps the management knew, even then, that the building was to be sold and gutted and all its ancient equipment thrown on the rubbish heap. We carefully closed that inner gate when we got out and, once on the landing, read the notice, perhaps the very one Jonny had been carrying up to attach to the mahogany door when he encountered Tudorlap for the last time. The lettering was huge, like *Sun* headlines, but apparently still not effective.

We climbed out of the small sash window on to the roof. The evening was fine and sunny and it was still hot up there at half past six. I could feel the heat coming off the roof through my trainers and when I touched the slates my finger tingled as if I had held it close to a flame. We meant to walk all the way down to the Edgware Road on the leads and the slates in one direction and back to the street that leads to Paddington Station in the other. But roof gardens and little cottagey fences put up to divide the plots from one another got in our way. We could get no further than the hotel next door and there something very odd happened. We were lying on the roof, looking down over the guttering and thinking of going back to the room and then home. I shifted along so that I could look through the top pane of a small window where the curtains were drawn back. In the room inside, in a double bed, lay a man and a woman asleep. I recognized the woman, though I'd only seen her once before. She was the cushion designer I had met at the birthday lunch Max and Selina had given for me.

So I had been wrong about people no longer using houses of call. Seeing them like that made me feel low, like a voyeur. I told Silver and he said, 'All right, we'll never look through windows again.'

'It's not really excusable, is it? Even if one's motive is just being interested in other people, it's still an invasion of privacy.'

'We'll try to be good,' Silver said. 'We won't just not be bad, we'll try to do positive good. How about that?'

I never have difficulty in remembering those words and what they led to. But at the time I don't believe we had any plans for the good we'd do. We never looked into rooms again, though, but the once. And that once was what precipitated us into disaster. I specially remember that night, not only because of our visit to the Gilmore and what I saw through that window, but because when we got back to Silver's we found Liv alone, convulsed with terror.

By then it was dark. She used to ask Jonny to buy candles for her, which he grudgingly did, but for once she had lit no candles, put on no lights. The whole house was in darkness. I could hear her mice scuttering about in the kitchen. Liv was huddled into a corner of the sofa, embryo-shaped, her arms round her drawn-up knees and her head on her knees. The only light came from outside the window and Silver's place was too high up for there to be much of that. She lifted her head when we came in and stared at us, her eyes bright with fear. It's odd how eyes can shine in a dark room, how they can be the only part of a face that's visible. Without a word she got up and threw herself into my arms. Silver struck a match and began lighting the stumps of candles left over from the night before.

'The doorbell is ringing,' Liv mumbled into my shoulder, 'and I go into Silver's room and look out of the window, there in the front, and is a policeman down there outside the door.'

'I don't suppose he'd come for you,' Silver said in that voice I always found so completely reassuring. 'He may have been after Jonny but most likely it was something about my dad's car.' Jack Silverman left one of his cars permanently parked, it seemed to me, in Russia Road. 'A lot of cars were broken into last week. He probably wanted to check the radio was still there.'

In fact, this was exactly what the policeman had called about, as Silver found out the next day. But Liv wouldn't believe him. She was sure Claudia and James had discovered her whereabouts. 'I trust you, Clodagh,' she said. 'I don't trust Jonny.' Silver she didn't mention, nor Wim. 'Will you take the money for me and hide it in your place?'

'I thought you were saving it to give back when they rumble you,' said Silver.

'Rumble? What is rumble?'

'Catch you. Bring you to justice.'

'I have told you, I cannot. My hands would not do it. My brain will but my hands, no.' Liv began to cry. 'I have to have this money. To live. To escape.'

I don't know what made me take a stand I'd most likely associate with people twice my age. Perhaps it was because I was happy and had friends, most of all had Silver, was never going to be a business manager or a secretary or married to Guy Wharton, and I had come to understand at last how worried Mum and Dad must have been over me after the pylon and when I was so ill and so totally apathetic and unresponsive.

'I'll look after your money,' I said, 'on condition you'll go and phone your parents now and tell them you're here and you're OK.'

Silver looked at me. 'You don't have to do this, Clo.'

'I know. I know as well that it's perfectly safe here and she's safe but she doesn't believe that.'

Liv said incongruously, 'It is too late, past eleven o'clock at home. Sweden is one hour ahead of here.'

'And it's broad daylight in Kiruna,' said Silver. 'They'll be enjoying the midnight sun.' He had come round to my point of view. If he never worried himself, he was aware that others did, and while he'd have liked to cure the world of anxiety, he knew it couldn't be done by feeding fear. 'Go on, give them a nice surprise, and when you come back we'll have lit fresh candles for you.'

The mice fled as I put on the kitchen light. The sink was full of filthy plates and cups, the table and counters a jumble of food packages and tins mixed up with empty packets and used, unwashed cans, ashtrays that contained pyramids of ash and stubs, smeary wineglasses, cups with brown dregs in them. Too many things had been spilt on the floor for anything to restore it to cleanliness but a complete scrub. I found some candles, we put them out and Silver lit them. The lights out in the kitchen and the door shut, the mice came back. We could always hear them come scuttering out from their holes. Liv fed them regularly but there was no need when there was so much from which they could help themselves.

She was using the phone in Silver's bedroom. We could just hear her voice and were pretty sure she really was talking to her parents, not from her words, which we of course couldn't understand, but from the placatory tone designed to reassure that was entirely familiar to us. We used it ourselves. Very soon she came back.

'They ask me to go home.'

'There's nothing to stop you,' I said. 'All you have to do is buy an air ticket and you've got the money.'

'My father will send me the money. He will send by tele-something if I have a bank account but I have no bank account.'

'Telegraphic transfer,' said Silver. 'You can use my bank account if you like.'

Liv had no reason not to trust Silver, rather the reverse. She had lived in his flat rent-free for more than two months, eaten his food and drunk his drink, smoked his cigarettes and used his water and electricity, all for nothing. In return she had given him a plague of mice. But she trusted no man, she had some deep-rooted prejudice against the male sex in practical matters. She gave me a sidelong look and her meaning was plain.

'You want to use mine?' I said. 'OK, you can, but wait a minute. If you've got the money why does your father have to send you your air fare?'

Liv sat down. She looked me straight in the eye. She put up her hands and pushed her long wispy fair hair away from her face. 'I am not using that money, Clodagh. That is my saving – is that right, saving? – for my future. It is to start. Then I put more with it and more and one day be rich.'

There was no more talk of keeping the money to give it back to Claudia and James. Or offering it to the police as a way of getting out of drunk-driving charges. She had learnt her lesson from Jonny. I had a curious feeling she would never spend the money, never even dip into it. And I felt then, perhaps for the first time, that people's attitude to money only takes shape when they earn or acquire or even perhaps steal their first sizeable sum. That's when you see generosity develop or profligacy, meanness or what psychiatrists call anal retention. Liv belonged in this last category. She had got the money and passionately needed to keep it, every penny, there should be no dipping into it, no spoiling or even touching the inviolate sum. It must be preserved intact, like some heirloom, in its entirety.

She hadn't kept it in any of the obvious places, that is, wrapped up in plastic and floating in the lavatory cistern or in a parcel under the mattress. It was in the bedroom she shared with Jonny, lying, unwrapped, between the television set and the video recorder on which the set stood. From a short distance away the notes, all of them lined up, edge to edge and corner to corner, were invisible. You'd only have seen them if you peered closely while sliding a cassette in and out, and since Jonny was uninterested in videos because he only watched sport, he'd never even looked in that direction. While Silver lifted up the television Liv slid the notes out. She began to count them.

I counted too. The sum was exactly £2,000. Now it's not really credible that Liv could have appropriated that exact amount unless she had stopped when the figure was reached, not at all a likely proceeding. The money she had on her when she ran away from the Range Rover crash was more probably just under £2,000 – I dismissed the idea of its being just *over* – so she must have acquired the shortfall somehow. It was typical of her compulsive nature to be satisfied only by a round sum. I wondered where she had got the rest since she had never been out of the Silvermans' house. She must have stolen it, and stolen it from Jonny – a dangerous act, I'd have thought, but I said nothing. Silver refrained from comment on that aspect of the matter too, but he did say one firm decisive thing.

'I know you don't trust me, Liv, but you'll have to trust me with the telegraphic transfer. Clo isn't going to take it into her bank account as well as looking after your two grand.'

Liv had to give in to that. Maybe she thought we'd settled this between us while she was on the phone, but in fact Silver's refusal on my behalf was the first I had heard of it. She didn't argue. She handed the money over to me. It made a not very thick wad but still I realized I had never seen so much in one pile before. I divided it into two and put one half in my jacket pocket on the left side and the other in the pocket on the right. Liv stared in a kind of anguish. I don't know whether this was caused by the apparently cavalier attitude with which I was handling her treasure or the act of handing it over at all.

I wasn't spending every night with Silver. In fact, though we'd usually be alone in his room until midnight or later, up till then I had spent few whole nights in his flat. For one thing, there was Mabel to look after and since her too adventurous sortie on to the roof I had never taken her back to Silver's. I felt too that Max and Selina would somehow know I wasn't there, conclude that I didn't really want old Mrs Fisherton's and throw me out. One weekend Jack and Erica Silverman came for the Friday and Saturday nights, a cue for all Silver's friends to stay away or, in the case of Liv, lie even lower than usual.

As it happened, I could have stayed every night at Silver's and Max would never have known. It was to be Liv's money that was my undoing. But that was a while ahead. On that night in June I felt perfectly secure, especially as I had been into college several times since the talk with Caroline Bodmer, the canal bank being open again a few days after the murder, and I had a feeling, which later proved true, that Dr Bodmer kept Max informed of my movements.

To find a hiding place for the money I braved old Mrs Fisherton's horrible green dining room. It was no gloomier by night than by day since almost no more light penetrated at noon than at midnight. The wallpaper and the green carpet gave it a subaqueous look, as if the room were part of an old wrecked ship. I was very uncomfortable in that room. I not only felt I was in a trap but also that the place was growing smaller while I looked for somewhere to stash the money. In the trolley had been my first idea, inside a kind of hotplate with a lid, and then I thought, suppose Beryl switches the thing on by mistake when she's hoovering.

Mabel came dancing in after I had turned my attention to the rest of the furniture. She seemed surprised that the door to the dining room was open and I inside, as well she might be, and pleased, she leapt on to the top of the sideboard and rubbed her face against my arm.

The sideboard drawers weren't full of silver cutlery and damask tablecloths as I had expected. I had forgotten for a moment that old Mrs Fisherton had been poor for the greater part of her life and not likely to have accumulated that kind of thing. The objects she had brought with her when Max installed her in the basement of 19 Russia Road were the kind you see on stalls at country antique fairs. I had been to one with my mother before the pylon and I recognized what in her words were 'old lady's paraphernalia': pokerwork napkin rings, cross-stitch matchbox cases, a pomander, numerous glass and pottery ashtrays, a pincushion, combs for the kind of hair you put up, egg cosies, a china toast rack in the shape of a row of butterflies, a pottery jam dish with a silver handle and a spoon suspended from it, and more, much more. Mabel, of course, got into the top drawer and began an ecstatic licking of one of the egg cosies. I lifted her out and tried the drawer below. It contained nothing but three plates, the kind some people hang up on walls, one white with a dark blue and red and gold pattern, one green and shaped like a layering of cabbage leaves and the third blue and white in what I suppose now was a willow pattern. The drawer below was full of neatly folded blue and white striped table napkins. I put Liv's money in the back of it.

When I'm working on a house that's been converted I always think about the metamorphosis of buildings, how they started one way maybe 150 years ago, were altered twenty years later, had another makeover early in the last century, were added to, divided up, split into flats, had other radical changes made to them and finally (only it won't be final) were practically rebuilt, as the Gilmore has been. I sometimes think that all the avatars of those buildings are still there, the Victorian versions, the Edwardian, the thirties flats, the mid-century apartments and penthouses, and that they might occasionally appear like phantoms or come in dreams. An earlier version of Max's house did come to me in a dream the night I hid the money. The yellow drawing room was divided by double doors and all three resulting rooms were small and crowded. In the smallest, overlooking a garden tenebrous with ilexes and holly, a little boy was sitting on a rocking horse, crying. I'd never seen him before, he was no one I knew, a dark brown boy with black curly hair, the tears on his cheeks like pearls. Before I could go to him and ask what was wrong I woke up, put out my hand and touched Mabel's wet fur, the raindrops on her whiskers. It had poured in the night and was still raining.

I've never had that dream again. It's Daniel who still comes to me. So was the boy Jason Patel? Was seeing him in tears a premonition? Hardly. Jason looked like a white boy, his skin was the colour of cream and his brown hair was straight. Only his eyes showed his Asian origin on the mother's side, dark brown irises floating in a white-blue like mother of pearl.

The dream was forgotten to surface again in memory a month or two later when I encountered Jason himself. First, I had other things to think about. I felt virtuous going off to college when there was strictly no need for me to do so, the lecture I might be expected to attend and Caroline Bodmer's tutorial not taking place until the afternoon. In fact, I went to neither. A message from the principal awaited me and was handed to me with a lowering look the moment I arrived in what, with fearful presumption, GUP called the Undergraduate Common Room.

Everyone had been on tenterhooks about their work assessments and whether they'd be considered good enough to come back the next year. Sometimes I thought dismissing me might be the answer to my problems and sometimes that this would be the worst that could happen. When the principal said, in highly uncompromising terms, that I could hardly be assessed on my course work since I had done none and I wouldn't be welcome back in October, I felt a marvellous lightness of being. They had done it for me, I need not do it, I need never see the place again, it was over. I even relished looking for the last time at the horrible view from that walkway, the old still soot-blackened warehouses, the new cuboid blocks of council flats, the ancient shot tower, the chimneys, the lock-up garages, the building sites and rubble heaps, the grey wispy grass between scabby brick ruins.

To tell Max or not? To tell Mum and Dad? As it turned out, the only person I told at that stage was Silver and then we were interrupted by Liv who came into his bedroom without knocking to ask if the money had come from her parents.

'Give them a chance,' Silver said. 'It's not much more than twelve hours since you gave them my bank details.'

By this time she knew what the policeman had come about and that it hadn't been about her. She was having second thoughts. Why had she panicked and phoned her parents?

'It is all your fault,' she said to me. 'Now they are knowing where I am.'

It was too wet to go on the roofs that night, a situation that was worse for Wim than the rest of us. Even he resisted braving the slates and leads, the dormers and parapets, when surfaces were as slippery as icy roads and the rain coming down in cataracts. He sat on the sofa next to Liv and told us how the night before, while Silver and I were on the modest heights of Sussex Gardens, he had climbed the green copper roofs of Whitehall, the ones you can see from St James's Park. I suppose everyone has stories to tell, but it seemed to me that the thing about us which drew us together was that we each had big experiences to recount. In Wim's case it was his ongoing escapade on the roofs, in Jonny's the murder he had attempted and in Liv's her abandonment of the children after the crash. That Silver had one I knew nothing of then, nor that when he told me his I would tell him mine.

Liv, of course, had a new story, though not much of a one in my opinion. Jonny, it appeared, had stayed away the night before, so hadn't heard about Liv's experience. Everyone supposed he had been burgling but perhaps not. At any rate no one asked and Liv launched into the tale of the policeman coming to the door and her subsequent terror. We were all there but it was Wim she looked at while she talked. Lounging back against the cushions, dressed in the yellow silk tunic and black jeans, he listened or appeared to listen with an expression of ironic calm, his habitual look when anything but his particular kind of mountaineering was being discussed.

'The bill was after me,' Jonny said with some satisfaction.

'No, he is coming because Silver's papa's car is broken into.'

'Not me,' said Jonny. 'That's something I never stooped to.'

Liv took no notice at all. She was looking at Wim, fixing her eyes on him with that undisguised intensity that was peculiarly her own. I don't think I've ever seen a woman gaze at a man with such naked longing as Liv, though it's true that men sometimes look at women like that. It was as if she wanted to devour him and the effort of keeping her hands from reaching for him made her clench them and brought a frown to her face. The effect was the same as pain but there was no mistaking this for pain, not when you saw that slack mouth and those widening eyes. Jonny saw it and was in no doubt what it meant, I'm sure of that. When Liv said her parents were sending the money for her air fare home, he suddenly put out his hand and took hold of her chin, holding it in a hard grip and turning her face by brute force.

'You're not going home. If you go anywhere, it'll be to my place.' By that he must have meant the room in Chichele Road, where perhaps he'd been the night before. 'Yes, that's a good idea. We'll have a bite to eat and then we'll go straight over there.'

'I won't,' Liv said.

Have you ever seen anyone stamp her foot from a sitting position? It's an extraordinary sight. Jonny took no notice. He fetched her a drink. It was whisky, I think, undiluted whisky, and it was half a tumblerful. I knew then and Silver knew that Jonny had been keeping her docile, keeping her for him to use, by feeding her alcohol, indulging a taste she already had and had developed when she was with James and Claudia. She began to drink it in the greedy way no one should ever drink, the addict's way. Wim remained quite still while all this was going on. Except that his long yellow eyes were wide open he might have been asleep. I suddenly noticed how beautiful his hands were, the colour of pale unpolished wood, sycamore or yew, and grainy like wood, the fingers long but thickened at the knuckles by the climbing and swinging he did. Liv drank her whisky, licking her lips so as not to miss a stray drop or two.

'I won't go,' she said again.

It must have been plain to Jonny that if she refused to leave with him he had no hope of getting her out of the Silvermans' house. Silver, having said in a very firm voice that she could stay with him until she went home to Sweden, was obviously not going to help Jonny manhandle her. Wim looked as usual as if helping anyone do anything was outside his design for living – though I was wrong there, as a later incident was to prove – and Jonny knew I disliked him as much as he disliked me. But instead of immediately caving in, he turned on Wim.

'You can keep your hands off her if you don't want your fucking legs broken.'

Broken legs would be almost worse for Wim than a broken neck. People are always talking these days about 'quality of life' and Wim's depended on the use of his strong long legs. I could quite easily imagine Jonny putting a bullet into each of his knees.

Wim said in his languid voice, 'Your meaning escapes me,' which was hardly honest of him since he had certainly slept with Liv once to my knowledge and probably several times. He moved only enough to cross one leg over the other, perhaps daring Jonny to carry out his threat. Jonny jumped up and stood over him in a way he could have done only when Wim was seated. There must have been ten or eleven inches difference in height between them.

'Leave her alone. I won't say it again.'

'That's a relief,' Wim said. 'I'm always glad not to hear your nasty cockney voice.'

Silver jumped up and grabbed Jonny from behind. Without this restraint the smaller man would have launched himself on Wim, fists flying and booted feet kicking. But it was perhaps Silver's saying in a clear firm voice that he wouldn't put up with this in his place and if they wanted to fight they could go out into the street, which did the trick. Jonny contented himself with muttering to Liv that she was coming with him, he wasn't having her defy him any longer. Once he was in a sexual relationship with a woman he believed he really owned her. Wim had closed his eyes, a half-smile on his face.

Everyone calmed down – Wim had never been anything but calm

– and after we had eaten and Jonny had rolled a couple of joints, we discussed my own dilemma, if and when I was going to tell Max I had got the sack. Nothing much else happened that night. I stayed with Silver, having left the window open at old Mrs Fisherton's for Mabel. Early in the morning, two policemen came, not this time about Silver's father's car.

13

When I got home Beryl was already there. She had fed Mabel and left her on my bed to sleep off half a can of Whiskas. She took one look at me and said she supposed I had been on the toot. I'm never quite sure what that means, though I've a good idea, and I said nothing but went to have a shower and wash my hair. Beryl had made coffee for both of us when I came out. She had opened the front door and all the windows. It was lovely and fresh, the rain had washed Russia Road clean, and so light I could almost kid myself I lived above ground.

'The Professor's got himself a lady friend,' she said.

I said she must be joking, I couldn't imagine anything less likely. It was a mystery how he had even managed to get married.

'I saw him having a coffee with her in the caff on my way in. He'd been doing his jogging, I reckon, and so had she. She had one of them shellsuits on. Shocking pink, it was.'

'Get away,' I said, lighting the first cigarette of the day. 'You're making it up.'

Beryl savoured the tobacco smell she liked so much. She sniffed and sniffed and smiled. 'I couldn't make it up, love. I haven't got no imagination. My kids are always telling me. Mum, you've got no imagination, that's what they say.'

That convinced me more than any protestations could have. 'What was she like?'

'Little and what you'd call neat, like. What my old man used to call a pocket Venus, dirty old sod. Got a worried face, though, lines round her eyes. Little prinked-up mouth like a baby's arse.' Beryl sniffed my cigarette once again and took a swig of her coffee. 'Not unlike Mrs, when you come to think of it, only younger. Mrs has had her face done, like, lifted, and this one hasn't, you can always tell. Men go for the same type, don't they?'

She began to talk about the neighbours, how Dr and Mrs Clark next door had become vegetarians. They said it was a matter of principle but Beryl thought it more to do with economy, the wicked price meat was these days.

'And how about the police knocking them up at No. 15?' she said. 'Last night and the night before. It's not going to be thieving from cars both times, is it?'

It wasn't but I didn't say so. Remarkably Beryl seemed to have no idea that I even knew Silver, still less that I was spending half my life round at the Silvermans'. 'He's got folks in there what are up to no good,' she said. 'Drugs, I shouldn't wonder. You seen the paper today?' She gave me a shrewd look. 'No, you'd better things to think about, dirty little stop-out.'

It was at times like this that I thought how nice it would be to have Beryl for one's mother and envied the son and daughter. 'What about the paper?' I said.

'That couple with the little coloured boy, they been seen taking him round a theme park in Ramsgate. It won't be long now before they collar them.'

'Won't you be sorry?' I said.

Beryl didn't know, she wasn't sure. Maybe Jason would be better off with brown people like himself. Anyway, Lane and Barrie had no business taking the law into their own hands.

'When I was young,' Beryl said, 'I mean, when I was a little kid, anyone could adopt anyone they liked, it was dead easy. And there was plenty of babies on account of it was a lot harder not to have them and a terrible stigma for those as did and wasn't married.'

I said that you couldn't call that a very desirable state of affairs and Beryl said no, maybe not, but at least you knew where you were, everyone knew their place and everyone was the same colour. Before I could rise hotly to the defence of the multiracial society she jumped up and set about vigorously vacuuming the living room. I went outside and sat on the iron staircase in the sunshine and looked at the moss and the rampant ivy and thought about what had happened the night before.

As Beryl had said, the calls made by the police at the Silvermans' could hardly both have been concerned with thefts from their car. The second had nothing to do with them and everything to do with Jonny. Two policemen had come to talk to him. Silver went down to answer the door, having first taken a look from his bedroom window at the one who rang the bell and the one who waited in the car, and they both followed him upstairs. They were making inquiries, they said, into the death of a woman called Sandra Furbank who had been found dead on the towpath at Paddington Basin. She lived on one of the boats. Whoever had killed her had taken her key, got into the boat and stolen the money she had there. Quite a lot of money apparently, though they didn't say how much.

Luckily two of the windows were open in Silver's room, in spite of the rain, but even so I could smell the lingering scent from the two joints Jonny had rolled. The taller of the policemen kept sniffing but he didn't say anything about the smell so maybe he just had a cold. They seemed uninterested in any of us, though they looked us over in a distasteful sort of way. It was Jonny they had come for. They had no reason to think he had known Sandra Furbank but plenty of reason, they said, to believe he had been down on that part of the canal that night. Silver said afterwards that they must have recently been given information by someone who said he or she had seen him there. After all, the murder had happened more than a month before. But the important point was that Jonny had a record. He had been in prison for causing actual bodily harm to someone. He had gone to the police station with them, the one at Paddington Green, I suppose.

'I wonder how they traced him here,' Silver said, and for the first time since I had known him he seemed worried. The anxiety state he warned others against he had fallen into himself.

'His landlady,' Wim said, 'or whoever he rents his room from. She'd have told them he'd an alternative address.' I'd seldom seen him look so happy. 'No doubt they'll keep him down there half the night.' The full force of his unaccustomed smile was turned on Liv. 'Maybe for good. Maybe we've seen the last of him. Bye-bye, Russia Road, hi there, Wormwood Scrubs.'

Liv laughed shrilly. Wim put out his hand. Not to her, not to take hers, but to beckon to her. He was smiling no longer. His long forefinger stretched out and curled up and he raised his eyebrows just a little. Liv stared at him, drops of perspiration forming on her upper lip and her forehead. She didn't look at all attractive then, all her rather ordinary prettiness was gone, disappeared under swollen features and the sudden smell of her sweat. But perhaps that *is* attraction, the real attraction of the female, not cleanness and sweetness and pretty clothes. She wasn't smiling then and nor was he. She yearned for him and he received her without moving, the beckoning hand still by then, only his neck extending a little as Liv fastened her mouth on his.

He was in perfect control of himself – when was he not? – and well aware of our presence, if unembarrassed by it, but Liv was lost, careless of whether anyone else was there or not. You couldn't call it kissing, what she was doing to Wim, it was more like the *guzzling* of a sea anemone first sucking in, then devouring, its prey. But Wim was no one's prey, more a passive but willing partner who suffered or enjoyed all this – it was hard to tell which – for just as long as it suited him. I think people of my age are less promiscuous than our parents' generation but also less inhibited. I wasn't very old but I had already encountered several couples who were indifferent to the presence of others in the room while they made love. It would hardly have suited me or Silver but we saw it as a phenomenon of our time. And now, for a few moments, it looked as if this was going to happen between Liv and Wim, or as if Liv, pushing him back against the sofa cushions and crouching above him, was going to make it happen. She pulled off her T-shirt and let her rather long full breasts hang udder-like and brush against his hands which he held clasped against his chest.

Then Silver spoke. His voice was cold. 'Please will you go and do what you're doing somewhere else.'

Liv would have taken no notice, she would scarcely have heard him, but Wim heard and obeyed. If he cared for anyone, if he cared about anyone, that person was Silver. It shocked me a bit that they didn't go into Wim's room but into Jonny's. The door closed. Silver put out his arms to me. 'Is it me?' he said, 'or are things getting out of hand?'

'Jonny won't be back for hours, will he?'

'I don't know. Ask me another. No, don't ask me anything but don't go home either. Stay here with me tonight.'

So I stayed and listened to the rain drumming on the roof and rattling down the closed casements and thought that, sharing Silver's bed apart, how much nicer it was to sleep up here in the heights than at old Mrs Fisherton's. But I slept less than well. I kept worrying about the window I had left open for Mabel and wondering if instead of her the rain was coming in and flooding the place. Although I hadn't said a word about it to Silver, he read my thoughts and said in his sleep, or half-sleep, 'Don't worry, Clo, sweetheart. Worrying never helps.'

I heard Wim's footsteps going downstairs and much later Jonny's footsteps coming up. The police had let him go after hours and hours, though they said they'd want to see him again. They had talked about searching the Silvermans' house because they hadn't yet recovered the money and the jewellery taken from Sandra Furbank's houseboat.

'They'll have to get a search warrant,' said practical Silver. 'They're not coming in here without one.'

I must be an optimist because I was sure they wouldn't come back. Perhaps, rather, it was because I found it hard to imagine the police attributing any dishonesty to Silver and his parents. But that is not the way they think. It's only in detective mysteries that policemen study human character and rely on psychology in their investigations. In life circumstantial evidence is the main thing and they must have had some, for they returned with that warrant, not to search the entirety of 15 Russia Road, but only Silver's flat. And to ask Silver about an alibi for Jonny.

While they were there Wim came in through the window from the roofs. Feet in black trainers came in first, of course, as he swung himself from the lintel of the dormer. He was dressed in black tracksuit pants and dark green sweatshirt and might just have passed for a roofer which was how, with his usual presence of mind, Silver presented him. Clearing out the gutters after the rain, Silver said, and neither of the policemen seemed to find anything odd. It would have been a different matter if it had been Jonny.

They wanted to know if Jonny had been here, in the flat, as he said he had, on the evening before the body was found. It was quite a long time ago now and maybe (they suggested) Silver would have difficulty in remembering. But Silver had no problem with that. Jonny had arrived at around seven and stayed all night. He had stayed till morning. Liv said the same, though her eyes shifted about while she talked, never looking directly at the policemen but giving them wary sidelong glances, which made me wonder if she would have found it much more satisfactory to rid herself of Jonny by saying he hadn't been there and she hadn't seen him that evening. But perhaps it was only that she was afraid. Afraid of *any* policemen, no matter what they had come about. She, like us, must have wondered what would have happened if she hadn't handed the Hindes' money over to me the night before and they had found it stashed between the TV and the video. It was on that visit that they told us the stolen sum was in the region of £2,000, exactly the amount Liv had accumulated.

She went into Jonny's bedroom after they had gone, from the way she looked at him over her shoulder obviously hoping Wim would follow her. He didn't. In his roofer role he joked a bit with Silver about mending the guttering and how about repointing the chimney stack while he was up there, and then he went back out of the window. He had only come in for a drink of water, he said. Silver put his arm round me and I laid my head on his shoulder.

'I remembered about Jonny being here,' he said, 'because it was the evening before the day we met. It was the last evening of my life without you. You went into the underpass because that woman's body was on the canal bank and they wouldn't let you through.'

'I remember,' I said.

'But d'you know what I'm asking myself, Clo? Would I have told them Jonny was here if I couldn't remember? Would I just have said it because it'd have been easier and because Jonny's a friend?'

'That's just speculation,' I said. 'You did remember. He was here.'

'You can't help wondering, though. And another thing I wonder is if I've made Jonny a friend of mine because I know my parents would hate it so much. Childish, isn't it? The superannuated rebellious teenager. D'you think Jonny will go once Liv has gone?'

I didn't know. I said he'd more likely find another girlfriend to bring here. But Liv was still there and by next day we knew she had no intention of going.

The money from her father and mother in Kiruna was late coming through. By now I have learnt money always is late coming through, whether it's a bill paid at last or a loan back or a fee, it always comes later than you expect. It's a rule of life. But I didn't know this then and I began to think Håkan Almquist had changed his mind. When eventually it arrived Silver asked Liv if she would like him to draw it out of his bank account immediately.

'D'you want one of us to get you an air ticket? We could go to the airline and that'd be cheaper than you phoning a travel agent.'

'I am not buying an air ticket, Silver. I am staying here.' It was I who received the look then, the wary elliptical glance so characteristic of Liv at her games. '*Mor* and *Far* are not worrying themselves, they know I am here. It is only that I am not going home.'

'Liv, if you're afraid to go out in the street,' I said, 'one of us will go with you. We could go early before anyone's about.'

'Oh, yes, I am afraid of that but that is not the matter.' Her English naturally got worse at times of stress. 'It is that I am not buying a ticket because I am keeping the money. I start saving again with this money, and again I have a little *redagg*.'

'A nest egg,' Silver said, guessing. 'All right. Do as you like.'

He told me later he'd have liked to throw her out but he couldn't. He hadn't the nerve or the callousness to put a frightened girl out into the street and leave her there, even though she had £2,000 in old Mrs Fisherton's dining room and £200 in his bank account. Liv seemed elated to have a new nucleus for her savings. She asked Silver to draw it out and give it to her. She had a shower and washed her hair, not a very regular proceeding with her, to make herself beautiful for when Wim came. Only he didn't come and Jonny did, for the first time in three days. She looked very taken aback to see him. I think she had made up her mind that he'd stay away for a long while after the police had been here and searched the place. He took no notice of her but opened one of the bottles he had brought to toast Silver and me in malt whisky. He was the only one to drink it until Liv reached for the bottle and poured herself a hefty slug into a glass she had been drinking gin from earlier in the day.

'Thanks a million, mate,' he said to Silver. 'You're a pal.'

'What for? You *were* here.'

'Of course I was. I didn't even know that Sandra bint. They should have got that Wim or whatever he calls himself helping them with their fucking inquiries. Some mate of his lives on a boat down there.' He gave Liv a vicious glare. 'I might tell them that next time they come sticking their dirty noses in my business.'

In fact, Wim only slightly knew the man who lived on the boat called *Cicero*. He was the one I had seen him talking to the first time I encountered him. But he knew him the way I knew Mrs Clark next door, just well enough to say good morning to and did she know there had been another lot of thefts from parked cars in the street. He had spoken to him no more than three times, as he told us that night, after Jonny had pulled Liv into his bedroom and switched the television on at top volume and we had gone out on the roofs and met him by chance on Peterborough Avenue.

Americans say you live 'on' a street and not 'in' it the way we do, but we really were 'on' streets, on top of the houses. It was midsummer, the longest day just past, and only twilight at nearly ten. We saw Wim a long way off, his head and upper body appearing first as he rope-climbed over a distant gable end. The sky still had a lingering stain of dark red and his black spider shape stood stark against it. Another scaffolding had been put up at the end of the last Torrington Gardens terrace before the first one had been taken down, so we could range a long way before coming to uncrossable abysses. We walked along the Peterborough Avenue leads, just inside the parapet, holding hands.

Wim met us halfway along the terrace, embracing us both in his strange silent way. He had been in Belgravia, on the roofs of Eaton Square, which is supposed to be the finest address in London. We sat on the stone shelf that formed the top of a dormer, in deep shadow high above the street-lamps in their net of plane-tree leaves, and Wim gave us chocolate bars. We lit cigarettes and looked down on the spangled map London becomes at night, lines and rings and studs and stars of light. Our cigarettes made three more, bright gleams of orangey-red in the dark.

There ought to be a period in everyone's life when time is of no account. It happens when you're a small child before you know about time. Your mother thinks about it for you, tells you when to do this and that and looks after you. But once you go to school you have to learn about time and that's when you may become its slave, always clock-watching, your fate determined, whether you're going to be a permanently late person or a punctual person. There's school and then there's some kind of further education and then a job and maybe a time never comes again when time doesn't matter. For us, our timeless time was that summer, when we had no need to get anywhere at any particular moment or count the minutes to something or set an alarm or even make a date. We never had no-time again, it went away in September never to return, and for the past eleven years I've been as much time's fool (Silver's expression, from Shakespeare, I think) as anyone else.

But that night we were in the midst of our timeless time. I don't know how long we three sat up there, not talking much and then not talking at all, smoking, eating Wim's chocolate and looking at the lights, watching the moon rise and set or just disappear behind a cloud, to be driven in through the window finally by the cold that comes stealthily after midnight. Silver came back with me for the first time to old Mrs Fisherton's and together we crept down the iron staircase. The following morning wasn't Beryl's day and Selina never put in one of her surprise appearances before ten. I still felt nervous about it, telling myself I was indulging in too much deceitful behaviour, and resolved to clear at least one matter up the next day. I'd tell Max I'd been given my marching orders from the Grand Union Polytechnic. While Silver was asleep with Mabel stretched out alongside his back, I went into the dining room and checked on Liv's money. It was in the drawer, quite safe, all £2,000 of it.

By a coincidence that might have been an unpleasant one, Selina did come downstairs and into old Mrs Fisherton's sometime during the morning. Silver had only just gone. From the front window Mabel had watched his departure up the iron staircase and then gone out herself. I had opened some windows to get rid of the cigarette smoke, so all in all I thought I'd had a lucky escape from many perils.

Selina brought me a letter which had come with the morning's post. The handwriting on the envelope was Guy's and this time no one had steamed it open. She was dressed and made-up as carefully as ever, her eyelids matching the dark blue of her trim little linen suit. I thought she looked far from well. For the first time I noticed a row of little vertical lines on her upper lip, the kind of wrinkles you associate with a much older woman. I told her I'd like to see Max sometime that day and would she arrange it, please. Any time would do.

'He hasn't come back yet,' she said. 'He takes much longer over his jogging these days.' She looked around her distractedly. 'You know, darling, what people aren't aware of is that it's not only my taste that's made this house the way it is today. Oh no, it's my *money*. I suppose you're like everyone else, you think it was Max that paid for all this.' She waved a hand vaguely above her head, presumably indicating the yellow drawing room. 'I mean, when I came here, the whole place was like that study of his, that *dump*. You thought that, didn't you, darling? Now be honest.'

I said, with perfect truth, that I'd never thought about it. I was still recovering from the shock of hearing her criticize Max, an activity I'd have thought impossible.

'Everyone thinks that, but nothing could be further from the truth. After all, when all's said and done he's only a lecturer at a university.' Selina made it sound as if such people were two a penny. 'And what they earn is cat's meat, chicken feed.' She seemed to seek about for more animals' meals metaphors but failed to find them. 'Anyway, he hadn't two halfpennies to rub together, darling, if you know what halfpennies are at your age. I've even heard people suggest I married him for his money when the truth is I married him for his *mind* and because I was so desperately *in love with him*. I've given him everything, my youth, my money, my love and devotion. I must have been mad. Oh, don't look at me like that, darling, just because you don't understand. You're so young, you haven't lived, you know nothing, nothing.'

At this point Selina really did begin to wring her hands. I said I was very sorry, though I didn't know what I was being sorry for, and could I get her anything? A cup of tea?

'I don't want anything. Not unless you've got some arsenic.' She laughed a peal of theatrical laughter. 'When you think, I could have bought myself a delightful little house in Chelsea, with a wisteria growing over it and window boxes. I could have been in the middle of things. Instead I spent everything I had on this barrack, up here, practically in *Kilburn*. For him. But he can go too far, he thinks I don't know what he's up to but I know only too well. I wasn't in repertory all those appalling bloody years for nothing. I've seen life, darling, and God knows it holds no surprises for me.' She seemed to realize quite suddenly that I was there, a flesh and blood creature standing before her, and that she hadn't been talking to herself and replying to herself but had had an audience. 'Oh dear, oh God, did you say you wanted to make an appointment with Max? He's very busy, you know. He's got the copy-editor's emendations to his book to go through and there are *zillions* of them.'

'I'd really like to see him today, Selina.'

Suddenly weary, she passed a hand across her forehead. 'Oh, I expect we can manage something. Why don't you come up about lunchtime? When he's having his coffee? He's always better, isn't he, when he's got some food inside him? Well, I think so, and God knows, I should know.'

Once she had gone I opened Guy's letter. He wrote that he was sorry to have missed me when I was home at Easter. He'd be in London on a certain date in early July and would I have dinner with him? It was another world he lived in, quite different from mine. Did I want that world, even occasionally? I'd have to borrow Beryl's daughter's black skirt again. Dinner would be in some other fine restaurant and I'm afraid all I wondered about was what kind of roof it had and how accessible that roof would be.

I took my washing to the launderette and found Morna there, reading *Harpers & Queen* and watching a couple of T-shirts and a lot of men's underwear spinning round in the dryer. I asked her what she was doing in Maida Vale at this hour, for no one ever called at Silver's before noon, and she said her brother lived in Elgin Avenue. He had sprained his ankle and couldn't walk so she was doing his washing for him.

'I think I've just seen Andrew Lane,' she said.

'Who?' I said, which was inexcusable since Beryl had been talking about him only the day before.

'That guy who took away the little boy when the social services told him not to. Him and his wife did.'

I asked her what she meant by saying she had seen him.

'I recognized him from his photo. Dark-haired guy with a sort of square face and thick eyebrows. It was in Elgin Avenue, the bit where the shops are. He was coming out of the supermarket with two bags of shopping.'

'Hundreds of people have square faces and thick eyebrows and dark hair,' I said. 'Thousands. It's quite an ordinary way to look.' I nearly said she looked like that herself but stopped myself in case she didn't think it very flattering. 'It could have been anyone.'

'No, it was him. I know it was. What d'you think I ought to do about it?'

Morna was always recognizing people in the street. Usually, famous ones. The previous week she had insisted she had seen Margaret Thatcher in Whitechapel. But although I didn't believe she had actually seen Andrew Lane, I felt a surprisingly strong urge to stop her telling the police. Up till then I'd thought very little about him and Alison Barrie, I hadn't considered what my attitude to them and what they'd done should be, but in that moment my sympathies were for them, perhaps only because one is usually on the side of the hunted.

'What d'you think I ought to *do* about it?'

'What can you do? You've only got to look at the papers to see the police get to hear of hundreds of sightings. They've been seen in a train in Scotland and on a ferry to Holland and in a Butlin's, but none of those people were really them. What makes you think you're different?'

'Because *I* saw him with my own eyes.'

'I expect that's what they all said.'

'He was nervous. He kept looking round over his shoulder.'

'Afraid of getting mugged, I expect,' I said. 'It can be a bit dodgy round there.'

Morna remained unconvinced. She asked me if we were still going on the roofs and when I said we were she told me we were all mad. On the way home with my washing I thought about Lane and Barrie and Jason and imagined them living in a caravan on a site on the Essex coast somewhere. Andrew Lane would drive for miles to do the family shopping, maybe fifty miles, which was about what it would be from Southend to Maida Vale. It was harder to convince myself that if he had driven fifty miles he wouldn't go to a bigger and better foodstore than a supermarket in Elgin Avenue. But then it hadn't been Andrew Lane that Morna had seen, had it?

I calculated that Max would have finished his lunch by half past one and be just reaching the coffee stage, so I went upstairs at twenty-five to two. Selina was outside the dining-room door, carrying a tray with used plates on that she was taking to the kitchen. She made the kind of face people do make when a conspiracy is afoot, a pursing of the lips and raising of the eyebrows. Yet we hadn't conspired together in anything. It occurred to me then that she was afraid of Max.

He was as he had been at our previous encounter, sitting at the table with his coffee cup in front of him, but this time with a book propped up against a tall pepper pot and open at a page of statistics.

As was his custom, he continued to read for a few moments before turning his eyes on me. His appearance surprised me. His glasses he seemed to have discarded. He looked fit and well and younger. His protuberant eyes were bright, the whites clear and porcelain-like, and his jowls seemed firmer. The tracksuit he inevitably wore was a new one, or new to me, the velvety chenille kind in quite a smart dark blue.

'I know what has brought you here, Clodagh,' he said. 'I'm one jump ahead of you there.'

'GUP told you?'

'Oh yes, the day before yesterday, and I was glad they did. It has given me a little time to think.'

I was none too pleased about this. After all, I was two years past my majority, I was a grown woman of twenty. Max wasn't my guardian or in any way responsible for me. The way I saw it I was just his lodger – but a lodger who paid no rent. It was this factor which kept me quiet when the truth was I wanted to ask him what business it was of his. GUP had wasted no time. The principal must have got straight on the phone to him.

'Of course, you were warned. You had Moses and the prophets but you refused to hear them.' I had no idea what this meant and have none now, but it has stuck in my mind. 'Now, frankly, I don't think the Grand Union Polytechnic would be too happy to have you back even if you changed to a different course. The long and the short of it is, they don't want any truck with you.' Max laughed, appreciative of his own wit. 'I must say I've revised my opinion of that establishment, it seems admirably run and with some excellent people on the faculty. But now to your future. History? English? Economics? I seem to remember you were not at all bad at history when you were a small girl. Now, shall I make some inquiries and see what kind of courses are available?'

I should have been grateful. In a way I was. But all I really thought about was that he obviously wasn't going to turn me out of old Mrs Fisherton's. Provided I went along with him and acquiesced in these educational plans, I could stay. Of course, I was never going anywhere to study the subjects Max had mentioned. It would only be the same story as at GUP all over again. By the time we were discussing this in his dining room I knew I wanted to turn my back on academe in any form and work in the building trade. I've said going on the roofs and being alone up there and silent had helped teach me to know myself and sort out what I wanted from life. What I wanted, I was beginning to see clearly, was to work with my hands and to do so with the utmost knowledge and expertise that could be achieved.

I knew what would be the result of saying any of this to Max. My steeplejack rejoinder still rankled, though he said nothing about it on this occasion but asked me if I'd told my parents. 'Not yet,' I said.

'Tell them, Clodagh. Tell them. Open confession is good for the soul, remember.' He sounded quite jolly all of a sudden. 'And better drop a word about spending at least a week with them in the long vacation. I know how keen you young ones are on London but your people miss you. Remember that.'

Who would have thought that only two weeks later he'd have evicted me?

14

A letter came from my husband this morning. He writes about the great heat and the conditions of a once green country drying up and becoming a desert. And he's bothered, as he sometimes is, as he probably always is, by the problem of aid workers having food while the starving population they're ministering to have practically none. Of course, he knows the Famaid people must be adequately fed if they're to do their job, and the food they have is very basic and not plentiful, but still it troubles him when he eats and the children in the camp cry with hunger. It makes him eat less because every mouthful is a reproach. He writes that he's losing weight and jokes about rapidly returning to the figure he had when first I knew him.

He'll be home at the end of July. I can't wait but I must. Writing this helps me when I start missing him too badly. And I tell myself – and I tell Mabel – that I mustn't be a fool, he's not in any danger, he has had too many inoculations to catch anything, and he won't be kidnapped. Those poor people are too enfeebled from want to try hostage-taking. And I have my work and good friends and this place high up in the sky.

By the way, I should clear something up now. If you thought Mabel was the same cat as I had at old Mrs Fisherton's, I'm afraid you're wrong. She's not. This one is also a tortoiseshell but she's only three and she's the second cat I've had called Mabel. She looks very much like her predecessor and she's just as affectionate but she has quite a different personality and, of course, she can't go out hunting. I must say, she has never shown any desire to do so. When my parents come here, Mum always says, 'The first Mabel you had, I often think she might be alive today if your father hadn't been so obstinate.'

And I always say, 'It's past and gone and it's no use regretting.'

They never talk about the pylon now. They never mention Daniel's name. Not long ago, when I was down there spending the day with them, Mum was full of a story she had read in the paper about two boys who were killed climbing a pylon in Wales. She told me about it artlessly as if it had no parallel in my own experience. I think she has forgotten it ever happened. She and Dad are proud of me now. I make quite a lot of money, you see, and I'm married with a home of my own. Whatever they thought of him once, they are extremely fond of their son-in-law, whom they regard as entirely selfless and a kind of saint. To their friends they refer to me as an 'electronics expert'. My virtual expulsion from the Grand Union Polytechnic, my banishment from Max's house, my subsequent disappearance, rooftop escapades and all the rest of it, have gone the way of the pylon, into oblivion.

Eleven years ago it was different. When I did as Max told me, rang Mum up and said I'd been asked not to come back to GUP in October, there was at first a dreadful silence. Then tears. I could hear her gulping and whimpering and I don't really know why I didn't just put the receiver down and run away and hide. Dad came on the line and said I had broken my mother's heart and he didn't know why people had children, they wouldn't if they had any idea what it would be like, just misery and bitterness and despair from the cradle to the – well, he couldn't say 'the grave', so he left the sentence hanging in the air. They told me to phone them again when they had had time to digest what I had said and were less upset. So I did, the next day, and Mum said she supposed I had better come home, there was no point in staying in London if I wasn't going to college. I told her Max had ideas about that and, plunging right in at the deep end, asked her whether she'd have my cat if I had to leave London. Another silence, then a sort of grudging assent, cut short by an explosion from Dad in the background, a bellow roughly decipherable as 'I'm not having her bloody mog here.' I thought I could safely leave that for the time being. After all, I still had old Mrs Fisherton's, I still had a home for Mabel, and it looked as if I would at least for August and September.

Silver and I always knew our time on the roofs must necessarily be short-lived, an adventure that would last for months rather than years, and would one day soon have to be abandoned to the pressures of the final stage of growing up. I had taken it for granted when I first met him that he and Wim had been roof-climbing for years and it was a surprise to discover that it was only in the previous July that he had been up there for the first time. A day is so much longer when you're twenty than when you're thirty, eight months is a lifetime, yet here's a paradox: nights pass fast in early youth, they go much more slowly for me now. When I sat on the rooftop with Silver and we talked and smoked and picnicked and talked and talked, the hours flew away. That summer it seemed that no sooner had the last red faded from the great wide open sky than the pale cold light of dawn was coming. And all the time we knew it must end, that there would be only so many long days and short swift nights before the practical world took over and we had to live real life.

Because what we had was fantasy and, if we didn't talk about it like that, we knew it was true. We knew it but Wim didn't. He was the only person I have ever known who lived life as if it were a dream, the sole one of us who appeared to have no past and no future but occupied only the present, and a present of his own creating. Convention meant nothing to him, nor ordinary social usage, nor manners. I doubt if he ever gave a single thought to Liv, or considered her as another human being with feelings and pride and the ability to suffer. Perhaps he never considered anyone like that. When he was away from her, as he mostly was, he forgot her existence. With her, that is in the same room as her, he became nothing more than an idle male animal, amiable enough, stirred to activity only when the female in heat came close.

He seemed to have arrived out of nowhere. You couldn't imagine him as being any different from what he was now or living any other sort of life, a child with parents, for instance, or a student. I could easily picture Liv as a little girl up there in that far northern place, going to school before it got light and coming home after dark, the world covered in snow for half the year; the house-proud prudent mother, the father a mining engineer, down quilts on her bed in the efficiently heated house, polished wood floors, perhaps a Lutheran text on the wall, done in cross-stitch by a grandmother. I could understand her longing to get away, escape the narrowness and the sameness of that life, first to Stockholm, then further afield.

Imagining Jonny's life was no more difficult, only a good deal less pleasant: the father and his brutish friends, their activities that make you shudder, the squalid flat on the kind of estate people are afraid even to walk past. But Wim existed, it seemed to me, in the here and now. He was only himself, single-minded, covert, a silent mystery.

Silver had met him on the roofs, but not as he had met Jonny. He was in the living room at the top of 15 Russia Road with his then girlfriend Judy, his parents being as usual away in the country. It was late, well past midnight. Judy was the first to hear sounds from above their heads. Wim said afterwards that what had happened to him on that roof was the first and only time he had ever slipped and dislodged a slate. Judy heard the slithering sound of his foot sliding and they both heard the slate skid down the mansard into the gutter. She was all for calling the police but Silver didn't like the idea of that and went to investigate. He opened the window and looked up. This incident was the end of things between him and Judy. She said that if he did any more mad things – Silver never told me at that time what other mad things she meant – they were finished, she was going home, she had had enough. Silver disliked being threatened and he thought it absurd when she said if he went out there he'd be killed, so he just told her in typical fashion not to fret, everything would be all right, and why not open the bottle of wine they had brought in with them.

Judy shouted at him that he was mad. Silver took no notice but levered himself up on to the mansard and then on to the flat roof. A man a few years older than himself was sitting on top of a dormer, holding a slate in his hand.

'Sorry about that,' he said. 'I'll put it back for you. I've never done anything like that before.'

Silver started laughing. 'Do you come here often?'

'As a matter of fact, it's the first time I've been further along this way than Torrington Gardens.'

'Come and have a drink,' Silver said.

Wim came in but he wouldn't drink the wine. He had a glass of water. He talked about the roofs and where he had come from that night and how, in his opinion, there were few roofs that couldn't be scaled with a rope and a bit of persistence. Judy went into the bedroom and slammed the door. Silver said he'd like to go up there with him and Wim said OK, fine, but some other night, not when Silver had been drinking. Tomorrow, Silver said, let's do it tomorrow, and I promise I'll be abstemious. So the next night Wim came in through the window and took Silver up on the roofs and slept at 15 Russia

174

Road when they came back at around three. True to her word, Judy left but they stayed friends.

And that was the beginning of the roof-climbing and the friendship with Wim, the two being coincidental. To Silver's surprise, the third time Wim came calling for him he greeted him by taking him into that curious embrace and a sort of intimacy was established. Wim never said how he felt but it was easy to see that if he ever loved anyone, he loved Silver. Sometimes his glance rested on him with a kind of tender yet ironic regard. It wasn't the way Liv looked at *him* but it had more affection and care in it. Yet in all those months since he and Silver had met, not far short of a year, embracing Silver, treating him as a best friend, daily bringing him gifts of chocolate or cigarettes, he had never confided in him, never imparted a detail of his past.

Silver felt quite flattered when Wim told him he had a job in a café and a room in 'sort of south-west London but north of the river'. Of parents, brothers, sisters, girlfriends, friends, he never spoke. If it wasn't too absurd a concept, you could say he had been born on the roofs and had grown up there. And there, when his body lost its suppleness and his eye its skill, he would die.

Morna came round to Silver's that evening and repeated her story of having seen Andrew Lane. Silver found an old newspaper among the stack in the kitchen and showed her the latest photograph of Lane and Barrie. That only made her the more certain it was him she had seen.

'Draw a beard on him,' Silver said.

While she was doing this, painstakingly working with a fine-pointed ballpoint, the phone rang. We all jumped. It doesn't sound much, the phone ringing. In most people's lives, I suppose, especially now, phones ring all the time. If it's not the one in your home or your office, it's your mobile. But nobody had any occasion to call Silver. The phone in his bedroom was an extension of his parents' and anyone who needed to call them got on to their number in the country. Silver's friends and acquaintances dropped in, they seldom rang first. But here was the phone ringing and in the peremptory sort of way it always seems to ring when you don't expect or want it.

Silver answered it and came back to say it was Liv's mother. Her English wasn't very good but that helped rather than hindered her, for Silver immediately guessed who it was. And guessed, of course, what she wanted.

'I am not wishing to talk to her,' Liv said. 'You must tell her I am not here, I am out.'

Silver looked at her and shrugged. That shrug said it all, that he wasn't telling lies for her. She looked at Wim and Wim smiled distantly, as well he might at the idea of him explaining anything to her mother. Morna pretended to be engrossed in an article in the newspaper that carried Andrew Lane's photograph.

'Clo?' Liv said in a piteous little-girl voice.

I got up and went into the bedroom and said Liv couldn't speak to her now (which wasn't exactly a lie) but she'd call her back in an hour. I always seemed to be an intermediary between Liv and her parents, and you couldn't have found anyone less suited to the role. Elsie Almquist refused to leave it at that. She wanted to know, quite naturally, why Liv hadn't come home two days before. Then Liv's father came on. His English was much better. Had the money for Liv's air fare arrived in Silver's bank account? I forgot all about lying and not lying and said I didn't know. Liv had better call him in half an hour, he said. If she didn't, he'd fly to London and fetch her, and I could tell her that.

I told her. She was sitting next to Wim on the sofa, that is, she was sitting on it at one end and he was sitting on it at the other. She gave a sort of sob, edged up to him and put her head against his chest and her arms round his neck. I couldn't see his face. At least he didn't fling her off. Perhaps it would have been better if he had because at that moment Jonny's key was heard in the lock and he walked into the room. Liv remained where she was, only turning a tearful face in Jonny's direction.

'What the fuck's going on?' Jonny said.

Liv said she had to go home. Her father was coming for her. Thanks to Clodagh – she cast a nasty aggrieved look at me – *Far* and *Mor* knew where she was and would come and take her away. She'd have to go home, she wouldn't have a choice. Jonny looked at Wim.

'Let go of her.'

'Better tell her to let go of me,' Wim said.

Jonny took Liv by the shoulders and pulled her away. She crouched with bent back, looking up at him with trembling mouth. Her hair hung down, long and lank. Liv's hair always had a shredded look, as if the ends had been torn rather than cut.

'If I find you've been screwing her, I'll kill you,' Jonny said, and to Liv, 'You're not going home and you're not staying here. You're coming back with me to my place.'

Liv began to scream, waving her arms and tearing at her hair with both hands. I understood how it came to look the way it did. Jonny slapped her face, not all that hard, not as hard as I'd have expected. Slapping the hysterical person's face is effective, as I remembered from the car wash experience. Liv fell on to the sofa, quietly weeping.

Silver intervened then. 'Jonny, Liv can stay here if she likes. I think she ought to go home but if she doesn't want to, that's her choice.'

'No, it's not. She doesn't have a choice. I make the choices. I saved her from the law and going inside and paying some fucking great fine, so she's mine now. Right? She belongs to me.' It was quite a long speech Jonny was making. I'd not have thought him capable of it. 'It's got nothing to do with no one else. She's mine. If I say she comes back to my place, she comes. And if I say she stays here, she stays.'

Wim got up while he was speaking and, though it was raining, climbed out of the window on to the roof. Liv's crying rose to a wail. I could see Silver wanted to tell Jonny that going or staying wasn't his choice, the flat was his and he made the decisions about who lived there. He didn't say it because he always refrained from asserting his rights or what he called 'pulling rank'.

Once more Jonny took hold of Liv but more gently this time. He sat beside her and turned her to look at him. Her red and swollen face looked as if it had been soaked in water. 'Things are going to change round here,' Jonny said. 'For one thing, you've got to hand over that money you stole.' He sang his nursery rhyme this time, something he didn't always do: 'You owe me five farthings, say the bells of St Martin's . . .'

I caught my breath but I didn't say anything. The rain was coming in through the open window. Silver went over to it and pulled it almost closed, leaving a gap between casement and architrave just wide enough for Wim to slide it open when he came back. Morna, who had been sitting on the floor, started to get up. 'I'd better go.'

'You can't go in this. It's pouring. Wait until it eases up.'

'I said I wanted the money,' Jonny said. 'I know you've got it hidden somewhere. I don't know what went on in your head if you thought you'd fooled me.' He looked from Liv to us. 'She thought she'd fooled me.' His tone was wondering, incredulous. A woman had actually thought she could pull a fast one over him. 'Where is it?' he said.

Her voice shook when she spoke. She put up a hand to her mouth as if she could stop the trembling but her hand shook too. 'It's in the bank. I put it in the bank.'

'You never. You haven't got no bank account.'

'Silver's account,' she managed to say.

Silver said, 'Take your hands off her shoulders, you're hurting her.' Jonny did, just about. His hands slid down on to her forearms. People usually did what Silver told them. 'All I've got in my account is the money her dad sent her for her air fare.'

'You sodding little liar,' Jonny said to Liv.

'Don't speak to her like that!' Morna stood over him, big, powerful, well-muscled Morna. He took no notice of her. The phone began ringing again. Quite a lot more than half an hour had passed since the Almquists phoned the first time and asked Liv to call them back. It was plain no one was going to answer it, but the ringing, from a source she was as aware of as any of us, seemed to give Liv courage.

'I put it on the roofs,' she said.

'You *what?*'

'I am wrapping it up in a bag, the bag of plastic food is in, and hiding it on the roofs. When I am up there I am hiding it.'

'You're mad.'

Liv shrugged. 'So I am mad. I hide it where no one ever find it.'

The ringing stopped. Silver and I looked at each other. Silver said, 'Give me your parents' number. I'm going to call them and tell them you're ill. You'll come home when you're better. OK?'

Liv hardly bothered to turn her head. 'OK.' She had the number in her head, of course, and reeled it off.

I went into the bedroom with Silver and Morna came with us. We sat on the bed, all three of us, and hugged each other and then Silver phoned the Almquists. I could hear Liv and Jonny arguing, then the sound of a blow and a scream from Liv. I went straight back and found her lying on the floor, holding one hand to her mouth. Blood was coming from between her fingers. Jonny was nowhere to be seen.

'What has he done to you?' I said.

'Nothing. I myself,' she said, a bit like Desdemona.

I couldn't imagine then why she lied, but later on I understood that if Silver knew Jonny had hit her she was afraid he'd turn them both out. She'd be obliged to go back to Jonny's room and be alone with him. For ever, was how she saw it. She'd lose the money and the air fare and become Jonny's slave. There would be no choice about it, for she was still afraid to go out in the street. She got up on to all-fours, then to her feet and spat something out into her cupped hand. It was a tooth, a molar, that Jonny had knocked out with his fist.

'Liv,' I said, 'you'll have to go to a dentist. You'll have to go out now and go to a dentist.'

She mumbled something about it being too late for that and what could a dentist do? 'It is at the back. It will not show.'

There's women for you. The prime concern is always for the look of the thing, for appearance. What will *he* think? What will other women think? I resolved in that moment, while I was fetching her a glass of water and a handful of tissues, that I wouldn't be one of that sisterhood and I have more or less stuck to it. If I lose a tooth, it's my health and ability to chew I think about, not the beauty I've never had much of anyway. Still, Mrs Clarkson has a lovely set of grinders now, by the look of them the whole lot capped, and wears the molar round her neck. I wonder what reason she gave the orthodontist for losing it?

Morna came back while I was giving Liv the water. I wiped her face and offered to take the tooth away and dispose of it. She wouldn't have that, she wanted to keep it, perhaps just because it was part of her. Morna said innocently, 'Did your tooth just drop out?'

Most of us lead such violence-free lives, all the violence we ever see is on television or in the cinema, that we're loath to believe people do kick and punch and hit other people, not at least the ones we know. Healthy young people's teeth don't just fall out but Morna would rather have believed Liv's had than that Jonny had knocked it out. Liv nodded.

'Jonny is out on the roofs. He looks for the money.' Her laughter set her mouth bleeding again. 'He is putting his hand down chimney pots, I expect, and lifting the lids off – what do you call them? – water tanks.'

'He won't find it,' I said.

She put her hands on my arms, she looked into my face. 'He must not, Clo, you are not letting him find it.'

This was beyond Morna and no one enlightened her. She went home soon after that. After he had seen her downstairs, Silver whispered to me, out of earshot on the landing, that maybe Liv would put the molar under her pillow for the tooth fairy in the hope of getting more money. We sat waiting for Jonny to come back. I suggested taking Liv back to old Mrs Fisherton's with me and Silver liked the idea but she wouldn't do it. It meant going down into the street and, although she'd be outside for no more than a few seconds, even that was too much. The fear of encountering James and Claudia was being replaced by a generalized agoraphobia, the opposite of what I had. Yet the roofs were exempt from it – then. She still saw those open spaces as safe.

I had been brought up to think nobody was all bad; in my mother's words, 'there's some good in all of us'. Human nature wasn't black or white but halfway between. Of course, I had reached a stage when I had lost faith in most of my parents' beliefs, but I still clung to that one until I met Jonny. Or, rather, until I came to *know* Jonny. There was no leaven of goodness in him. He was bad, evil through and through. I tried to make excuses for him on the grounds of his awful childhood, that early life I could barely imagine, those dreadful things happening to a baby, a child of four or five, while his abuser sang nursery rhymes. And I did make those excuses, I told myself that losing his mother so young, losing her love and never receiving love from any other source, he was bound to be unable to give it. I told myself that his greed and meanness came from early poverty, his ill manners from a total lack of instruction in social usage. A lot was still left out. There seemed no accounting for the absence of any sort of empathy in his nature, any thought for others or even of camaraderie with his fellows. Once I had thought he must be in love with Liv to want her so exclusively and feel jealous of her, but he wasn't in love, he was incapable of love. She was simply his woman, that he had found and intended to keep for his use. She told us that night that sex freely sought and given had ceased between them. Jonny came close to raping her. She gave in to him to save herself being beaten.

*

At last, when we'd been waiting for about three hours, she went into the bedroom. As she put it herself, she had nowhere else to go. Silver's firm, 'You can go home to Sweden, I'll call a cab and take you down to it and go to Heathrow with you,' had no effect. After she had gone I asked him why he liked Jonny. What is it you see in him, was what I said.

He sighed. He suddenly looked much older. That extreme fairness fades early, the skin reddening, the shining blond hair turning to straw. I put my arms round him and hugged him tight. After a while he said, 'You know that money I've got, that came to me from my grandmother, it's a capital sum that yields 10,000 a year. It's not really very much, it's a starting salary for lots of people, but it's a hell of a lot when you're seventeen and you don't have to work for it. Getting it is like having a door opened for you on to unlimited freedom. And having this flat handed over to me, that's another freedom opener.'

In the silence I asked him what that had to do with Jonny.

'It made me able to know people like Jonny. I mean, I had my own place and I had my money. I'm a fool, Clo, but my excuse is that I was young, I *am* young. When I met Jonny coming out of that flat, up on the roofs, I mean, I just thought what experience it would be to know a burglar. A real-life burglar. It had been the same with Wim, a strange person, a sort of human spider, who treated the roofs of London the way other people treat mountains. The difference was that Wim's OK but Jonny isn't. If I hadn't been able to afford him, if I hadn't had this place and I wasn't able to afford to let him live here when he wants to rent-free, if I couldn't afford to buy wine and food and have his girlfriend here, if I couldn't do those things, he'd have come once, I expect, but never again. And now I'm stuck with him. Aren't I? If there's a way out, I'd like to know what it is.'

I said thoughtfully, 'It's wrong for young people to have money come to them too soon, isn't it?'

'I expect it's all right for people with very strong characters.'

'But you *are* like that.'

'No, I'm not. It's just the impression I give. Not worrying or telling other people not to worry, being calm and steady, it's all a front. I could seem to be that way because I had money. And money that'll never stop, that'll always keep coming whatever happens and whatever I do. Look at it like this, I need never work. I wouldn't do very well,

I'd just rub along, but I'd have the life thousands have on just that amount, only they have to work for it. I can lead a life of leisure. Ambition needn't be in it nor much hope. And I've got this place too. I pay my parents, but let's face it, it's a nominal rent I pay.

'There's only one way out of it. Give it away. I can do that. I can make it over to anyone or any charity, say, I choose. I haven't the nerve. That's the truth of it, Clo. I know it would be better for me to do that, better in every way, but I haven't the strength of will. Not yet. I will one day.'

Did I believe him? Probably. I was starry-eyed and idealistic in those days. And if I believed him my faith wouldn't have been misplaced, for he did give that income of his away, or most of it, and he did give up the flat. We had come a long way from why he let Jonny live there. I kissed Silver and held him for a while but we didn't make love that night. I went home, creeping down the iron staircase at three in the morning, having no premonition, of course, of the strange events that were to take place the next day.

15

The sight of Selina gave me a shock. She was sitting in old Mrs Fisherton's armchair in old Mrs Fisherton's living room, holding Daniel's photograph in her hands. I walked in, having been shopping in Clifton Road, and there she was, beautifully dressed as usual, this time in a jade-green silk suit with puffed shoulders and bead embroidery round the skirt hem, her curvy little legs crossed at the knees, her feet in green shoes with stiletto heels. She looked up from studying the photograph with some puzzlement but made no excuses for treating the place as her own. Well, I suppose it was her own.

'There was a cat in here when I first came, darling. I shooed it out. If you leave windows open down here, cats will come in. And you don't want that, do you? It isn't as if we had mice.'

Poor Mabel. Still, she had come to no harm. Selina's face was painted like a piece of porcelain or one of those concubines you see in Chinese pictures, white and pink and pale green and scarlet and black. Her nails scuttled about like red beetles. She couldn't keep her hands still. I took the photograph from her, laid it on the table and offered her coffee. She shook her head vehemently.

'I'm not stopping. I don't know why I came. The thing is, darling –' she smiled brightly – 'I've so much to say and I've no one else to say it to.' Suddenly, without warning, she launched into an account of her sex life with Max. People of the age I was then never consider the elderly or middle-aged as having sex. It all stops at forty, it *must*. The alternative would be too grotesque. 'He isn't very marvellous in the bedroom department, darling, but what else really would you expect? I'm not sure if you'll believe this but he was nearly fifty when we met and he's never slept with anyone before. Never. I was the first. I can see from your face you don't believe me but my answer to that is, why would he lie? It's not exactly something to be proud of, is it? If he says he's never had a woman till me, he's not lying. I mean, I know young ones like you and that lovely boy in the photo, whoever he is, you're having sex at school, twelve or thirteen, that's normal, and even when I was your age – well, I think I was eighteen. No, seventeen. But forty-eight! Naturally I taught him everything.'

By this time I really was staring at her, aghast. I didn't know what to say. I said nothing. Her porcelain face had flushed pink but otherwise she seemed not a bit discomposed.

'I can't say he was a very apt pupil. Men are so selfish, aren't they? Let me tell you, they are, whether you've learnt that yet or not. If only they'd be patient, if only they'd wait a little, postpone their own pleasure, find out what pleases *you*, but they won't. They're scared. If they don't do it at once, they're afraid they won't do it at all.' She paused and looked searchingly at me. 'Oh well, I expect it's different for you. Everything's different now, everything's changed. Women rule the world now. But me, I've missed the boat. It's too late.

'The worst part is that he's using what I taught him on others. You didn't know that, did you? I can see from your face you didn't. We'd only been married two years when he got himself a girlfriend. Once they start, even when they're late starters, there's no stopping them. Of course, that time I did stop him. I said he couldn't go on like that when I'd spent everything I had on his home. Beautifying his home. Basically he hadn't a bean. Twenty thousand, our drawing room cost me, you should have seen it before, a real ratbag. There were moth grubs crawling in the upholstery, I mean *worms*. I had it all ripped out and burnt. The carpet fitters were here, laying that top-quality Wilton carpet, the "vibrant veridian", it's called, and he was off somewhere with that woman.'

'I'm sorry,' I said, all other comments failing me.

'But I stopped it. And he's been faithful to me ever since, at least I suppose he has. Well, he has, if you don't count ogling people and sort of half-baked flirting, and you can't really count that, can you? Until now, that is. Until this one. I didn't dream till Beryl let it drop she'd seen them. Unintentionally, I mean, in all innocence, she'd no idea I wasn't fully aware. What am I going to do? That's what I ask myself. I can't spend another fortune on his home, I've just done the dining room in "ebony" and "papaya leaf", as you'll have noticed, and even if I redid the morning room, I expect it would be to no avail.'

'I'm sorry,' I said again.

'So you should be, darling,' she said inexplicably. 'Though I've no doubt it was as unintentional on your part as it was on Beryl's.' She got up and flung out her arms in an actressy gesture that wasn't very good acting. 'The trouble is, I love him, fool that I am. I'm his slave.' I thought of Liv and Jonny, though it wasn't at all the same thing. 'I try to make myself lovely for him and the upshot is that he goes overboard for scruffy academics.' A rueful smile followed this. She was absurd but I really did feel sorry for her. 'I must go, darling. It's been a help to me talking. Talking always helps, don't you think? Like crying.'

That seemed such a pathetic thing to say that, though I'd never done it before, I put an arm round her shoulder and gave her a kiss. She smiled tremulously. 'And on top of all this I'm having a dinner party here for him on Saturday. His publisher and a lot of people connected with his wretched book. Well, no, I'm sure it's a marvellous book, I shouldn't have said that. But I just don't feel up to entertaining hordes of people. Not *her*, though, thank God, there are limits.'

I couldn't imagine what she'd meant by saying that I should be sorry, and that it was unintentional on my part. What was? What had I done? I put it down to simple hysteria. In any case, I didn't want to think about it. I'm afraid I found it deeply distasteful, the very idea of tortoise-necked Max with his bulging cheeks and fluffy tufts of white hair having sex with anyone. I thought of Silver and me and how strong and beautiful we were and I shuddered. Twenty-year-olds think like that, always have, I expect, and always will.

It amused me and made me a bit cross too that Selina had driven poor Mabel out of her own home. I called to her out of my bedroom window and whistled the special whistle I had for her and she soon came. In a way I couldn't explain Selina's attitude towards her worried me, so when the time came for me to go up to Silver's I took her with me. I carried her up the four flights and into Silver's flat. It was rather a chilly day and no one was out on the roofs – Wim may have been but his whereabouts were seldom known – so I closed the windows, not wanting to run the risk of Mabel escaping that way.

Jonny was at work, Liv asleep on the sofa, as she so often was. Mabel wandered about restlessly, marking all the furniture as if she hadn't done it before. Then a terrible thing happened. The kitchen door being ajar, she pushed her nose round it, went into the kitchen and caught a mouse.

I was afraid Liv would wake up, discover what had happened and start screaming the place down, but Silver said Mabel might as well be allowed to eat the mouse once she'd caught it. Quoting someone who wrote a ghost story about a cat, he called her 'the redoubtable adversary of the genus *mus*'. Liv slept on. Mabel ate the best part of the mouse and we wrapped up the remains in newspaper and put them in the waste bin. Then we went into Silver's bedroom and lay on the bed with Mabel sitting on the end of it washing herself, and talked about my future, what I was going to do instead of Psychology and Business Studies and whether Max was really hunting up suitable courses for me in something I might want to do or if he was too busy with his 'scruffy academic', whoever she might be.

'What are you going to do, come to that?' I said.

'Have you any suggestions?'

'With you it'd have to be something in social sciences.'

'Would it?' he said. 'I suppose you're right. But it's no use worrying about it, is it? No use at all. I know worrying's no good to anyone but I've been doing it lately. I found a white hair on my head this morning and I'm only twenty.'

'But all your hairs are white, Silver,' I said.

'This one was whiter.'

Liv was awake when we went back into the living room. She'd been lying with her head buried in the cushions and now we saw her face for the first time. It was all over bruises and one of her eyes was black. Jonny had finally come in at half past three. He hadn't been able to find the money. Liv said that gleefully, though his failure had resulted in a good many blows to her face, and in spite of the fact that he couldn't possibly have found it no matter where he'd looked since it was all the time in old Mrs Fisherton's sideboard drawer. He meant to go on looking that night. Liv he had accused of giving the money to Wim for him to hide. And that of course implied that it might be almost anywhere, Wim having access to heights and levels none of us dared scale. It was when she denied this that he had started punching her face.

Silver looked grim. The bruises and damage to Liv's eye had finally settled it. He was going to speak to Jonny. And as soon as Jonny appeared, early for him, at around half past five, he took him aside. They went into the third bedroom, and Silver told him that if he hit Liv again he'd have to go. She could stay but he must go. Jonny said he'd been provoked beyond bearing or he'd never have done it. Liv was two-timing him with Wim, he was sure of it, and she had lied and lied to him about the money.

'It's not your money,' Silver said.

Jonny was indignant. 'It's not hers either. Look at it this way, I've as much right to it as she has. She stole it, mate, you've got to admit it, so it's not hers, is it?' Evil Jonny might have been but he wasn't unintelligent. 'It belongs to them two she worked for but they don't even know she nicked it, that's all a load of bollocks about them looking for it out in the street, that's crap. So it don't belong to her and it don't belong to me but it's here in this place somewhere or up on top of this place and when I find it *I'm going to nick it again*. That's nothing to me, all in the day's work, you might say. I've been a thief since I was a young kid.

> 'In and out the City Road,
> In and out the Eagle,
> That's the way the money goes,
> Pop goes the weasel.'

He had it all worked out. Silver couldn't gainsay him. The whole business had taken on a kind of metaphysical or ethical slant and it seemed beyond ordinary argument. All Silver could do was repeat what he had said about Jonny having to go if he struck Liv again. Then he suggested he take this bedroom which was seldom used, and leave Liv to the one they had been sharing. Jonny agreed to that, pretended to be delighted at the idea – 'to have a bit of peace from that bitch whingeing'.

That evening he behaved impeccably, or as impeccably as he ever could, producing two pizzas he had brought in for our dinner, as well as wine which Silver and I didn't drink because we were going on the roofs. Jonny never observed Silver's rule about this. He used to say he managed better up there when he was 'pissed' and evidently intended to be an excellent manager that night, for he drank a whole bottle of wine and a fair amount of whisky too and sang an obscene version (his own?) of 'Three Blind Mice'. Liv, of course, hated any version, especially the bit about cutting off their tails with a carving knife. Of Wim there was no sign.

Liv had washed and polished her tooth and asked if we thought she could have it mounted to hang from a gold chain round her neck. She seemed delighted with the new bedroom arrangement. I think her pleased acceptance was due to the increased chances (as she saw it) of entertaining Wim than to getting rid of Jonny. She hadn't, of course, got rid of him. There were no locks on the doors of any rooms in the flat, Jonny could have got to her any time he wanted to, and he certainly would want to when he was sure the money was nowhere on the roofs. The fact that I had hidden it made me feel very uncomfortable and when I went down to take Mabel home I checked in the sideboard drawer. It was there. Of course it was. But I was dissatisfied with my hiding place and I considered moving it. On Sunday, two days away, I was to wish I had. But that Friday evening it seemed safe enough, as safe as anywhere.

Silver and Liv and I went up on to the roofs, all the way along Peterborough Avenue as far as the first intersecting street. When you're on the leads or the slates, coming to where a street branches off is like walking along downland to the edge of a cliff. Or reaching a precipice. The street isn't just an ordinary useful roadway but an uncrossable canyon. We turned round, we had no choice, and sat down in the middle of a flat area where someone had once tried to make a roof garden. They'd probably found it too much bother to climb up a ladder and get through a trap door every time they wanted to water the plants, for the tubs were full of brown twigs and stems with dead seed heads on them, very like the dried flowers people pay a great deal of money for. There was even a dead birch tree, its silver bark hanging off in rags, its branches dangling threads. The moonlight made everything grey and black and frost-white, though it was a mild windless night, as warm as a London night can ever be.

Sometimes, far down below us, a car passed, taking the through-route from the Harrow Road to St John's Wood. Usually the cars were driven quite slowly but one came very fast. We heard a squeal of brakes and then a revving of the engine as the car moved off again. We looked over the parapet at the street lined with cars on both sides and Silver asked us if we realized that for the whole of our lifetimes we had never seen streets without cars parked nose-to-tail between the kerb and the roadway, we had never seen streets looking the way they did when they were first built. The problem with traffic was more than vehicles jammed to a standstill or crawling in a close-packed herd. It was also the covering of streets by day and night, endlessly, with shiny metal capsules, millions of them edging the pavements like the permanent scarring left by a wound.

It was better up on the roofs. No cars there, no danger and no noise. We sat down by the dead tree and smoked. Liv asked if her money was safe and I said I had checked earlier in the evening, when I took Mabel home. She had an idea, she said. Did we think that if she gave him the money, all of it apart from her air fare home, Jonny would go away and leave her alone? Go back to his room in Cricklewood and forget her? It was quite a lot and he was always wanting money, more and more of it.

I didn't know, I couldn't imagine it would be as easy as that, but Silver said he'd had more than enough of that money, he was sick of hearing about it, it wasn't hers to keep or give away. He had said in the beginning she ought to send it back to Claudia and James. If she did that she need not be afraid of them any longer. She'd be able to go out into the streets without fear, get a job or go home to Sweden if she wanted to.

'But it is all I have,' she said. 'I need it. Besides, if I am giving it back they will know I steal it before.'

This seemed unanswerable. Silver refused to talk about it and soon after that Liv went back on her own to the roof of 15 Russia Road and in through the window to savour the pleasures of having a room to herself and without Jonny. She had only been gone five minutes when he appeared, walking along from the opposite direction and just inside the parapet. He had searched the roofs from the Castlemaine Road end of Russia Road, across the Italianate house that stood alone, all along Torrington Gardens and Peterborough Avenue as far as the cross street.

'She's got that slippery bastard to hide it for her. I'll kill him.'

I said, 'Oh, grow up,' but Silver said nothing till he had gone. Then, 'I can't see any answer to this apart from throwing Jonny out. Sometimes I think Liv will be living in my place until we both get our bus passes.'

'Don't worry,' I said and that made us both laugh.

The moon had gone in and it was dark and warm up there at midnight. Silver said, 'Tell me about the grasshopper.'

I was almost frightened, it was such a surprise. 'The *what?*'

'You said it in your sleep. You have several times. "Don't go any higher," you say and sometimes, "The grasshoppers leap across the fields."'

'Ah,' I said. 'The pylon. That's what someone once called the pylon.'

'We all have one big story in our lives,' Silver said. 'I expect we accumulate more stories as we get old but maybe there's always just that one big one. That's yours, isn't it?'

So sitting with his arm round me, under the dead birch tree, I told him about the pylon and Daniel, how he'd tried to light his cigarette from the corona, and the fireball that engulfed him. I described how I'd held on to him and how, at last, I'd had to let him fall, how Guy Wharton had seen us and run off to get help but it had all been too late. It took a long time. Silver listened in silence, looking into my face for a while and then away at the hands folded in my lap.

'Now tell me your story,' I said.

'I will but not till tomorrow.' Then, as we got to our feet to return first to 15 Russia Road and straightaway to old Mrs Fisherton's together, he said in a voice so serious that it seemed to commit him for life, 'I love you.'

We didn't kiss. Not then. I carefully chose my words, not wanting to seem simply to be replying to him. Not just giving him some rejoinder. 'I love you, Silver,' I said, 'with all my heart.'

It was a profound moment, a plighting of troth, up there on the roofs in the half-dark. I believe we both thought we had made a solemn pact that could never be broken. What could part us if we wanted not to be parted? In silence we went back and through the window, down the four flights of stairs and out into the street. Among the glittering parked cars and the scattered litter. And on the opposite side, between the back bumper of a van and the front fender of some big expensive car, there was something dark and soft lying close up against the kerb. I don't like writing 'in the gutter', but that's where she was.

She was still quite warm, her fur smooth and sleek, the green velvet collar untouched. It had happened not long before. Maybe the car that raced down Peterborough Avenue and braked and revved had come this way, down this street, and come just as fast and carelessly.

I held her body in my arms and Silver stroked her head. The golden eyes were dull and glazed. Silver did something for which I would love him for ever if I hadn't already loved him. He closed her eyes with his fingertips.

There was no blood. I couldn't see a mark on her. We carried her down the iron staircase and into old Mrs Fisherton's and there we wrapped her up in a sweater of mine, a nice one I loved, not an old thing to be discarded, and next day we buried her in the garden of 15 Russia Road. But that night, weeping, I asked Silver if it was my fault for not keeping her up there in his flat with me. Or did he think that by carrying her into No. 15 I'd introduced her to that dangerous road?

We'd never know the answers to those questions, he said. Speculating was useless. The likelihood was that she had often been out into the street. After all, to find me in the first place she had apparently come all the way from Sutherland Avenue, and unlike us, had avoided the safe highway of the roofs. He never once said she was 'only a cat' or advised me to get another immediately. We went to bed and I cried and he held me in his arms until I fell asleep.

16

Silver and I went along to the Clifton Nursery and bought plants for Mabel's grave. July isn't the best time of the year for planting anything and it's too late for sowing seeds. I didn't know any of this then but Silver did. Being young, we wanted instant results the way children do, so we bought coleus with leaves striped in red and green and chocolate and a pink and white fuchsia and a red geranium already in bloom. On my latest visit to No. 15, only a few weeks ago, I went to look at the grave for the first time in eleven years. The coleus had all died in the first of that autumn's frosts and the geranium had withered the way geraniums do, but the fuchsia was going strong, a big bush three feet high and covered in buds.

Mabel's death left me feeling gloomy and depressed. Jonny's telling me 30,000 cats were killed on the roads of Britain every year and singing 'Ding, dong bell, pussy's in the well' didn't help. It was Saturday so he wasn't at work but he seemed to have left Liv alone. Of Wim there was again no sign. No one had seen him for two days. Morna and Judy came round in the late morning. We had no plans to go on the roofs until the evening. It was a hot steamy sort of day, the air heavy and smelling of diesel and roses, a curious sickly mixture.

Silver said he'd take us all out to lunch in a pub in Blenheim Terrace where we could eat outside. He meant it as a treat for me because I was sad. Jonny had gone out somewhere by then and Liv, of course, wouldn't come with us. Morna had her mother's car with her and Liv would only have had to cross the pavement and get into the back seat but even that was too terrifying for her to contemplate. So we all went down without her and there, parked behind Morna's mother's car, was a van delivering wine for Selina's party. Selina came running out to shout instructions to the driver. She didn't see me. By then I was sitting in the car, watching her in the rear-view mirror and telling myself not to hate her just because she had shooed Mabel out of old Mrs Fisherton's on the last day of her life.

I had never felt so close to Silver as I did that day. I wanted to be physically near him too and he seemed happy about that. At lunch and afterwards we sat side by side with our bodies pressed close together and holding hands when we weren't actually eating. I drank a lot of wine and so did he to keep me company. We'd have to sleep off its effects before we went on the roofs but that was all right too, we were soon desperate to be alone and in our bed and making love.

It was quite late when we woke up, dusk if not dark. Liv was asleep on the sofa in the living room, her shaggy hair all spread out over the cushions in tails like the ones on her mice. Silver called me over to the window and we looked down and across the back of No. 17 to Selina's guests disporting themselves in the garden. Max's guests, I suppose I should say. Some were sitting on the bulbous white-metal garden furniture, all were drinking wine or brandy – we could tell by the glasses – and two, a man and a woman who looked enormously old to us, were dancing. Faint ancient music came out from the open french windows, and they were dancing, this aged couple, some long-lost dance, a quickstep, Silver said it was, or maybe a foxtrot. The moon that had disappeared so early the night before now showed itself in the pale lilac sky, a shape like a segment of an orange, its light unable to compete with Selina's bright lamps and the dazzling blue circular element that hung on the wall to kill mosquitoes. From high above I imagined them dashing themselves against it, the sizzling sound as it electrocuted and destroyed them, and I shuddered.

There were no mosquitoes on the roofs. They never fly so high. The music reached us distantly and the carefully muted civilized laughter of elderly academics who hated to disturb the neighbours. It all seemed remote, a different and unreal world, the same place Guy sometimes took me to, where all the people were unlike me and Silver, and all the things they did nothing we'd ever care to do.

'Can you dance?' I said.

'I've never tried. I expect I could learn if you really wanted me to.'

'I don't want to dance,' I said. 'I want to hear your story.'

He had to tell it as it had been told to him over the years by his parents and his brother and sister, for he had no memory of what had happened. When he was fifteen his mother had been very keen on the idea of Repressed Memory Syndrome and had coaxed him into encounters with a therapist who claimed to be able to dredge up out of the unconscious everything that had ever happened to the subject. Provided, that is, she was given plenty of time and she could catch her client young enough. Silver had been very taken with the idea of inventing experiences and had thought up blood-curdling events he claimed to have taken place in his early life. And when, later, he confessed that everything he had told her was a hoax, she'd have none of it, saying he was making excuses because he was afraid to confront the dreadful magnitude of what he remembered. Of course, he saw that he couldn't win. He was bored with it anyway and was going to tell her at their next encounter that he had had enough when his mother read in a magazine (and immediately believed what she read) that an eminent psychiatrist had denied the validity of RMS and called it a cruel deception which destroyed relationships and split families. That was the end of any outside intervention in recapturing what had happened to him. He went on trying privately to remember but most of what he ever brought up out of his unconscious was a cliff with pink flowers on it and very green grass, his sister running, white gulls swooping and wheeling.

'When I see gulls now,' he said, 'those gulls we get on the canal, that's what always comes back, the flowers on the cliff and Rachel running down the slope. Birds and a boat come into it too. But nothing much else.'

He was three years old. His brother and sister were much older, Rachel nine and Julian eleven. The family, the parents and the three children, were on holiday in a hotel on the Cornish coast. It was high summer, the middle of August. Silver wasn't called Silver then, that came later, when he was at school, but by his given name, Michael. They were all out for a walk along the cliffs before going on the beach.

The cliffs are very high there, limestone escarpments, overgrown at that time of the year with Livingstone daisies and at the top with bilberry bushes and gorse. The bottoms of the cliffs are rough with sharp pointed protuberances, like the feet of reptiles, but the sand, when the tide goes out, is smooth and hard and ochre-coloured. How high, I wanted to know, and he said just about as high as the terraces in Russia Road.

He was in the care of his brother and sister, though neither of his parents had expressly said this. It was simply taken for granted that if

194

the children ran on ahead, and they always did run on ahead, Julian and Rachel would look after Silver. Afterwards, neither of the older children remembered separating from him. They said they hadn't taken their eyes off him, and then Rachel remembered the butterfly. She had seen it alight on the flower head of a purple thistle and called Julian over to look at it because she was interested in butterflies and this was one of a kind she had never seen before. It was quite large, a rich tangerine colour with green underwings, patterned in black, and Silver, again researching, thought from his sister's description that it must have been a Dark Green Fritillary. This is an insect that feeds on thistles and prefers coastal districts but it is quite rare, which would account for Rachel's never having seen it before. Julian wasn't much interested in *Argynnis aglaia* but he gave it a glance. He and Rachel said they took their eyes off Silver for maybe half a minute. The butterfly disliked their scrutiny and flew off and when they turned round their little brother had vanished.

He had been nowhere near the edge, they said. He had been with them, no more than a dozen yards from them, in the meadow that lay between the cliff path and the strip of woodland that separated it from the road. They and their parents ran in all directions calling him. First, of course, they went to the edge of the cliff. To reach it Silver would have had to get over or under a wire fence, admittedly flimsy, push through a dense mass of bilberry bushes and prickly gorse and brambles. But they looked over the edge, it was the first thing they did after shouting in vain, it was the natural thing, and there was nothing to be seen, no little figure lying face-downwards on the smooth yellow sand.

It was a beautiful clear day, the sun shining, visibility as good as it could be, the sea calm. No one was about except themselves. They ran across the meadow where Rachel had seen the butterfly and they searched the little wood. They called Silver's name, 'Michael, Michael, where are you?' Julian went back in the direction of the hotel in case Silver had decided to return there on his own, a most unlikely thing for him to have done, but possible. Rachel ran on ahead, calling him. Jack Silverman found a way down the cliff, one of the zigzag paths that wound between the bushes and the mats of pink and yellow daisies, but Erica decided enough time had been wasted and returned to the hotel where she called the police and, for good measure, the coastguard. No mobile phones in those days, at least none in private use.

All the hotel guests, or all those who hadn't gone off somewhere for the day, joined in the search. One party took the two miles of beach, another the cliff top and a third the wooded hinterland and the coast road. That road, on the far side of the wood, not far away, was the most terrifying of all things to Erica Silverman, worse than the sea. Traffic went along it quite fast, as in those days there was no speed limit on it.

There were four houses at that point. They had no view of the sea, for the woodland interrupted it. At the end of the row was a shop that sold newspapers, basic groceries, ice cream and beach toys. No one in the houses or the shop had seen Silver. No one came upon a little body on the roadside verge or on the sands or caught up in the dense mass of vegetation that covered the cliff. He had been with his brother and sister, they had looked elsewhere for a few seconds and in that fraction of a minute, he had disappeared. It must have been longer, of course, but people always minimize time in these situations. The Silvermans were distraught, the parents despairing, the brother and sister guilty and frightened. All of them passed a terrible day and an even more dreadful night. Silver's disappearance was on television, reporters appeared, cameras were everywhere. The weather continued glorious, even hotter than on the day he vanished. Some sort of regatta was scheduled for the day after and it went ahead, but amid protests. Silver's mother said she could never see a sailing ship after that, not a picture of a yacht, or even a painting of a three-masted schooner, without the whole of that terrible weekend coming back to her in all its details.

By that time the police knew Silver had been abducted. It was the only possible explanation. They interviewed known local paedophiles. They began house-to-house investigations in the nearby town. On the Monday morning – Silver had gone missing on the previous Friday – a woman called Diana Lomax found him on the sands in a little cove about a mile from where he had vanished. He seemed fine, not distressed or even puzzled, but then he was always a self-contained level-headed child. He was dressed as he had been on the Friday, in exactly the same clothes, but they were clean, they had been washed. In his hand he held a small plastic spade with which he had dug a little pit in the sand and when Mrs Lomax found him he was watching the water fill it, standing there, intently looking at the level rising.

She knew what construction would be put on her appearing with him but she was afraid to leave him there. Never mind the questioning and the implications of blame, she couldn't leave a little child alone on that beach while she went up the cliff and called the police. Besides, his abductor might be nearby. Because he took some persuading to leave his newly dug pit, she bribed him with the chocolate bar she had in her beach bag with her swimming things. He refused to walk, of course, little children always do, so she carried him all the way up the zigzag path and across the meadow and into the hotel, where she sat him on the reception desk while she called up to the Silvermans' room. Silver's father came down. Silver laughed when he saw him and said, 'There's my dad.'

Jack Silverman called Diana Lomax 'one of the Righteous among the Nations'. He seemed to worship her. He tried to give her money, then when that was refused, buy her some expensive present, a car or a valuable piece of furniture. That was refused too. Every Christmas he wrote to her and thanked her afresh for saving his son's life, which was what he was sure she had done. He was always asking her to come and stay because he knew she liked visiting London. She appeared to prefer staying with her friends who lived somewhere near the Silvermans, but she managed to avoid telling Jack exactly where. It would have been apparent to anyone but his father, Silver said, it *was* apparent to his mother, that Diana Lomax wanted nothing more to do with the Silvermans. Reluctantly she agreed to Jack and Erica's taking her out to dinner while she was in London and, protesting, let Jack pay for a car to take her to Paddington Station when she went home. She left without saying goodbye, but even that discourtesy made no difference to Jack.

A couple of years later Diana Lomax had her first operation for cancer. A year after that she died. Jack wept when he heard the news as he had done when he came downstairs that Monday morning and she lifted Silver off the counter and put him into his arms.

'I don't really like to say this,' I said, 'but have you ever thought that maybe it was Diana Lomax who took you away?'

'Of course. Often. When I was fifteen and got keen on finding out,' he said. 'I thought my dad was going to hit me when I suggested it. I still suppose it's possible. But if she did what did she want me *for?*'

That was something else I hadn't liked to ask, and hadn't asked.

'A couple of doctors examined me, if that's what you're thinking. Nothing. And not a mark on me. Diana didn't want a child, she'd had three children, all grown up by then. She had two grandchildren she saw a lot of. She had a job, she had a boyfriend in the same village, she wasn't lonely or frustrated or psychologically disturbed. The police questioned her for hours, they investigated her background, searched her house. There was nothing.'

I asked him what he personally thought had happened to him. 'I don't know. I haven't an idea. I'd like to know, though I never will now. Sometimes I think I remember a boat, being in a sailing boat or seeing a sailing boat, and sometimes I see a room with a green armchair and birds on a mantelpiece, but I only think I do. I may have made those things up. There are three days of my life unaccounted for, a sort of lost weekend like people have from heavy drinking. Alcohol amnesia, except that all I used to drink in those days was milk and orange juice.'

Both our stories – you could hardly call them 'peak experiences' because they were neither good nor pleasurable events – involved heights. I asked Silver if he thought that significant and he said it must be. We walked around the roofs a bit after that, going in the other direction towards Castlemaine Road, jumping over the chasms between the terraces nearly as well as Wim would have done. Both of us, it appeared, had had our baptism of fire and it had left us with a lifelong yearning to be high above the world.

Max and Selina's party was over. We looked down at the deserted garden where empty and half-empty glasses stood about on the white furniture, gleaming faintly in the half-dark. The lights had all been put out and the mosquito zapper switched off. The trees swayed a little in the wind that had risen while we were up there and their leaves trembled and shivered. I thought that if I shut my eyes and wished hard enough, I'd see Mabel when I opened them, stepping daintily across the lawn and jumping on to the wall outside my window. I shut them and wished and nothing happened. Silver put his arms round me and held me tight.

We looked over the front then and saw all the people going home, kissing Selina, some kissing Max, car doors slamming and the civilized academics wincing because the noise they made might wake the neighbours. 'Good night, ladies, sweet ladies, good night, good night,' said Silver.

It wasn't very late, not much past eleven. No one was about in the flat. I suppose it's hindsight that tells me the calm silence felt expectant, as if waiting for something to happen, but I think I really sensed this at the time. Perhaps all interiors feel like that when there's no activity going on in them, no wind to rattle windows or rain to dash against glass. Quiet, calm, stillness. The sound of traffic on the Westway was a distant hum, not unlike the sea.

We had been in the living room about ten minutes, made ourselves tea and put the radio on very softly, I talking of going back to old Mrs Fisherton's, when Wim came in at the window. He gave Silver one of his usual hugs and then he hugged me. I fetched him a mug of tea, strong and black, the way he liked it. Liv must have been listening for him, maybe had been listening for him for three days, for she came out of the bedroom and although he only nodded to her, saying 'hi', sat down on the floor at his feet. Her position seemed designed for resting her head against his legs, and if she failed to do this it was probably because she feared a rebuff.

Wim's silences often seemed enigmatic or profound but it's possible they only indicated an empty mind. Yet he had the ability to be with people, part of the company, while taking no part in the conversation. When he did speak he was articulate and fluent. He never made small talk, would have scorned asking how someone was or commenting on the weather or the temperature. That evening he drank his tea, set the mug down and made the statement that was to change our lives.

'I've seen Andrew Lane and Alison Barrie,' he said.

Silver smiled. 'You and Morna both.'

'Who is Morna?'

'The girl I was at Queen Mary's with. You've met her a couple of times. Morna, remember? Big dark girl, beautiful face.'

That was the first jealousy I felt with Silver, a thin shaft of it going into my side like a long pin, and I resolved to crush it if it came again.

'It doesn't matter,' Silver said. 'The point is only that she said she saw him, Andrew Lane, I mean. Coming out of a shop in Elgin.'

'He wasn't coming out of a shop when I saw him,' said Wim. He lit a cigarette and passed round the pack. 'He was in a room in a flat and she was there. Not the boy, though. I expect the boy was in bed.'

I hadn't expected an interest in people from Wim, and perhaps the kind he had was more anthropological than social. He liked to see how they behaved when they didn't know they were being watched. He wanted to see their faces when they thought they were alone. Jonny, bent on a rather different assessment of flat-dwellers, best pleased when they were absent from their homes, made his reconnaissance from balconies. Wim lay on the mansard, head-down, and peered over the top edge of dormers. It was much to his advantage that few people on the top floors drew their curtains or pulled down their blinds.

He had been on his way back to Silver's after a night and a day and half a night on the roofs. Sleeping up there, drinking orange juice and eating cold pizza on the tall terraces of the Bayswater Road after scaling the asymmetrical heights of Park Lane. He'd walked along the canal from Paddington Basin to the bridge at the Paddington Stop and then climbed on to the roof of a terrace in Formosa Street, some builder having thoughtfully left a ladder behind for his use. Wim never admitted to physical tiredness, he never admitted to anything, come to that, but by the time he had climbed the scaffolding on to the gable end of Torrington Gardens, he paused to drink the water he had with him and to eat a bar of Cadbury's Whole Nut chocolate. Then he lay on the slope of the mansard and edged his way along. Each time he came to a dormer he hung his head down over its lintel and looked through the topmost pane of glass. It was dark outside, the feeble orange moon drifting in and out of cloud masses, but bright with light inside except in those flats where the occupants had already gone to bed. Some of the residents used the dormer room as a bedroom but in all but one of these the curtains were drawn. In the odd room out, where there were no curtains to draw, a lone old Chinese man in striped pyjamas slept on a futon, lying on his back, his arms outflung. The time was just past eleven-thirty.

Wim, apparently, observed all this with interest. It was from the fifth window from the Peterborough Avenue end that he saw the missing couple. They were sitting opposite one another across a table, holding hands on its surface and talking. The window was closed and what they said was inaudible. The positions they had chosen to sit in were such that, in order to see the face at the window, the man would have had to turn his head to the left almost in a half-circle and the woman hers sharp right. Only a noise at the window would have alerted them to move like this and Wim never made a noise.

He watched them for a few minutes, half-expecting the boy Jason to come into the room. But it was too late for a child to be up. The man was fully dressed but the woman wore a dressing gown over a long nightdress. Her hair was fair, dry and brittle-looking, her face strained and networked with lines. Andrew Lane was less easy to identify because before he had disappeared with Alison Barrie and the child he had worn a beard. But the square brow and the thick black circumflex eyebrows were unmistakable.

'Have they been there all the time?' Silver asked. 'It's been months. Since March, hasn't it?'

'February,' I said. 'They went away from wherever they lived a few days before my birthday.'

All those people talking about it at the lunch party Max and Selina gave for me, and Silver's parents there, only I knew nothing of whose parents they were then, or what he would mean to me.

Wim shrugged. Who knew how long they had been there? The point was that they were there now.

'Are you quite certain it was them?' Silver asked.

'If you mean, would I swear to it in a court, no. But it was them, just the same.'

'Well, they're all right there at the moment, aren't they? They're safe there. We won't worry about it. We'll go and take a look tomorrow. Not tonight but tomorrow.'

'They switched the light off before I left,' Wim said. 'They went to the door together and the guy turned the light off.'

It was at this point that Jonny arrived. We heard his feet on the stairs and his key in the door, but before he had even appeared we all knew, by some silent sharing of thoughts, that it would be best for him to know nothing about it. As usually happens in a case like that, no one could think of anything to say. Jonny smelt of drink. His face was red and climbing the stairs had made him sweat. His eye rested contemptuously on Liv who by now had managed to press herself against Wim's legs.

'Polly, put the kettle on,' he sang in a slurred voice. 'We'll all have tea.'

Liv didn't move.

'Don't think,' Jonny said to her, 'that sleeping in that room on your tod is going to save you. I can get in there any time I want. You put the chest of drawers against the door and I'll bash the fucking chest of drawers to bits.'

'Make your own tea, Jonny,' Silver said. 'You're pissed out of your mind.'

'Pissed,' Jonny admitted, making a fine distinction, 'but not out-of-my-mind pissed. My mind is clear. I know what I'm doing.'

Wim yawned. I thought I could read what he was thinking. For two pins I'll go in there with her, and by the time you come bashing down the furniture I'll be fresh for a fight. But Jonny forgot about his tea and went off to bed. The stairs had winded him and he staggered, grabbing the door handle to save himself from falling. I told Silver that I was going home. He came downstairs with me, leaving the other two – to what? Nothing, probably. Too many things happened the next day for me ever to find out.

It was one in the morning and the whole of 19 Russia Road was in darkness. I crept down the iron staircase, the cold fronds of ivy tapping against my face, and let myself in. Once Mabel would have been there to greet me or, uncurling her body and rolling on her back with waving paws, have welcomed me to bed. The place seemed disproportionately silent and dark. Having been out in the open for most of the day and up high in the sky for half the night, I felt more oppressively than had become usual with me, the dull misery of life in a basement. It was deep night, the beginning of the small hours, but it might as well have been a spring morning or summer noon, nothing of the sky and nothing of sunlight was ever visible down there. I got into bed and lay with the light on, thinking about those two, Lane and Barrie, to stop myself mourning Mabel. How long had they been in a top flat in Torrington Gardens? Was the boy with them? Precisely which house was it the flat was in? Had Wim taken the number or simply counted the dormers? And how were they living in there? On what? Had they money? Morna had seen Andrew Lane out shopping, so presumably they had enough.

Thinking about money reminded me. I had omitted to check on Liv's £2,000, something I did most days. I got up. Walking through old Mrs Fisherton's to the dining room I felt the whole weight of that big tall house pressing on me and it suddenly seemed remarkable that a house like this one should stand and go on standing for 100 years and more. It was quite fragile, it must be, bricks on timber, bricks on bricks, thin slivers of mortar, top-heavy surely. For a moment I was almost afraid of its sudden collapse, a soft rushing sound first, increasing to a rumble and a roar as the whole edifice came tumbling down, engulfing me in broken bricks and debris and splintering wood. Of course, I knew it was only my claustrophobia that made me fancy such things, that I could be buried under the falling house, suffocated under it, my mouth full of plaster dust and sticky cobwebs, but I really did feel a terror of it for a few seconds. I had to stand still and breathe deeply before I opened the door that was always kept closed and let myself into old Mrs Fisherton's nasty dining room.

I switched the light on and immediately saw that things were different. Things were not as I had left them when I was last in there two days before. The trolley had been moved a few feet away from the wall, a dark green tray patterned with various species of tropical birds lay on the table. Most troubling of all, most *sinister*, was the torch that stood on the sideboard, lamp end downwards.

Quickly I opened the table napkin drawer. Liv's money was gone.

17

It's a strange feeling you have when you discover you've lost a sum of money, a sudden hollowness inside, as if something has fallen out of your body. Not just money, though. I expect you feel it when you have lost any valuable item, jewellery, something expensive that you've just bought. Last evening, leaving the former Gilmore Hotel in Sussex Gardens, I went to find my car which was parked quite a long way away, on a meter in Praed Street. Several times that day I had been back to the car to feed the meter (when no traffic warden was looking) and moving the car and putting cash into the new meter (when one was). Someone must have watched me and seen me feel for change in my jacket pocket, for, when I got to the car at just before six, not only the remaining change but my wallet which was also in it were gone. Mugging has never happened to me before and I didn't like it, though the sum involved was only £30 and credit cards are quickly replaceable. I suppose that what I hate is being made a *mug* of, not being streetwise enough, not being sufficiently on my guard.

I had no such feelings when I understood that Liv's £2,000 was gone, no hollowness as of having expelled well-being and contentment, but pure panic. I searched every drawer in that room, though I knew perfectly well where I had left those wads of notes. But that is always done in these circumstances, it comes of not trusting oneself, doubting one's own memory. I desperately wished I had asked Silver to stay with me that night, just to have him there, his comforting presence. I thought of going back to him. If I did that I might find Liv still up, still in that room with her head against Wim's knees. Sooner or later I should have to face her but not then, not *now*. In the end I just went back to bed. I even managed to sleep, waking early to a pounding on the door at the foot of the interior staircase.

It frightened me more than when Beryl appeared in my bedroom or when Selina just turned up, walked into the flat when it pleased her or was to be discovered sitting in one of my armchairs. This time it couldn't be Selina, for Selina never knocked, it must be someone with a message to say one of my parents was ill, or someone from next door to say Silver had had an accident. I jumped up, in the absence of any sort of dressing gown threw the bed quilt round me, and called out, 'Come in, come in,' and 'I'm coming.'

It couldn't be Selina but it was. She had a hangover, there were pouches under her eyes and red veins branching all over her round cheeks. But she was as beautifully dressed as ever, the pink pearls round her neck and in her ears. She looked at me as you might look at someone who has just kicked you hard on the shin for no reason, with disbelief, bewilderment and pain.

'Oh, Clodagh.'

I didn't connect her tone with the missing money. Not then. I simply supposed I must have done some awful thing, or awful in her eyes and Max's, been seen by one of their friends smoking in the street, or holding hands with Silver or burying my poor cat.

'What's the matter?' I said, preparing to defend myself.

'Max wants to see you. Now. He hasn't had his breakfast yet, he couldn't eat, he says.' I hadn't had mine either. It was only eight o'clock in the morning. 'It was as much as we could do to entertain our guests last night. And as for food, it would have choked us. I drank too much, of course. I *had* to.' She had never uttered so many sentences to me without the 'darling' inserted. 'He's in the drawing room. Please go up at once, will you?'

I had come a long way since last October. 'I'll have a bath and dress first,' I said. I did and I took my time. Not without great anxiety, of course, and not without some self-reproach. I had constantly to remind myself, I did so every day, that Max had let me have this place rent-free. It was because I lived there that I had met Silver, and Silver was my treasure, the most important person in my life, the only one who could have taken Daniel's place and more. All this had happened through Max. He was concerned about my welfare, he was even now, or so I supposed, doing his best to find a university course for me that I might like the sound of and want to take. I ought to be grateful and I was. But I also felt there was no reason to treat me like a bad child showing early symptoms of psychopathy.

No one had cleaned up the drawing room after the party. Sticky glasses stood about, a full ashtray overflowed on to a black and gilt ormolu table and someone had spilt syrupy orange liquid on the emerald carpet. It made a livid patch of what looked like an ineradicable stain. Max in sepulchral black tracksuit – a kind of mourning assumed for me? – was sitting in an armchair, one of the uncomfortable kind upholstered in shiny satin. In front of him stood a round table and on the table was Liv's money laid out in ten neat piles, rather like cards for a game of patience. He looked happy, pleased with himself and several years younger than when I had last seen him. But the voice in which he spoke to me was deep, heavy and loaded with doom.

'Sit down, please Clodagh. Sit down over there.'

'Over there' was another satin armchair, but chestnut brown instead of yellow. I felt something sticking in my side and pulled out from underneath me a silver cigarette holder from which, into my hand, trickled a little stream of black tar.

'Oh, put it down, put it down,' said Max.

I laid it on the table a few inches from the notes and, in the absence of anything else to do, wiped my hand on my jeans. Max stared as if he had never before seen such a disgusting act. There was silence now of the kind that is always intended to intimidate the accused, to force them to ask what's the matter. I looked at Max, I looked at the money, I did what the silence expected of me.

'What is it?'

'Can you think,' said Max, 'of any reason why I shouldn't call the police?'

I couldn't. 'I'd like to say something,' I said.

I spoke slowly because I was quaking inside and if my hands began to tremble I didn't want him to see. I closed my fists, something which always looks aggressive, though it may be a defence measure. 'You very kindly let me have the flat and you let me have it for free, but I don't think that should mean I don't have any right to privacy. I'm over eighteen, I'm grown up, I ought to be able to keep things in the place where I live without other people –' I nearly said snooping – 'looking for them and taking – taking them away.'

It wasn't very well put. Max's lips twitched. Inwardly he was laughing at my inability to be articulate, to find the cogent phrase. But in the same cold tone he told me I'd abrogated – that was the word he used – my right to privacy through my behaviour. Instead of asking me where the money came from, he told me and then denied the implication.

'It hasn't escaped my notice that this is precisely the sum taken from the houseboat when that poor woman was killed. However, I am not for a moment suggesting you were involved in that appalling business.'

What was he suggesting, then? That it was the kind of thing I might be associated with? I understood, then. I saw how he and Selina saw *me*. As a criminal. The first instance of my criminal behaviour was not only climbing the pylon but taking a younger friend up with me and killing him. I smoked, though they had told me not to. I played truant from my polytechnic and lied about it until I was chucked out. And now I was a thief or at least a receiver of stolen goods.

'Well?' he said. 'What have you got to say for yourself?'

'I'm looking after that money for a friend.' It was true but it sounded feeble. The truth sometimes does. 'She asked me to look after it because it wasn't safe where she was and she hasn't a bank account.'

'You'll have to try rather harder than that.'

'I can't try harder than tell the truth,' I said. It wasn't a bad answer on the whole. It made him angry.

'Oh, nonsense, nonsense. Now listen to me. You've made something of a mess of the first twenty years of your life. Do you have any idea of what you want to do in the future? Or are you set on becoming one of those down-and-outs one sees sleeping on the streets? But, no, you're a woman. You'll marry the first man who's willing to have you and you'll make him miserable as well as yourself.'

This picture was so unlike me I couldn't take it seriously. Not the last part, at any rate. It didn't even make me cross. 'I want to be a roofer,' I said. 'I'll do a City and Guilds building course and then I'll apprentice myself to a roofer.'

'Really?' In order to get up, Max pushed the table a little further away from him and nearer me. This was a mistake on his part. 'I hope you don't imagine you can remain here while you train to be an artisan. I have other uses for Grandmother Mabel's apartment. I'd like you out of here within the week.' He was longing for me to beg him not to call the police. 'Within the week, Clodagh.'

'I'll go today,' I said. 'Thank you for letting me live here. I *am* grateful, though you may not believe it.'

With that, before he could stop me, I snatched up the notes, two fistfuls, and ran for the door. Max was athletic for his age and he was wearing a tracksuit and trainers, but his age was sixty and mine was twenty. He made an awful roar, the kind of noise you imagine a wounded bison might make. I slammed the door behind me, ran downstairs and out of the house by the front door. Luckily, as usual, my key was in my pocket. It was early and it might have been that no one was up, but I rang Silver's bell and Wim came down to let me in. He came surprisingly fast, but then he was a surprising person. The great thing was that you never needed to explain anything to him, just as he never explained his own conduct to anyone. I raced up the stairs, my hands full of money, burst into the flat and into Liv's room. Whether she had been alone all night I couldn't tell, but she was alone then. And asleep.

I shook her. It wasn't very kind of me but I had to wake her. She was one of those slow surfacers who take ages to rouse themselves, but while she was making wa-wa-wa, what's-the-matter noises, I held up the money for her to see before stuffing it under her pillow.

It was strange how exhilarated I felt. I had been thrown out of my home, I had been insulted – even someone with less *amour propre* than I had would have seen Max's words as insults – and for all I knew the police sirens might be sounding for me any minute, but I felt full of happiness and energy. Adrenalin, I suppose it was, released by the running and the snatching of the money. I rushed into Silver's room. He wasn't asleep. He put out his arms to me and I got into bed with him. Quite a long while after that I told him what Max had said and how I had been evicted. I seemed to make a habit of being thrown out of places and wondered what establishment would be next to do it.

'Not this one,' said Silver. 'I'll come back with you to collect your stuff.'

No, I said. That might not be wise. I'd do a Liv, I thought, and keep my refuge a secret from Max and Selina. But first I'd talk to them.

Max is dead now. He has been dead for three years. After Selina left him, perhaps I should say was forced to leave him, when he brought his lover into their home, after what's usually called an 'acrimonious' divorce, 19 Russia Road was sold and the proceeds divided between them. Max bought a little house in a Bayswater mews and married the woman he had been living with, and it was there I went one evening to have dinner with them. By that time we were on friendly if guarded terms. A ring main on the ground floor failed while I was there and I was able, to my great pleasure and with a certain secret triumph, to find the fault and put things right. Max was astounded. Thanking me, he said I obviously had intelligence and what a pity it was I had made so few intellectual demands on it. Six months afterwards he was dead.

As for Selina, she never remarried. I sometimes read about her in the papers, in the gossip columns or diary notes. The profile some journalist did of her for *The Times* last year mentioned a partner, so she's not alone in the hi-tech ultra-modern flat she's bought in Docklands. *Streetwise* is of course still running and likely to run for many years.

When I went back into their house that morning, I thought that not only was I descending the iron staircase and entering old Mrs Fisherton's for the last time, but that this would be the last time I'd speak to Max and Selina. I never imagined – how could I? – that I'd go to Max's new home and, ultimately, visit him in hospital when he was on his deathbed. Nor that Selina and I would regularly exchange Christmas cards and that she, unable to accept the invitation to my wedding, would send me a handsome present of the most expensive kind of food mixer. No, that morning, I thought I was turning my back on them and the house for ever.

Feeling no animosity towards Mabel Fisherton herself, though I wished she had furnished her flat more cheerfully, I said goodbye to her and, when I had taken my clothes off them, jangled the wire hangers in her wardrobe for the final time. If her namesake had lived, what would I be doing about her? I'd have found a way, I thought, and wished I had a sweet cat to take away with me. When I had packed my case and Dad's trunk I went upstairs to look for my landlords, if people can be landlords when you aren't paying them.

They were both in the kitchen. I had never been in there before and hardly imagine Max was there very often. He looked rather out of place, sitting awkwardly at the table with a cup of coffee in front of him. Too upset to drink it in solitary state in the morning room, I supposed. Selina was at the sink, washing, of all things, one of their big Chinese vases. Over her dainty lilac skirt and sweater, she wore an apron with the faces of local heroes Robert Browning and Elizabeth Barrett printed on it. Both turned to face me and Selina slowly stripped off her yellow rubber gloves. We're all inconsistent about our expectations and prejudices. I had never expected young men to get up when I came into a room, I'd have been astounded if one of them had, but I knew men of my father's generation and Max's rose to their feet for women and thought it good manners to do so. Max stood up for Selina and for Erica Silverman and the cushion designer, I had seen it, and I'm sure he did for his mysterious lover, but he had never once stood up for me. I didn't want him to, I didn't care, but I knew he stayed put because he despised me and thought I merited no courtesies. He sat tight and scowled at me with dislike.

I was no longer frightened. Not in the least. Euphoria made me want to be rude to them but I knew I must restrain myself.

'What is it now?' Max said, as if I had been popping in and out of the kitchen for hours. 'Since you're leaving I've decided not to inform the police.'

Selina looked as if she was going to cry. 'Oh, Clodagh, how could you?'

'I came to say goodbye,' I said. 'I'm going now.'

'Is that all you have to say?'

Teachers at school had occasionally talked to me like this but more politely. 'I'd like to know how you found my friend's money.'

Max shook his head in exasperation and turned away but Selina answered me. 'I was looking for table napkins.' She gave her husband an injured look. 'We've only got paper ones but Max wanted real ones and said his grandma had some.'

'My grand*mother*,' Max corrected her.

I wanted to laugh but kept a grave face. I also wanted to say that I hoped the napkins had been starched and folded into waterlily shapes. 'Well, goodbye,' was what I actually said. 'And thank you very much for everything.'

'I shall be phoning your parents this evening,' said Max.

I left the kitchen and started down the stairs. Selina came after me, tottering on her stilettos. I stopped and we faced each other halfway down. 'Why didn't you stand up for yourself, darling?' she asked in a stage whisper, something she was presumably practised in. I understood

I was reinstated in her regard. 'Why didn't you say you wanted to keep the flat?'

'Because I don't.'

'He wants it for his woman. She's got nowhere to live and he's going to put her in there. He will now. You'll see.'

'Goodbye, Selina,' I said, and once again I ran out of the front door of 19 Russia Road.

Out in the street, observing for the first time that it was a lovely day, I stood breathing what passes for fresh air in Maida Vale and staring appreciatively at Mrs Clark's geraniums and the plaster face of a woman in a tiara above her triple window. A more important first time was the realization that I need never live below ground again. My troglodyte days were over. I opened the gate of No. 15 and had taken a single step on to the paved path when a voice behind me called out, 'Excuse me!'

I turned round. The man who had spoken had no need to introduce himself. Liv looked exactly like him.

'You're Mr Almquist?'

'How did you know?'

'There's a strong family resemblance.'

'You are her friend? She lives here?'

I nodded. 'Please to take me to my daughter,' he said.

I'd have liked a half-hour's warning, a chance to get Liv up and dressed and remove both Jonny and Wim. Silver was all right, he always made a respectable impression. But I had no warning and it was too late to lie. The arrival of Mr Almquist seemed an unnecessary and certainly unwanted complication. For some reason, halfway up the first flight of stairs, I thought about Max phoning my parents. I wouldn't be there, would I? Was I too about to turn into a missing person, like Liv?

Going up those stairs with someone from the outside world, a 'grown-up' (does one ever think of oneself as grown up? Do I now? Did *Max*?) was a new experience. It made me look around as we reached each landing and perhaps see what I saw through Håkan Almquist's eyes. I had never really looked around before, I had always been too keen to reach the top, but now I saw carpeted hallways with small tables standing on them or a single chair, doors open on to rooms prettily furnished but deserted, nearly always empty, immaculately cleaned by Beryl, a flower vase filled with dried grasses on a gilt table, a red and white striped settee with perfectly plumped-up cushions where no head ever rested, a glass bowl with fruit in it, but even from this distance you could see the apples and oranges were made of wax.

If Håkan Almquist thought he was going to find his daughter in a room like one of these, his expectations were soon dashed. But I suppose he took very little notice of his surroundings, for when Liv saw him she screamed. It must be disconcerting for a parent when his child reacts like that and Liv's father certainly seemed distressed. He sat down heavily on one end of the sofa. Wim was on the other end, wearing his plum-coloured tunic, and consuming a breakfast of Cadbury's Fruit and Nut chocolate and what looked like a banana milk shake. Liv's screams turned to crying, the tears rolled down her cheeks, while she shouted, 'I am not going home, I am not, I am not!'

There's a saying that home is where they have to take you in, which to my mind implies that it's a last resort. You don't want to go there and they don't want you but there's really no option. I hadn't reached that point (though I did eventually) and if Liv had, she was still fighting it. Mr Almquist spoke to her in Swedish and she replied in that language until, suddenly, she said, very loudly and clearly, 'I am British now. I stay here and become a British person.'

Sweden was not in the European Union at that time and in order to stay Liv would have needed a work permit, which she must have had while working for James and Claudia. Mr Almquist, still speaking Swedish, mentioned their names, and Liv began shouting again.

'They are never giving me a reference. I tell you, they hate me. They like to see me dead. That is why I never can go in the street. Do you understand now? I never can go down into the street.'

Plainly the poor chap didn't understand. Silver tried to explain, but of course he knew better than to mention the money or the car crash, so Håkan Almquist became more and more mystified. All the while Wim sat there finishing his milk shake and the last square of his chocolate. I won't say I never saw him eat anything but chocolate but it was his staple food, his rice or his potatoes you might say, and the occasional slice of pizza or packet of crisps was just garnish. Liv seemed to be directing her sobs and cries at him as much as at her father, perhaps she thought it made her attractive. He ignored her. He might have been quite alone in the room. I wouldn't have been surprised if he had got up and climbed out of the window, but Liv's father would have been.

Silver whispered to me to come into the bedroom and leave them to sort it out. We sat on the bed while I told him all about my encounter with Max and Selina and he, eventually, drew my attention back to what Wim had seen through the dormer window. It was natural enough, in the light of what had been happening, that I had almost forgotten it. Silver asked me if I had any ideas. What, for instance, were we going to do about it, if anything?

'I'd like to see for myself,' I said.

Silver had asked Wim for precise directions and he had been down Torrington Gardens himself this morning to locate the house. The fifth window on the top floor from Peterborough Avenue was in the second house from the end, there being three dormers on this level to each house. A balcony ran along this floor just below the dormers where the mansard ended and it was bordered by a low parapet of bottle-shaped pillars. If hanging upside down on the mansard was beyond our powers, we could walk along this balcony. The house was of dark grey brickwork with cream facings and red bricks in a Greek key pattern running along just below the parapet and again between the bay windows on the ground floor and the sash windows on the first floor. It would be easy to slip down on to the balcony from the roof.

This particular house, 4 Torrington Gardens, was divided like its neighbours into five flats. Silver had gone up the path into the porch and read the names beside the row of bells. The top bell and the one below it were for Flats D and E, both apparently occupied by some-one named Robinson. No style or initials, just Robinson. Some people called Nyland lived in Flat C and an S. Francis on the ground floor.

'If it's them,' I said, 'what are we going to do? Are we going to do anything?'

'Let's make sure first.'

'Yes, but are we going to creep up on them or – well, boldly reveal ourselves?'

'We're on the side of the hunted, not the hunter, aren't we?' Silver said and I nodded. 'So is being on their side giving them up or keeping them hidden? I suppose it's keeping them hidden because they could give themselves up if they wanted to. Anyway, it's wrong to do good to people against their will.'

'Is it?' I thought about that one and ended up by no means certain. It surely might be right to force someone into a rehabilitation programme even if they wanted to keep on injecting heroin, or make a family live in a hygienic new house no matter how much they might prefer their dirty cottage. I told Silver this and he said he didn't know but the family analogy was a bad one because only the parents probably would make the decision while the children, who benefited or suffered as much as they, had no say in the matter.

'You're thinking of Jason, the little boy,' I said.

But he hadn't been. He had forgotten about Jason and said he'd only believe in him when he'd seen him himself. He was speculating as to what Lane and Barrie were doing there, if they had been there from the first or recently moved on from some other hiding place that had proved unsafe, if indeed it was them at all, when there came a shattering scream from the living room. We rushed out to find Håkan Almquist trying to manhandle Liv out of the flat. He had two plastic sacks into which he had presumably packed her clothes and these he was pushing across the floor with his feet, necessarily very slowly, while he dragged Liv, pulling her by the welt of her sweater. The sweater welt stretched as if made of elastic and Liv, straining backwards and trying to dig her feet into the thin old carpet, reminded me of a shaggy dog dragging on the end of its leash.

Mr Almquist stopped pulling when he saw us and Liv broke free. A furious altercation between them was incomprehensible to us but we knew very well she was saying she wouldn't go with him and he telling her she must. 'I shall call the police,' he shouted at Silver, 'and they will make her come home with me.'

At the idea of the police Liv looked as if she was going to faint. She crawled on to the sofa and huddled into the far corner of it, hugging her knees. Silver was very polite, but what he said was unlikely to please Liv's father. It would be useless calling the police. Liv was over-age, an adult woman, and no one could take her anywhere if she wanted to stay.

'But she is my daughter. She lives in my home.'

'I expect you'll find the law is the same in Sweden,' Silver said.

Håkan Almquist's response to that was to slap Liv's face. Poor Liv was always getting smacked. As she cried out he seized her by the shoulders and started pulling her off the sofa. She screamed. I have never come across anyone, unless you count three-year-olds in supermarkets, who could scream so loudly and penetratingly as she could. It was a sound which rose and fell and rose and fell like a police siren, and it roused Wim, who had retreated to another room. He came out, quickly took in the situation and surprised me by seizing hold of the older man from the rear and, walking backwards himself, propelling him towards the door. Silver and I held him, taking an arm each. I didn't like doing this, it felt like violence, though it was only restraint. Wim picked Liv up in his arms and without a word carried her into her bedroom. He came back immediately, closing the door behind him.

'What am I to do?' said Mr Almquist.

He had calmed down. He looked despairingly at Silver. We released his arms and he dropped into an armchair. 'She doesn't want to go,' Silver said gently. 'You must see that. She can stay here, she's all right here.'

'But what is wrong with her? Is it her mind?'

We said we didn't know. No one said anything about her refusal to go out into the street and no one mentioned Jonny. Håkan Almquist sat there for a few minutes, staring at Liv's bedroom door and casting sidelong glances at Wim. Then he got up, sighed, and said he'd go. Not home, not back to Sweden, but find himself an hotel and come back the next day to try and make her change her mind.

All this reminded me that unless I did something about it I'd be in Liv's case myself, a missing person whose parents hadn't known where she was for months. But do what? It wasn't likely Dad would behave like Mr Almquist but could I take the risk? He and Mum were already angry enough with me for getting myself thrown out of GUP and we had spoken only once since that piece of news was imparted. I told Mr Almquist I'd come with him and help him find somewhere to stay and Silver and he and I all went downstairs together.

The only hotel I knew of was the Gilmore. We could hardly recommend it, having tested its lift ourselves, and we eventually found him one in Elgin Avenue, the Edgware Road end. By this time he was talking about the air fare he had sent Liv and saying he wanted it back. She wasn't to be trusted with money, he said, suddenly confiding

215

in us. She stole from her mother's purse when quite a small child and there had been trouble at school over her shoplifting. Silver told him he had the money safe in his own bank account and then we left him, I to find a callbox and phone my parents, not relying on the anonymity of any call reaching them from Silver's flat.

The ensuing trouble was worse than I had expected. Oddly enough, Max and Selina came in for as much rage and blame as I. Dad would phone Max as soon as I had rung off. A piece of his mind would be delivered. Mum wanted to know what I had done that was so disgraceful (her word) as to deserve summary eviction. Where was I now? When was I coming home?

'I'm not,' I said and had to back away from the receiver, the outburst was so violent.

Silver kept feeding the phone with 20p pieces. When I too was threatened with the police I said goodbye and put the receiver down, but carefully and not with a crash. Hand in hand we walked back to 15 Russia Road. It was my home now, a place where they didn't have to take me in. They wanted to.

18

Håkan Almquist's arrival and his violence towards her, even more than that, his threat of calling the police, made Liv's attitude to the outdoors worse. Now not only Claudia and James were out there looking for her but her father as well. She stayed in her bedroom, only coming out at sunset. The sun streamed into Silver's living room on a fine day, and it was as if she was afraid of its rays seeking her out as in wartime an airman might fear the beam of a searchlight. Even when those rays had dulled and reddened, she flinched from them, covering her face with her hands.

Jonny came in as the red light was fading from the walls. He brought in a bottle of whisky and two bottles of wine, but Liv wouldn't drink, saying she felt sick. She told him about her father's visit, constantly appealing to us for confirmation of this threat or that. Jonny made matters worse by telling her she had committed a criminal offence. Once her father went to the police, as of course he would, they would know where to find her and be able to prosecute her for driving over the permitted limit, leaving the scene of an accident and endangering the lives of three young children. This last was an offence I believe he invented on the spur of the moment. Liv was terrified. Jonny told her the only way she could make sure of not being sent to prison or heavily fined and deported to Sweden was by coming back to Cricklewood with him. She lay on the floor and cried.

Jonny sat there, occasionally prodding her with his toe, and drinking neat whisky. We were a pair of 'fucking wimps' because we wouldn't join him. I was desperate for a glass of wine but had to refuse it. We were going on the roofs. Of course, we wanted to go alone, but Silver, whispering to me in the bedroom, said he disliked the idea of going at all if it meant leaving Liv alone with Jonny.

'He could get her out of the house on his own if there's no one around to hear her screaming. Or he could stun her first, he's capable of that. You don't know how often I've wished I'd never met him.'

'Then we'd better take him with us,' I said.

Would it have been better if we had? Or worse? Perhaps no different. We went alone because Morna arrived just as we were thinking of leaving. Sure, she'd stay with Liv till we got back, there was something she wanted to watch on television. Jonny was far from pleased to see her. He became antagonistic when she suggested she and Liv go and lie on Liv's bed to watch the episode in her serial. He asked them if they were a 'couple of lezzies'.

'And what I want to know is, what you done with that two grand?'

I had been wondering that myself. Liv smiled at him. She had what I thought of as a dangerous way of behaving when defying him – when defying any man, I expect. She'd stand up, stretch her neck and drop her shoulders, thrusting out her breasts and pulling in her waist. Liv's breasts were big and her waist tiny, so the attitude was highly provocative.

'It is where you will not find it,' she said, confident now she had big strong Morna to protect her.

They went off into the bedroom and Jonny lit a cigar. It was to be days before the choking throat-tingling smell of that cigar disappeared from the flat. I changed my shoes for trainers and put on one of Silver's sweaters.

Two days before, Silver's newspaper had carried another Lane and Barrie story – they had something about them, some so-called new angle, two or three times a week – and this one had the usual photographs, Andrew Lane anonymous behind his black beard, Alison Barrie looking lined and anxious, and the little boy Jason beautiful as only mixed-race children can be when one of the races is Asian. No new discoveries as to their whereabouts had been made, but Andrew Lane's father had died and that was what occasioned the story. A whole article inside was devoted to how much money John Lane might have left and to whom and who would inherit his house: Andrew, his only child, was the opinion of the newspaper, speculating as to whether he would come forward to claim it.

We went out at the precise time, I calculated, that Max would be phoning my parents. In days gone by, before I became a delinquent, when he had had occasion to phone them, he always did so after nine in the evening. Fond as she had been of Max, nearer a brother than a cousin to her, Mum used to say he did it deliberately to stop Dad seeing the start of the nine o'clock news. At two minutes past nine, when we opened the casement and climbed out on to the mansard, Max and my parents would be tearing me to shreds and spitting out the pieces.

I could almost hear the conversation, Max detailing my iniquities, Mum and Dad asking him where he thought I had gone, he telling them that as far as he knew I was at home with them, all of them concluding that I was a lost soul who would end up on the streets. But their conversation wasn't as I had imagined it. Mum's anger had gathered and accumulated and festered throughout the afternoon, Dad took his cue from her, and by the time Max phoned at two minutes past nine both of them were ripe to accuse him of irresponsible behaviour and criminal negligence. How dare he turn a young girl out of his house with nowhere to go? And in what everyone knew was a rough area, no matter how pretty it looked? Mum had by this time changed her mind about Maida Vale being a 'nice part' of London. How could anywhere be nice that was between Kilburn and Paddington Station? Max, of course, countered with a catalogue of my sins and the result was that he didn't speak to Mum and Dad or they to him for a year afterwards.

It was a while before I found out about this conversation. While Silver and I climbed up the mansard on to the flat part of the roof I had no idea they were quarrelling over me. I'd have been rather flattered if I'd known, but I didn't know and I didn't think about any of them for long. It was a fine calm night, the sky clear. An immensity of purple was spread out above us, unbroken by cloud or aircraft lights or streak of cirrus. Yet it was veiled by a hood of vapour dense enough to hide Venus and Mars and the Plough and the Seven Sisters, which I'd grown up with and become so used to that I only noticed them when they were gone.

We climbed down the gable at the end of the last terrace in Russia Road and on to the house that stood alone, then up the nailhead steps on the first gable of Torrington Gardens, and walked all the way to the terrace end. There, out of sight from any window, we dropped over the edge on to the balcony. The parapet with its bottle-shaped pillars was very low, less than three feet high, which made me think it was designed for show and not for anyone to walk out on. Besides, the dormers above it contained sash windows, not casement windows.

The plane trees in the pavement were very tall here, their leafy crowns reaching far beyond roof height. Anyone walking down the street might look up in this direction without seeing us. The street-lamps seemed very far below us, we were in the dark up here, but still we crouched down. We lay down and worked our way along, snake-fashion, Silver going first. It was dirty on that balcony with drifts of the dead plane leaves from autumns gone by and the accumu-lated dust of years. When we got up on to our knees our hands were black and our clothes covered in sticky dirt as dark as soot.

Curtains had been drawn in the first three windows we passed, and in the fourth a piece of cloth had been pinned up against the glass to exclude the light. We were now under the windows of 4 Torrington Gardens. Was the cloth there because it was Jason's bedroom? At the second window in the flat, the fifth one along, Silver got cautiously on to his hands and knees and I did the same. The window ledge was quite low down and when I lifted my head I could see into the room Wim had looked into, see the circular table with chairs around it, two armchairs, one red, one black, a television set, a picture on the wall facing us of a tiger in a rain forest. In the red armchair sat a little boy in blue pyjamas. Silver's indrawing of breath was just audible. I shifted so that I was closer to him and he took my dirty hand in his dirty hand. The boy wasn't looking in our direction or at the television but gazing at something on his lap and slowly moving his fingers.

'He's doing a jigsaw puzzle,' Silver said.

It was on a bean-bag board resting on his knees. The board was blue and the bag part dark blue with a pattern of rabbits on it. On the television screen a car chase was in progress, up and down the steep streets of San Francisco, but it wasn't exciting enough to distract him from his jigsaw. He looked like his photograph, exactly like. His skin was a soft golden cream and his lips red as a rose. We couldn't see his eyes, they were so intent upon his puzzle, but his hair, which looked black in the photo, was a dark-sepia brown. His bare feet dangled, not quite reaching the ground, and they were the most perfect small feet you could imagine, the toes as smooth and straight as fingers.

'What do you think?' Silver whispered. 'Is it him?'

A woman had come into the room. We dodged down a bit in case she saw us, though it was quite bright in there, a central light being on as well as a table-lamp, and fairly dark where we were. She didn't even glance at the window but went straight to the boy, her anxious face softening as she smiled. She held out her arms but he shook his head quite vehemently. What she said to him couldn't be heard but it worked, it persuaded him to put bean-bag and jigsaw aside and stand up as she squatted down, so that their heads were on a level. She put her arms round him and kissed him, and for a moment he rested his cheek against hers. It looked as if she was trying to lift him and failing. He was too heavy now. Both of them shook their heads ruefully and laughed.

Hand in hand they left the room but not before I was able to see her quite clearly. For a moment she had looked unseeing in our direction. She resembled Alison Barrie, though younger and prettier than in the photograph. Perhaps the wrinkles were ironed out by artificial light, for her forehead was smooth and the lines about her mouth less obvious. In spite of this her face was a mask of anxiety, as if acute fear lived with her day and night, and she looked very much in need of Silver's panacea: 'Don't worry.' If it was Alison, if it was Jason.

A moment after they had gone a lamp came on behind the cloth hanging at the first window. It was some sort of green floral material and the light showed up its pattern of poppies and daisies. We waited for something more to happen, for that light to go out perhaps and for her to come back into the living room, perhaps with Andrew. Or for Andrew to come in alone. If it was she, if there was a man there at all. The car chase was long over, the film itself was over, and a quiz show had begun. Silver said that we must take into account the fact that the flat was probably quite big, consisting of as many as six rooms, three along the back as well as these in the front. He and she could be in their kitchen or even have gone to bed.

'They wouldn't go to bed leaving the telly on,' I said.

I lit a cigarette but Silver told me to put it out. The window was open a little way at the bottom and if they weren't smokers themselves they might smell it. It was almost ten and I was wondering if we were to stay there all night, when the woman came back. She was barefoot, wearing a dressing gown of pink and white checked cotton. She began to tidy the room, plumping up cushions, blowing dust from the table top, picking up cups by inserting a separate finger in each one.

She switched off the television, took the cups away, came back and carefully laid puzzle and bean-bag on the table. We ducked down as she came to the window and closed it. She was so near us that, looking up, I could see the golden down on her forearms, the little snag in the material of her dressing gown at the waist, the gold watch on her wrist. We held our breath. She had only to look down – but she didn't. She went to the door, switched off the light and left the room.

The backs of the houses in Torrington Gardens can be seen from Torrington Road. We wriggled back along the balcony, climbed up on to the roof, and instead of returning in the Russia Road direction, made our way down the scaffolding between the end of this terrace and the start of the first one in Peterborough Avenue.

'Don't you think it's strange,' I said as we were walking home, 'that Morna still recognized him even though in the photos he had a beard and now she says he hasn't?'

'There was a picture of him in one of the papers,' Silver said, 'without a beard. That is, what some artist thought he'd look like without one.'

'I wish we'd seen him.'

'We will.'

I wrote some diary pages that night after Silver was asleep. It was my first night as an occupant of his flat rather than a visitor. I lived there now. I wanted to record my status as a resident and record too our first sight of the people in the flat we began calling simply 4E, the way we went about things and what we said. I'd have forgotten details of our conversation and the precise sequence of events if I hadn't. Besides, much as I loved Silver, I enjoyed being alone sometimes. I enjoyed being on my own for a while in that room that was so high up, its windows open on to the night, a little wind rustling the leaves of the gum tree and the catalpa whose branches made a canopy over Mabel's grave. That night I sat there for a long time, writing sporadically, thinking about my life and the strange turns it had taken, about Daniel too and all the people who believed me wicked beyond redemption. I wrote ten pages and thought of Silver and me and our luck in finding each other, until the blackbird began to sing, establishing its territory in the tea bush, as it always did at four in the morning.

19

In most houses socket outlets – you probably call them 'points' – are mounted quite high up in the wall, so that flexes have to trail at knee or hip level to appliances on furniture in the centre of the room. This is a system I avoid whenever I can and I'm starting to get a reputation with architects and builders as someone who installs floor socket outlets. Darren and Lysander and I are mounting this kind of wiring accessory in the floors of the Gilmore Hotel wherever possible and equipping them with a spring-loaded cover flap to keep the outlets free of dust and debris. It brings me a lot of pleasure and satisfaction to see how elegant the matt (but not dull) stainless-steel rectangles look, even though the tongue-and-grooved wood floors aren't yet laid.

My system is safe too, about as far from a fire risk as any wiring can be. It makes me think of its reverse, the hit-and-miss electrics in Silver's flat where there were still old-style five- and fifteen-amp outlets, flexes trailing from wall outlets, two of these at head height, I never found out why, one flex looped up and hung over a curtain rod. I knew nothing of wiring in those days, couldn't have mended a fuse, still less changed a plug, but even I sensed it might not be too great an idea to have an electric heater standing on a stool in the bathroom, its flex running across the floor, waiting to be tripped over, and an iron in the kitchen whose cable stretched across the sink. We never had a fire but there was one in a house in Torrington Gardens, and it was caused, people later said, by a similar kind of carelessness.

The fire started while we were up on the roofs, Silver and Wim and I. We had twice been back to the balcony outside the flat where the people Wim was positive were Andrew and Alison and Jason lived. We had been in daylight but had seen nothing of them. Eight hours later we went again but this time the whole place was in darkness. If they were indeed who Wim thought they were, it was inconceivable that they could all have been out. Perhaps they were in bed, though it was only just after ten when we got there. Silver and I had a great feeling of let-down because we had given a lot of thought to what we meant to do about them. Reveal ourselves? Make contact? We even thought of *writing* to them. We had come to no conclusions at that point, being certain only that our conduct would not include giving them up to the police or the social services. But when we went back that evening, Silver and I once more crawling along inside the parapet, we had made up our minds that if they saw us it was essential they recognize us as friends and not as hostile voyeurs.

Wim remained on the roof. He hung over the dormer from the top and announced in a whisper as we approached that all the lights were out in the flat back and front. For all that we waited a while, hoping and half-expecting that table-lamp to be switched on. The truth was that we could scarcely imagine people voluntarily going to bed at ten at night. But after a while we left and Wim said, perhaps by way of consoling us for our disappointment, that he'd help us on to the roofs of Formosa Street. He had brought his ropes and with the help of them and a chimney stack would get us up the gable at the Warrington Crescent end. We walked along the almost flat roof. The shops below us were all closed but a restaurant was open, its lights making window-shaped patterns on the pavement. The sound of talk and laughter and the rattle of plates reached us. To the west rose the pagoda-roofed blocks of flats built to replace slum streets, their windows brighter than the yellow moon, and on the far side of the canal the byzantine spire of St Mary Magdalene, its nave fitting with such architectural cunning into the triangle beyond the gleaming grass of Westbourne Green.

We heard the sirens before we saw the smoke and flames. Their wailing was commonplace round there and might have come equally from police cars or ambulances as from fire engines. Some extra sense must have alerted the people in the restaurant to excitement, for they poured out into the street. We were wary about climbing down with all that crowd to see us but we moved back to the end of the terrace and it was from there that we saw the thick black smoke billowing and surging into the night air from what seemed, shockingly and awfully, to be the top of a house in Torrington Gardens. Bright red sparks leapt and roared through the column of smoke. By then we could hear a crackling and a roar, quite different sounds from the dismal howl of the sirens.

'Is it them?' Silver said.

We both knew exactly what he meant. Was this inferno in the top of 4 Torrington Gardens?

'It's more like 20 or 22,' said Wim and we breathed again, for we trusted him to know. The idea of those people we already called 'our three' being smoked out of their home like bees from a hive seemed a dreadful ineluctable fate, for it precluded all possible escape. 'We'll go to the other end and climb down where no one can see us.'

A crowd had appeared from somewhere and was surging towards Torrington Gardens. Smoke and sparks and the sirens had summoned them. There was even one woman in a dressing gown. They were uninterested in us and no one looked in our direction when we went over the wall into a wilderness of ilexes and tall weed flowers. We climbed up the scaffolding on to the roof above Flat 4E. Wim had been right and the fire was quite a long way away, in the second terrace from where we stood and beyond three chimney stacks.

Did the sirens wake 'our three' and did they suppose the vehicles that wailed and brayed were coming for them? Wim did his hanging upside-down act and told us the table-lamp had been switched on in the living room below but no one was to be seen. We stood and watched what we could see of the fire, which wasn't much, the whole expanse of roof down there being shrouded in dense dark grey smoke. The crowd on the opposite pavement had a better view than we did and we a better view of them than of the fire. Three fire engines had arrived, arcs from their hoses shot into the dark shining air like fountains from artesian wells. A plane tree had caught fire and burnt like a torch until some kind of flame-quelling foam was sprayed on it, leaving a pitiful black skeleton behind.

No one had been hurt, though we knew nothing of that till the next morning. The tenants of the two top flats were all out, returning home somewhere around midnight to find themselves homeless. Someone, I don't know if it was ever discovered precisely who, had overloaded the system. I didn't understand it then, though I was already quite interested, but I imagine that what had happened was that there were old radial circuits in the house and though each was supposed to feed just one socket, extra sockets had been added and too many powerful appliances used. Whatever it was, it badly damaged several houses in the middle of Torrington Gardens.

We slid off the roof on to the balcony, all three of us this time, and slithered along among the dry leaves until we were under the window of the room where that dim light still shone. Wim went first and was first to get a glimpse of the room. 'Look. He's there.'

A dark-haired man was sitting at the table. He wasn't much like the newspaper pictures. His face was weaker, the jaw less square, the forehead narrower. Where he sat, if he had lifted his head, he would have faced the window, but he kept his head lowered. In front of him, on a red and black checked tablecloth with which the table was spread, he had a mug of some hot drink. We could see it steaming. The fire and the sound of the fire engines and his consequent fear had awakened him, he had gone into the kitchen and made himself a cup of tea. Made it for himself only, it appeared. Perhaps the others were asleep. He was doing nothing but drinking his tea, reading nothing, watching nothing. From time to time he lifted the mug to his lips and drank but when he set it down again he continued to stare at the red and black squares on the tablecloth. His face had a deeply worried look, sad and despairing.

'Is it him?' I said.

Silver took my hand and squeezed it. 'I don't know. We can't even be sure the others are who we think they are. We have to be sure before we can do anything.'

Wim got up. He stood on the balcony, leaning against the wall between the dormers. 'Why do you have to do anything?'

'I'll tell you,' Silver said, 'when we've decided.'

Wim nodded. He wasn't very interested. 'I think I shall spend the night on top of Clive Court. I've got some chocolate I left up there and a bottle of orange juice.'

We watched him as he headed off for Sutherland Avenue, knowing he could use the roofs for a highway at least as far as the end of Lanark Road before beginning his ascent of the tallest block of flats in north London. Inside the room the man switched off the lamp. For a moment he and the interior were lost to us and then, as he opened the door, light flooded in from some hall or landing outside. We saw him in that light, the whole of him, hesitating for some reason in the doorway, a rather thick-set man of average height in grey trousers and white open-necked shirt. Had he dressed to come to this room? Had he no dressing gown? It was strange to us not to be naked in bed but we knew there were those who wore nightdresses and pyjamas. Why wasn't he in pyjamas? At the time we kept these questions to ourselves, so it wasn't our voices which alerted him, if alerted he was. He turned sharply to look at the window. We ducked down quickly and he seemed not to see us. Almost at once the door was shut and the light excluded.

'I thought he'd be taller,' Silver said.

'And I thought he'd be thinner,' I said. 'Come on, let's go back.'

When we got home, intent on baths or most probably a shared bath, for we were coated in balcony grime, Liv came out of her bedroom, whimpering that the sound of the sirens had frightened her, she had thought they were made by the police coming after her. Told by Silver that the sirens belonged to fire engines, not police cars, that there had been a bad fire in Torrington Gardens, she became exultant in a quite unseemly way, jumping up and down and clapping her hands. While we had our bath she sat in the bathroom and talked to us, something we disliked as we had our own prudishness and objected to being seen together naked. But there was never enough hot water to take two baths in succession and no one had ever thought of equipping that bathroom with a shower. Liv sat on the stool where the dangerous electric heater usually stood and talked to us about her money. Or Claudia and James's money.

'Where is it now?' Silver asked and, seeing her wide-eyed frightened small-creature look, said, 'You needn't mind telling us. Jonny isn't here. Come to think of it, he hasn't been here for a while, has he?'

'No, thank God. And perhaps will never again?'

Silver said he wouldn't bank on it and where was the money?

'It is under the floor!'

She explained. The floors at Silver's were all covered with fitted carpet, a different colour in every room, greenish and fawnish and reddish, all very worn and battered by then, with threadbare bits covered up with rugs. In Liv's room that had been Jonny's room, this carpet was in a worse state than anywhere else and there were several rugs. While Jonny was at work, Silver and I out somewhere and Wim no doubt on the roofs, she had lifted up a rug, pulled out whatever fastenings there were to pin a corner section of the carpet to the floor and found floorboards of raw unpainted wood beneath. These she had prised up with a tool, probably a chisel or an abused screwdriver, she had found in a toolbox in the utility room on the lower-ground floor.

'The *basement?* You went down to the basement?' said Silver. 'Congratulations. It must be the first time.'

It was. Liv looked proud of herself in a shamefaced sort of way. 'I am very scared when I am doing this. But I do it – did it. And I am taking up a bit of floor and putting my money into the hole and putting the bit back again and then the carpet and the thing on it.'

'The rug.'

'Yes, the rug. And now I am making a plan for what I am doing about the money and *Far*, my papa, and getting away.'

'Getting away?' I said.

I hoped I didn't sound too elated at the prospect but she seemed not to notice. 'I am being, have been –' she struggled with her tenses – 'out of here and down the stairs and I am not dead, no, I am still here, I am survivor. One day, if I am being very strong and brave, I will go down again and a taxi will be there and you will help me walking over little bit of path on to little bit of street and into the taxi!'

'You're doing very well, Liv,' Silver said, grabbing a towel and wrapping it modestly round himself. 'Where's this taxi going to take you?'

'To Sweden. To my home. But not yet. Yet I am not ready. First I am giving my papa the money to take home and then I am following him when I am brave and strong enough.'

English is peculiar in this usage it has of continuous present and continuous future tenses. They're probably not called that but my husband isn't here to set me right. Silver could have told me. But while I was writing it I never showed him my diary. Whether Liv meant she had given her father the money or intended to give it to him was unclear. But she was sure he'd consent to go home and take the money with him, provided she promised to follow.

'But why not just go with him?' I said. I should have known better.

'Because I am telling you I am not ready, Clodagh. I am not so brave yet. You know that I am having agoraphobia, it is not so easy to – to –'

228

'Overcome,' said Silver. 'Conquer.'

'Yes, conquer. One day I am conquering and then I will go. First I am glad to take away the money and Jonny cannot find.'

We got her back into her room and then we went to bed, but first we looked out of the window we usually climbed out of and from which most of the back of Torrington Gardens could be seen. The fire was out and the smoke was all gone. Down in the garden pale-faced dahlias had closed their petals for the night. The grass was growing long and it was time for one of Beryl's sons to come and mow it. Silver and I lay in bed and discussed the question of the occupants of the top flat at 4 Torrington Gardens. If they were who we thought they were, the time had come to make ourselves known to them. They had friends, notably 'Robinson', who must have lent or let the flat to them, and who must know their identity, but had they any others? If they had, if they had someone looking after them, would Andrew have risked discovery by going out shopping?

There was a parallel there with Liv's behaviour, Silver said. She never ventured outside owing to an unfounded fear of being seen and apprehended, while Andrew, if this was Andrew, who had real grounds for caution, had no choice but to go out if his family weren't to starve. I said that wasn't a parallel but a contrast, and then, because it had only just occurred to me, I asked him if the damage to those houses would cut off our passage along the Torrington Gardens roofs.

He had already thought of it. 'There are other roofs,' he said, 'there are other ways of reaching them. We'll see. Don't worry,' and then we went to sleep.

I've given the impression, I know, of being irresponsible and uncaring of my parents' worries. The fact was that at this time, a week or so after Max had turned me out, I daily expected one of them to arrive at Silver's and attempt to take me back. Another parallel with Liv's situation, I suppose, though fear of being caught didn't stop me going out. By then Beryl knew where I was. I was too proud to ask her not to say anything to Selina, I was sure she and Max must know my whereabouts and have passed this information on to Mum and Dad. As it happened, Beryl hadn't said a word. She who was such a tremendous gossip about her employers drew a line at what she would have defined as betraying a friend.

'You and me is pals, love,' she said when I spoke to her about this a couple of weeks later and thanked her. 'I keep me mouth shut when it's them as I'm fond of.'

I was so touched I almost cried. It was then that I persuaded Silver to let her in to clean the place, mainly to have her there for me to chat to. Silver said he would on condition I'd let him give her more money and I didn't dispute that. In some ways we were like a happily married couple, he and I, weren't we?

But before all that I phoned Mum and Dad again. Most of their anger was for Max. Mum said she had never been so disillusioned about anyone in her life and Dad said people were so strange it just made character judgement impossible. They both took it for granted that I'd come home.

'You mustn't be afraid to come back here, Clodagh.'

This was a novel view of the situation I had failed to see before. Where did they think I had been? In a *hotel*? I who had hardly any money and was close to letting Silver keep me?

'We shall let bygones be bygones,' my father said. 'No one will say anything to you about that pylon business, so there's no need to worry about that. Of course, we must have a talk.'

I could imagine that talk. I said I'd think about it but at present I was staying with friends 'in north London'. I was all right. They must remember I was twenty years old. It was a measure of my youth that I said 'nearly twenty-and-a-half years old'.

'There isn't anything you're not telling us, is there, dear?'

Plenty, but not the things you mean, Mother, not pregnancy or a sexually transmitted disease or trouble with crack and smack or even climbing a pylon. It was that phone call and what they said, or didn't say, that made me decide to get a job. Not to think about it, not to do it next week or even tomorrow but *now*.

Silver's daily paper was on the table in the living room but I dismissed consulting its Situations Vacant columns. More out-of-date pictures of Andrew Lane and Alison Barrie on its front page had put me off that paper, these and the story it carried of the couple and Jason being seen by a 'member of the government' while campaigning for a forthcoming by-election in north Wales. I thought a bit about this and what it was that caused otherwise intelligent people to make these misidentifications, apparently want to make them and go on making them all the time. I wondered again if *we* could be mistaken and how we could put this to the test. Then I went out to look for a job.

Although I wasn't paranoid about this sort of thing the way Liv was, I steered clear of any possible sighting by Max and Selina by always walking in the direction of Torrington Gardens. Apart from Max going for his runs, they never went anywhere on foot, so there was little chance of an encounter. I was thinking more about the fire damage than about them. On my way to the newsagent I had a look at the houses where the fire had been. Because of the damage to the roofs of Nos 22 and 24 our route to the end of the terrace had been cut off for several days, but now I saw that the tarpaulins and battens Silver had forecast would soon go up there were in place. Men were working on the roof, not to begin repairing it but to protect what lay below from rain and wind damage. A scaffolding had been put up. It looked temporary to me. It would come down once the roof area was made watertight.

This particular section of the terrace had a dismal aspect, the two top floors of those three houses black and damp, a grim combination, their charred interiors still exposed. The poor plane tree was just the bare bones of itself. Its branches were like the remains of a wood fire that has been put out because it has begun to rain and its shrivelled blackened leaves lay in drifts all over the pavements and the gardens. Silver had already been round there several times on reconnaissance and reported back that the fire must have been under control before there was too much structural damage to the roofs. The struts, though burnt black, seemed intact. Once the tarpaulins were up we'd be able to go up there again and Silver, as was often the case, had been right to say don't worry.

Maida Vale lacks a real shopping centre but it has several little groups of shops, the largest of these being in Clifton Road where there are two newsagents. Each had glass cases of advertisement cards but there were no jobs on offer, only babies' cots for sale at bargain prices and bookshelves as good as new and women with dubious motives offering French and German lessons. I walked up to the Edgware Road but the café on the bridge had no situations vacant. For once, the only time I really wanted one, which I suppose is what Jonny would have called sod's law. It was then I decided that as soon as I saw a job on offer, provided it wasn't disgusting or potentially criminal and, of course, within my powers, I'd do it. Maybe that was less a decision than a prayer because ten minutes later it was answered. The newsagent's window in Lauderdale Road had a card advertising for a gardener.

I had never done much gardening except for once or twice mowing the lawn at home and I had even been persuaded to pull out a few weeds. Dad had taught me the difference between a weed and a cultivated plant and because I was quite interested I'd learnt. Perhaps I'd have been wiser to go home and smarten myself up a bit, but I was clean and wearing clean clothes and I had just washed my hair. Besides, I told myself, no one wants a designer-dressed gardener. It made no difference, anyway, for they said they'd take me on. Provided I could produce two good references.

The house was in Randolph Avenue, one in a long terrace. I'm afraid that before I even went up the steps to the front door I lifted up my eyes to the rooftops and was pleased with what I saw. The people were a Mr and Mrs Houghton, well-off, elderly, owners of the whole house. I never discovered their first names or much about them except that they had five children and twelve grandchildren. That I was a woman amazed them at first but I think they came to like the idea, believing, as many people do, that while women may be weaker and more capricious than men, they are less likely to be criminals or vandals and are more reliable. They showed me the garden, which was large with big unpruned fruit trees, a shaggy lawn and weed-choked flowerbeds. If my references were satisfactory, they'd want me four days a week.

Job applicants, I know by personal experience, are totally unscrupulous about references. I was. Silver gave me one, though the only gardening I'd ever done at his place was to help dig poor Mabel's grave. He wrote that I was an expert on the unique flora of Maida Vale. The other came from Beryl, who surprised me with her beautiful italic script, not to mention the headed cream-laid writing paper. Up at the top of her tower block Beryl hadn't even got a garden, only two window boxes, which shows the depravity to which we had all sunk.

I worked for the Houghtons for nearly two months. They paid me well and I think I did a good job for them. It was the worst time of the year for gardening, involving as it did no planting at all but only cutting down and mowing and pulling out weeds. Still, I made that large garden neat, got the lawn back into shape with trim edges and revealed in the flowerbeds, once the nettles and thistles and bindweed were gone, unexpected treasures, the pink lily flowers of *Nerine bowdenii*, a Himalayan blue poppy and a snow-white blossomed *Romneya*, struggling to bloom in the darkness under the dock leaves. And I learnt a lot about flowers, mugging up plant lore from Silver's father's books on my days off. 'What if?', as you know, is what I sometimes like saying. So what if I had stayed on at the Houghtons' and got to love it as I might have done? Would I have eventually left and done a horticulture course somewhere? Or gone to university to study botany? I might have become a park keeper by now. More and more women do.

But I was only to have seven weeks as a gardener. It was during those seven weeks that we came to grief.

20

It was the first week of August.

As soon as the tarpaulins were up on the burnt roofs, the temporary scaffolding down and the workmen gone, all of which happened in the space of three days, we went up there to see how safe it would be to walk on. Of course, we hadn't absented ourselves from the roofs on the nights immediately following the fire. We had several times climbed the scaffolding between the last terrace in Torrington Gardens and the first in Peterborough Avenue and walked along to assess what the builders had done that day. And we had twice crawled under the topmost windows of No. 4, but without catching a glimpse of the people who lived there. Silver and I were afraid this particular scaffolding might soon be taken down. The painting, which was the purpose of putting it there in the first place, was almost done. Once the scaffolding went, approach to 4E would be nearly impossible for us.

We failed in our attempt. The tarpaulin was there and the battens which held it in place. None of us was heavy but when we tentatively tried standing on the temporary roofing it sagged and a creaking sound came from underneath. Wim ran lightly across the tarpaulin from roughly the top of No. 24 to the top of No. 18 and back again. It was all right if you did it fast, he said, if you had a contingency plan in your head for what you'd do if the floor started to give way under you. He didn't say what contingency plan he had and we didn't ask. We sat inside the parapet on the top of 26, ate the Mars Bars he had brought with him and smoked his Marlboros. Since the fire the weather had been wet for part of every day – sod's law again, for it would have been helpful if it had rained the night of the fire – and even the safe parts of the roof were slippery. Rather reluctantly Silver and I decided not to risk crossing the tarpaulin. Not, at any rate, on a dark wet night.

So we sat up there and talked about how to be sure the three in 4E were indeed Andrew Lane, Alison Barrie and Jason Patel. Until we were certain of this we felt we could make no progress. We had seen the woman and the boy at the same time and we had seen the man alone but so far we had never seen all three of them together. And we were unsure about the man. Morna had seen someone out shopping that she identified as Andrew Lane but, as Silver reminded us, Morna tended to give well-known names to people she saw in the street.

'You mean, we mightn't have thought the man we saw was Andrew if Morna hadn't told us about him first?' I said.

'I mean that if Morna hadn't told us she'd seen him, Wim mightn't have jumped to the conclusion the half-Asian boy and the blonde woman he saw were Jason and Alison. Sorry, Wim, I'm only saying we took our cue from you. We *wanted* them to be those people and we jumped to a conclusion too.'

Wim said slowly, 'There's a way to prove it.'

We listened.

'We show ourselves to them.' His strange pan–European accent had become more marked. 'The boy's not important. That is, not for our purposes. *Your* purposes. We go to the balcony and show ourselves to the man and the woman, preferably together but one or other of them will do.'

I must have been very slow that night for I asked what for. 'They won't recognize *us*.'

'I think I know what Wim means,' Silver said. 'If they see us, and remember they'll be seeing three young people, dirty and in grotty clothes from crawling along that balcony, if they see us outside their window looking in, maybe even threatening to break in, and if they're law-abiding respectable people called, for example, Robinson, they'll ring the police. Anyone not afraid of the law would.'

Wim smiled. 'But if they're who I think they are, they'll be more afraid of the police than of us. They won't call them. They'll prepare themselves to put up a fight.'

'We may as well do it now.' Silver got to his feet and put out his hand to pull me to mine. 'Down one lot of scaffolding and up the other.'

It was dark and windy, the sky covered by a lumpy wrack of cloud that, lit from below, looked like cottage cheese stained with purple juice. The wind came in occasional sharp gusts, bringing a short splash of rain with it, but otherwise the air was still and damp. It was dangerous walking on the slates, though nothing would have made me say so. I was relieved when we slid off the mansard on to the narrow walkway between parapet and house wall.

Why did we want to do it? To identify them? Most of all, why did we want to help them? We didn't know them. We knew virtually nothing about the way adoption worked in this country, I don't suppose we even knew that no central agency existed and that adoption was managed by local authorities – if, indeed, we knew what a local authority was and did. Such knowledge as we had came from reading about Andrew Lane and Alison Barrie in the newspapers. So why did we place ourselves so firmly on their side and against those forces that wanted to take Jason away from them?

I suspect our reason had something to do with the cause the young always espouse: justice. It seemed unjust to us that some power in the land should have the right to deprive two people of the child they loved and who loved them. Needless to say, we never questioned at that time their kindness and their love, we took it for granted. We never asked ourselves or one another if they were fit to be parents nor if Jason's best interests were served by living with them. It was justice we saw. Not with the scales in her hand, for we were uninterested in weighing up pros and cons, but crusading, with a flaming sword.

No one was in the street below us. The usual cars were lined up, nose to tail, all along both sides, and because Torrington Gardens was a wide road, down the centre as well. On the opposite side many windows in the equally high terraces were brightly lit, their blinds up or curtains drawn back, but I had never seen a face looking out of any of them. What, after all, would a watcher have seen but the familiar opposing façade glimpsed through a network of branches, thready twigs and leaves?

'We needn't crawl,' I said. 'We can walk. There's no one to see us.'

Silver agreed but said we needed to make ourselves dirty, so we picked up handfuls of last year's plane leaves and the black grime of many years and rubbed it over our faces and hands, wiping our hands down the front of our T-shirts. We looked quite sinister, especially Silver, fair and pale-skinned as he was, now with his ice-grey eyes peering out of dark whorls.

'I'm sorry we have to frighten them,' he said, but I said that perhaps they'd just be angry.

'They'll only be angry if they're not who we think they are.'

'And then we shall have to get out of here fast,' said Wim.

Instead of dropping on to our knees, we walked along the balcony. The room in 4E was lit but empty. It had been a cool day with hourly showers and not much sun but still the window was open about four inches at the top. We sat down and speculated as to what they might be doing. It was just ten, so too late for them to be putting the boy to bed. Washing dishes, said Silver, to whose lot this task most often fell at home in Russia Road. One of them was having a bath, I said, and the other one was sitting with Jason who refused to sleep. Wim offered no suggestions. He lit a cigarette, saying that the smoke would drift in at the window, they would smell it and come. So we all lit cigarettes. The smoke was visible, little grey wisps of it slipping and curling into the gap between sash and lintel.

It did fetch them, both of the grown-ups. We heard their hasty tread behind us and heard the window being raised and shut. A catch clicked. We got up, then stood, the three of us, side by side, and Wim, taking a penknife from his pocket, as if he had rehearsed this, reached up with it and made as if to insert the blade between the top of the sash and the architrave. The two people inside – they had retreated to the far side of the room behind the table – stared at us in horror. They were clinging to each other, not in a graceful embrace, but each clutching at the other's clothes, the woman's hands making frenzied grabs at the man's chest and shoulders. Her face was such a mask of pain and terror, her eyes huge, her mouth half-open, that I resolved in that moment I'd never again take part in a hunt for anyone or anything. Then she let out a loud scream.

We didn't move, beyond Wim withdrawing his hand from the window and putting the penknife back in his pocket. The scream had awakened the child and the sound he made equalled hers. We stood our ground. We had to if this was going to work. Her screams changed to cries of 'I'm coming, it's all right, Mummy's coming' on sobs of terror, and she ran from the room. He followed her, slamming the door behind him. I thought I heard a key turn in the lock of that door.

'There's no phone in the room,' Silver whispered. 'It must be somewhere else in the flat.'

I shivered. 'She called herself "Mummy", did you notice?'

'Of course she would, of course she'd do that.'

We ran back along the balcony this time and climbed on to the roof. Wim said it was the safest place to be, but I thought that up there would be the first place the police would look. If there were any police. I thought of that evening a week before when the fire engines had come, their sirens blaring, and waited for that sound again. This time it would be from police cars. What Wim had done I rather disliked, not so much the smoking out of the occupants of 4E but his act at the window, the penknife inserted between wood and glass, as if he meant to break in and enter. I watched him as we waited, his inscrutable sallow face, the yellow-green eyes like those of a big cat. It was then I noticed for the first time how strange his hands were, the fingers disproportionately long, the backs short and narrow and the wrists as fine, symmetrical and honed as machine parts.

We smoked one more cigarette. We watched and waited. Nothing happened for a long while. Wim, who had stubbed his out, had snaked to the edge of mansard and hung over it. He turned his head to us and put one of those exaggerated fingers to his lips. I heard the window go up, perhaps to its full extent, a rasping rattling sound. Then a grunt as from someone not as used to clambering out of windows as we were. Wim mouthed, in a soundless whisper, 'He's on the balcony.'

I suppose we knew then. We knew our test had worked. We heard him walk along, picking his way, treading cautiously, as if this nineteenth-century walkway would disintegrate when obliged to carry twelve stone of twentieth-century humanity. He walked a little way to the right, then back and a little way to the left. Law-abiding he might not be but in the past he had been. This was a man who would baulk at trespassing on his neighbour's property even when he had seen three desperate villains attempting to break in. He gave another grunt as he climbed back into the room. The window rattled and closed with a bang.

'Isn't this going to make it harder for us to show ourselves to them when we do?'

I asked this after we'd gone down the scaffolding and were walking back along the street. To our surprise Wim was still with us. I always thought there was something incongruous about seeing him at ground level, though that was where I had first seen him. He turned to me.

'I shan't be there. You'll do it alone.'

'Is that why you won't be there? Because you think it was you who principally scared them?'

Wim first yawned, then smiled. 'Not really, Clo. I'm not interested.'

I was still on the alert for police sirens, knowing too that the three of us, with our dirt-smeared faces and grubby clothes, would be prime targets for the police to stop and question, to ask what we were doing out at that hour and where were we going. But there were no sirens and no police. I hoped that the three in Flat 4E were in bed and asleep, no longer frightened, but somehow I doubted that. We climbed the stairs at 15 Russia Road, I especially feeling weary after my hard day's work in the Houghtons' garden.

'We know it's them now,' I said.

'We know it's them.'

Silver went to make us tea while I washed my hands and face. Wim went into the bathroom immediately after me and emerged with his long sheepskin coat covering his nakedness. He disappeared into Liv's room, closing the door behind him. Silver looked at me and put up his eyebrows.

'It makes a change for him to go to *her*.'

'Yes, but where's Jonny?'

'Gone for ever, maybe. I guess he's found someone else. Or some scam that's more important than sex.'

Owing to my great tiredness, it was the next day before I asked Silver what we were going to do now we knew the occupants of 4E were who we thought they were.

'Go and look after them,' he said.

But not that day. The rain was torrential, pouring down in relentless straight rods. It was too wet to venture out and go to the launderette. Instead I went downstairs and chatted to Beryl while she pursued her pointless task of dusting rooms no one had occupied for weeks and no one else would enter for months. The 'new girl' had moved into old Mrs Fisherton's and it was her belief we should soon see 'Mrs' moving out.

'D'you mean she's Max's *girlfriend*?'

'He's always down there, love,' said Beryl, 'and I'll tell you something else. His side of the bed's not been slept in this past week. You can always tell. It's a king-size and his side's all straight and smooth. His hairs used to be all over the pillow, handfuls of white hairs, reminds me of a sheepdog we had when my old man was still alive, always shedding, that dog was, but there's no hairs there now. He's doing his moulting down in the basement.'

'A bit tough on Selina, isn't it?'

'If she'd any self-respect she wouldn't put up with it,' said Beryl and then the doorbell rang.

She went to answer it – 'to save poor Mr Silver's legs' – and let in Håkan Almquist.

Liv's father had been in London for nearly a fortnight. It must have cost him a fortune even at the not very luxurious hotel in Elgin Avenue. But his motive for staying seemed only partly his concern for his daughter's welfare. It was true that he called at 15 Russia Road every day and while he was there harangued and scolded Liv, but he never stayed long and, according to her, spent the rest of his time at drinking clubs, pubs and dubious places in Soho. All his life, in Kiruna, he had been a quiet, respectable, upright sort of man, devoted to his family and hardly ever having a day off work. This was his annual holiday he was taking, though the original intention of himself and Liv's mother had been to spend it on Gotland and Bornholm. It was twenty years since he had been to London and it had apparently gone to his head. Apart from those daily hectoring visits, he seemed to have forgotten why he had come in the first place. If London was such an attractive holiday place, Liv's mother could have joined him, for she too was taking her annual leave. As far as I know no one suggested this and perhaps Håkan Almquist, breaking out and letting rip at last, felt her presence might have interfered with his pleasures.

That rainy morning he arrived carrying a large and rather beautiful umbrella, the silk on its steeply domed frame printed with a picture of the Basin of St Mark's in Venice, all done in glorious colours on a deep blue background. He shook it out in the hall, splashing walls and carpet and leaving the mess for Beryl to clear up. He also carried or wore, as usual, one of those smallish backpack bags that today are fashionable for women but which at that time I had never seen on the back of man or woman. I went ahead of him upstairs with the intention of alerting Liv before he got there in case she was still in bed with Wim, though it was past eleven. But Wim was nowhere to be seen and she was up and about, far more brisk and cheerful than usual, bathed and dressed, her hair newly washed and looking its shining blonde best.

Instead of showing her usual sullenness, she greeted her father with enthusiasm and broke at once into rapid Swedish. He, frowning in a schoolmasterish way, reproved her for the 'unpoliteness' of speaking in what was to me a foreign language, but she only laughed. I knew what she was saying, anyway. She was talking about handing the money over to him. I observed his look of wonder, then calculation. Liv said, 'Come with me,' and took my arm.

We went into the bedroom. She lifted up a corner of the carpet and one of the boards underneath it. Her excavations with an unsuitable tool had made a mess of that floor. A package was underneath, wadded and wrapped in cling-film. I thought of the curious existence those notes had had since they were so carelessly and prodigally handed over by James or Claudia, first living in a chocolate tin in a bedroom cupboard, then travelling everywhere with Liv in a money belt, later packed between a television set and a video, hidden by me below ground in a table napkin drawer, parcelled up in food wrap and buried under floorboards, finally – or would it be finally? – handed over into the safe keeping of a presumably responsible person.

Håkan Almquist took the package in silence, turned it over and back again, unharnessed himself from his backpack, opened one of its many flaps and put the money inside. He seemed to have forgotten all about 'unpoliteness', for more rapid interchanges in Swedish took place. Liv told me afterwards he was once more urging her to come back with him while she was telling him that she would, she soon would, but she had to get herself used to going down to ground level and then to the ultimate bugbear, the street. To that end she went downstairs with him, I following because I was afraid she might have some nervous crisis the further she descended and I feared Håkan Almquist would do nothing to help if she did.

He told her, in English, I suppose for my benefit, and in a gloomy tone, that he'd go back to Sweden the next day. I don't know whether his reluctance stemmed from returning without her, facing his wife after his long absence or leaving the pubs and pleasures of London. In the hall he kissed Liv austerely on both cheeks and shook hands with me. He seemed to regard me as some kind of stabilizing influence on her, in which regard he could hardly have been more wrong.

The front door was opened, the rain had almost stopped and greyish damp air came in. Liv turned pale. She shrank back from the airy void where the door had been as if some threatening thug stood on the step. I closed it quickly. We went into the Silvermans' living room, newly dusted and vacuumed by Beryl, and watched the bearer of Liv's hoard make his way through the drizzle across Russia Road in the Torrington Gardens direction. A taxi with its light on appeared from Castlemaine Road, cruising slowly. I expected him to take it but he let it pass him and turned towards the roundabout and Elgin Avenue.

'He will not spend his money on a cab,' said Liv, speaking, it seemed, from experience.

I congratulated her on her fortitude in being able to stand there at ground level and contemplate the street. She nodded, her expression still dismal.

'I am a brave woman. Perhaps you did not know this. I am working to overcome my handicap.'

'That's good,' I said.

'But always I am thinking, Clodagh, what will I do now if Claudia and James come and ask for their money? Now my papa, my daddy, has it. This is not easy.'

Back at Silver's I phoned my parents, then Guy Wharton. It was weeks since I had spoken to him or heard from him, not surprising since I had moved out of 19 Russia Road and left no forwarding address. There was no reply and he had switched off his answering machine.

This wasn't one of my days at the Houghtons'. When the rain had lifted and a weak sun come out, Silver and I did something very unusual for us. We went down to the pub, the Prince Alfred, and had beer and sandwiches, and then we walked along the canal from the St John's Wood side of the Maida Hill Tunnel. Passing through Regent's Park, we saw a zoo keeper with a lynx on a lead. It was more like a dog than a cat, trotting along and sniffing at every tree trunk. I recorded its appearance in my diary that evening along with all the experiences of the day and the day before, because it was once more too wet for roof-climbing. Rain descended in torrents, streaming down the windows and rattling on the slates. I wrote and read what I had written and asked Silver for a history of the canal and he told me how the coming of the railways had made this once busy commercial waterway into no more than a route for pleasure traffic. Then we talked about the denizens of 4E. They would never let us in, Silver said. We must enter the room by the window and sit there quietly, waiting for them to come in, and then assure them of our good intentions. But I said they would be too frightened and there must be another way.

All the time I had been writing, Silver had been reading and, while we talked, Liv had been going into our bedroom to use the phone and call the hotel where her father was staying. She must have done it five times and by then it was past eleven at night. Wim came in at the window off the wet roof and sat with us, drinking wine, a rare departure for him. I could see a lot of her weight of care fall from Liv's shoulders at the sight of him. She was suddenly lighter and prettier and much happier. If he drank wine, he must intend not to go back on the roofs. Therefore he'd stay here and sleep with her.

But she still needed to speak to her father. To check on the money. Had he put it in the hotel safe? Surely he hadn't carried it down to the West End with him? Was he there now? She could hardly believe it, not at almost midnight. His flight was due to leave before nine in the morning, which meant he'd have to leave for Heathrow at seven. He had always been an early riser and early to bed. What had come over him? What had London done to him?

Liv phoned for the last time at exactly midnight. The night receptionist at the hotel told her Mr Almquist wasn't in his room. The hotel bar was closed. When had he last been seen? The receptionist knew nothing about it. He'd only come on at eight. Liv asked if he had put anything into the hotel safe, for the place wasn't of the standard to have private safes in rooms, but the receptionist said in a shocked tone that he was in no position to tell her things like that over the phone.

Liv came out of that room looking thoughtful, but when Wim beckoned to her she went to him as a needle goes to a magnet and I saw that her arms and hands were faintly trembling. He took her on his knee and held his wineglass to her lips.

21

I've spent the day at a dolls' museum in Hampstead, rewiring one of its prize exhibits, a doll's house valued at £12,000. It's a perfect facsimile in miniature of a Victorian Gothic mansion, three storeys high and with pitched roofs and castellated turrets. It was made in the twenties so had electric light installed, which the museum's curator had decided needed renewing. Driving home up Downshire Hill from South End Green after completing this enjoyable and peaceful task, I saw Håkan Almquist and his wife. Truth to tell, I had purposely gone that way when South End Road and Fleet Road might have been the better option, in the hope of catching a glimpse of Liv or even of Angus Clarkson himself, it being seven by then. What Liv had become from what she had been exercised a kind of fascination over me. It seemed such an unlikely success story, if you measure success in those terms. But I didn't see Liv or her husband. I saw her parents.

They were in the front garden of her extravagant house, apparently waiting for something or someone. I pulled in a few yards up and on the opposite side. Håkan Almquist looked just the same as when I had last seen him and he still carried his little bag strapped to his back, perhaps even the same little bag into which he had placed Liv's package that day eleven years ago. He was dressed in the kind of casual clothes Scandinavians wear on holiday, even when that holiday is in a city, jeans and open-necked shirt, anorak and walking boots. His wife wore the same sort of gear and looked the same, the only difference between them being that her hair, though short, wasn't crew cut and her anorak was blue not green. The front door opened and the au pair came out with the two children, retreating immediately as if glad to see the back of all four and shutting the door rather loudly. Almost simultaneously a taxi drew up outside and they got into it, propelling the children in front of them, the little girl yelling in protest. I wondered where they were going. To some theatre or cinema? It was too late for Madame Tussaud's or the zoo. This, at any rate, was one cab Liv's father hadn't minded spending money on. But perhaps Mr Clarkson paid.

Parents notoriously put aside all resentment and reproaches when their children succeed in life. Or succeed according to their judgement criteria. I think mine would have respected me more if my life had followed Liv's course, if I had found a rich husband and had a boy and a girl, instead of what Dad called my 'messing about with wires and fuse-boxes'. Still, they're proud of me now, if in a grudging and puzzled kind of way ('But, *why*, dear? How did you ever come to want to do such a thing?') just as Liv's parents would have become proud of her and probably without such reservations.

I asked myself how she had managed to prevent those parents from revealing, by a chance remark, the kind of life she led and company she kept while living at 15 Russia Road. Had she bought their silence as she had tried to buy mine? I imagined them subjected to a daily nagging, constant adjurations from Liv, while Angus Clarkson was off stockbroking or entrepreneur-ing, not to dare say a word, not even to hint at events of that past time.

On the other hand, Håkan Almquist knew very little about what went on, despite his daily visits. He had met Jonny and had good cause to remember him. But would he particularly link him to Liv? And the chances were that he had never recovered his lost memory. To Liv's great relief, surely, he might retain only a confused recollection of that fortnight in London on his own, a trip which had started with the aim of fetching his daughter back to Kiruna, turned into a living-it-up he might prefer to forget, and ended in a hospital bed.

That night eleven years ago, when Liv failed to get hold of him at the hotel, we were none of us particularly concerned about his fate. No doubt he had left the money in his room or in the hotel safe and was even at that moment enjoying himself at Stringfellow's or some such place. The fact that he had to make an early start the next day counted for nothing. He could sleep on the plane. Liv said that sounded very unlike *Far*, but as Silver put it, did fun and games in Soho sound like *Far*?

Her anxiety wasn't enough to wake her early the next morning. Wim came out of the bedroom before she did and set about cooking eggs and bacon for himself and me and Silver. When Liv finally emerged at about ten she began at once on her phobia therapy, for which she required my support, creeping down the stairs with me ahead of her to shield her view of what lay below. Silver said it reminded him of a girl he had once seen on an underground escalator being escorted down this phobic staircase by a railway official. Only she had had another one behind her as well. I, of course, had only one tube memory to revert to, but having an irrational fear myself, I could understand Liv's.

The rain had cleared and it was a fine misty morning. I asked her if going down into the hall on the ground floor would be sufficient for today or would she like the front door opened? She shook her head vigorously, so I took her into the living room as I had done the day before and raised one of the windows a couple of inches. Whether it was the feel of the air coming in or the sight of Russia Road from this level which reminded her – how could she have forgotten, even temporarily? – I don't know, but she suddenly exclaimed that she must phone the hotel, she must find out if her father had come back the night before.

Perhaps because she refused, from some obscure paranoid motive connected with James and Claudia, to tell the receptionist she was Håkan Almquist's daughter and had consistently refused to do so the night before, he would tell her nothing beyond the fact that Mr Almquist was not in the hotel at that moment. She asked if he had caught his flight and was told they were in no position to tell her. Liv looked thoughtful. She nodded her head once or twice, then said to me, 'You must go there and find what is happening.' She seemed to realize that this was rude even by her standards and flushed a deep mottled red. 'Please you will go, please. You know that I cannot, I cannot go in the street.'

It was Silver who went to the hotel. He spoke to the manager. No one knew if Håkan Almquist had returned to the hotel in the night. The night receptionist had no memory of seeing him but this man was not behind his desk for every minute of every hour.

'He's got to go out for a pee sometimes, hasn't he?' the manager said.

The key to Room 12 was missing from its hook but Mr Almquist was one of those who carried his room key about with him instead of handing it in. They had made the key fobs as heavy as they reasonably could, the manager said bitterly, but that never deterred these people. He had never been able to understand what was so fascinating about a key with a great lump of metal hanging from it that you had to carry it about with you wherever you went. Silver went home and told Liv she ought to phone the police. Or he'd do it if she liked. This brought on a storm of raving and tears and in the end he had to promise to do nothing.

None of us, that is Wim, Silver and I, knew what Håkan Almquist was really like. All we had to go on was visits from a man who mostly spoke in an incomprehensible foreign language and the testimony of his daughter who described him as dull, staid and respectable, and his London behaviour as exceptional. But Liv was an unreliable person and perhaps all this was exaggerated or outright untruths. So Silver and I concluded when we discussed it in private in our bedroom. Far from being the well-conducted clean-living mining engineer we had been led to believe he was, he might be exactly the kind of man who would defraud his daughter of a large sum of money and, once it was in his possession, abscond, leaving his hotel bill unpaid. But perhaps what we really wanted was to be rid of it all, not have this added complication in our lives, so that we could concentrate on the occupants of 4E.

A fine hot summer's day was in the making. The sun began to burn the mist away. Leaning out of the window, I could feel the heat on my skin, already intense. We'd go to 4E before dark, Silver said, and while Jason was still up. And we'd take presents with us as a token of our good faith and friendliness, things they probably never got, a newspaper maybe and a bottle of wine and something for the boy. Chocolate, Wim said, which seemed a good idea.

I was due at the Houghtons' at midday. It was really too hot for gardening, with a dangerous heat the English are unaccustomed to. I put on a cotton hat, which was a discard of Silver's father, and sun cream on my face and arms and got down to dead-heading, cutting back and weeding. I don't know if you have ever tried clearing a nettle plantation. It's not a pleasant task in the heat, for nettles have root systems like a close-woven fishing net, yellow and tough. If you leave a bit behind the whole ramification grows again and with remarkable speed. Mrs Houghton brought me a cup of tea and Mr Houghton a glass of Perrier and both admired what I had done, saying

247

they didn't know how they had got on without me, something that is always gratifying to hear. It was just after six when I got home and learnt what had happened in my absence.

Liv greeted me calmly enough but with staring eyes, and told me how she had twice tried to phone her mother in Kiruna and twice got the answering machine. She claimed to have been ignorant of the fact that her parents had one. The message she had left said only that it was Liv calling from London. Silver had tried to persuade her to go to the hotel herself, though he knew before he began that this was hopeless. All he had accomplished was to get her to stand on our front doorstep. He had taken her downstairs again, opened the front door and put the catch on. Then he had very gradually opened it wider with her standing beside him. Trembling all over, he said. It was relatively cool inside the hall. As the door came open waves of heat seemed to roll in and settle on their arms and faces. This was rather comforting to Liv, apparently, and enabled her to step over the threshold. She stood at the top of the steps under the porch overhang, where she followed Silver's instructions and breathed deeply. She clung to his arm, tottering as if the damage done to her was in her bones rather than her mind. Sweat streamed off her, actually dripping from her face and making damp patches on her clothes, and he could smell her, an oniony, salty scent like frying.

No cars went by. In the flats opposite windows were wide open and music drifting out, something quite unusual in Russia Road. But the weather was unusual, even for that warm summer. The sight of a man riding past on a bike set Liv shaking again. Silver suggested she walk down two steps but she was adamant she had done enough. He shepherded her upstairs again, if that's the word, for shepherds don't actually hold on to their sheep and manhandle them, which is what he had to do if she wasn't to collapse on the stairs and go into one of her foetal positions. Once back in his flat he made her have a bath, actually running the water for her. Being a nurse must be like that, he said to me, only nurses do it all the time and he had only had one afternoon of it.

It would be good for her to come out with us that night, he said. She hadn't even been up on the roofs for weeks.

'She could get the same attitude to the roofs as she has to the ground level,' he said. 'It could get to be a phobia of any sort of outside.'

I asked him what he thought had happened to Håkan Almquist. 'Gone off with someone he met while he was here on his own,' he said. 'Woman or man, I don't know. The temptation of that money was too much for him. Liv doesn't know her dad as well as she thinks she does. Maybe we don't any of us really know our parents. After all, they don't know *us*. But don't worry. He'll turn up.'

After we'd eaten some of Silver's bean soup (very unsuitable for the weather) and a not very successful lentil dish of my own with multi-grain bread, Liv attempted another phone call to her mother. She went into our bedroom and, this time, her mother still being away from home, left a long message. We could hear her but of course we couldn't understand. She translated for us.

'I am saying to her, *Far* has disappeared, he has stolen my money. I trust him and he is doing this terrible thing to me. All this I am telling her because she should know it. But she cannot do anything for me, for she is there and I am here. But she should know what he is doing to me.'

Silver sighed. 'Did you leave this number?'

'She is knowing it. Don't you remember *Mor* is phoning me here when Clodagh is *making* me tell them I live here?'

'Come on,' said Silver, 'we're going to make ourselves known to 4E Torrington Gardens.'

Liv demurred a bit. Her excuses were plainly just that, excuses. Her mother might call back, the hotel might phone to say the money had been found, she was too tired and ill with the worry of it. It looked as if Silver had been right in forecasting an extension of her agoraphobia to the roofs. But he really wanted her with us, not for her company, of which both of us were weary, but because presenting Andrew and Alison with a man and two women rather than a woman and two men would make them feel more secure and encourage them to trust us. He told Liv this and she seemed flattered. At any rate, she agreed to come.

I was rather pleased Wim was still absent. Present in my mind and constantly recurring was a picture of those two people clinging to each other at the sight of us. Alison's scream still rang in my ears. It was Wim who had done this, I believed, who had provoked this reaction, his startling face and physique, so attractive to Liv, his shaven head, his eyes and the black clothes he wore. And of course he had made the threatening gesture of breaking in. Even though it was he who had discovered them in the first place, we'd be better off without him.

The problem we hadn't thought of was how to get her on to the top of 4E without crossing the tarpaulin that covered the burnt area of roof. The only way was the one we intended to take, that is by way of the street and the scaffolding. But Liv, of course, wouldn't go down into the street. We all climbed out of Silver's window and followed our usual route. It was about nine, later than we had meant to be, but much time had been taken up in arguing with Liv and persuading her to come. The evening was warm, almost all light faded from the clear deep purple sky. Liv lit two candles and carried them along, one in each hand. Down below us lay a greenish-golden sea, the glow of street-lamps shimmering through spread plane leaves. There was no wind, not even the faintest chill in the air, and strangely no smell of exhaust or cooking or humanity, only the scent of lavender from one of the gardens down there, where they grew that pleasant herb to the exclusion of all else. We walked along inside the parapet and stopped when we reached the tarpaulin to survey what lay before us.

'I can walk across,' Liv said. 'I am not so big. I am not so many kilos.'

But Silver wouldn't let her. He had brought a torch which he shone down on to the front of the building below us. Each house had its own individual balcony, separate from next-door's, and the railing was not dumbells of stone but an ironwork trellis. Those of 18 and 22 had only been blackened by the fire, as the whole upper part of the façade had been, and looked structurally sound but the one in the middle, on 20, had been damaged by some other agency, the firemen's ladders perhaps. Those balconies were not intended for standing on or climbing over, nor used as repositories for heavy equipment, and this one was sagging from the wall, its floor actually split away from the main fabric and showing a wide crack.

We all dropped down on to the balcony, feeling our way gingerly and holding on to the lintels in the dormers. It was perhaps as well we did for when we got on to 20 the floor groaned and creaked under our weight, especially under Silver's. He wasn't heavy for his height but he was a lot heavier than Liv and me and when he took a step a piece of masonry broke loose under his tread and went clattering down into the front garden below.

Hastily we climbed back up again. By then we realized we were going to have to leave Liv behind. We went all the way back with her, using up more valuable time, and left her in the flat with the intention of once more phoning her mother, though by this time, in Sweden, it was almost eleven.

Silver had his doubts then whether we should abandon the whole venture until the next night but I dissuaded him and we set off once more, this time along the pavements. The final painting of the terrace in Peterborough Avenue had begun, there was quite a strong paint smell in the warm still air, and we wondered if perhaps we might make ourselves known at 4E only to have to abandon them through lack of access.

Though a light was on in the room we had decided must be Jason's, the flowers on the makeshift curtain showing up red and yellow against the gleaming green background, the living room was in darkness. Still, the window was open several inches at top and bottom and inside it was rather untidy, a newspaper lying on the floor, cups and a glass on the table, cushions in the two armchairs flattened and a pair of women's shoes on the rug in front of the fireplace, as if Alison had kicked them off and let them lie. If this had been Silver's place, it would have been quite normal for a room to be left like this overnight, indeed much worse than this, but we had had evidence of Alison's need to tidy up before she went to bed. She'd be back and probably Andrew would too.

Should we wait outside in silence, go away and come back, or do as we had done before and light cigarettes to attract their attention? Go in, said Silver, go in and be there waiting for them. It would be a shock but it would soon be over and better than letting them see us through the window again. We opened that window as far as we could, raising the inner sash until its top and bottom bars were parallel with the outer sash, and climbed inside. The air in there felt the same as outside, warm, still, but without the smell of paint. It was darker, though. Our eyes had to become accustomed to a different kind of darkness. A mirror hung above the fireplace and I turned my head away from it, afraid that if I looked into its shiny greyness I'd see not myself but someone else's face. We sat down each in an armchair and, leaning forward, I picked up Alison's shoes and set them side by side, their toes pointing towards the window. We looked at each other in total silence for a minute or two.

Silver got up and opened the door. Light came flooding in, light and voices. They were somewhere, talking. The words weren't distinguishable. He looked at me, looked away again, and spoke that phrase I've told you is what I say when I want to attract the attention of a customer whose name I don't know, though I didn't use it in those days and maybe never had used it.

'Are you there?'

He didn't call it or speak it very loudly, but in a quiet gentle manner that no one who wasn't completely paranoid and terrified would take as threatening. There was silence. The voices that had been in conversation were stilled. Silver pressed the switch by the door and I stood up, blinking at the flood of light.

Everything happened very quickly after that. I didn't see him come, I didn't even hear him, but he was upon Silver before either of us could move or make a sound. He leapt on him out of the hallway. He threw his arms round his neck and flung him to the ground, scrambling on top of him and punching his head, screaming, 'I'll kill you, I'll kill you!'

22

We pulled him off, Alison and I. She tugged at him as much as I, she was as anguished and upset as I was. And suddenly, as we pinioned him and had to let him go because he was too strong for us, Silver leapt up from the floor in a single bound and flew at Andrew, grabbing him by the throat. My Silver, that I'd always thought of as gentle and easy-going. They fought and sprang apart, confronting each other, snarling like dogs. I shouted out that we were friends. I roared at them, I could have been heard in Swiss Cottage, I yelled that we sympathized, we'd come to help.

'By breaking in?' Alison cried on a bitter note.

'We never broke anything,' I said, and then I saw the piece of porcelain Silver and Andrew had knocked on to the floor while they were fighting. It had been a china bird, a bullfinch with grey wings and soft pink breast, but its head was broken off and its delicate feet were shattered. I picked up the pieces and held them in my hand.

Alison looked at its fellows on the shelf above a radiator, a wren, a greenfinch and a thrush. She made a deprecating gesture with her right hand. 'I brought them with me when I came here. They made it home. Well, no, they helped to make it home.'

The men had stopped. The fighting was over. Andrew's neck was bruised red and purple as if someone had tried to strangle him and Silver's face, his poor pale skin, was a mess of blood and dirt, his left eye the colour of raw liver and swelling fast.

'I suppose it's all over,' Andrew said. He sat down in the red armchair and laid his head back and closed his eyes. 'You'll have told the police or the social services. Whatever. They'll be here soon.' He gave a sigh, the like of which I'd never heard before and have never heard since, it was so heavy and profound, a great exhalation of breath, loud and rasping. 'It was a good try. It lasted six months. It's over now.' He turned on Silver, then on me, vindictive looks. 'I hope you're pleased with yourselves.'

Alison said, before the utterance of that word 'yourselves', 'Would you like a drink? You may as well. I want one. We've been through enough. We've one last bottle of wine.'

'What's that called?' Andrew looked at her, casting up his eyes. 'Heaping coals of fire on one's enemies' heads?'

'I'd like a wash,' said Silver, and he went out to find a bathroom. No one tried to stop him. Somewhere in the flat a clock chimed eleven. Outside in the street, as if on cue, the fire engine (or police cars or ambulance) sirens began to howl. Andrew went over to the window and stood there as if giving himself up.

'They aren't coming for you,' I said. 'We're not your enemies. We've come to help you. We thought we could do things for you.' I introduced myself, adding that we lived together. 'I'm Clodagh and he's Silver. We're on your side. And we haven't told anyone.'

It was plain, naturally, that Andrew didn't believe us. He nodded, he stared at me, saying nothing. Alison came back with the wine, already opened, and four glasses on a tray. Before pouring it she went up to Andrew and sat on the arm of his chair. She did a strange unexpected thing – well, strange to do in company. She put her arm round his neck and kissed him full on the lips, an open-mouthed kiss, a kiss of passion, as if she was saying to him, this may be the last time, or the last time before things change so terribly that we shall become different people.

He responded, but less warmly. Perhaps he was embarrassed. I had a feeling that if it went on he would push her away. She drew away from him and got up. The wine was poured. As she filled the last glass, finishing the bottle, Silver came back, his face clean but covered with angry blotches. Suddenly the boy in the next room cried out, a piercing yell. It was the sound a two-year-old makes in fear, in a bad dream, but with the volume of which a child of eight is capable. Alison ran to him.

'He's quite disturbed and he doesn't sleep well,' Andrew said. He sounded very tired. 'He wants to be in his own home. He hates not being able to go out.' Lifting his glass, 'Cheers,' he said. 'Did you mean that? About being on our side?'

'Of course. Why not?'

'How did you find us?'

'Our friend saw you. He recognized you.'

'We go on roofs,' I said. 'That's what we do, it's our thing. We've watched you through the window. We didn't mean to frighten you.'

'Everything frightens us,' Andrew said.

Alison came back with Jason. She couldn't carry him, he was too heavy for her, but she held him close against her as he walked beside her, her arm round the boy's shoulders as she pressed his head against her waist. His face was stained with tears. He lifted big dark eyes to look at us, to stare aghast or fascinated, it was hard to tell. I thought then that we must have been the first people he had seen, apart from Andrew and Alison, for six months.

It was as if Alison read my mind. 'We see no one. We live here isolated. Andrew goes out sometimes, not often. He goes to buy food. We live out of tins.' She glanced at her wineglass. 'And bottles.'

Then Silver said it again, that we were friends, that we wanted to help them. They must trust us.

'But why? Why help us?'

'I suppose because we think you ought to have him. We don't like the rules. Isn't that enough? Trust us.'

'I trust no one,' Andrew said.

He took Jason on his knee. He drew him towards him and looked solemnly into his face. Everything those two did seemed ritualistic, studied, as if they believed they were doing it for the last time. Andrew gently eased Jason into his arms, letting the boy lean back into the crook of his elbow. Alison crossed the room and closed the window. Jason was quiet then, sleepy, content.

'We'll prove our – our good faith,' Silver said. 'We'll go now.' He finished his wine and, as if on cue, I too emptied my glass. 'You'll know we mean what we say when you hear nothing. We'll come back tomorrow, we'll come back at nine. Nine in the evening, I mean.' He stood up. I stood up and he put his arm round me, but he was still looking searchingly at the people he was talking to. 'If nothing has happened by then, and nothing will, when we come back you'll know we're friends. Right?'

Neither of them said anything. Jason had fallen asleep in his foster father's arms. We said, 'Good night.'

Still no one spoke. They watched us. Silver said, 'We'll replace your wine. We'll bring you lots of it.' And, characteristically, 'Don't worry, please don't.'

Silver opened the window. He pushed down the top sash and pushed up the bottom sash. We climbed out. We walked along the balcony. The light inside the window we'd come out of went off almost immediately, but though we waited a while and listened, no one shut the window.

'They've left it open,' Silver said, 'because they think nothing matters any more, they think this is the end of the world.'

The night was still warm. We went down into the street and walked home in an ecstasy of love and triumph. Upstairs, in the flat, all was still and silent, the living room empty, the windows wide open. Silver smiled at me, his face a mask of bruises, his cheeks skinned and scraped and his left eye like a boxer's after a fight when the other man gets disqualified. In spite of always saying not to worry, he was concerned about Liv and he opened her bedroom door very quietly to check she was all right. She and Wim lay side by side on the bed, the covers on the floor, their bodies gleaming with sweat in the half-dark.

We went back on to the roofs. It must have been by common consent, for no word was spoken. We took blankets with us and the pillows from our bed and slept up there under the stars. The blurred, vapour-cloaked stars. But first we made love and in spite of what Silver had said about limits, there were no limits. It was the one and only time on the roofs. We were awakened terribly early by the singing of birds that has become so much louder and richer in town gardens than in the sterile countryside. I watched the dawn come but poor Silver could hardly see out of his swollen eye.

We had nothing else to talk about. To Wim, to an uncaring, uninterested Liv, we poured out our news and our discoveries the next morning.

'I might come with you this evening,' Wim said.

Liv looked up. 'I can never come. I have my problem.'

'So you do,' said Silver. 'Time for therapy.'

And he took her downstairs and outside once more. I followed and together we walked her down two steps before she stopped, dug in her heels and refused to move. Curing her of her phobia, if that's what we were doing, was a slow process.

Her mother hadn't called her back and when she'd tried again, as soon as she'd got up, the answering machine was still on.

'Doesn't your mother work?' Silver asked her.

'She is still on her holidays. Remember she and my papa are going to Gotland, *was* going to Gotland, I am meaning, but he is coming here instead. Where is he? What shall I do?'

In the light of what we discovered later, I think Liv really was more concerned about her father than the money. Or was she most intent on giving an impression of concern? I said I'd call at the hotel on my way to work at the Houghtons' but first I wanted to write my diary. The difficulty was always in finding privacy. Silver alone left me undisturbed while I was writing. I usually went into our bedroom and closed the door, but that morning Liv kept coming in to make more attempts to reach her mother. The answering-machine tape would soon be used up, I thought, for every time the unmistakable voice of Håkan Almquist came loudly out of the receiver and the long beep sounded, she left a message. All at Silver's expense too.

'Are you sure she still has this number?' I said when she'd made the fifth call.

'You are right, Clodagh. It is possible she is losing it. I will give it.' And she made a sixth call.

Soon after that I heard a shrill scream from the living room. It was hard to tell whether it was uttered in pain or pleasure but there was no doubt it was Liv's scream. Her father's come, I thought, he's come back from wherever he's been and, please God, he's got the money. But it wasn't Håkan Almquist, it was Jonny.

'The bad penny is back,' he said when he saw me.

'Why aren't you at the car park?'

'Listen to her. You'd think she was a schoolteacher.' He curled back his upper lip. '"Why aren't you at the car park?"' He used a shrill affected voice, not much like mine, I hope. 'I'll tell you why, Miss Brown. I'm not proud. I'm not at the car park because I've resigned. I've left. Asked for my cards. Does that satisfy you?'

Instead of the top half of a suit, he wore a black leather jacket, jeans into which someone had ironed creases – highly unacceptable to Silver and me, to whom creases in jeans were in as bad taste as high heels with trousers would have been to my mother – and black suede designer trainers. Wim, who'd seldom taken much notice of him, stared in fascination and only with difficulty took away his eyes. As to Liv, she had retreated to the end of the sofa and her English–Swedish dictionary.

When I left, Silver walked part of the way with me. He was going to shop for wine, biscuits, crisps and bananas, further evidence to 4E of our good faith. 'I won't come to the hotel,' he said. 'They know me. But you could say you're Almquist's daughter.'

'I'm not Swedish.'

'They won't think about that. They'll tell you more if you say he's your father.'

He was right. I went into an office and talked to the manager. Håkan Almquist had never returned. The previous afternoon they had cleared his things out of his room and packed his suitcase. It was currently in a side room. I could see it if I liked. He showed me a not very large blue Revelation case.

'Weren't there any other bags?' I asked, thinking of the black leather backpack.

'Only this. All his things went into it. Oh, and we have his passport.'

At that time I had never stayed in an hotel on my own, I had scarcely stayed in an hotel at all and certainly not abroad. I didn't know if this was standard practice on the part of an hotel, to retain a foreign guest's passport. The manager explained.

'We don't usually hang on to passports. Of course, we collect them and give them back to the guest next day. Your dad –' I had to think who he meant – 'asked us to hold on to his. He seemed to think it was safer with us.'

This document was shown to me. It wasn't helpful. As usual with passports, the photograph was unrecognizable. 'May I look in the suitcase?'

He shrugged. It was all the same to him. I lifted the somewhat scuffed canvas lid. I was looking, of course, for the money. Mr Almquist's clothes held little interest for me. I'd have been very surprised to find £2,000 in notes lying between the jeans and the sweatshirts. Suddenly I thought of his hotel bill. I didn't want to ask about it in case the manager expected me to pay it. That was what might come of saying I was his daughter. But I did ask.

'We've an imprint of his credit card. You needn't worry about that.'

After this I went to the Houghtons'. It was going to be as hot as the day before. I pulled out more nettle root systems, I grubbed up more groundsel and docks with tap roots eight inches long. Mrs Houghton brought me out a long cold drink whose principal ingredients, she said, were lemongrass and ginger. I didn't expect Silver to come round and fetch me but as I was putting the tools away he appeared, walking down the path with Mrs Houghton.

'Such a nice boy,' she said the next day. 'Is he your fiancé?'

I couldn't answer that, for I didn't know what was requisite and what had to happen before a betrothal was finalized. Mrs Houghton looked sympathetically at the bruises on his face and his black eye, now quite closed.

'Have you been in a fight?' she asked in the sort of tone that indicates the speaker is joking. Silver said that was exactly right, though it wasn't of his making, and Mrs Houghton, still disbelieving but amused, fetched arnica – whatever that may be – and dabbed it on his bruises.

At home nothing more had been heard of or about Mr Almquist. Silver called it the Case of the Disappearing Swede, which he said sounded like the title of a Sherlock Holmes story. As we walked along I told him about the suitcase and the passport.

'That means he can't have left the country.'

'He'll have to come back for his passport sometime,' I said, 'and then I suppose everything will be explained.'

When we saw Andrew leaning out of the window waiting for us, expecting us, we both felt things would be all right now. For him and Alison and Jason everything was changing for the better. We set out our wine bottles on the table, the chocolate finger biscuits, the crystallized fruits, the bananas and the Battenberg cake. Jason, who had been kept up to meet us, though wearing the teddy-bear pyjamas ready for bed, saw the bananas and reached for one, hesitating and looking at Alison as he remembered he had to say please.

'Of course you can!' she said. 'They're for you. Our new friends brought them for you.'

That made Andrew frown. Hardly a mark, souvenir of the fight, showed on his dark skin. He might have been waiting for us and been quite welcoming when we arrived, but he hadn't yet reached the stage of calling us friends.

'Why are you doing this?' he said.

Why were we? I'm not sure if I could have answered. 'I suppose because we think you're right and the social services are wrong,' Silver said, and then, changing the subject, 'Who's Robinson?'

For a moment they seemed not to know what he meant. Then Andrew said, 'Ah, yes, Robinson. Just someone we know, someone who presumably feels as you do. That we're in the right and they're not. Would you say that was so, Alison?'

'He's a dear friend who lent us this flat for as long as we want it. He owns the house but he's hardly ever here. He's a widower and he's mostly in the south of France.'

'And how long will you want it?' Silver asked.

She looked distressed. 'I don't know. We've got some ideas – would you like to see over the flat?'

Jason finished his banana and skipped on ahead. The flat was his little world, the only one he had now, and he knew every inch of it. As well as the living room there were three bedrooms, a bathroom and quite a large kitchen. From the bedroom that was Andrew and Alison's you could look down on to a neglected garden, worse than the Houghtons' before I started. Elders and buddleias, the weed trees of inner London, grew where once there had been flowerbeds and a field of hay where once had been a lawn.

'Who lives underneath you?' I asked Alison.

'No one in the flat immediately below. That's for Louis Robinson's use when he's here. An elderly couple on the two floors below that, and on the ground floor a young man. The basement's used as a store for some of Louis's furniture.'

The flat had the unmistakable look of a place in which transients have lived, no one having any interest in how it was decorated or furnished, scarcely noticing these things. Not that it was particularly shabby, the pale fawn carpet looked quite new, you could see that Louis Robinson was no slum landlord, but that everything was bland and bleak, the predominant colours cream and buff and that fawn, the furniture the sort that appears in a chain store's autumn sale. In recent years I have seen pictures like the ones on those walls in motel bedrooms, photographs of famous buildings, St Paul's, the Arc de Triomphe, the Empire State, the Audubon bird prints, and of course the tiger in the rain forest, all in frames that looked like steel but were probably aluminium.

Plainly Alison had added touches of her own. It was a home-making effort which must have been restricted by how much they could bring with them and carry up those stairs. Most of the improvements, I guessed, had taken place in Jason's room. This small area, perhaps eight feet by ten, he showed me with great pride, the bookshelves, his own paintings on the walls and his newspaper and magazine cut-outs pinned to a cork board. He had rather a small box for his rather small toys, miniature cars and trucks mostly. Bigger things wouldn't have been portable. Silver took a particular interest in the ship in a bottle, which stood on the top shelf, studying it with his good eye. The bottle was of pale blue glass and the ship a three-masted schooner with a painted hull and yellow sails.

'It was mine,' Alison said. 'It was given to me for my sixth birthday and I was terribly disappointed because I wasn't allowed to play with it. I got to like it later on.'

'I'm not allowed to play with it,' said Jason, but not as if this prohibition much bothered him. 'I'm only allowed to look.'

'When you're older you'll find there's plenty that comes into that category,' said Andrew and I decided that I didn't like him much. He'd spoken in that tone some men use for certain kinds of sexual innuendo, wry, worldly wise, cynical. He had looked at me appraisingly and as if we were entering into a conspiracy.

We went back into the living room. Silver stopped Alison opening the wine. It was for them exclusively. Jason said good night to us, coming up first to Silver to say the words gravely, then to me. He hesitated as I bent towards him, then kissed my cheek.

'I should be so lucky.' Andrew cast up his eyes in mock envy. Then, before I could say anything, though I had no words ready, he took Jason off to bed.

There was silence. Silver broke it by asking Alison how long they had been there. It was really an invitation to tell us the circumstances of their flight, and this was how she took it. She sighed. But first she said, 'I think we can trust you, but of course I don't know. You may be just very clever actors. You may be criminals. For all I know, because we hardly ever see a newspaper, there may be a reward offered to whoever finds us and you may be after that. But I reason this way, if you are, you'll give us up and our story will all come out, while if you're not, you're the best thing that's happened to us since Louis let us have this place. Either way it makes no difference if I tell you what happened or if I don't. So I shall.'

She looked from one to the other of us and nodded. 'When they said we'd have to give Jason up they fixed a date for when they'd come and fetch him. All this has been in the papers, I think, only the papers didn't always get it right. Anyway, what do I know about the papers? There's not much of it on television, though I expect there would be if we were caught. They made this date and we decided we'd have to get out two days before. By then we'd stopped protesting, not because we'd given up, far from it, but we knew that if we made public protests our – well, our intention to escape would be known. The bank, for instance, would have been suspicious when we drew out everything we had. Maybe the building society would when we sold our shares. So we didn't tell anyone except Gordon, my half-brother. He lives a long way away, in Exeter. I wasn't sure I could trust my half-sister but I know I could trust him. I told him everything and up to a point we've kept in touch. We told the woman who cleans for us we'd be away three months but not why or where and we paid her in advance for that, so no doubt she's stopped coming.'

'According to the paper,' I said, 'she's still going into your house to keep an eye on things.'

'Bless her. She's got a kind heart. We left everything, nearly all our possessions, our books, our clothes. We left our car behind. We just walked out of our jobs, we didn't resign, we didn't give the requisite notice. That too would have attracted attention to us.'

'One thing,' Silver said. 'You may not know this. Andrew's father died.'

She put up her hand to her mouth, took it away in a fist. 'Oh, no, Oh God. You mustn't tell him, I must tell him.'

'We won't say a word.'

'They were very close. He was an only child and his mother died years ago. He'll take it very hard. It'll be worse because he wasn't there. I wonder if he asked for him – oh, I hope it didn't break his heart Andrew not being there. What did he die of?'

'The paper didn't say.'

262

She was silent for a moment, a pause in time during which Andrew came back. She lifted her head and gave him too bright a smile. 'I'm telling them about our great escape.'

He nodded, if not very enthusiastically, but he evidently felt the same as Alison. Revealing everything to us would make no difference to the final outcome.

'I was saying how we left everything behind and how we'd only told Gordon and, up to a point, our cleaner. We knew someone who had a caravan on a site near Orford in Suffolk, we'd been there in the summer and we still had the key. We reasoned that no one would be there in February and we were right.'

But the bitter cold of that North Sea coast in winter had been too much for them, that and the fear that the very unlikelihood of anyone's wishing to live in a holiday caravan at that season and in that weather would draw attention to them. They had already aroused the suspicions of the caretaker who made the rounds of the place a couple of times a week. Ironically, among all the false sightings by people with active imaginations, this man who had had a true sighting and who probably knew it told no one. They went by bus, a train, a tube train, another train and another bus to a place near Guildford and into an hotel. All this, of course, was an adventure to Jason. The hotel was a place people went to to play golf. In the winter the few guests played bridge. Andrew, who had been a keen bridge player some years before, joined in, mainly not to draw attention to himself. He had shaved off his beard and Alison had managed to buy a brunette wig in Ipswich from a shop near the station while they had an hour-long wait for the London train. Only Jason eluded disguise and this frightened them.

The hotel was comfortable and warm, the food good, and no one seemed suspicious. But it was too expensive. They had no income now, only capital to live on. They moved into a cheaper place, a B and B in Bognor Regis, one of the few open in winter. By this time it was the beginning of March. Alison kept in touch with her half-brother by phone. When she and Andrew were thinking of moving on again, Jason attracting too much attention from the woman who ran the B and B – she was always asking about him, where did he come from, he couldn't be their child with that colouring, did he come from 'one of those places out East' – Alison got a letter from Gordon. He had spoken to Louis Robinson about their plight, pretty sure he could trust him, but saying nothing of their whereabouts or the name they were using.

'OK, but who is Louis Robinson?' Silver asked. 'An old family friend or something?'

'His wife and my mother were at school together, it goes that far back. She died and he went to live in the house they had in France. He's quite old, about seventy. This house is where they used to live.'

Louis Robinson had been just about to leave Cannes for London when Gordon spoke to him. They arranged to meet and did so two days later. Louis offered Alison and Andrew this flat rent-free for as long as they wanted it.

'He apologized for its being on the top floor,' Alison said. 'We were so grateful we didn't care about things like that, we were just so happy to have a place of our own.'

Andrew raised his eyebrows. 'It hasn't been the most convenient option, though, has it? I mean, if he'd let us have the lower-ground floor, we'd have had the use of the garden for Jason. I suppose Robinson didn't want the hassle of moving his furniture out.'

Alison seemed a bit embarrassed by this show of ingratitude. 'We came here in March, a month after we left our own house. We've never seen Louis, he went back to France, and we've never seen the old people, I think they lead a very quiet life. Andrew's seen the man on the ground floor, but he's lucky, people don't recognize him without his beard.'

Silver told her about the picture in the paper, the identikit, if that's what it's called, which showed a very passable likeness of Andrew as he now was.

'Maybe I should grow my beard again and fool them. After all, I've all the time in the world and I hardly ever go out. I won't be able to go out at all now and no doubt we'll starve to death.'

We'd shop for them, we said. We'd do their shopping, get anything they wanted and bring it in somehow. That reminded Andrew, he said, that he owed us for the wine and the chocolate and stuff, but Silver said that was a present, a token of goodwill. We'd get supplies for them tomorrow and they could pay us when we brought them. He told Alison to make a list, and while she was doing this, asked what their plans were for the future.

'You can't stay here for ever.'

'We know that. For one thing, Jason will have to go to school. At present we teach him ourselves. Alison's a trained teacher and I've got a BEd. But he needs friends, people his own age. He needs to be in the open air and at the moment he never is.'

'What we'd like,' said Alison, handing Silver her shopping list, 'is to go and live abroad. My father's in Australia, in a suburb of Sydney. He was a few years younger than my mother, he's only sixty-five now. They were divorced when I was twelve but we've written to each other, I've seen him every time he's been over here, I'd like to see him again. I'd like to live near him. But we can't get out of this country.'

'We've very little money left,' said Andrew. 'We can't sell our house without its being known where we are. If we went I'd want to take *my* father with us, he's getting on now and he's not a well man.'

I dared not look at Alison. Silver dared not look at me. We obviously weren't going to get any further with settling their future, so we said it was time for us to go. Andrew opened the window for us and, leaning out after we'd climbed on to the balcony, said he still wasn't sure about us, he couldn't understand our altruism, it wasn't what he was used to.

'How about Louis Robinson, then?' Silver said.

Andrew didn't answer. 'If you betray us I'll never forgive you, I'll get you. The mess your face is in is nothing to what it'll be. And that applies to her too.'

Silver said gravely, 'Good night. See you tomorrow. Don't forget to leave the window open.'

'That wasn't very nice,' I said as we climbed down the scaffolding.

'I suppose he's under a lot of pressure. I couldn't very well tell anyone in his situation not to worry, could I?'

It was from that night or perhaps from the night before that our interest in the roofs underwent a change. We no longer climbed on them for their own sake. Our passion for them, never anywhere near Wim's, cooled. From that night scaling the roofs had really only one purpose for us: to get to 4 Torrington Gardens and into the flat without being seen by the other occupants.

We walked home a different way. The wine bar in Lauderdale Road was still open. We sat at a table outside and each had a glass of

Merlot. Silver raised his, we clinked glasses and he said, 'To you. To love.'

Returning in this particular direction, we entered Russia Road from the other end, the way I seldom went by day for fear of seeing Max or Selina. But by then I no longer much cared whether I saw them or not. I had Silver, I had a place to live, I had work. And I was always afraid of becoming even a little bit like poor Liv.

But as we passed 19 I couldn't resist glancing at the house. And I was rewarded, if that's the word. Max was coming furtively up the iron staircase from old Mrs Fisherton's. He was wearing his chocolate-coloured tracksuit, as far as I could see by the street-lamp's light. I heard the woman he had been visiting close the door behind him. Instead of looking in our direction, he kept his head lowered and let himself in quietly by the front door. I began to laugh, I couldn't help it, and covered up my mouth with my hand.

23

Silver was firm. 'I can't let you phone her any more, Liv. I'm sorry. I can't afford it.'

'When I am finding my papa I will pay you back.'

'It's still no.'

She began to cry, a fierce bawling. Wim had disappeared again. There was no sign of Jonny. When she had recovered a bit and was only snivelling I walked her downstairs and down the front steps. She set foot upon the path itself, lifted up her head and looked into the bright sunlit street. It was another fine hot day. The sun shone on her swollen tear-marked face and made her blink. But I think she was really making progress, might within a week or so have reached the point when she could have been got across the pavement and into a taxi − if the police hadn't come. But that was later. That wasn't till the afternoon.

At the time I was optimistic, though my cheerfulness took a downturn as we mounted the staircase and she told me what had happened the previous night.

'Jonny has violated me.'

She must have looked that word up in her dictionary. 'Rape', which she certainly knew, wouldn't do for her, she saw it as too mild and perhaps too hackneyed. I asked her when this was and she said it had been soon after we had gone out.

'Nobody cares about me. Wim doesn't want to hear. To Jonny I am prostitute.' She added, as if remembering it was expected of her, 'My money is gone, stolen by my own father.' She looked at me, her mouth working like a crying child's. 'I am thinking I must kill myself.'

'You mustn't say that,' I said. 'I care about you and Silver cares. Oh, Liv, don't start crying again.'

'I am not first with anyone,' she said through her tears and sobs.

We sat down on the stairs between the third floor and the fourth. My thoughts went back to a year past and I remembered how I had felt like that, not first with anyone. With Daniel gone and my parents so condemnatory, I'd thought everyone had someone they loved more than me. Even with Guy Wharton, who was kind to me, I could never have said I came first in his thoughts and heart. I put my arms round Liv and hugged her. Presently we started up the stairs again and once we were in the flat and she'd gone to her room, I told Silver about Jonny's rapist activities. He knocked on Liv's door.

'I can't keep him out of here, Liv,' he said. 'He's got a key. And if he hadn't, he'd use the window. I'm sorry about this, I know how it sounds.' It was useless telling her to call the police and complain of rape, he had said to me. They'd want her to go to the police station with them, go to the rape crisis centre. 'I'll have a locksmith round to put a lock on your door. I don't believe Jonny would break the door down.'

I've sometimes reflected since then that almost every helpful suggestion made to Liv she rejected. Oh, no, she couldn't lock her door. There might be a fire. She might lose the key. It was my opinion, later confided to Silver, that in locking Jonny out she feared she'd also lock Wim out. Poor Silver was beginning to feel his non-paying tenants a great trouble to him. It comes very hard on young people when they have a sneaking suspicion their elders may have been right all along. Apparently his father had warned him, when letting him have the flat, that while having a girlfriend to stay with him was all very well (Jack Silverman, though cranky, was an enlightened man), bringing home dubious homeless pals might be a mistake.

'My chickens are coming home to roost,' Silver said, 'though why that should be a hardship I don't know. I'd have thought one would have wanted one's chickens at home, not laying eggs for someone else.'

'Your chickens don't lay any eggs,' I said. 'They just peck each other to bits.'

He laughed and said to Liv, who had listened to this exchange with angry suspicion, that the best solution was for her to persevere with her therapy so that she could get herself back into the outside world. Even if the £2,000 was lost, he had her air fare in his bank account, and she should get back to Sweden as soon as possible.

'My money is not lost. My money will come back to me.'

It seemed doubtful.

'You don't want me here,' she said dolefully.

He couldn't deny it. He said nothing. Liv, who had been crying again, dried her eyes and said she'd like to go all the way down to the basement and try how it would be going up the area staircase. She said it as if it was an inspiration of her own rather than Silver's idea. It was a Saturday and I didn't have to go to work, so we both took her all the way down to the lower-ground floor. It wasn't a bit like old Mrs Fisherton's but bare of furniture, all the walls painted a stark white that made it seem fairly light. I still felt the walls and the whole mass of the house above us as oppressive weights and the absence of the sight of a sky as suffocating. But I said nothing of this to Liv in case she decided to become the world's only claustrophobic agoraphobe. The area door was unlocked. We got her outside into the moss-grown well, always damp as these places are even in the heat, and slowly mounted the stairs.

There was a gate at the top, exactly the same as at Max's, a wrought-iron gate in a wrought-iron railing. I went first with Liv behind me and Silver following her. Things seemed quite promising as we stood on the paving, feeling the sun lay a skin of heat on our faces and looking over the low hedge at the street beyond. Then the last thing Silver and I wanted happened.

Two people appeared on the other side of Russia Road, walking along from the right-hand side towards us, a man and a woman in their thirties, she too well-dressed for a Saturday-morning stroll, in a smart blue-silk trouser-suit, he in jeans and a sports jacket. Liv screamed when she saw them. She covered her mouth with her hand but too late, as such gestures always are. Her scream brought them to look in our direction, but as far as I could see they gave no sign of recognition, simply checking, I suppose, that no one was in trouble.

Whether they were James and Claudia Hinde I had no idea, but Liv thought they were. She turned and fled down the staircase, tripping on the bottom step and falling flat on her face. Luckily she wasn't hurt apart from grazes on her hands. We picked her up and between us carried her up as far as the second floor, where we set her down and told her to walk. She sat down and refused to budge. She must hide, she said, she must be hidden somewhere secret in the house. At any moment James and Claudia would ring the front-doorbell, either that or come back with a policeman. Silver said there wasn't any secret place in the house and he wouldn't hide her. We all sat there for about ten minutes, which is a long time when you're not doing anything and don't know what to say. Liv kept looking at the grazes on her palms, from which a little blood was trickling. At the end of those ten minutes the doorbell did ring. I've seen plenty of people jump but never the way Liv did, leaping galvanically off the stair, all her muscles locked, her hands clawed. She gave a wolf-like howl.

Silver went down. I said to Liv, like some awful old-time psychiatric nurse, that she must get up, pull herself together, get up those stairs. For some reason it worked and she began to run, surprisingly fast for someone who had taken no exercise for months. It was only Morna and Judy at the front door. Silver brought them upstairs. Their arrival was a godsend, for after what had happened we'd never have been able to leave Liv alone while we did our shopping, and they seemed quite willing to stay with her. If only Wim were a more reliable person. We both thought it but we didn't say it aloud. We were beginning to feel like the parents of a two-year-old, except that most parents love the child and happily bear the curtailment of their freedom, while we felt ours as an intolerable burden.

We couldn't ask Morna to stay behind while the rest of us lunched out. Besides, I didn't care for a threesome with Judy. She was very pretty. Now I knew she had been Silver's girlfriend she seemed much prettier than she had at first. I resolved firmly, as I had done before, not to be jealous, but it was a struggle. We ate at home, conjuring up something from what we had. Scraps, said Silver. That was what it meant, ends of two loaves, cheese rinds, two stale eggs and half a dried-up fruit cake. We had shopped for Andrew and Alison but forgotten to get anything for ourselves. It was about half an hour after Morna and Judy left that the police came.

Silver and I were in bed. Desire had seized us simultaneously. I hoped very much that on his part it wasn't actuated by seeing Judy again, but I didn't seriously think this. Liv was in her own room and we were lying side by side having a post-coital cigarette when the doorbell rang. Silver can get dressed faster than anyone I know. He pulled on a T-shirt and stuck his head out of the window. I heard him say, 'I'll be right down.'

I followed him, fastening my jeans, running my fingers through my hair. He didn't really think this could be something to do with James and Claudia, did he, I asked him as we ran down.

'I'm wondering if it could be about Liv's father,' he said.

He was right. The hotel manager had told the police. They didn't tell us how they discovered where I lived but Silver thought it probable the manager had spotted me in Mrs Houghton's garden, it being quite near the hotel, and asked her where I lived. This in fact was the case, as Mrs Houghton herself told me rather apprehensively the following Monday. Had she done the right thing? She hadn't known what to do. For my part, I was quite gratified to learn that she was unwilling to lose her gardener.

Silver took the police into his parents' charmingly furnished living room, all cleaned and polished by Beryl, and they were obviously impressed by its respectability. There were many facts we'd have liked the answers to that they didn't reveal. I suppose they never do. For instance, it was a long time before we found out why the manager had called the police. They took me, quite reasonably, for Håkan Almquist's daughter. I denied it at once. Silver and I hardly knew what to do, how to act. Why did they want his daughter?

'He's in the Royal Free,' the older policeman said. 'He was mugged. Hit on the head. He's got a fractured skull but he'll be OK. His wife's come over and she's with him.'

Something, at any rate, was explained.

'We know his daughter,' Silver said. 'We'll tell her.'

That was the end of the police responsibility, apparently. Looking round him, the younger one said that was a nice picture, he was fond of landscapes. Silver said, 'Was he robbed of anything?'

They looked cagey. Then the older one said, 'A wallet perhaps. When he was found he hadn't a wallet on him. He had loose change in his jeans pocket and a Swedish identity card and driving licence in his jacket breast-pocket. That's how we knew who he was.'

'You'll let the daughter know, won't you?' This was the younger one. He cast a longing look behind him at Erica Silverman's painting of a Scottish glen.

They gave the impression of not caring much now Elsie Almquist had been located. Had she been sent for? Or, informed, had decided she wanted to be with her husband? I had the mean thought, not expressed aloud, that all those phone calls made to Kiruna had been a waste of money.

'No mention of a black leather backpack with £2,000 in it, you'll

271

have noticed,' said Silver as we went back to the flat. 'Do we tell them?'

'I suppose so. I don't know. We'll have to tell Liv.'

She was still asleep. Wim turned up before she woke, descending gracefully through the window in spite of carrying a bag of cans of fruit juice in one hand and another full of chocolate biscuits, crisps, cakes from the patisserie and pizzas in the other. It was unusual for him to cross the roofs resplendently clad, but that afternoon he wore a new (or new secondhand) tunic of lemon-yellow silk embroidered with birds. I said it reminded me of a vase Max had called *famille jaune* and he laughed and said he had never been called fragile before. I was to remember that remark of his – with bitterness.

We made tea and told him about Liv's father. You could see he didn't want to know. He never treated her the way Jonny did, he had too much finesse for that. He never used her and I'm sure he gave her great sexual pleasure, but he wanted nothing serious to enter their relationship, nothing that might hint at commitment. Perhaps any liaison he had with any woman would have been the same.

'She'll have to go out now,' he said, bored. 'She'll have to go and visit him. Have another biscuit, Clodagh. The coconut ones are great.'

Of course Liv soon appeared, fetched out by the sound of Wim's voice. She had washed herself and combed her hair. The tear marks were eradicated and she had put on a clean white T-shirt, more a low-necked vest, that showed off her splendid breasts and tiny waist. Wim's boredom went and he looked interested. Strange he might have been but he was, after all, a man.

Giving me a resentful glance, presumably because I was sitting next to Wim, Liv got down on the floor at his feet and when he showed no reaction beyond giving her a small smile, leant her head against his knees. Silver drew breath and told her about her father, that he was in hospital with a fractured skull. I expected a violent reaction but she only stared, nodded and said, 'So that is where he has been.'

'Your mother's here. She's with him. I don't know where she's staying.'

'Oh, she has a friend in Elstree.' It was the first we'd heard of it. 'My papa isn't liking her a lot,' she said by way of explanation, I suppose, for Håkan Almquist's staying in an hotel. Then the inevitable, 'Where is my money?'

Now Silver and I didn't exactly know. We only knew that the police hadn't mentioned the backpack. But there were a lot of things left unmentioned. Silver said Liv would have to go to the hospital. She'd have to go to the police and tell them the whole story, or part of the story presumably, leaving out the fact that she had stolen the money in the first place, if she wanted answers to that.

Liv became hysterical. I had never seen her like this before. She was crying and laughing at the same time. She rocked back and forth, uttering short sharp yelps of laughter, the tears pouring down her face. I knew she wouldn't go to that hospital. Even if her father was dying she wouldn't go. We looked at each other in despair. It was Wim who saved things. He took hold of her, pulled her up, said, 'I can't stand that noise. Come to bed. That will shut you up.'

She was taken care of for another hour or so. Silver and I decided to take our washing to the launderette.

'Why haven't your parents got a washing machine?' I grumbled.

'They did have. It wore out and when they got a new one they took it with them to St Albans.'

I emptied pockets and turned socks inside out. In the right-hand pocket of the jeans I had worn two nights before, I found the fragments of the little china bullfinch broken by Silver and Andrew while they fought. Silver looked at the pieces in my hand with a strange expression on his face. If I hadn't known he never worried and was seldom afraid, I'd have fancied I saw anxiety there or even fear.

'Are you thinking it might be mended?' I said.

'No, no, it's beyond repair.' He sounded as if he was talking of something entirely different, of a quite other possibility, which struck a little chill into my heart. Then he smiled at me and gave me a quick kiss and all was well.

24

Going through that eleven-year-old diary, I find that Silver and I visited Andrew and Alison that Saturday evening and on three occasions in the following week. Once Wim came with us, at first frightening them inexcusably. They thought we had betrayed them and brought the police, though anyone less like a policeman it would have been hard to find. Apparently they saw his yellow tunic as a disguise. Then Alison identified him as our friend, who had been with us the first time we showed ourselves to them.

Once the confusion about Wim was over, we were established as their shoppers. They need never go out again until the time came for them to leave. I was going to say that we wanted no gratitude but of course, privately, we did. Still, expecting people to be grateful is such a shameful thing that Silver and I left any feelings we had about it unexpressed, even to each other. Alison was always profuse in her thanks, saying she didn't know what they'd have done without us, that we were 'life savers', and Jason's face lit up when we brought him chocolate or a half-melted ice cream. There was something pathetic and, more than that, distressing, in the way he liked us, always kissed me and put his arms round my neck, not, I'm sure, because of our personalities or something in us he found attractive and charming, but purely because we brought him delicious things to eat.

It was different with Andrew. At first he actively disliked us, though from the first he showed a very unwelcome sexual interest in me. Gradually his defences went down but never very far. I doubt if he ever came truly to trust us. And perhaps it was because of this, because distrust begets distrust, that when Alison asked for our surnames I said we were both called Brown. I didn't want them to look up Silverman in the phone book, find our address, our phone number. Neither of them seemed to see anything odd in this, or perhaps they thought we were married to each other.

Our shopping for them, carried out solely to save the family from discovery, Andrew only grudgingly admitted to be of assistance. Strange as it sounds, I think part of his mind rebelled against what we were doing. Going out was dangerous for him but just the same he had enjoyed it, it was a brief taste of what freedom might be, it took him out of that flat and into the open air. It allowed him to see other people, other faces apart from Alison's and Jason's. I used to wonder (according to the diary) if, while cautiously going from shop to shop in Elgin Avenue or Clifton Road, he had ever had a wild thought of never returning but of filling his pockets with the money they had brought with them and running away.

For they too, like Liv, had a secret hoard. Where they kept it no one told us for a long time. But it was unlikely they had taken up a floorboard and hidden it underneath. After all, it was legitimately theirs. It was a substantial sum, it must have been, for they had emptied their joint bank account and sold all their assets before they left, and, after that early staying in an hotel and a B and B, had spent very little. But having no income, only this capital, they were anxious about it. They watched it dwindle. They had nightmares, Alison told me, about having nothing left, about need compelling them to give themselves up.

Meanwhile Liv's worries obsessed her. Someone must find out what had happened to the black leather backpack. Did we think an insurance company would pay the money she had lost? I find it extraordinary how many people think insurance companies will compensate you for any loss, almost irrespective of whether you have a policy with them, that this is what they exist for, to keep irresponsible wastrels happy. Liv had no insurance of any kind but she still seemed to think application could be made to someone or other for repayment of the lost money. When we said it was impossible she shrugged and smiled as if she had secret knowledge and turned her attention to her father. He must be visited, someone must go to the hospital. She couldn't, she was ill again, since seeing James and Claudia she was worse than she had been before her agoraphobia therapy began.

The locksmith came on the day Silver and I went to the hospital to visit Håkan Almquist. We had to ask Morna to come so that there was someone there to let him in. Liv's father was getting on quite well, dressed and sitting in a chair, though with a big bandage round his head. He remembered nothing about the attack on him and very little about what had gone before. The name of the hotel he had recalled only when the police reminded him, but he had forgotten where his daughter was living and Elsie Almquist seemed never to have known, beyond the fact that it was in London. Into the great gaps in his memory had fallen everything to do with the backpack and its contents. The first the police knew of its existence was when Elsie asked them where it was. She insisted that her husband had taken it with him to London and suggested that the hotel had stolen it.

Treading carefully, Silver and I introduced ourselves as friends of Liv's, come to inquire after Mr Almquist because his daughter couldn't. Naturally Elsie wanted to know why she couldn't. Where was she? Didn't she know about her father? Was she ill herself? Elsie's English was inferior to her husband's but she managed to convey to us that, having rushed to London as fast as she could get a flight, she had had the added worry of her daughter's irresponsible behaviour.

Håkan Almquist sat there in his chair beside the high white bed, one of many men in that ward, some walking about on Zimmer frames, others helped to take a few steps by a wife or girlfriend, two or three in bed with cages holding the bedclothes up off their legs. His Liv-like face was rather pale but otherwise he looked well. The holes in his memory seemed not to trouble him. I looked at his left hand and noticed that his wedding ring was gone.

'I forget,' he said, resuming his seat and stretching out his legs. 'What can I do about that? At first I try to remember – for the police, you know – but it is hopeless. Everything is gone for four, five days before I am mugged.'

Elsie said something to him in Swedish and he, apologizing to us, answered her in that language. Silver and I were in a dilemma. If we told them where she was, Liv would be sure they'd tell the police and consider we had betrayed her. But the alternative was worse. She trapped us in a corner by asking the crucial question.

'So, where is my daughter?'

Silver answered. He said to me afterwards that he had to answer and he had to tell the truth. We weren't in the business of protecting Liv to the extent of lying to her parents. 'Her address is 15 Russia Road, London w9.'

He wrote it down and wrote the phone number too. It gave him an uncomfortable feeling of laying his private sanctuary open to unwanted investigation and exploration. How would he cope with Liv if the police came and asked to talk to her? Suppose she locked herself in and threw the key out of the window? Suppose she tried to kill herself? Even while we were speaking and he was unwillingly betraying Liv, the locksmith was in Russia Road, making her bedroom door secure.

Elsie wanted to know if she lived there alone, if she was still an au pair, and once more, why couldn't she come and see her parents instead of her parents having to go to her?

'You must ask her yourself,' said Silver, who had had enough of this.

The one bright spot seemed to be that if Elsie came round that evening, as she said she would, she could be a sitter with Liv while we went out. We discussed this on the bus going home, and we also discussed the black leather backpack. It wasn't a comforting thought that, apart from the person who had stolen it, no one knew what it had contained but Silver, Liv and me. If we told the police, if Liv let us tell them, would they believe us? We enumerated to each other what it must have contained. The Russia Road address and phone number among other things. Håkan Almquist's wallet, if he possessed one. Traveller's cheques and credit cards, surely. The hotel door key and the door key to his own house, only this was so far away up in the Arctic Circle that its absence presented very little threat. And had his wedding ring been in there too?

'I don't see why he'd carry his wedding ring around in a backpack,' Silver said. 'Anyway, I thought only women had them. Are you sure he had one?'

'Positive. Of course it might be in that locker drawer in the hospital. As for carrying it about in a backpack, if he did he may have been in the habit of picking up ladies he didn't want to know he was married.'

'Oh, you are so sophisticated,' Silver said, laughing.

'Aren't I? And you are so untouched and pure – I won't say naive.'

We walked through from Lisson Grove hand in hand along the canalside. The place was thronged with people. It was very hot.

'One day, when you marry me, will you have a wedding ring?'

My heart thudded a bit, which was absurd because I knew he loved me. 'I will if you will,' I said, and a kind of excitement welled up inside me, threatening to choke me.

But I grew calm again, I was able to speak in my normal voice, and we talked, only half-seriously, about how good it would be if you could get married anywhere you wanted (you couldn't, then), not just in a church or a registry office. Silver said our ceremony could be on the roofs, the priest or registrar could be hauled up in a hoist and the witnesses standing on the balcony below, but that was the last time he spoke to me of marriage. The next proposal I had came, as it might have to some Victorian miss, in a letter, and my wedding was conventional enough, a quiet affair at St Michael's, Highgate.

Not that evening but the following one Alison talked confidentially to me. We were in her bedroom, sitting on the bed. Silver and Andrew were in the kitchen, arguing about the cost of the provisions we had brought. Well, Silver never argued, he just stood his ground, saying he knew food was expensive, it was more expensive in London than up north where Andrew and Alison came from, and especially so when bought at these small local supermarkets. Andrew moaned about what would become of them when their money ran out. As it happened, Silver had offered to pay for some of what we brought, a generosity that angered me and made me tell him afterwards that this was what came of having money left one when one was too young to understand how to manage it. Andrew grumbled and scrutinized the receipts we had given him and Alison and I went into her bedroom, closing the door behind us.

She told me how she'd had an abortion when she was seventeen. Something had gone wrong, this was just before the 1967 Act legalizing abortion, and her fallopian tubes were blocked. She didn't know until she got married and tried to have a child.

'That wasn't Andrew, though?' I said.

'That was my first husband, Charles Barrie. We were divorced, but I kept his name. My mother didn't like the idea of me using my maiden name – well, things were different then.' She made a face. 'Later on I lived with Andrew and we got married when we wanted to adopt a child.'

I said I knew that, though admitting this knowledge made me feel like a gossip, memorizing details from newspaper stories.

'Men often don't care whether they have children or not,' she said. 'It's been my luck, or maybe my ill-luck, that the two significant men in my life both wanted children. Charles didn't. Life's strange, isn't it? Between Charles and Andrew I had a boyfriend who was a doctor from Kerala. If he hadn't wanted children so much we'd maybe have married.'

'Kerala? That's India?'

'That's in the south of India. If I'd married him, the social services wouldn't have stopped us adopting Jason. We'd have been the right mix for taking a mixed-race child. Ironical, eh?'

That was 'what if' if ever I heard one. But I thought, as I always do, even when dwelling on 'what ifs' of my own, how about all the imponderables, the different places you might have lived in, the different people you'd have known, the quite other way your thought processes might have developed, not to mention your desires and needs and the level of your happiness or its reverse? The possibility Alison cited scarcely seemed ironical to me but just appeared the complicated way life arranges itself.

'Jason's not really a mixed-race child at all,' she said. 'He had an Asian mother but he's been brought up – if you can call it that – by white people exclusively. In the children's home where he was there were black children, but if he'd been white, I mean if he'd been one of the white children, black children would have been there as well. I didn't put that very well.'

I said I knew what she meant. I put my hand over hers and she gave me a watery smile. 'I told Andrew about his father. He was very upset. He had a sort of wild idea he could go to the funeral in disguise. Of course that was completely stupid, he didn't really mean it. Has there been anything more in the papers?'

'Nothing about you for two or three days,' I said and then we went back into the living room. Andrew got out an album they had brought with them and showed us photographs of the street they lived in and Jason in their garden and their house. It was very much like my parents' house, thirties Tudor. I made the comparison in my mind and I think that was the first time I thought of my old home as my parents' house and not 'ours'. The car on the garage drive was a Mercedes. This was middle-class prosperity, to which the social services would have objected less if Andrew had been that doctor from Kerala.

Looking about me at the contrast, at Louis Robinson's bleak fourth floor, I reflected on what some people will risk for the sake of having a child and what they will sacrifice. Would I? What made it harder to understand was that surely most of such ventures failed, perhaps all failed. I said something like that to Silver on our way home. His reply surprised me, for he said that this wasn't so, we only got to hear about the ones that failed because that made a better story. For instance, the parent of a child or children who failed to win custody, usually the father, often successfully managed to abduct those children and take them abroad. I must have read of cases that only came into the news when the mothers tried to get those children back. Their efforts were usually in vain.

Handing back the photograph album, Silver asked Andrew how they proposed leaving this country. He didn't answer at once. Alison's sigh was audible. Her talk to me had left her in a state of heightened emotion and she said almost passionately, 'If I could keep Jason, if *we* could, I'd be willing to stay here for ever. Even in these circumstances, even never being able to go out, see our friends, talk on the phone to people, I could put up with that for him.'

'Well, I couldn't.' I suddenly noticed how much rage Andrew was suppressing. Veins that stood out on his forehead looked as if they'd split under the pressure. 'And he couldn't. He has to go to school. Oh, all right, we teach him but we need books, we need a school curriculum. We're prisoners here. And things happen outside that we're powerless to do anything about. I mean, my father dying. I can't even go and bury my father.' The anger began to pour out of him, but in measured words, not incoherently. His face was very flushed. 'I'll tell you what a typical day is like here – in this place. In prison. Starting first thing in the morning. It's like this. We might as well stay in bed but we can't because Jason gets us up at seven. One of us makes tea, usually me because I'm a morning person and Alison isn't. She and Jason will be having their morning love-in, their cuddle.' This rather pretty sentence he uttered scornfully and Alison looked away. You could see how imprisonment was straining their relationship. 'Then it's getting up and having showers and getting breakfast. Once, at the beginning of April, by the way, and April was bloody cold if you remember, the heating went off. We hadn't any hot water. We couldn't send for a plumber and the downstairs people have their own water heaters. We had to get in touch with Louis in Cannes and eventually he sent his grandson round. He's not a plumber but he fixed it. We'd been without hot water for a week. And then we had the added worry of someone else now being in the know.'

'Now, darling, you know Joel Robinson is completely trustworthy.'

'You mean he'd lie to the police for our sake and they'd believe him? I don't think so.' The scathing tone he used chilled my blood. 'I'll go on with the timetable. We have breakfast, we do some housework. This place is very clean, I don't know if you've noticed? It's clean because we've nothing else to do, and when the vacuum cleaner packs up, as it's threatening to do, housework will take up more of our time because we'll have to use a dustpan and brush. Jason's probably watching a video while this goes on. We record our own videos for him, children's programmes, animal stuff, so-called classic serials –' he looked at me – 'so long as they don't have too much bum and tit in them.

'Then we start lessons, not great fun for him, since he's all alone with no companions. As to the one who's not teaching, say it's me, I look out of the window. I know more about the structure of plane trees than anyone now living, I've charted the life cycle of their leaves from day to day, I could write a thesis on it. When I've done my leaf study, sometimes I just lie down and sleep. We both sleep a lot, it ought to be doing us good but it doesn't seem to. I'd sneak out to the shops before you so kindly took that job away from me.' His resentful tone made it sound far from kind. 'Now I don't have to I use the time for reading, only we've read all Robinson's books, none of which in any case would have been my choice.'

'We're lucky to have any books,' Alison said. 'We're lucky to have the video.'

'Oh, lucky. We're not lucky, my dear, we're bloody wretched.' He looked back at Silver. 'When we've had lunch, the other one of us gets on with the lessons. We can't remember the things we should without textbooks, so very likely we're giving him the wrong information. Never mind. We're *lucky*. Afternoons always drag, don't you think? Well, ours drag twice as slowly as most people's. We have tea with biscuits, cake, anything. There are no scales here, thank God, but I can tell I'm putting on weight fast. I've put on a stone, I reckon, since we've been here. Alison's always been one of those scraggy women. She could live on cream and chips and still stay thin.

'Things are a bit grim after tea because there's nothing left to do, nothing. Sometimes I just walk round the flat, into every room, in and out again, marching along, back to where I started from and then do it all over again. It drives Alison crazy.'

I could tell from her expression that it did. She closed her eyes, shook her head a little.

'Or I recite the multiplication table, which must be good for Jason if for no one else. He usually enlivens things at this time by asking why he can't go out, he wants to go out, why can't he see his friends, why can't he go in the park? He can see the trees of a park from the kitchen window. We explain as best we can for the fiftieth or maybe the hundredth time. Then he says that if "the policemen", I quote, want us to go back home it's wrong, it's breaking the law, not to go. I don't know who told him there was such a thing as law, I'm sure I didn't.

'Thank God for the news at six. Thank God for the happy hour of six to seven. I try not to ask myself what we'll do if the TV starts going the same way as the Hoover. Evenings are long, especially in this heat, we usually both have cold showers – like the flat, we're terribly clean – and we still have unbroken television. What I like best are those programmes where you see happy sun-kissed people on beaches or hikers striding across the free hills of Derbyshire. Or drivers in fast cars disappearing into the sunset or birds in flight or –'

'Don't!' Alison said it sharply, in an end-of-one's-tether voice. 'Don't keep on about it. You must stop, I can't stand it.'

It was his turn now to close his eyes. He'd clenched his fists and bowed his head. We looked on helplessly. Alison got up and laid her hand on his shoulder. I thought he might shake it off angrily but he didn't, he covered her hand with his own.

Silver broke the silence by asking what we could get for them apart from food. He mentioned books, maybe a Walkman and batteries for it. Andrew's diatribe had been quite enlightening and gave us ideas. How about writing pads and coloured chalks, flowers and plants, though these would be difficult to bring up the scaffolding, a chess set, patience cards, more jigsaws for Jason, news and comment periodicals like the *Economist* and the *Spectator*?

'We have to watch our money,' Andrew said in a chastened tone. Or perhaps getting all that off his chest had left him drained and tired. 'But books, yes. They'll have to be paperbacks.' He wrote the titles on the food shopping list. 'I've a Walkman but the batteries *have* run out.'

'Could you possibly buy Jason a pair of trainers? If his feet go on growing at this rate, I'll have to cut holes in his shoes.'

We added shoes to the list and Andrew told us Jason's size. 'If only there was a way I could sell my father's house. It's mine now. It'll fetch half a million. I've never needed the money so much.'

'In ten years' time,' Alison said, and her words were cool and considered, 'Jason will be eighteen. Then you'll be able to sell it. No one will be able to take him away from you then. It's only ten years.'

Sitting here, writing to my husband in Africa, rereading his last letter and then transcribing these pages of diary very nearly word for word, I ask myself who I'm writing this account for. For anyone in particular? For anyone at all? Perhaps for my husband, who knows so much of it already. But there may be something peculiarly enjoyable in reading something one already knows, particularly if it's a beloved person's version of events, just as there is in rereading a book one is long familiar with. I read *Jane Eyre* at school, I did it for my GCSEs (called O-levels then), and it's bringing me far more pleasure the second time round. Don't think for a moment that I'm comparing myself to Charlotte Brontë. The only parallel between her writings and mine is in the pain and suffering. So neither can be an entirely pleasurable read, I fear.

Still, we had had no unhappiness in our relationship up till then, Silver and I. Misery and discontent were for others. The occasional presence in the flat of pretty Judy cast only a faint shadow at first, as perhaps for Silver did Guy Wharton. From him I hadn't heard for weeks, not surprising really since he'd no idea where I was. What became of the few letters which must have been sent to me at old Mrs Fisherton's? Beryl never saw any. I asked her. So were they never taken down the staircase to the basement? If I thought about it, and I didn't much, I supposed that Max or Selina forwarded my post to Suffolk. But this wasn't so either. With a strange unaccountable (then) vindictiveness, they must have destroyed everything.

I encountered Guy by chance, walking round the Clifton Nursery. The weather had cooled a little, it had rained, and Mrs Houghton wanted shrubs planted. I suggested a solanum and a climbing hydrangea, believing erroneously that my reading had made me an expert. Guy was at the counter paying for a pot plant and a birthday card. He said he was going out to lunch and the plant was for his hostess but since he was staying at his South Kensington flat and the lunch party was in Pimlico, it seemed unnecessarily out of his way. I wondered, though it was only romantic guesswork, if he had come on the off chance of seeing me. For all I knew, he paid frequent visits to Maida Vale with that end in view. His obvious delight at seeing me made it quite likely.

We walked down to the canal and sat on a seat in the gardens at the top of Warwick Avenue. Because it was windy as well as sunny the water sparkled and danced. The houseboats bore their loads of flowers in tubs and boxes, lush by then and overgrown. Guy said, 'I wrote to you a couple of times.'

'I've moved. They didn't send on my letters.'

I told him I had dropped out of the Grand Union Polytechnic and become a gardener. The shock that piece of news gave him was plain to see. When his face was flushed he looked more than ever like Andrew Lane.

'Don't you think you should have done what I suggested and come and worked for my father?'

'I won't be a gardener for ever,' I said. 'But I might be sitting behind a desk for ever if I became a secretary. Besides, Guy, can you see me in an office?'

I was in my usual garb, jeans and trainers, a T-shirt with a face or an animal or slogan on it. My hair had grown very long, a great black cloak of it hanging halfway down my back. Needless to say perhaps, no make-up ever touched my face or varnish my nails and I smelt of Camay soap. He looked at me and said, 'I can see you anywhere. I mean, in a dress and nice shoes and – well, I don't know, the things girls wear.' That made me laugh, but he was quite serious. 'You'd always look lovely to me, Clodagh.'

I'd have to tell him, I realized that, and I was seeking about for a form of words when he suggested we take the boat trip from Jason's Wharf to Camden Lock. If we walked up there now we could catch the eleven-thirty boat. Or how about dinner that evening or tomorrow or the next night? Or dinner on all of them, he said.

'I can't go on a boat trip, Guy. I have to go and be a gardener. Besides –' I looked at him, knowing he'd be hurt – 'I have to tell you

I'm living with someone at 15 Russia Road. I met him in April.'

He nodded. 'It was inevitable. Will it last?'

What a question. For a moment I disliked him for asking it. 'I don't know. How should I know? I think it will.'

'If we got engaged,' he said, 'I wouldn't ask you to live with me. I wouldn't think it right.' I could think of no answer to that. 'You might change your mind about this – this friend of yours. If you do, I want to be there.'

I kissed him as we parted, though it was he not I who made that kiss intense. I broke away from him, shaking my head.

'Can I still write to you sometimes?'

I didn't answer, forgetting I had given him my address. So we parted, he with his pot of calceolarias to the Warwick Avenue tube station, I to the Houghtons'. All afternoon, while I gave the lawn its weekly mowing and cut its edges as neatly as I could with a sharp spade, I thought about Guy as if I was in love with him, which I certainly was not. I dwelt on him with regret because he was so kind, so tolerant, so affectionate and so suitable. And I found him attractive. When he'd kissed me, as he had done once or twice, I'd been excited, I'd wanted more, only he was too proper to expect more on what he would have thought of as a short acquaintance. He was the only one who had stuck by me after the pylon. I believed he truly loved me and, in time, when I had cured him of a sexism he didn't even know he had, I thought he'd have made an excellent husband.

He would have wanted to change me, sit me at a desk, put me into 'the things girls wear', and I'd have tried to make him more open-minded, less prudish and conventional, freer, more laid-back. What I didn't know then was that you can't change people. Women, especially women, go into marriage expecting to be able to change their husbands, fit them into the desired mould. They are in for disappointment. The only man to marry is the man you wouldn't change if change were possible, the one who is exactly what you want just as he is.

Guy did write to me rather a lot after that. His letters embarrassed me and made me feel guilty and the last one I stuffed into my jeans pocket unread. Sitting on the roof with Silver the evening after my meeting with Guy, I told him all about it. He said very gently and, I thought, a little coolly – too coolly? – that we shouldn't be totally exclusive, we had to have other friends. It wasn't as if Guy expected sex with me – or did he? Not really, I said, not as far as I knew, though (and this I didn't say) those kisses had been passionate enough.

'You must do as you like, Clodagh. I've no rights over you.'

That was hardly the reply I wanted, of course. It was the first time Silver had said anything to me that jarred. But did I really expect a relationship of perfect unblemished accord? We said no more. We picked up our bag of books and writing pads and jigsaw puzzles and our bag of videotape cassettes and magazines. Jason was waiting for us, actually outside the window. He made me squat down so that he could put his arms round my neck and hug me. I didn't think it very safe for him to be on that balcony, which wasn't really a balcony at all but an eighteen-inch-wide shelf with a three-foot-high parapet. The ground, a concreted area supporting a few wilted plants in stone troughs, lay fifty feet below. I marvelled at these parents, for it was as parents that they saw themselves, who sacrificed everything, home, careers, income, liberty, for the sake of a child yet failed to take the elementary precaution of warning him against risking his life on that narrow shelf.

Of course, you could see how much he loved being out there. That ridge of masonry with its dusty floor was his garden, his park, his playground, his freedom. The fresh air, and it was fresh enough up above the treetops, made him unconsciously take deep breaths. But he came in with us willingly enough and the pair of red and blue trainers we had bought him distracted his attention from the open air. His large dark liquid eyes widened and he smiled, then laughed out loud. The book we had brought specially for him was a real book without illustrations and, wearing his new shoes, he settled down immediately to read it. Alison said it was past his bedtime and he asked her if he could read his new book in bed.

Rather reluctantly, after Jason had been taken away, Andrew started to pay us for what we had brought. I say 'started' because Silver tried to stop him, saying that many of the things were our idea, he hadn't asked us to get them. I don't know if Andrew was mean by nature or if circumstances had made him cheese-paring, but he accepted Silver's offer with relief. Deeply disapproving, I said nothing but the indignant glance I gave Silver told him everything I felt. With Alison's permission, I went into Jason's bedroom to say goodnight to him and, giving him a kiss, reflected on how much he undoubtedly loved Andrew and Alison, how happy he was with them, and wondered what would become of him when he was taken from them, as inevitably he would one day be.

Or was it inevitable? Was there perhaps a way?

25

Elsie Almquist came round to Russia Road while I was conducting an agoraphobia therapy session with Liv. I was standing just inside the front door, trying to cajole her into taking a step outside. Clinging to my arm, she had begun shuffling over the threshold, her entire body shuddering, when her mother came across the road and up to the gate.

The previous evening, before we went on the roofs, I had been to the Hindes' house, rung the bell and, when a girl answered the door, said I was from Westminster City Council. I said I was carrying out a survey into what residents thought of the council's waste-disposal system. At this point a woman came down the stairs and a man came out from the doorway on the left. Perhaps they had learnt something from their experiences with Liv, for James Hinde asked me to produce identification. I retreated, quite satisfied. Whoever that couple Liv saw in Russia Road might have been, they weren't James and Claudia.

But when Liv heard I had been to the Hindes' house she was aghast. They'd have followed me, they'd trace me here, there was probably someone watching the house even now. We could only get her downstairs by posting Judy at one end of the street and Morna at the other. But neither of them, of course, were on the alert for a middle-aged Swedish woman with a worried expression and a London A–Z guide in her hand. Liv, who these days reacted like this to almost anything unexpected, screamed shrilly. I pushed her back into the house, asked Elsie Almquist in and got them both up the stairs.

I know now that Liv was ill and that we were quite wrong to try and treat her ourselves. But we were very young. Getting her to a doctor was virtually impossible, while bringing a doctor or some psychiatric social worker to her never occurred to us. We never realized how close to the edge of paranoid schizophrenia she was. And her mother simply thought she was being difficult, 'being a teenager', when she rolled herself up into a ball in the place at the end of the sofa we had come to call 'Liv's corner'. She went over to her and shook her, taking her by the shoulder and jerking her arm back and forth. Liv reacted not by lifting her head or uncurling herself but by lashing out, striking her mother who was still bending over her a sharp blow on the chin.

For poor Elsie this was an impossible situation. She eyed the room we were in, turning her head and swivelling her eyes, with an expression of pained dismay. What Elsie saw must have made her feel far worse than when she set out with her daughter's address and her London guide. I don't know that there were actually any mouse droppings on the ancient, greasy, grey, worn and deeply stained carpet, but there may have been. Cigarette ash sprinkled the top of every surface. Every chair had its woodwork scuffed and its upholstery threadbare, while the sofa might, if the vendor was lucky, have fetched £5 if sold from a Church Street pavement. The wallpaper was coming off and one evening Wim had hastened its disintegration by peeling quite a large area off in strips. At the open windows the high wind that had sprung up blew the frayed and dirty curtains out almost horizontally and tumbled on to the floor a week's accumulated newspapers.

Elsie couldn't stop herself from shaking her head and shutting her eyes in despair. Judy and Morna came up the stairs, Silver came out from his bedroom, while she gazed, aghast. The next thing will be Wim arriving through the window, I thought. But he didn't come and gradually Elsie seemed to take comfort from Silver's presence, accepting a cup of tea from his hands (and sending it back because it had milk in it) and at last taking her eyes off her daughter.

It was hoped her husband would be discharged from hospital in two days' time. She managed to say this in quite good English, while apologizing all the time for her failure to master this phrase or that. Her husband and she would go back to Sweden very soon. She was due to return to work the following Monday.

'We will go back and we will bring Liv with us. That is the best way.'

By then Liv was looking drowsy. She quite often fell asleep in the middle of the day with conversation going on all around her. But her mother's words electrified her. She leapt up off the sofa, stood there, convulsed like someone on TV who has been shot and at any moment will fall, and began shouting at her mother in Swedish. No one could understand a word but we all knew what she was saying: she wouldn't go, she was unable even to go outside, and someone had taken her money. At least she had stopped accusing her father of stealing it.

Summoning up what English she could remember from her school-days, Elsie threatened Liv with the law. 'I will ask a policeman to come here and make you.'

But all of us, Elsie included for all her brave words, knew that was impossible. Liv was nineteen, she was an adult and could live where she pleased. She muttered something to her mother, then addressed everyone, 'I stay here, in this flat. Silver is liking me here and Wim is.' She looked sternly at me. 'Wim is, very much. Maybe it will be years and years. I don't know. I must get back my money. But it is here I stay.'

With that, she went into her bedroom and we heard the key turn in the new lock. It was then, at this point, Silver told me later, that he understood what had happened to the £2,000. He didn't know how he understood, it just came to him out of the air in a sudden revelation. We were on our way to Cricklewood on the bus, it being one of those evenings we didn't go to 4E Torrington Gardens. The day had been sultry and humid, very warm but sunless, and now at eight the sun shone at last, low in the sky, a dark red globe glaring out between bars of black cirrus. We sat on the top, at the front, the better to contemplate awful Kilburn High Road and the incongruously pretty streets that turn off it, the dusty trees, the sari shops and secondhand clothes shops, the squalid clubs, the supermarkets absorbing and disgorging crowds, the Tricycle Theatre and the pubs. The bus stopped approximately every thirty seconds at a red light.

'It was Jonny,' Silver said. He looked into my face. 'You're not all that surprised are you?'

'I'm not surprised,' I said.

'He knew about that money from the first. Well, we all did, but none of us had designs on it. I think he knew everything that happened to it, you taking care of it, you bringing it back, Liv hiding it for a second time. I don't think he knew where it was hidden the first time but he did the second. He was probably thinking of taking it when I exiled him from her room.'

'He must have kept watch on the house. But he still had his job then. I don't see how he could have.'

'He was just lucky. He saw Liv's father come and knew the sort of time he came. As for the date of his return to Sweden, Liv very likely told him herself. He guessed she'd hand the money to him the day before. And he need not even have guessed. She may have told him everything, that her father was going home and taking her money with him.'

We sat in silence, reflecting no doubt on the unwisdom of Liv's behaviour, and never seeing that we ourselves were just as foolish and improvident, never understanding that in our whole policy towards Andrew and Alison, our attitude to Liv and our dealings with someone who was, after all, a criminal, we were quite as imprudent as she if not as unbalanced.

The house in which Jonny had a room lacked the graciousness of Maida Vale terraces. It was tall and solid with a ponderous bay on the ground floor and three pairs of sash windows above, its façade unadorned by anything but heavy stone windowsills and branching drainpipes. A man of about Jonny's own age came to the door. He was as unlike Jonny as could be, being skeletally thin and with a sparse fair beard and long straggly hair. Jonny wasn't there, he said, he'd moved out the week before. He hadn't himself seen him leave but the man who owned the house, his landlord, knowing he wanted a room for his friend, had told him Jonny's was vacant.

'You don't know where he went, I suppose?' Silver asked.

'You suppose right, mate. I've never even spoken to the guy.'

So Jonny had no job and no known address. 'What are we going to do?' I asked as we went slowly back to the bus stop. 'We could tell the police.' I said this very doubtfully, not yet cured of the Lawless Teenager Syndrome. 'I suppose we *could*. But then they'd come and question Liv. D'you think it's possible for someone to die of fright? I sometimes think Liv could.'

Silver said he didn't know but he knew what I meant. Besides, Jonny had been his friend. He couldn't betray his friend, it would be wrong. On the other hand, Jonny hadn't just stolen the money and treated Liv brutally, he had hit Håkan Almquist over the head as well and fractured his skull. If he had, if he did.

'You see, we don't know. It's all guesswork,' he said. 'We haven't any evidence. It may have been someone else. All we really know is that Jonny's left his job and moved house, but that proves nothing.

Oh, and he's got some new clothes. He may not have known about the money, he may think Liv let you or me put it in our bank accounts.'

Silver, who had only half an hour before been so certain of Jonny's guilt, had now half-persuaded himself he was innocent, or innocent of this particular offence. And so we argued ourselves out of our strong belief. We did nothing. Jonny was somewhere, probably still in London, but we'd no idea where. Liv was still in the flat and likely to remain there perhaps, as she'd said, 'for years and years'. Three days later, Håkan Almquist was allowed to go home to Stockholm and thence to Kiruna.

Wim too had apparently vanished. The pattern of occupation of the flat was changing. A friend of Morna's called Niall, a student at the School of Oriental and African Studies, had also come to stay. Failing to persuade Silver to let her have Jonny's room, Judy camped in the living room. I tried very hard not to mind Judy's being there, but I did mind.

I've heard older people say that my generation, born in the late sixties and early seventies, is the first to grow up free from sexual guilt and sexual pressures. We don't need to clock up a lot of partners, we don't need the experience that comes from variety. Free to enter a relationship without shame and without concealment, we are open about our sex lives and frank with each other about our feelings. Jealousy is absent and so is subterfuge. The notion of passion being heightened by tension and danger is foreign to us. In the age of Aids we accept a full and rewarding sex life with just one person without covert longings or secret desires. All I can say is, I haven't noticed it. No one I know is like that and I'm not myself, though we might wish to be. As everyone, I imagine, since the world began has wished to be.

So Judy's occasional presence in the flat was a cloud across the sky of my sunny days, as Wim's was across Jonny's. And although I never knew it till the end, my presence was a threat to Liv, for she feared Wim's obvious fondness for me, as Guy's very existence was to Silver. None of us brought these things out into the open. We never discussed them. They festered and oozed inside us. Particularly bad for me were the days when Judy spent the night in the flat, on the living-room floor, and was still there when I had to go off to work at the Houghtons'.

As I mowed the lawn and dead-headed the dahlias, I'd imagine her and Silver sitting there talking about old times (those were the days and do you remember?), unchaperoned, Liv locked in her room fast asleep. And that week Silver never once came to Randolph Avenue to collect me at the end of my day's work.

My consolation was that Judy could never accompany us on to the roofs. She was much too afraid of heights. But Silver had told her about the occupants of 4E Torrington Gardens, which I thought a risky thing to have done.

'Don't worry,' he said, in that mantra of his. 'Judy's all right. She won't talk.'

'But *why* did you tell her?'

'Because she's a friend of mine. Because I like her.'

'Because she used to be your girlfriend?'

'If you like,' he said, but in the distant tone he used when voicing his disapproval.

They were rather alike to look at, he and Judy. They might have been brother and sister. (How I wished they were.) She too was white-skinned and fair-haired, though her hair was darker than Silver's. Their eyes were the same shade of bright silver-grey. And, what I found most deeply disquieting, she was Jewish. I hardly knew Silver's parents then, I knew nothing of their views, but my imagination supplied a semi-orthodox couple who expected their son not to 'marry out', who in the past had looked with favour on Judy and would like to do so again. Even her name seemed in her favour. In some feminist book I'd read while still at school, Judith was praised as a great heroine. 'Strengthen me this day, O Lord God of Israel!' she cried as she plunged the sword into Holofernes. Sometimes I felt I couldn't compete.

But she never came on the roofs with us. We left her behind to look after Liv, though the possible threat from Jonny seemed to grow less every day. And up there we were united again, close again. Because crossing the burnt roof had made us nervous that first time, we hadn't tried it again but, in the third week of August, on an evening when we had nothing to carry to 4E, we decided to make another attempt. The masonry was warm to touch, although the sun was now gone, and the slates under our feet were dry and smooth, not at all slippery. No rain had fallen for so long that drifts of pale dry dust lay in the guttering inside the parapet. An early drop, heralding that later fall two months off, had shed leaves from the plane trees and some had blown up here. They lay on the tarpaulin, yellow-green, shrivelled, but still as big as dinner plates.

Silver set first one foot, then the other, on to the tarpaulin. The timbers underneath creaked but they held. I followed, trying to tread lightly, as if going on tiptoe would somehow reduce my weight. Safe on the other side, he put out his hand to me, I took it and jumped the last bit on to the firm slates. We went into each other's arms, hugged and kissed because we had achieved the crossing without coming to harm. It must be rare in life to regret *not* meeting with an accident but later I had good reason to be sorry that the tarpaulin had held that night, that it didn't sag and give way, dropping us, perhaps without serious injury, in among the burnt joists and ruined masonry beneath. And that the broken balcony hadn't subsided under the shock.

We let ourselves into the flat to find Andrew and Alison sitting in the living room, clearly doing nothing but waiting for us. Jason had gone to bed. Silver and I had no idea how much our visits had come to mean to them. We thought of ourselves in this context as simply messengers and carriers of provisions. To them, though, as Alison later told us, we were messengers of the gods, angels, which she said is what the word means. Our appearance on the balcony and our entry through the window was the high spot of their day, while the times we didn't come were lifeless and dreary. We were something to look forward to in their prison, the long hot summer waning away outside, life going on but inaccessible to them, suspended as they were in that place, the innocent Jason serving time for an accident of birth.

We asked for their shopping list, we told them what the papers said about them, we reported that they had been seen in Aberystwyth, in Columbus, Ohio, and in Paris. The *Mail on Sunday* had published a letter purporting to come from Andrew, setting out conditions under which they'd be willing to return home. The *Sunday Mirror* carried a photograph, taken on a Leeds shopping mall's closed-circuit television, of a man and a woman and a little boy hurrying through the crowd as if afraid they'd been spotted. Andrew said he had written no letter. If he had, we'd know because we'd have posted it. As for Leeds, they had none of them ever been there.

Principally we wanted to talk to them about the plan we were formulating for getting them out of there. First of all, it would be necessary for us to find out more about the people who lived on the lower floors, the young man on the ground floor and the elderly couple who had what Andrew called the 'duplex'. How much did they know? Had they guessed anything? What did they think about these people who never went out? Did they know there was a child up here?

Passports would have to be acquired and air tickets bought. Silver revealed for the first time – he hadn't explained this to me – that he had told Judy about them because she was a good amateur photographer and could take pictures of them for their new passports.

'I don't know how,' I said, 'if she's scared to come across the roofs.'

'She'll come up the stairs. By then we'll know the movements of the people on the lower floors. We'll know if they're likely to see anyone coming up to the top flat.' He said to Andrew, 'Do you know any of them? According to the bells, there's a couple called Nyland and an S. Francis.'

'Mr and Mrs Nyland are quite elderly,' Alison said. 'The man on the ground floor's an actor.'

'He's quite famous.' Andrew began sneering. 'In TV circles, that is, by TV standards. He's the baddie in some sitcom.'

I thought of Selina, who perhaps should be thankful she was the goodie. Andrew said they had never seen any of these people, all they knew of them they had from Louis Robinson. In the days when he used to go out shopping he had once encountered someone visiting Mrs Nyland. A younger woman had put her head round her front door just as he was crossing the landing.

'The daughter, I expect it was. She must have heard me coming down the stairs, they're not carpeted, they're sort of marble stuff. She calculated just when I'd pass her mother's door. People like that, they've nothing else to do but poke their noses into others' business.'

'We'll go home that way,' Silver said. 'Down the stairs instead of up on to the roof.'

'Where exactly do you live?' Andrew often sounded very suspicious. 'Not far away, I suppose?'

'Not far,' Silver said, smiling.

They saw us out. For a moment they were like ordinary people saying good night to friends who had dropped in for the evening. But they closed the front door rather quickly behind us. The light went off. We waited, taking a while to get used to the darkness. Through windows in the stairwell a little dull moonlight leaked in. Silver went first. There were two flights to every storey and we went down four, bypassing Louis Robinson's unoccupied flat, then two more to the inhabited part of the house. It was about half past ten by then and all was silent but for the patter of our feet in trainers on the treads which were, as Andrew said, made of 'marble stuff'. If the old people slept upstairs in their two-storey apartment they were very likely to be asleep somewhere behind that newly painted black front door. Someone, probably that very day, had polished the brass knocker and letter-box and doorknob so that they shone like eighteen-carat gold. Caught in the letter-box, under the flap, was an envelope.

Silver pulled it out slowly and gently, one finger under the flap lest it slam shut. Why the letter was there, why it hadn't been properly put into the outside box with the rest of the post, there was no telling. Perhaps it had been wrongly delivered to the man downstairs and he had brought it up here. It was addressed to Mr and Mrs J. L. Nyland, Flat C, 4 Torrington Gardens, Maida Vale, w9, confirming what we already knew.

We pushed it through the door and went on down through the silence. When we were outside and looked back, we saw that no lights were on there or above. The actor was more likely to be out than in bed. We walked home through the streets, both perhaps feeling we'd have been happier and more comfortable fifty feet above. Liv and Judy and Niall were in the living room and Wim had come after an absence of nearly two weeks. Watching him with Liv, I asked myself if he was less detached, if he might even be growing fond of her, for as she pressed herself up close to him on the sofa as she often tried to do, he had his arm round her and let her rest her head on his shoulder. If he was staying, he'd have to share her bed, for Niall now occupied his usual space. Judy announced that she wouldn't stay the night, she was going home, and I told myself it was wrong to be glad, to hope she'd never come back.

It was my idea to try asking Selina if she knew anything about the actor. Silver agreed, though he was surprised that I was willing to renew contact with her and Max. But I was changing, and with the rapid progress that happens when one is twenty. Whatever I may have told myself about my feelings, I realized that I had been afraid of Max. He had embodied all the authoritarian figures I'd ever known. Selina hadn't frightened me but all the time I was with her I used to feel alienated and confused, as if I was trying to understand a foreign language spoken by someone who could have talked English if she had chosen to.

Should I try to avoid Max? I was no longer up early enough to call at the house while he went out for his morning run. Besides, even if I stirred myself and managed to be outside by seven, Selina would still be in bed and would look less than kindly on someone who fetched her to the door in a dressing gown and without her make-up. I decided I'd have to brave Max and face the consequences. I bundled up our dirty clothes into a pillowcase for Silver to take to the launderette and I went out into the street just before ten. But as I looked across at No. 19 from the top of our steps, something it was quite possible to do above the low porch walls and between the narrow pillars, I saw an astonishing sight. A woman in a blue tracksuit was coming up the area staircase. She paused at the top to close and fasten the gate just as Max, in his chocolate running gear, came out of the front door. The woman was my former supervisor, Caroline Bodmer.

They met on the path and kissed. Max held the street gate open for her and the two of them set off at a jog trot in the direction of Paddington Recreation Ground. No doubt on her account, Max had changed his exercise time. What I had seen gave me much to think about. Certain unexplained remarks of Selina's fell into place. I understood her reference to 'scruffy academics'. I watched Max and Caroline Bodmer disappear round the corner into Lauderdale Road – they hadn't once looked in my direction – and walked round to No. 19. Selina opened the door so quickly she must have been standing just inside it. Her face was grim, more lined than I had ever seen it, the make-up on her skin like plaster applied with a trowel. She wore a skimpy silk suit in that hardest of all colours to wear, lemon yellow, and a lot of gold jewellery.

'Come in,' she said, in the voice of an undertaker talking to the bereaved. 'I suppose you saw them?'

'I'd no idea *she* was his girlfriend.'

She spoke to me as if we had parted from each other half an hour before. 'Well, darling, I did say I didn't blame you. I'm sure it was done in all innocence, you introducing them, I mean. But it was on your account she was always phoning here. And once they'd met, if you can credit it, but he swears it's true, it was love at first sight.' We might have been close friends on intimate terms. 'Come up to the drawing room. My poor drawing room that I loved so much and that I'll have to leave behind. I'm leaving, you know. I'm going on Friday, and I suppose I shall have to look on all this for the last and final time.'

I looked about me. There were fluff and hairs on the emerald carpet, dust on the once shining surfaces and the flowers in the Chinese vases were dead. The ashtrays, surprisingly in that household, were full of ash and cigarette ends.

'It hasn't been cleaned for weeks, darling. I haven't let Beryl clean it. I couldn't really tell you why, it was a sort of gesture on my part. I suppose I feel I shan't mind leaving it so much if it's all filthy and spoilt. Do you remember the party we had for your birthday? We were all so happy then, weren't we? You and me and Max, just like a family. I mustn't cry. I've used up all my waterproof mascara and I haven't replaced it. There are so many things that have just *lapsed*, darling.'

This hardly seemed the time to mention the actor, but when would be the time? She was leaving at the end of the week. I asked her tentatively, trying to think of a reason for wanting to know and failing to find one. This mattered not at all as Selina was quite uninterested in me, in what I might be doing, where I was living or anyone I might have seen or met.

'Oh, him, darling, yes. He's called Sean Francis. Terribly dishy, don't you think? Lovely eyes and those sort of soft features. He was the guest star on *Streetwise* for two episodes. Not that he's a star, just amazingly fanciable. I only wish I was ten years younger, but that's all water under the bridge or ships that pass in the night or something, isn't it? I've given Max my best years and he's thrown them aside like an old fag end. Did I tell you I've started smoking again? It's a great comfort. I only gave it up to please His Majesty.' She passed me the silver cigarette box as if we'd never had those inquests about the smell of smoke in old Mrs Fisherton's. 'It keeps me thin, too, I can get into a size six.'

I asked her where she was going to live and she said she'd taken a flat in Dolphin Square for six months. 'It's packed with Members of Parliament, darling, and you never know, do you?'

Returning home in reflective mood, I thought about Max and Selina and saw that though I was in no possible way to blame for Max falling in love with Caroline Bodmer and she, presumably, falling in love with him, but for me they'd never have met. But for the towpath being impassable on a certain day and this leading to my failure to keep my appointment with Caroline, she'd never have phoned 19 Russia Road. And another result of that was that I had met Silver. So I'd found my love and Selina had lost hers because a woman had been murdered on the canal bank. I thought of the great causal chain of events, trying to get back beyond that murder to the man who had carried it out, perhaps just someone who had flown into a rage because the dead woman had refused him money or sex. Or been unfaithful to him. As Max had been to Selina and perhaps Silver would be to me.

Letters had begun arriving from Sweden. The Almquists, who had never written to Liv before, now bombarded her with daily admonitions. Håkan wrote in English. I can only suppose this was so that Liv could show his letters to the rest of us and he'd thus win our support in sending her home. They phoned too, and almost every day. One morning, when I answered the phone, Håkan launched into a great defence of himself in respect of the missing money. He had no memory of ever having been given it, I must believe that, he said, he couldn't remember coming to 15 Russia Road that day or leaving it or carrying the money with him or being mugged. He knew only that he had been told these things were so. I had to fetch Liv out of bed. Since Wim had been sleeping with her on an almost regular basis – that is, for the past three nights – she had been calmer. She got up now with a smile on her face and stood there quite naked, rotating her body, showing off its magnificence. I think she was saying to me, look at this, you can't compete with this, and to Wim that it was all for him. He watched her with greedy eyes, a look on his face I had never seen there before. She bent over and kissed his mouth before pulling the T-shirt he had discarded on to the floor over her head and going off to talk to her father.

Wim's attention to her and his love-making were the best therapy she could have had. Or so it seemed then, so it seemed. And when I took her downstairs – it would never have crossed his mind to do this – she took almost jaunty steps down the path, stood at the gate and looked quite boldly up and down the length of Russia Road.

'Soon I am walking in the street, Clodagh.'

I said optimistically that this meant she'd soon be able to go home to Sweden.

'That is a possibility, yes, but I don't think so. Better Wim and I go somewhere away from here, a long long way, and get work and are happy.'

Very unlikely, as far as Wim was concerned. I tried to imagine him in a domestic situation, being a breadwinner, or even half of a breadwinning couple, having an ordinary conversation, eating proper meals, watching television. I tried and failed.

That was the day, according to my diary, meticulously kept at this time, that Silver saw Jonny. He saw him in a street off the Holloway Road where he had gone to buy something for Andrew Lane, an attachment for the shower at 4E, something that couldn't be found nearer home. Jonny was coming down the front steps of a shabby grey house in a terrace of such houses in a street without trees or anything green and where the front gardens were full of dustbins and chained-up bicycles. Silver called out something, hi or hello, but Jonny wouldn't look at him and passed him by as if they had never met before.

'Did he look prosperous?'

'Not so's you'd notice. It's not very salubrious where he's living, if he's living there, not what your mum and my mum would call "a nice part".'

I said that perhaps it was just as well Jonny had ignored him. He had said himself, I pointed out, that it would have been better for everyone if he had never been friends with someone like Jonny and invited him into his home.

'He's not "someone like", he's himself.' Silver's tone was cold and remote. 'And it's not the way I want to be, only knowing respectable people.'

His coldness I attributed to the presence of Judy in the flat, although she had been absent since the night we began on our Andrew and Alison exit plan. I didn't know, he never said a word at that time, that it was Guy Wharton coming between us, that Silver was beginning to believe I was deceiving him with Guy. And it wasn't only that Lucy, coming round with Tom while I was at work, had told him, perhaps with no malice, that she had seen me kissing Guy that morning in the Warwick Avenue gardens after we had met at the nursery. There was more to it than that.

So much for the openness and frankness of young people, the absence of jealousy and recrimination in their liberated lives. So much for their new attitude to sex, suspicion fled and passion simplified. Silver and I slept in the same bed and sometimes made love, though as I imagine middle-aged people, tired of a long marriage and of each other, make it. Dutifully, almost sadly, a simple preface to sleep.

Sometimes I thought that all that held us together was our determination to do what we could for the escape of Andrew, Alison and Jason, to carry out the plan we were formulating. And I remembered with sadness Silver's talk of marriage as we walked the canal bank and our love-making that warm evening on the roof.

26

August came to an end and on its final day a newspaper carried a big story about Andrew and Alison and Jason. We had taken little notice of the recent accounts of sightings. This story was different. This time a woman who lived in Inverness Terrace had told the police and the newspaper she had seen Andrew shopping in Westbourne Grove.

If you get there by way of the underpass, the one where I was so frightened and where I met Silver, Westbourne Grove is about half a mile from Torrington Gardens. This was serious, this was getting very near home. But Andrew had stayed in since we had started fetching things in for them. Or had he?

The scaffolding between Peterborough Avenue and the first terrace in Torrington Gardens was still there, though the redecoration was long finished and the new paint already spattered with pigeon droppings. Though this seemed unlikely, we wondered with optimism if the removal of the scaffolding and repair of the burnt roof might coincide.

Jason was once more on the balcony waiting for us. I put my arms round him and he kissed me soundly on both cheeks. At the moment all was well enough, he was hidden behind a screen of leaves, but in autumn when they fell the people in the houses opposite would be able to see him. I had failed to understand then what risks prisoners will take for a glimpse of liberty, a breath of air, a sight of sky not looked at through glass.

We had brought the newspaper with us and we showed it to Andrew, certain then that the woman who claimed to have seen him had just made a guess that was unlucky for them but a breakthrough for the police. He took a defiant stance. Yes, he had been out.

'I couldn't stand being everlastingly cooped up in here. I felt I was fighting for breath. I'll tell you something. Before all this started I promised Jason a mynah bird, he was crazy to have a talking bird, but if we ever get out of here he won't. I'll never keep a caged bird. Every time I looked at it or heard it talk, I'd think of this place, this *dump*.'

Jason began to whine. 'Dad, you promised, you promised, Dad.'

'I know how hard it is,' Silver said, 'but you mustn't go out. That's the way you'll be found.'

'No, you don't know how hard it is. No one knows who hasn't been through it. I didn't need to go shopping. You do that for us and I'm sure we're very grateful.' He didn't sound grateful, he sounded resentful. 'I had to go out. I had to be free just for half an hour. I felt that if I didn't go out, I'd have a breakdown, I'd start screaming out of the window.' He added, in a few words taking away my impulse to shout at him, what about Alison, what about her having a breakdown, 'It was such a lovely day.'

'You'd better get a false beard,' said Silver, 'or grow one. But then you'll look the way you did before you left your home. How about a moustache? Could you do that? In time for when my friend comes to take your passport photos?'

'My' friend, not 'our'. 'When's that going to be?'

'I don't know. I'll have to ask her. Meanwhile, could you just not go out? You won't be here much longer, you won't be here for the winter. I promise you that.'

It was a promise that would be fulfilled. Even then I was sure it would be. I had faith in Silver and you could see they had, or Alison had. Andrew said no more. Did Alison ever reproach him? Had she ever said a word to him about his imprudence, about the danger he ran into through his need for immediate freedom? She laid her hand on his arm, caressing it for a moment before sitting down at the table to read the newspaper account. Silver gave them the outline of our plan.

The greatest risk was from Sean Francis on the ground floor. There was a good chance of his seeing them if they went downstairs with their suitcases and waited in the hall for a taxi. The elderly couple he thought we had no need to worry about. He meant to get to know Sean Francis, find out what sort of a person he was and if, even, we could take him into our confidence. Here Andrew interrupted to say he didn't care for that. You could trust no one.

'You trust us,' Silver said.

'Only through force of necessity. Did we have a choice?'

Silver turned his head so that he seemed to be addressing only Alison and Jason. I could see the red flush on the back of his neck.

Judy would take their photographs, he said. He was pretty sure he could get passports for them through someone he knew. There was one thing he had to say to them they might not like. But that could come later. It must be Jason's bedtime and we'd like to take him to bed, have a look at his new curtains.

No one objected. Each holding a hand, we took Jason into his bedroom and were shown the curtains Alison had made to replace the strip of floral green cloth that had covered the window. With no sewing machine she had stitched them by hand and lined them. The material was patterned with zoo animals. Jason said Alison had found it, carefully folded and laid in the bottom drawer of a chest.

'She said Mr Robinson wouldn't mind. She said he'd have forgotten it was there.'

He looked incredulous. Such a failure of memory was beyond him. He put on his pyjamas and got into bed. I read to him for ten minutes, disappointed because Silver, who would once have stayed to hear of the activities of hobbits, went back to join Andrew and Alison. I kissed Jason good night, careful not to let my tears touch his face. I wiped my eyes before returning to the living room.

With Jason absent, Silver explained his strategy, or explained what he'd like them to consent to. The stumbling block, the difficulty, in any escape plan was Jason. His looks put him outside the possibility of being their natural child. He might, just, be taken for Spanish or Portuguese, but never of Anglo-Saxon parentage. So, if the escape was to work, they must be split up.

'No!' Alison shouted.

We all listened for some sound from Jason. There was nothing. 'Hear me out,' Silver said. 'My idea is that I should take him. I don't need a new passport, I've got one, and I've got an Australian visa. I went there a couple of years ago with my family. I'll never pass Jason off as a relative. He looks even less like me than like you. But I think I could say he was my stepson I'm taking home to his mother. That's just an idea. I may come up with a better. I did say this was an outline plan.'

Alison was staring at him. She kept her eyes on him the whole time he was speaking.

'You'd travel together, of course. No one will question you. Why should they? The only one to attract attention is Jason and he won't be with you. We won't go on the same flight. I'd suggest I go with Jason on, say, a Sunday and you follow on the Monday. We meet by prearrangement – in a hotel, say – I hand him over and go back on the next flight.'

'I can't agree to this,' Alison said.

Andrew gave her a cold look. 'Why not? What's wrong with it apart from the expense? It's going to be bloody expensive.'

'The money doesn't matter.' She made a throwing-away gesture, flinging out her hands. Her lined face contorted into wrinkles. 'If this makes us destitute, my father will look after us. But I can't be parted from Jason. And even if I could be, if I could bear that, Andrew and I couldn't travel on the same plane. Suppose it crashed? Suppose we were both killed? Jason would be left alone again.'

'You know, I'm amazed sometimes at the nonsense people talk,' Andrew said. 'Have you ever known someone set out on a car journey and ask what would happen if they were in a smash-up? No, of course you haven't. But they've only got to get on an hour-long flight from London to Edinburgh to start imagining it's going to crash.'

Silver looked from one to the other of them. 'Would you think about it? Discuss it? You may be able to improve on it.' He paused. 'And don't worry. Don't worry about the money.'

Once more we went down through the inside of the house. It was just after ten. There was no way of telling whether the Nylands were in bed or not, but as we passed on down the last flight of stairs, trying to be silent but not succeeding, the soles of our trainers slapping on those marble treads, the front door of Flat B opened. A man came out into the hall and looked up the stairs. Looked straight at us.

There were other people behind that door as we could tell by the sound of voices and laughter, but I supposed from Selina's description that this must be Sean Francis. He was tall and thin and dark with that sort of feminine face that later became so fashionable, short nose, full mouth. I saw him in a television play last week and he seemed not to have aged at all. I suppose he was in his late twenties at that time. He said in a sharp voice, 'What are you doing here?'

'Calling on the Nylands,' Silver said promptly.

'No, you can't have been. They're away.'

One of the great things about Silver was the way he always rose to the occasion, kept his cool, was never wrong-footed. 'Clodagh Brown

305

and Michael Silverman,' he said. 'How do you do? Mr Francis, I presume?'

'Well, yes.'

'My friend and I have been watering Mrs Nyland's houseplants. We run a home-tending service for clients away on holiday.'

Whether he swallowed this we'd no idea at the time, but he went back into his flat and closed the door. I said to Silver as we came out into the street, 'Can we talk? Can we go on the roofs and talk?'

He nodded. He seemed to understand. Not only were the roofs our element, they were also almost the only place, apart from his bed, we could go and be sure of being alone. We climbed up the scaffolding and walked along inside the parapet, not holding hands this time. While we were together in the past we had talked all the time, we could never make an end of finding new things to say to each other, but that night we walked in silence, looking upwards at the heavy clouds, lit to a deep sepia brown by the yellow chemical lights below. The wind was warm. It carried with it the faintest scent of green curry from a restaurant in Sutherland Avenue. We sat on the slates between a chimney stack and the tarpaulin. Silver gave me a cigarette.

'I know what you're going to say. That I shouldn't have said I was Michael Silverman when we've told Andrew and Alison we're both called Brown. It was a slip of the tongue. But the chances of their ever meeting and comparing notes are pretty remote.'

'I wasn't going to say that,' I said. Once he had always been able to make a good guess at what I was going to say.

'What, then?'

There were so many things. The one I most wanted to ask I shied away from. 'Who's going to pay for your proposed trip to Australia with Jason?'

'Andrew and Alison have money. They'll pay for themselves.'

'I expect they will, but I'll be very surprised if they finance a separate flight for you and Jason. You're planning to pay for it yourself, aren't you?'

'What if I am?'

'It'll cost thousands. And there'll be a hotel to pay for and cars to and from airports. And these passports, who's going to pay for them? False passports – have you any idea what you'll have to pay for them?'

He looked away from me. 'You think having money is bad for

someone my age. This would be a way of getting rid of it. You can't have it both ways.'

'D'you care how I have it? D'you really think the way you go on, the way you shut me out, I'm going to be there to have it one way or the other?' I'd started shouting, forgetful of the people not far below us. 'We were happy and you've made us miserable. You never told me a word of this plan of yours, you never consulted me. It was as much of a surprise to me as it was to them.'

He could be so cold and quiet. '*I've* made us miserable? I think you're forgetting your hand in it.'

I should have asked then but I didn't. I jumped up and ran away from him across the tarpaulin, not going carefully, not troubling where I set my feet, but running as if I were on solid ground. The damaged timbers creaked. I jumped on to the slates on the other side, making a lot of noise about it. He was watching me, blank-faced, not as if he cared what happened to me but out of mere interest in folly. I had looked back once but not again. I ran on, crying while I ran, the tears still coming while I climbed through our window. Judy was back, sitting with Niall, sharing a bottle of wine and a joint. Hours passed before Silver came to bed. He lay quite still for a minute or two, then turned his back on me.

It was Jonny Silver intended to ask about the passports. He told me this in the neutral cool voice he had begun using when he spoke to me. It was a far from ideal plan but it was the only one he could think of. Jonny was the only criminal he knew.

'And don't ask me what it's going to cost,' he said.

'I was going to ask you if it's wise to let Jonny in on this.'

'Probably not but who else is there to ask? You have to remember that whatever happens and whatever he does, he'd never, *never*, go to the police.'

I took Liv down the stairs, out of the front door and down the path. How about going out of the gate and taking a few steps down the street? She looked fearfully at me, then nodded as if agreeing to do something that took great courage. Perhaps it did. There was very little difference between the texture and surface of the path and that of the pavement, both being of Portland stone, but Liv behaved like someone attempting to step from firm ground on to a quicksand. I had a moment's anxiety when the front door of 19 opened and Selina came out, not because I was afraid to see her but on Liv's account, in case she mistook her for Claudia or some other avenging fury. But Liv seemed untroubled, concentrating now on taking a second step. Selina was carrying a big suitcase in each hand. She put them down on the path, went back and returned with two even larger cases. A taxi drew up. Apart from a little frisson passing through her neck and shoulders, Liv seemed unfazed. She was proceeding along the pavement like an amputee learning to use artificial legs.

Selina beckoned rather imperiously to the taxi driver. Taking his time about it, he got out of his cab and strolled up the path. Liv took him in her stride too, her eyes just flicking over him. Making sure the driver knew what was expected of him, Selina watched him pick up, with much panting, two of the cases. She came over to us. The complete solipsist, she showed no surprise at seeing me there, nor at seeing me the escort of someone apparently disabled, but cried out, 'I'm going, darling. I'm off to fresh woods and pastures new.'

I said goodbye to her and Liv did, though as far as I knew they had never before set eyes on each other. The taxi departed for Dolphin Square. At the gate of 17 Liv and I turned round and came back again. I was pleased with her and said so. She nodded complacently as if this was only her due. I could see she had taken a huge turn for the better, something largely brought about by Wim's attentions, it seemed. We no longer had qualms about leaving her alone. Wim would come to her and Jonny wouldn't. That was how we saw it – but how can I say 'we' like that when it was becoming impossible to use that pronoun, implying as it does a couple, a union, a closeness? *I* saw it like that and I believe Silver did too, that's all I can say. Yet we were still together and still united in our plan to rescue that imprisoned trio. But Silver went on his own to find Jonny, back to Holloway and the little grey house with a disproportionately large and high flight of steps reaching up to its front door.

I tried to make myself like Judy and be nice to her. My efforts must have worked, for she seemed happy to come with me to take her passport photographs at 4E. We all walked together to the end of Russia Road where Silver left us to get the bus to Swiss Cottage. Judy watched him go, rather wistfully, I thought, and said with some nervousness that I didn't expect her to climb on roofs, did I? We'd let ourselves in at the front door, I said. Andrew had given me a key. It was then that we had an unlooked-for piece of luck.

At first it seemed like disaster or near-disaster. We were on the doorstep of 4 Torrington Gardens, Judy with camera, tripod and a bagful of photographic stuff. I was fishing the key out of my pocket when the door was opened by Sean Francis. We took a step back. He looked at me, half-recognizing me as the Nylands' houseplant minder, then at Judy. An uncertain smile hovered, he put his head on one side, said, 'Hello. I know you, don't I? Can't remember where from.'

'Norroy,' Judy said. 'Norroy House. *The Ghost Child.*'

'That's *right*. How extraordinary. How are your mum and dad? And the terribly nice lady who used to make endless cups of tea?'

'They're fine, they're all fine.'

'Look, are you living round here? I'm in a mad rush, I'm late before I've started, but give me a ring, will you? We might have a coffee or a drink or something.'

Judy said she would, she'd like to. He ran off down Torrington Gardens. Not a word had been said about me or watering the houseplants or the Nylands. We stepped inside the hall and closed the door behind us. 'What was all that about?' I said. 'How d'you know him?'

Her parents had lent their house to the television production company that was making a film Sean Francis was in. The company paid them a lot of money, refurnished the house and partly decorated it but the family remained in what had been a housekeeper's flat. Judy and her brother got to know some of the cast quite well, a state of affairs helped by their grandmother, who lived with them, luring some of the actors away from their mobile canteen and plying them with tea and cakes.

'It was just before I started going about with Silver. I told him about it but I expect he's forgotten.'

I decided not to comment on that. We started up the marble staircase, eight flights of it. 'Would you have a drink with him? You wouldn't mind?'

'It would be a funny sort of girl who'd mind,' she said.

'Because we have to get him in on this. We have to take him into our confidence. The ideal thing would be if you could sort of pave the way and then maybe we could all meet and – well, tell him.'

'I'll call him tomorrow.' She grinned. 'Who knows what may come of it?' Outside the Nylands' front door she stopped, turned and said to me, 'I just want to say, Clodagh, you know I'm not interested in Silver any more, don't you? I love him, I really do, but not like that. Not any more. And he doesn't like me like that. I just want you to know, though I expect you do already.'

Honesty is mostly best. 'No, I didn't already. Thanks. Thanks a lot.' I felt like laughing and singing, though I knew this didn't solve everything or even anything much. I smiled at her.

'Only I thought you'd been a bit cold with me and you're not really a cold person, are you?'

'No. No, I'm not.'

I don't know which of us made the first move. But she put her arms round me and I put mine around her and we hugged each other there on the marble step halfway up the empty echoing house. It's a good feeling, your enemy turning into your friend in the twinkling of an eye. Just a few words said, a misunderstanding cleared up, the world changed.

Andrew's eye looked out at us through the tiny glass hole in the door. Bolts were drawn, a chain removed, and he let us in. He had managed to grow a small moustache about as thick as his eyebrows. It did quite a lot to alter his appearance but his suspicious nature was unchanged. He had been prepared for Judy's coming but he was still apprehensive and later, while she was going about the flat with Alison looking for a suitable place to take her shots, he questioned me – in fact, he interrogated me – as to her trustworthiness. How well did I know her? How could he know she wouldn't just take her pictures to the police?

'I can only tell you she won't do that,' I said. 'If you don't want her to take your photographs, you'd better say now and we'll go. But there's no one else and you have to have photos for your passports.'

He nodded, not entirely convinced. Where was Silver? Why hadn't he come? Did I realize this was the first time Silver hadn't come?

I said he had gone to see someone about the passports. Someone he knew on the other side of London who he hoped would be able to get them. Judy came back and the photography session began. Jason, who might have made a fuss at being expected to sit still, enjoyed posing and faced the camera with an engaging smile. Andrew consented to comb down his hair into a fringe across his brow and when this was done looked even less like his former self. Alison had been cutting his hair and not very successfully but this way the chopped-off pudding-basin effect worked. We got Alison to make herself up heavily and use a dark lipstick Judy had brought with her. It aged her, making her seem more tired and worn than ever, but at least she looked quite unlike all the newspaper photographs. They were both dubious about their appearance in these shots. Did such small subterfuges really create a disguise? I reminded them that, without Jason, no passport official was likely to give them a second glance, but all this did was to start Alison off again on the horrors of being parted from him.

We took their shopping list, promised to report back on how Silver had got on and then we left, Andrew muttering as he accompanied us to the door that we did understand, didn't we, that he wasn't made of money, he couldn't pay some ridiculous price for false documents, it wasn't as if he had a regular income.

'They're not very nice, are they?' Judy said as we clattered down, not bothering to muffle our footsteps with no one to hear us. 'He's no charmer and she whinges all the time.'

I thought how odd it was that the oppressed, the disadvantaged, the victims, are always supposed to be nice people. To be virtuous and lovable, almost saintly. If they're not, and they're just as often not, there's resentment, a feeling that they don't deserve rescuing. But people can't change and become perfect overnight as soon as they find themselves in a trap or in peril. I said some of this to Judy and she laughed and said it was all very well in the case of hostages but Andrew and Alison's situation was of their own making. If they expected help, they ought to be pleasanter to their rescuers.

'You haven't rescued them yet, anyway,' she said.

Silver hadn't returned. I didn't expect him for a long while. Judy said let's go round to the Robert Browning or the Warrington Hotel and take Wim with us. But he was evidently behind that closed door in bed with Liv, so we went alone. Max and Caroline Bodmer were at a table outside the Warrington but once they had seen me they left quickly. We stayed until the pub shut and went home slowly through the warm streets, making a diversion to the canal to watch the dine-and-dance boat go by, its coloured lights glittering, its music drifting across the water.

'I really fancy that Sean,' Judy said. 'It's not going to be a punishment getting to know him better.'

Five years later she married him, and when I last heard they had two babies and were very happy, but that was all unthought of then. Silver came home in the small hours, I think it was about three. He sat on the bed and told me in a tired voice – or was he just tired of me? – that he had seen Jonny and got a promise from him to produce three passports.

27

When he got there Jonny was out. The house was a warren of single rented rooms. No one living there knew where he was or when he'd be back, but several confirmed that he was a tenant. Silver sat down on the wall outside to wait for him. The neighbourhood, not far from Holloway prison, was very different from ours. Not so many people owned cars but everyone seemed to want to be out in the streets, either walking about or sitting on their front doorsteps. The night was warm for early September but the sky overcast and the atmosphere sultry as if a storm threatened. Men's shouts and women's shrieks, which always seem to start when darkness comes, had begun and bursts of rock music thudded out of passing cars, their windows open or their roofs down. Silver told me all this as if I didn't know it already or as if there was no one there and he was talking to himself.

He kept his eyes turned away. I suddenly understood that he was deeply unhappy but when I put out my hand to touch his hand he withdrew it. He had sat in the corner café opposite and drank coffee. Tiredness had come over him and he needed something to keep him awake. Jonny came when he was on the point of giving up. The café had closed and he was back on the wall, almost stunned by the volume of someone's music belting out of an open window behind him. It was ten to one.

Jonny was carrying a black leather backpack, not on his back but with one of its straps hooked over his shoulder. He said hello to Silver and called him mate. Silver asked if they could talk and, after a momentary hesitation, Jonny nodded. They went upstairs through that dilapidated house which smelt of grass and tobacco and curry but most overpoweringly of decay from the wheelie-bin in the hall. If they left it outside, someone would nick it, Jonny said, as if stealing garbage containers was the most ordinary thing in the world. His room was at the top of the house. Silver noticed that access to the flat roof would be easy through the single sash window.

The coffee had done its work and he felt wide awake and very aware of his surroundings. He suspected the black leather backpack was Håkan Almquist's, yet he couldn't have positively identified it, not if, for instance, the police had asked him. Nothing in the room gave any clue to Jonny's affluence, if affluent he was. He was dressed much as usual, the room was furnished as such places are, drearily and sparsely. It was dirty and untidy. For Silver to make that comment meant it must have been in a bad state. Since it looked as if he wasn't going to be offered anything, he asked if there was any tea or instant coffee. Jonny looked as if about to say a blunt no, but eventually produced an electric kettle, two mugs and, in the palm of his hand, two teabags.

'Liv been out in the street yet?' Silver shrugged, taking the mug of milkless tea. 'Because when she does I'm fetching her back here. I'll be over to fetch her in the van. You can tell her that, so as she's ready.'

Silver made no reply to that. He went straight into the middle of things and asked Jonny about the passports. Could he get passports for a man, a woman and a child?

'I might be able to.'

Silver wanted yes or no but he knew better than to ask directly.

'It'll cost you,' added Jonny.

'How much?'

'Couple of K each.'

Silver had no means of knowing if this was, so to speak, the standard rate for false passports, if it was too high or even too low. The trouble with dealing with criminals if you're not one yourself is that the language is unfamiliar to you, the country they inhabit, all the terms of reference. Would Andrew Lane be willing to pay this sort of money? Would his wife agree? And if they weren't willing but still wanted to leave the country, would he pay it out of his own pocket?

'Would you?' I said.

'If I have to.'

I wanted to say, in one of my mother's pet phrases, that there was no 'have to' about it, but I could see that would have no effect on him.

'The fuss people make about a couple of thousand,' he said, thinking, I suppose, of Liv's lost money as well. 'It's not megabucks, for God's sake.'

Not to you. And there lies the difference. 'So you told him to go ahead?'

'I told him I'd bring him the photographs as soon as Judy has them ready.' This was tantamount to a yes. 'I didn't tell him who they were for. I was putting off doing that, I know, even though he'd never go near the police.'

Silver was leaving, he was at the door, when he turned round and asked Jonny straight out if it was he who had assaulted Håkan Almquist and taken his backpack. He said he wouldn't have been surprised to get the old answer, 'It might have been.' But Jonny just looked at him. You read in thrillers about a man giving someone an 'ugly' look – well, that describes a frequent expression of Jonny's quite well. He gave Silver an ugly look. Silver was about six inches taller than he and six years younger but Jonny would still be a formidable opponent. He looked as if he was going to make for the door and head-butt him.

When nothing happened Silver thought, nothing venture nothing have, and that if Jonny moved he could get outside and slam the door on him. He said, 'What did you do with the money?'

'Don't you worry about that,' Jonny said in a parody of Silver's own often repeated advice. 'I know where the fucking money is. It's where no one else will find it.' And he started laughing.

It's not megabucks, for God's sake, I thought. Silver went downstairs and out into the street. All public transport but night buses had stopped and there were none of those about. He had got as far as Archway when a taxi came.

'That's another way of getting rid of your capital,' I said, more nastily than I had ever spoken to him.

He didn't say any more.

What is seen can't be unseen. What is said can't be unsaid. The cruel epithet, the insults and accusations, these may be forgiven but not forgotten. And surely forgiveness implies forgetting, because without forgetfulness all that was said and seen remains. It's said that when the Catholic receives absolution for the sins he has confessed, he knows not only that they are forgiven but that they have passed utterly from the mind of God.

Silver and I were unable to forget but we could accept. I've accepted and now I can look back and, remembering, smile.

We had few private places of our own in Silver's flat, no sanctums, but I did have the old desk which was a reject of his father's and which stood in a corner of our bedroom. On its scuffed red leather inlay I laid my notebooks and wrote my diary. It was there, the next morning, that I found the letter from Guy in its envelope, rather creased, lying on the red leather and precisely lined up alongside the right angle of its lower left-hand corner. I took it out and started reading it, immediately realizing that I hadn't read it before. In it, in an old-fashioned courtly way, he proposed marriage.

Guy knew I had someone else, yet in this letter he had seemed to assume that Silver – he didn't know him by name – was just a stopgap while I and he made up our minds, or else that he was someone used to make him jealous. He took it for granted I wanted to be married, that I was waiting for him to ask. When I read that I wondered how much he had talked to my mother and what she had said to him of her own hopes.

I read on, sitting on the bed in which Silver lay fast asleep. Guy wrote that he understood I needed time to make up my mind. But he reminded me that we had known each other a long time and that he alone (according to me) supported me when everyone turned against me after the pylon. He made it sound as if he had *kept* me, I mean given me money. Then he wrote about the job in his father's firm and again he referred to this as if it had been seriously proposed and seriously considered by me. I had no real job, no training, only a truncated education, but if I married him I'd never need to work again, a way of life he put to me as if it was the answer to my prayers, the ideal, any woman's ambition. Besides that, we loved each other. We had been so close, he wrote, that giving each other up now would be impossible and wrong. We belonged to one another.

It shocked me very much. In a way it frightened me, because I wondered what kind of a man this was, who could insinuate to a woman that being her friend was supporting her and that eating a few meals together, sharing a drink and parting with a kiss was passion. But that was all I was afraid of. If I thought about it, I supposed Liv or Wim or Niall had found the letter on top of the wastebin, suspected it had been thrown away in error, rescued it and put it on my desk. And opened it first? I didn't like that but there was nothing I could do about it then, so I went off to the Houghtons' before Silver was awake.

Judy developed the photographs herself. She showed them to us that evening. No one could have identified Andrew and Alison as their true selves from those pictures. Somehow, very cleverly, while taking shots which were plainly the kind acceptable to immigration officials, that is full-faced, looking straight into the camera, she had made them look subtly different due to the angle of their heads, Andrew's hair and moustache and Alison's make-up. But Jason looked like himself. This was the boy of the newspaper prints. Not just any handsome Asian or part-Asian child but entirely himself, unmistakable to any observant person who had taken minimal interest in the media versions of the case.

He was good-looking, but not with the rather dull good looks that show themselves in classical features. His upper lip was short, his mouth full and tilted upwards at the corners. In spite of the undoubted trials of his short life, he seemed always on the brink of a smile. His eyes were large, bright and steady, not shifting away or furtive but always fixed on whomsoever he was listening to. These things couldn't be disguised. If his skin in the photo looked paler than in reality, there remained plenty in his face that could never have had its origins in Europe. He was the Indian youth in the wall painting. Except that it sounds too fanciful, I'd say he was Krishna dancing with the milkmaids.

'Shall I take another shot of him?' Judy asked.

Silver had been scrutinizing the picture. He said he didn't think it would matter as when the escape began Jason would be with him, they'd be travelling first and alone together. He looked at me, perhaps waiting for more inquiries as to where the cost of it was coming from. I say 'perhaps' because, sadly, I could no longer intuit what Silver was thinking, just as he could no longer guess my thoughts.

We went to 4E, Wim accompanying us, not that we had any news to impart or any shopping to carry beyond that day's papers, but because we had got into the habit of paying nightly visits. For reassurance, for comfort, to relieve the monotony of their dreadful days and interminable evenings. And we wanted to show them the pictures, the several versions Judy had produced. Andrew seemed fascinated by his own face, so greatly changed by the moustache (now more luxuriant) and the fringe of hair covering his forehead. With one of his laughs which were shrill and unkind, he called Alison a 'painted hussy' and hinted he might find her more attractive if she looked like that all the time. Silver asked what they wanted to be called on the passports and Alison suggested Blythe, her half-brother's name. It was Wim, rather surprisingly, who objected. The police would know everything about their backgrounds, he said, all their past, all previous names and connections. It didn't mean they hadn't got it fully documented just because there was no mention of it in the papers. There were things they would keep dark in case revealing them hampered their inquiries.

Andrew sat at the table and looked through *The Times* and the *Mail*. For the first time since the hunt for the three of them had begun, Jason's natural mother had appeared on the scene and given her story to a journalist. The newspaper was weary of reproducing the stale old photographs and no doubt delighted to feature instead this portrait of a very good-looking woman in her twenties. Nelima Patel looked a lot like Jason, or perhaps I should say he looked very like her. I was desperate for him not to see this picture, not to ask who it was and perhaps guess without being told. Eager to read anything he could get his hands on, he often snatched the papers we brought. Andrew and Alison had told him a good deal about their escape with him, they'd had to, they'd had somehow to justify the hiding away, the necessity of staying indoors, his lack of companions. He was fond of reading about himself. Especially when he had been seen on the seafront at Weston-super-Mare, say, when he knew perfectly well he had been in Maida Vale. But this time his attention was held elsewhere, concentrated on the photographs. There were twenty-four of them from which three must be selected. He shifted them about on the table as if they were cards in a patience game.

A name they chose, Silver said, had better be one that had no connection with their past or present. Not even a cousin's name or something taken from a W9 street or a current newspaper story, nothing that rhymed with their names or simply had the initial letter changed. Not, for instance, Fane or Parry. Alison fetched the phone book and finally they chose to call themselves Mr and Mrs Rogers, Gerald and Pamela Rogers.

Jason, who wouldn't be travelling with them, would seem to

have no connection with them, would become James Robert Desai.

His mother's story, which I read while they picked the photographs they thought approximated least to the reality and most to their disguised selves, sounded like the invention of a romantic novelist, and an old-fashioned one at that. It read as if the words had been put into her mouth by someone whose whole concept of present-day existence involved hard-done-by young women, virtuous, brave and selfless, and attractive, callous, mean-minded men bent only on seduction. Nelima Patel had been married and divorced since Jason's birth, her husband also having deserted her. She had three more children and a new partner, was unemployed as was he, living on the dole, bitterly regretting, according to the journalist, abandoning Jason into the care of the local authority. Once he and his abductors were found, she would fight to get him back. While no one was looking, I took the double page on which the story appeared out of the paper and stuffed it, all screwed up, into my pocket.

'I saw you. You did the right thing,' Silver said to me when we were climbing down the scaffolding. This was the only sign of approval I had had from him for some time.

'What would Jason have thought if he'd seen it? I can't imagine it. People fighting over – well, ownership of you. Your real mother with three more kids but not with you.'

We dropped to the ground. Wim had gone. His new interest in Liv couldn't keep him from the roofs and he had departed along the highway of Sutherland Avenue towards the Harrow Road. Silver started talking about the lost three days of his life, the time someone had taken him away, hidden him, cared tenderly for him, and then, inexplicably, returned him near the place he had been snatched from. For Diana Lomax to find and take back to Jack Silverman. He talked as if to himself or to an unseen audience, not to me.

'Suppose the person or people who took me hadn't taken me back? I often wonder what made them take me back. After all, they might have got away with it. Andrew and Alison have. Or they have for seven months. When we've got them out of the country they'll have got away with it for good. It would be easier for me to understand my own situation if the police had burst into wherever it was and arrested whoever it was and restored me to my sorrowing parents. But she – he – whoever – took me to that little beach, precisely under the cliff where I was taken from, and left me there. I was *three*. What kind of a person leaves a child of three alone on a beach, in a cove, with the tide coming in?

'Suppose instead they'd kept me and I'd never have been found. What would they have done for me? How would I have been brought up? And where would I be now? A fatalist would say everything would have been the same in the end, because that's my destiny, to be walking along Torrington Gardens, w9, at ten-thirty on 3rd September, come what may. But I don't believe that. I think maybe I'd have grown up in Cornwall or south Wales or even America with a different name and different parents and different siblings too. Now I'd be at the University of Cardiff or New York State and I'd never have walked on the roofs.'

I waited for him to say that he'd never have met me, but of course I was disappointed in that. He spoke not another word until we got to the end of the street where the house on its own stood amid its shadowy garden of evergreens and fading roses. Then he said, quite abruptly, that he wasn't coming back with me but going straight to Holloway to hand the photographs over to Jonny and tell him the passports were to be for Gerald and Pamela Rogers and James Desai.

I've been with Darren and Junilla and his children to Disneyland, Paris, on the Eurostar. We stayed overnight and came back the next day with carrier bags full of wine and packs of cigarettes for him and Lysander. Both children were with us so that Campaspe could have a weekend with her new man.

I had a good enough time but I don't really know why I went. Because I was invited? Because I was lonely? These last few weeks, only three now, are dragging badly. When my husband comes home I should throw a great party to welcome him, Junilla says. She'd have a party every weekend if it was practicable. But I don't want anyone there but me when he comes home. I'm hungry to see him. It's as if my eyes ache from not seeing him. I devote a lot of mind-space between working and writing this to imagining the cab bringing him home draw up down there on the drive-in and to seeing him get out and pay the man and hump his bags. I ought to go down and help him up with them but I don't – in my vision of this, I mean – but I wait here to hear the faint slithering hiss of the lift as it brings him up to the penthouse floor. The doors slide open and click shut behind him, and then he comes to this door, his bags bumping and sliding, and I hear his key turn in the lock.

'*Hiss*' is Swedish for a lift. Niall said it must be an onomatopoeia, a term I'd never heard until he brought it out, the word echoing the sound a lift makes. But Liv, who had used it, saying ungratefully that 15 Russia Road was impossible without a '*hiss*', insisted that was nonsense, it came from the old Norse.

'What, those old Vikings had lifts? In their ships maybe?'

Liv didn't much like Niall. She said he was always picking on her. And it's true he was a pedantic person, always saying things like, 'It all depends on what you mean by so-and-so,' and 'Can you define that?' He's a professor of something or other now at one of those universities that come very high up the league tables. But at that time he was a spotty boy with red hair who boasted that he passed his exams without doing any work. I suppose he fancied Liv. They say that men who trump up arguments with women and are critical of their appearance and way of life are really attracted by them. Perhaps Niall was. At any rate, he took over my job of escorting Liv downstairs for her therapy walk, though bullying her in a whiny voice and nagging her to do better. The walk now extended as far as 7 Russia Road, which was in the next terrace. Liv probably walked a yard more every day, but she wouldn't cross the road. She had some idea that a favourite contract-killing method was to run the victim over. James and Claudia, in her feverish imagination, were just the kind of people to employ a hitman in a big Mercedes.

Silver, of course, thought it wiser and kinder not to pass on Jonny's message to her. It would only upset her. Besides, when she eventually left his place she'd naturally go back to Sweden. With no money but her air fare, still in Silver's bank account, she had very little choice. Jonny had received the photographs, at first with no comment. But he returned to them after a few minutes, staring long and hard at the shot of Jason. Silver knew he never read a newspaper, on account of reading being a problem for him, but he had watched a lot of television while in Russia Road and might have access to television still, though there was no set in that room.

'He's that kid,' he said at last. 'The Paki kid.'

Usually so calm, Silver was filled with rage at this description of Jason, whose mother, according to the paper, had been born in Bradford, the child of Brahmins from Varanasi. But he had to hold his tongue if he wanted those passports.

'These two are the folks that kidnapped him, are they?'

Silver nodded, not trusting himself to speak. Afterwards he thought he should have said, 'They might be,' which Jonny would have understood.

'A real dog, that one,' he commented of Alison. 'There's some ugly women make me sick, I mean puke. Don't tell me you've got this lot up in your place.'

'I wasn't going to tell you that.'

'Come on, Silv, where are they?'

Silver had to tell him. He had to tell him and explain. He wouldn't have put it past Jonny to go calling at 4E and perhaps try some blackmail, always supposing anyone let him in. He told me, he was bitterly regretting ever having befriended Jonny, ever having let him have a room in his flat, and the worst of it was that at the time he had thought it dashing and rather smart to have a friend who was a burglar. And the consequence was that he found himself plunged into crime in that foul room at two o'clock in the morning, Jonny's grin cold and his expression full of contempt. So much for friendship, so much for having an open mind.

But he needed those passports. Of all of us I think it was Silver who was most committed to the protection and ultimate rescue of the people at 4E. Wim and I, Judy, even Liv, wished them well, felt they had been badly treated and wanted to get them out of there and safely bound for some distant freedom. But if the difficulties had seemed too great, the odds too stacked against us, we'd have given up. We'd have told them there was no more we could do beyond bringing them food. Silver went much further than that. Rescuing Andrew and Alison and keeping Jason with them was a passion, nothing deflected him from his object. So however bad Jonny might be, however nauseating it was to listen to his insulting words and understand that everything he did was motivated by greed and a compulsion to take revenge on society, Silver knew he needed him and that without his help he couldn't proceed with our plan. He waited for Jonny to ask for some of the payment in advance and Jonny did ask. He had upped the figure and now wanted £7,000 for the the three passports, £2,000 to be a down payment.

'I thought I was a sort of citizen of the world,' Silver said, 'free and classless. A Robin Hood/Scarlet Pimpernel kind of character, equally happy in the company of villains as of nobs. As at home with the crooked as with the straight. I'm learning how deeply conformist I am. I offered him a cheque. He laughed. That laughter taught me a lot, among other things that my belief he liked me was just illusion. He never liked me, he never thought about it. I was useful and he used me. Of course he wouldn't take a cheque. He was amazed, he said, that I hadn't brought cash with me. As soon as the bank opened this morning he came with me and I drew the money out.'

'If it's invested,' I said, knowing very little about these things, 'didn't you have to give them notice you wanted to draw such a large sum? Didn't you have to get your stockbroker or whatever to sell some of them?'

He didn't answer but turned away and went into the kitchen. I saw then, I don't know how, that he had taken those steps weeks before. He had prepared for this rescue, laying his plans in advance. I went to the Houghtons' and while I worked on building a structure with wooden uprights and chicken wire to house a compost heap, I thought about Silver and me and wondered if we were coming to the end of the road, our road. If what had been so lovely, a real passion and joy in one another's company, had worn itself out because we were so young and perhaps hadn't worked at our relationship. And perhaps too because I had said things that implied Silver had too much money, couldn't handle money and failed to understand what the lack of it meant to others. So I was sad and maybe seemed sullen. I kept thinking that the time was coming when I'd have to leave this place and live alone once more. Yet life was unthinkable without him. I wondered how I had existed before I met him, all those lonely months at old Mrs Fisherton's. I see I've written in my diary for that day that only the job we had to do together, our rescue mission, kept me there with him. We had to see that through but when it was done I'd go. Unless things changed, unless he came back to me.

Another sad thing was that we seemed to go on the roofs less and less. There was no real need to approach 4E along the balcony and enter through the window. It was quicker and simpler to walk to the end of Torrington Gardens, go up the steps to the front door and let ourselves in with the key Andrew had given us. The roofs were just for the fun of it and we had fun together no longer.

Once inside the house our only fear had been of encountering Sean Francis but in the few days since she had made herself known to him, Judy and he had spent a lot of time together. He accepted our visits to the house, still I suppose believing we were there to water the Nylands' plants, for Judy had said nothing to him about who lived on the top floor. One disquieting thing, though. He knew someone was up there. Once, before we began to do the shopping for them, he had seen Andrew, seen him only from the back as he let himself out of the front door, but that had been enough to intrigue him. Up till then, he had believed the top floor unoccupied. The next time he had spoken to Mrs Nyland he had asked her if she had heard anything overhead and she had told him that once or twice she had been aware of a child's running feet. One very warm day when her windows were open she thought she had heard a woman's voice, but it might have come from the house next door. All this had been imparted to Judy, who was waiting for the right moment to tell Sean who was actually up there. Or not to tell him if she sensed his sympathies wouldn't be with us.

The Nylands were due back in the following week. That meant, of course, that our excuse of watering their plants would no longer work. Judy would have to tell him the truth or we would have to resume our visits from the roof. And if he remained in ignorance of what we were really doing in the house, he might, almost certainly would, mention us and our activities to Mrs Nyland.

But none of this worried us much that evening. Upstairs, on the top, we always rang the bell, though we had a key to Flat E as well. It was as if we now only went there as invited guests. We had a code for the doorbell, two long rings and a short one. Jason let us in, ecstatic as usual to see us. We were invited into his bedroom to see a painting he had done that day, which Alison had stuck on the wall with the Blu-Tack we had brought in with the rest of the shopping. It was a picture of a ship in a bottle, he had used the real one he had as a model, but on the deck stood a boy obviously intended to be himself, waving at something or someone, the shore perhaps, a desert island or a crowd on the beach. Who knows? A psychologist might have said that instead of just drawing a boy on a boat he had drawn a boy on a boat in a bottle because the bottle represented his prison walls, transparent but also impassable. Silver picked up the bottle itself, seemingly fascinated by it as he had been when we were once before in that room.

'I've read about these things,' he said, 'how they put the masts on hinges and attach strings to them so that when the boat's been got in they can pull the strings and the masts and sails stand up, but I don't think I've ever seen a real one before. And yet I seem to remember one. Looking at Jason's picture, I feel as if I can remember being where he is, standing on the deck of a ship in a bottle – but it's all nonsense.'

He put the bottle down and we went back into the living room and told Alison and Andrew the cost of the passports. Andrew said it was impossible, he couldn't pay that. Suppose the whole venture went wrong? He had had in mind less than half the sum Silver had mentioned.

'But we've got it,' Alison said. 'Is there anything better we could spend it on?'

'A car,' Andrew said, 'a house, or the start of paying back a loan on a house, clothes, schooling for Jason. Hundreds of things, our fares to Australia included.'

'We can't go at all without passports.'

Silver promised to try and get the cost reduced. He'd never succeed with Jonny and I knew that, while telling Andrew, as he would, that the price had been cut, he'd pay the surplus himself. He so passionately wanted to get these people and this child safely out of the country and safely received in Sydney that, if necessary, he'd impoverish himself to do it.

28

I still have those passports. They're in front of me now. How they came into my hands and remained in my possession I'll tell you later. They're no use to anyone, you might say they're not *real* passports, they're false, illegal documents, but they cost so much, they represent such a sacrifice and such resolution that I have kept them as a memento of those things and of the best-laid plans going wrong.

When I look at the photograph of Alison, I wonder how we ever thought it could be accepted as of a real woman who naturally looked like that. The make-up on her face, the mouth drawn wider and fuller than her natural mouth, the eyes painted with black lines and the eyelashes caked with mascara. Andrew's is almost as bad, for his has that rogues' gallery wanted-man's look as he glowers from under an eyebrow-overhanging fringe. Jason looks beautiful, he looks flawless, and when my eyes rest on his photograph with a kind of pity and longing I can understand why makers of commercials and advertisements want to use younger and younger models.

Alison's passport describes her as being called Pamela Mary Rogers, a British citizen, born on 19 March 1949. In his passport Andrew is Gerald Rogers, born on 3 June 1951. Jason has become James Desai, and because he was tall Silver had decreed his date of birth to be ten not eight years before, but kept to its true date of 7 November lest anyone ask him. In some circumstances you could ask a child to lie but not about his birthday. It must be the most important date in his year. Each passport has an Australian visa in the appropriate place, or perhaps I should say a false Australian visa. Only in Silver's was the visa authentic.

We took the passports round to 4E as soon as Silver had collected them from Jonny. Andrew contemplated them in silence, shaking his head.

'Five thousand pounds,' he said at last, and repeated it. 'Five thousand pounds.'

'We don't have a choice,' Alison said.

'When I was a child, a man earning £5,000 a year was rich. You could buy a very nice house for £5,000. You could buy a house and a car.'

This seemed irrelevant to me. After all, when his father was a child you could probably buy a house and a car for five *hundred* pounds and in his grandfather's youth for fifty. What was clear was that he was going to demur at the cost and not just demur, refuse to pay. Silver, who had already taken £2,000 off, said, 'I negotiated a price. It's come down to £3,000.'

Of course he hadn't negotiated a price. He was going to pay it out of his own pocket. If Andrew saw this he gave no sign of it. He just said a grudging 'all right', picked up all three passports and put them in the table drawer. Alison asked about flights to Australia. How? When? Silver suggested two weeks' time. It might be a good idea to fix a date immediately and he would buy the tickets. Economy class, Andrew said, he hoped that was understood. Silver was on the edge of anger but he controlled it.

'Look, I'm taking it that you do want to do this? You want to get away from here and to Sydney?'

'Of course we do,' Alison said, 'and we're enormously grateful to you. I don't know why you should have done all this for us, we think it's angelic of you. You must never think we don't appreciate it.'

Silver nodded, unsmiling. 'So shall we say September 18th? It's a Saturday, just over two weeks from now. I'll take Jason that day and I suggest you follow twenty-four hours later on the Sunday.'

'If you like.' Alison looked nervous now things were becoming so definite. 'I don't mean that, I mean anything you say, we're in your hands.'

I saw that she was afraid to go. More than that, she wanted to remain where she was. It was too big a step, they had suffered enough, the venture might fail and all be lost. Here they were safe. Departing was to come to the edge of the abyss and leap blindfold. I looked at Alison's face and thought, you won't sleep much till September 18th, you'll lie awake worrying all those nights between now and then.

'Does he, I mean Jason, does he have to go with you?' she asked.

Silver said those words we should be very careful about saying, the words that make too enormous a promise unless we're absolutely confident we can fulfil it. 'Trust me.'

'I trust you. I'm only saying you ought to know how hard it will be for me to – well, surrender Jason into your hands.'

'Think about it less melodramatically,' Silver said. 'Better still, don't think about it. Don't let it bother you. Leave it to us. I'll book the flights, I'll buy the tickets.'

Andrew made no move. As I have said, we had no idea where they kept their hoard except that it wasn't in that room. Unless it was in the table drawer, but all that had seemed to contain was their passports. A memory came back to me from five or six years before. A man, a former friend of my father's, had come to our house ostensibly to repay a loan. Dad had lent him £1,000. He stayed for hours, he drank tea, he ate biscuits, he drank gin and tonic, beer, and at last got up to go without mentioning the loan. He was halfway to the door and then Dad had to speak, embarrassed, hating it, saying what I now said.

'You owe us some money.'

'All right, all right. I was going to give you something.' Andrew sounded quite irritable, as if we were beggars who had approached him in the street. 'I'll just remind you that we can't earn, we don't have jobs like you, we don't have an income. What we have diminishes a bit every day. Even when we get to Australia these visas you've got us don't entitle us to work. If we work, we'll have to do it illegally.'

'You should be used to that,' I said. 'You've been doing something illegal for seven months.'

None of them thought me capable of speaking like that and I had rather surprised myself. Alison said, 'Please don't be angry. Please don't think we're ungrateful. It's just that we're in – well, a very nervous state.' She looked near to tears. 'Andrew doesn't mean it,' she said when he'd left the room to fetch their contribution to our expenses. 'I wish you could hear what he says about you when you're not here. He's always singing your praises.'

This I found hard to believe but I said no more. I used to wonder a lot about Andrew Lane. It was plain that he loved Jason, and loved him as much as Alison did. Once he must have loved Alison. He must have wanted to draw their money out of the bank, leave home, run from hotel to B and B to caravan, make arrangements with Louis Robinson, hide up there. But the way of life he had chosen was more than he could cope with. He longed for freedom, and he was unsure that he wanted Jason at any price. Imprisonment was destroying his love for Alison. He simply wasn't strong enough, steadfast enough, and perhaps he was always tugged by the memory of what they had had before, good jobs, an income, a nice house, friends, neighbours, freedom. But no Jason. Was Jason worth it? I was thinking all this when he came back with a wad of £20 and £10 notes. He dealt out £2,000, put the notes into Silver's hands and asked him to count them.

'I'll give you some more when you've got our plane tickets.'

This meant, of course, that Silver was going to have to buy the tickets out of his own pocket. Neither Andrew nor Alison showed any surprise that a boy of twenty could find the sort of sums we were talking about. It seemed not to occur to them. I suppose that when they lived in the real world they had both earned so much that they assumed those still out there did also.

The letter from Guy was still on the desk where I had left it. Wondering why I had bothered to keep it once I had read it, I tore it up and dropped the pieces in our wastebin.

Silver, watching me, said, 'Are you going to?'

'Am I going to what?'

'Marry him. This guy Guy.'

I could hardly believe it. I stared at him. 'Of course I'm not going to marry him. I'm too young to get married.'

'Is that the only reason?'

What I knew wasn't pleasant. 'Have you read my letter?'

He sat down on the bed and lit a cigarette. He didn't give me one. 'You left it in your jeans pocket. I took your jeans to the launderette and when I was clearing out the pockets I found it. Classic, isn't it? It's what women are supposed to do when their husbands are unfaithful. I've read about it in books.'

'And you read my letter?'

'I did. Dreadful, wasn't it? You must be very shocked. It's something to be ashamed of, isn't it, reading other people's letters? I don't care. I don't give a shit. I opened it and read it. It didn't give me any pleasure reading it, or any sort of satisfaction. In fact, it made me bloody miserable and bloody angry too.'

'Is that why you've been all cold and sulky?' I said.

'What do you think?'

He said he was going to sleep on the sofa. I could have the bed but he'd prefer me not to invite anyone else into it while he was in the flat.

I lay in that bed feeling all sorts of guilt and all sorts of resentment. I wrote nothing in my diary. What I've set down here is what I remember. I may not have got every word and every phrase right. How deeply engraved on our concept of what honour ought to be is the principle that however you may deceive and lie, prevaricate and deviate, you must never never read someone else's letters. Silver had seemed to me the soul of honour. If anyone had asked me what I saw in him, I'd have said I found him attractive, I found him funny and clever and the best company in the world, but first and foremost I loved him for his integrity. What became of that when he had read my private letter?

And I didn't care for Guy at all. I felt a sort of loyalty to him and a great deal of gratitude but that letter, which implied I was looking for a husband and a home and what I believe is called a meal ticket, had killed the little affection I had. Silver, my calm and laid-back, clever and funny Silver, had been perturbed by that letter? Did that mean he was less than what I had thought and I had been deluded? Or was it that I had no understanding of jealousy? You must understand that I'm asking myself this now, I didn't ask it then. But I remembered Judy and how I had been afraid of her and I fell asleep feeling less furiously indignant than I had when Silver first left me to spend the night on the sofa.

We made it up the next day. He said he was sorry he had read the letter, he knew it was an awful thing to do, and I explained it was so unimportant to me that I had no interest in who read it. I hadn't even done so myself for ages.

It wasn't one of my Houghton days, so I sat down and wrote to Guy, saying no to his proposal and that it might be best if we didn't see each other again. I offered to show the letter to Silver who said I was like a Victorian bride, writing to former suitors under her husband's instructions, and refused to look at it.

'Come up on the roof,' he said.

We climbed out of the window. Dusk was violet-coloured and

warm, untouched as yet by any chill of autumn. We spread the blanket we had brought with us on the slates and sat side by side up against the chimney stack, watching the lights go on across west London and the aircraft cross the darkening sky, like meteorites homing on Heathrow. I said that we had made it up, and so we had. Each had forgiven the other but not forgotten. The roof at twilight was our place of romance as others might have some restaurant or beauty spot where they had been happy. We made it up but things were not the same.

That, of course, doesn't necessarily have a forlorn meaning. For me, with the quarrel and the hard things that were said (harder, I think, than I can now remember), the innocence had gone out of our relationship. Perhaps it was also the case for him, but I could no longer delude myself that I read his mind and guessed his thoughts. That had gone too. Perhaps it was only that we had grown up a little more but in a leap and a bound instead of at the usual gradual pace. Eve looked on Adam as a god when she first came to Eden. 'He for God only, she for God in him,' Silver once said to me, quoting something. But I think that after they were turned out of the garden in disgrace, their life together became more real because there was no more illusion and she knew he was only a man. Silver was only a boy and I wasn't sure if my love could withstand knowing that. He knew that another man had wanted me and thought that I had wavered, so that I was changed in his eyes.

But we were happy up on the roof, kissing and talking (and apologizing), and neither of us said a word about money, spending it, lending it or trying to rid oneself of inheritances. And when it got very dark and we had smoked all our cigarettes we went back into the flat and to bed.

Young people feel enormously magnanimous and kind when they go home to visit their parents. I still feel a bit that way, though it's now something I sternly repress. I had been regularly speaking on the phone to Mum, and Dad too when he was at home or it wasn't news time. They had my phone number at Silver's and somehow they had learnt the address. From Guy, was my guess. I had been intending to go home for a long time. You'll have realized what stopped me, that the major stumbling block was how to get to Liverpool Street Station.

Nothing would have got me down into that tube again and a taxi costing £15 was beyond my means. In the end I took the No. 6 bus to Oxford Street and the No. 8 from there to Liverpool Street. It took nearly an hour.

More buses at the other end. A taxi there would have been far more than £15. The third bus dropped me in our village four hours after I had left Silver's and I was very late for Mum's lunch. Conversation at first centred on the extraordinary circumstance of my still living in Russia Road and only next door but one to Max. This led to a digression on the subject of Max. Mum was sure he must be ill, possibly mentally ill – she subscribes to the ancient theory of psychiatric problems being the result of overloading the brain – but even that could hardly excuse accusing me of theft and being an accomplice to murder and turning me out of the house. I was quite willing to talk about this for as long as they liked. It postponed what I had to tell them, what I had really come here to tell them. The moment wasn't long delayed.

Dad began bemoaning the fact that I'd dropped out of GUP. I had told them I was working. Working at what? I took a deep breath, said I was living with my boyfriend and had a job as a part-time gardener.

They had grown up in the sixties, so the idea of cohabiting with a man didn't upset them the way it would have upset their own parents. They didn't like it. They'd rather I'd been married – oddly enough, they'd rather I had been *engaged* – but they accepted, my mother saying what a pity it wasn't Guy. It was my occupation that really troubled them. Jobs, training, courses, in my parents' estimation, should always lead to something. 'Leading to something' was their touchstone, and this, I think, was why when I decided to become an electrician they gave grudging approval. It so plainly would lead to something. Artisan's calling it might be, it was in fact my own grandfather's occupation, and Dad muttered things about clogs to clogs in three generations, but at least it led to security and a reasonable income. Gardening was something else entirely. Gardening was dirty, weather-dependent, notoriously badly paid and a dead end. It wasn't a trade you could go back to after you were married and had a couple of babies.

'It's a stopgap,' I said. 'I needed the money.'

The afternoon was unpleasant, as I knew it would be. There was, of course, little else to talk about. Nothing had happened to them, nothing ever did, and that was the way they liked it. The last big event in their lives, apart from my departure, was what had happened on the pylon. That was referred to, Mum expressing the opinion that everything which had gone wrong for me, and she evidently felt that nothing had gone right, dated from the pylon. It was, as she put it rather poetically, the top rung on the downward ladder. She and Dad talked exhaustively on the subject of *what was I going to do next?* Wouldn't it be better for me to come home and start again? Had I considered retaking my A-levels? Then followed a series of comparisons with the children of people they knew. One who had been a 'late starter' like me, had at twenty-two gone into the City and was reputedly making £200,000 a year. Another, whose first degree had been taken at a 'humble' (Dad's word) polytechnic, was now studying for a DPhil at Oxford. It wasn't for themselves they were worried, they insisted, but for me, my future, my personal happiness. To this end Mum lay awake at night, worrying.

Sometimes I contrast this with the way we are now. I saw them at the weekend, I went down to stay a couple of nights. I truly believe they have forgotten those worries they had, those sleepless nights, dead-end jobs, clogs to clogs, and everything that was said and thought. They have forgotten the pylon. We are the best of friends. We are approaching the situation of a mutual admiration society. Two particular activities take place during my visits, they have become routine, expected, almost rites. I take Mum and Dad out to dinner on the Saturday night at the best restaurant the neighbourhood has to offer, a very grand converted manor-house in which the dining room is the former banqueting hall with an outlook on deer grazing on parkland, and I undertake some small electrical job for them. This may only be to mend the kettle or it may be rather more complex, putting in a new power outlet, for instance, or servicing the lawn-mower. I think they save up these little tasks for me, probably denying themselves for weeks the use of some appliance, refusing to call in the local man, so that they can have the pleasure of watching me perform the job for which I'm trained.

But all this was a long way off that day in early September eleven years ago. We came close to quarrelling. I couldn't stand two rows in a week with the people I cared for most in the world, so I left early.

More buses, a very slow train that kept stopping because of signalling failure, two more buses. It was nearly eleven before I got home.

Silver had been out most of the day, shopping around for flights to Sydney. He was in a dilemma. In one way he wanted the cheapest possible seats, especially for himself, as while he thought that, ethically, Andrew and Alison ought to pay for his round-trip flights, he knew they wouldn't. Or, rather, Andrew would argue about it and plead poverty, which he couldn't stand. On the other hand, he had determined that this was the starting point of ridding himself of his grandmother's legacy. So wouldn't the most straightforward thing be to buy the most expensive seats possible, even buy *first-class* seats, a method that would use up everything he had at one swoop?

'Why are you getting rid of it anyway?' I said.

He looked me straight in the eye. I couldn't read his expression, which was blank and calm, the way he could often make himself look.

'You'll lose this place. You won't be able to pay your parents rent. Unless you ask them to let you stay on rent-free. After all, they're hardly ever here. They've only been here once since I came.'

'No, I'll lose this flat,' he said. 'I've thought of that. I think I've thought of everything. The funny thing is, I feel quite excited at the prospect. Of not having it, I mean, the income, this place, *private means*.'

'But why?'

'Well, since you ask, for you.'

'For *me*?'

'You don't like it. And I like you too much to keep on doing something you don't like. Or maybe I should say I love you too much for that.'

Who could ask for a fairer commitment?

The following day we both spent phoning airlines and calling at the kind of travel agents that looked as if their only reason for existing was to undercut each other's prices. I'd managed to persuade Silver that wasting his money, throwing it away on first-class seats for people who'd be too worried to appreciate them, wouldn't be an ethical way of getting rid of it. Give it to the charity you think the most worthy cause, I said. You used to tell people who stole or cheated to get money that they should give a tithe to the poor.

'I don't tell them that any more,' he said. 'If it wouldn't sound moralistic beyond belief, I'd tell them not to do it at all.'

'Give it to something worthwhile.'

He did. After we had parted. It was a long time before I heard that he had given half of what remained to the famine relief organization he now works for. But that day we went shopping for cheap seats to Sydney and in the end managed to get three singles and one return for rather more but not much more than Silver gave for the passports. Saturday 18th and Sunday 19th were impossible. We had to settle for midweek, less popular days for travel, when seats were cheaper. September 22nd and 23rd, the Wednesday and Thursday. The woman in the travel agent pointed out that if we had booked Apex flights three months ahead, the price would have come down far more. We even talked of it. But there were too many imponderables. Would Andrew stand being cooped up in there for a further three months? By December it would be cold. Would the heating in 4E function for the winter without servicing? And what of the woman who had seen Andrew shopping in Westbourne Grove? We had heard no more of this but that didn't mean nothing more had happened. The police would certainly have questioned her. They might even know by now that it was likely their quarry was living in the Bayswater–Paddington area. The obvious best thing was to get them away as soon as possible.

Then there was Sean Francis. We went to see him that evening in Judy's company. Sounding him out carefully, calculating the kind of man he was, she had decided that taking the risk of telling him was a very small risk. He had reacted to the news with surprise but not enormous astonishment, having believed for a long time that something fishy was going on up there. But he was unable to give Judy the unqualified approval of our support for Andrew and Alison and our activities on their behalf she had hoped for. He was older than we were and perhaps the seven years between us made him less impulsive, less passionate for a cause and more inclined to see the law as good.

'I'm only saying you don't know all the facts. You only know what they say and what the media say. They may not be the ideal parents they think they are. From what Judy says he's a selfish bastard and she's a nervous wreck.'

'But you wouldn't do anything to get in the way, would you, Sean?'

Judy was sitting next to him and he had his arm round her. 'You wouldn't sort of tell anyone? I mean, the law, the police?'

'I've already told you that as far as anyone who inquires is concerned, I don't know anything about it. If they come downstairs or I hear them leave, I'll stay inside here.'

'But you won't lie for us?' said Silver. 'You won't help if we need you?'

'That's right. I'll be shooting my new series the week before and from the 20th to the 24th anyway. And by the 22nd I'll be too knackered to notice what's going on.' Sean smiled. To show something or other, I suppose. That he enjoyed his uninvolved status, maybe, or that he was lazy. Judy smiled too and I could see that he already meant much more to her than the fate of the people in 4E.

We went back to see them, ringing the doorbell in code and finding them about to go to bed, Alison in a dressing gown, shivering from the cold shower she'd just taken. Their water heater had gone wrong again. It made us see even more strongly how right we had been not to consider postponing their escape till the winter. The weather was warm still and washing in cold water would be possible for ten days without too much anguish. Andrew also saw it that way. They must go as soon as it could be arranged and he made less fuss about the cost of the flights than I had expected. That didn't mean he could give us the money there and then, though. They kept their money, he said, in a safe in Jason's room. Jason was asleep and mustn't be disturbed. Confirming what I had suspected, Alison said she'd have been quite willing to stop there till December. They had been there for six months, they could stay another three. Showing a touching faith in us, she said she was sure we could find someone to mend the water heater. We had found a photographer, so why not an electrician?

'We're going,' Andrew said. 'Jason's going on the 22nd and we're going on the 23rd and that's all there is to it. If I don't get out of here soon, I'll go out head-first and they can pick my body up off the pavement.'

He flew into a rage when Silver told them Sean Francis knew. Knew and would keep quiet, but not deny them and defend them if circumstances came to that. They wouldn't have a quiet moment, he shouted, they'd not sleep. Every ring at the door, every time the phone rang . . .

'But we often can't hear the doorbell, darling, and the phone never rings.'

'That's just it. That's what I'm worried about. How we're going to be when it does ring, when the phone does go.'

She told him, very gently, to calm down and, surprisingly, he did. We said good night to them and went home by way of the roofs. The scaffolding between the last terrace in Torrington Gardens and the first in Peterborough Avenue was still there, though weeks had gone by since the builders had last used it, and no scaffolding had yet gone up by the burnt houses. We examined the tarpaulin once more. It was untouched, apparently, since we were last there, unmarked except by the grey-white splashes of pigeon droppings. Silver asked if we should try the crossing again. I nodded. We both crossed the tarpaulin with no more to worry us than a few creaks from below and a showering sound that was probably powdered plaster falling from a crack we had caused to shift a little.

Things were calm and peaceful in the flat. Niall was somewhere playing music, but very softly. Liv's door was shut but we guessed that she and Wim were on the other side of it. Glasses they had been drinking from stood on the table with an empty bottle of Bulgarian red and a carton of orange juice. Silver closed the windows. No one would come. It had begun to rain.

He had a bath, I wrote my diary. Niall's music stopped. I'd never known it so quiet at the top of 15 Russia Road. No voices from the flat or the street, no unearthly cries some people seem impelled to make once midnight is past, no wind blowing, only the gentle regular patting of rain on the leads. I listened but could detect no traffic sound, sea-like, from the Edgware Road. The silence was heavy, as if night itself slept.

29.

He's not in any danger but I worry when I haven't heard for a week. It was a double bonus when his letter came this morning and at eight he phoned. In just a bit less than two weeks he'll be home. I don't want him ever to go away again but I know I lack the will or the nerve to stop him if he needs to go.

When I started writing this I said I didn't know any poetry. I don't, but he does. This is what he wrote to me, a quotation from I don't know what, except that it's by Browning and he used to live in Maida Vale.

> So, I shall see her in three days
> And just one night, but nights are short,
> Then two long hours, and that is morn –
> See how I come, unchanged, unworn!
> Feel, where my life broke off from thine,
> How fresh the splinters keep and fine, –
> Only a touch and we combine!

I must finish before he comes home and I have quite a long way to go. And I have to come soon to the dreadful thing that I can never think of even now without a shudder and a twisting and turning inside me.

When Silver went to collect the passports, he asked Jonny for the keys to 15 Russia Road. Jonny, after all, came there no more, he'd a home of sorts of his own and probably could have bought himself something far better. But Silver said nothing of any of that, he made no excuses for asking for the keys back nor tried to justify himself and his request just because Jonny had produced those passports. He had been well paid for that, it wasn't a favour. Jonny didn't argue. He gave Silver the keys without hesitation, which made Silver wonder if he had had copies cut. It was the day after we had bought the airline tickets that Silver asked me if he should have the locks changed. If he did this, he'd have to explain matters to his parents. He'd have to tell them some approximation to the truth, which was that he had invited a burglar into the house, let him have a bed in his flat and permitted him to bring his girlfriend with him.

September 22nd and 23rd were a watershed in our lives, until which we hoped everything would pass in a calm and serene manner, quietly leading up to those two days. Afterwards all would be changed. But the changes we didn't foresee were enormous, monumental cataclysms in our lives, against which the small ones, such as Jack and Erica Silverman returning to the house some weekends as they did in winter, Liv's departure either with or without Wim, Niall's three-month tenancy (a grand word for it), were insignificant. We did a lot of sitting about in the flat or on the roofs or in canalside cafés in those days, talking about the double escape and about what we'd do after it had been successfully accomplished. We started calling it the Exodus.

Silver had made a booking for two single rooms at a hotel in Sydney. He found it among the cheaper one-star hotels in a guide book called *Australia on a Shoestring*. On Wednesday 22nd he'd go to the taxi rank in Warwick Avenue and take a taxi round to 4 Torrington Gardens. He wouldn't have Andrew or Alison bring Jason down but would go up himself to fetch him. We still had no idea when the Nylands would be back, Sean didn't know, but it was most likely they would be home by the 22nd, Exodus Day One. I know this sounds ageist, but there's no doubt it's much easier dealing with old people in this sort of situation than with young ones. Mr and Mrs Nyland's eyesight and hearing would be less good than ours, they would probably need to rest at times during the day, they would move far more slowly than we did, be less quick to react and less vigorous. Taking Jason downstairs must involve passing their front door but Silver would hear their footsteps inside that door, hear the no-longer-quite-steady hand fumble at the catch, and either race Jason down or pull him back up. They were not a hazard.

Sean would be away shooting his series. In any case, he had more or less undertaken a passive role. We hoped for a wet day or a foggy day. Darkness would be even better but the flight was a mid-afternoon one. It was a pity we had to take a taxi but we knew no one with a motor vehicle we could take into our confidence except Jonny and we both thought he was far enough into our confidence already. Morna could drive. We decided to ask Morna if she could borrow her mother's car and drive it to Heathrow; it would be a better idea than the taxi.

The biggest danger was passing through passport control. Silver thought a lot depended on keeping one's cool while the man or the woman scrutinized Jason's passport, looked them both up and down, and maybe went away briefly into some inner office. He could only do his best, he said. Once they were through and on that plane, most of their troubles were over. My task was to get Andrew and Alison out on Exodus Day Two, and I must first check that they looked like their passport photos, then that the baggage they were taking wasn't over the weight limit. We hoped that nothing untoward would happen, such as assessing how much extra they had to pay on the surplus kilos, which might draw attention to them.

The taxi risk would be smaller this second time. Anyone looking for Andrew and Alison would be looking for Jason too. I'd accompany them to Heathrow, though I couldn't see what use I'd be beyond bolstering up their courage. When I had seen them into the passport control queue I'd leave them, go back home and wait for Silver to return the next day. Andrew and Alison would have collected Jason from the hotel and, if everything had gone according to plan, we'd never see any of them again.

'We won't know how to pass the time,' I said.

'Oh, yes, we will. This is our crossing point, remember? Life begins afterwards.'

It had to be another go at university for both of us. This year we were too late for the October intake but some places would take you in January or we could postpone things till next year. Do some sort of course perhaps, or voluntary service overseas. Silver wanted to read social sciences, he couldn't understand why he hadn't known that before. I wondered about agriculture. I knew the countryside, I enjoyed growing things. We both decided we had had enough of communal living, we'd have a single room somewhere that we'd share. If we could get to the same university or to colleges close together.

So we made firm plans for the Exodus and vague plans for when it was past. One afternoon, it was September 16th, after we'd been sitting at a table outside a café in Clifton Road drinking cups of tea, then coffee, we trailed slowly home by way of Randolph Avenue to find Jonny's van parked on a meter at the Castlemaine Road end and Jonny sitting in the cab, smoking a cigarette.

You hear a lot today about the prevalence in London of unmarked white vans. There are allegedly thousands of them about, no one knows who buys them or who owns them and there's generally said to be some malign reason behind possessing one. None of this was thought of, as far as I know, eleven years ago. If Jonny's white van, which he always kept immaculate, looked sinister to me, this was only because I associated it inevitably with him, and later came to be reminded of him by every white van I saw. He waved cheerfully at us and opened the driver's door.

'Let us in, will you, mate? I need a word with Liv.'

I suppose Silver reasoned that she could come to little harm with the rest of us there. Anyway, he said yes, all right, whereupon Jonny got down, carrying two bottles of wine and a bottle of Jack Daniel's. He preceded us up the path and Silver unlocked the front door.

Liv was walking short distances in the street now without screaming or shivering or passing out. But at this point she seemed to have called a halt. It was plain she didn't want to go home or, come to that, go anywhere. She was a bit like Alison in that respect. Both of them felt safe where they were and very unsafe elsewhere. Before we came along, Alison was presumably waiting for the unlikely event of the social services relenting. Liv was waiting to see what Wim would do. That he would do anything requiring a positive decision on his part, anything in the nature of setting up house with Liv, was even more improbable than Alison's local authority letting her keep Jason. But Liv hoped. And meanwhile she was staying put.

We found her in the living room, lying on the sofa asleep. The windows were shut. It had been a chilly day in comparison with the weather we had had in August. Wim usually had to tap on the glass when he came unless Liv had opened one of the windows for him, something she often did far too early in the evening, making the rest of us shiver. Jonny, first making a face of disgust at the sight of her lying there on her back, her mouth open, her skirt rucked up around her thighs, stamped his feet and let out a yell that made us jump.

'Wake up, you lazy cow!'

She shot upright. She blinked at the light and, when she saw Jonny, screamed. She rolled over on to her front, hiding her face in the sofa cushions. He spoke to her fairly gently for him.

'Come on, girl, there's nothing to be scared of. It's only Jonny, it's only your old Jonny, right?' He resorted to nursery rhyme. 'Only old Jonny who never did you any harm but killed the mice on your father's farm.'

A sentiment hardly likely to appeal to Liv. But she sat up and asked him what he wanted. Silver went into the kitchen to make tea but Jonny said we should have a drink, let's open one of his bottles. Liv was never averse to alcohol, though she was drinking a lot less than she must have done while with the Hindes. Silver had wineglasses but Jonny never used them. They were too small for his taste and it was four tumblers he filled with his Portuguese green wine.

'I've come to take you back with me, my love,' he said.

'I am not going. I am telling you over and over I am not going. I go home to Sweden.'

I had never known Jonny so reasonable. He started speaking almost like a rational, socially aware human being. 'Now listen to me, Liv, my love. What are you going to do with yourself back there? Have you got work there, have you got a place to live? Nope. I can get you good well-paid work, not bad hours, and no questions asked about permits and NI number and all that shit.' The unpleasant idea came to me that what he meant was prostitution. I dismissed it because I thought I was too inexperienced to know about these things but now, looking back, I'm pretty sure I was right. Jonny the cat burglar, Jonny the mugger and now Jonny the pimp. 'I've got a place to live. It's not grand. To be perfectly honest with you, it's a dump. But I'll change all that. I'll buy a place, a nice little flat in a nice neighbourhood. How does that grab you?'

If only it had been Wim talking. We who knew could read that in her face. It was a much prettier face by then. Love and nights with Wim must have done that. The red blotchiness was gone, her nose was no longer pink, the cold sores to which she'd been prey even in summer had disappeared. She washed her hair every day and it was golden and glossy. Never cut, allowed to grow, it was even longer than mine. My grandmother used to say that teenage girls had what she called 'puppy fat' that melted away when they got older. I don't know if this is true but Liv, in spite of taking no exercise and eating and drinking quite a lot, had become slimmer in these past weeks. She was very nearly beautiful. Jonny looked at her with hungry eyes.

'I am thinking about it,' she said. Her English too had improved a lot. 'I *will* think about it,' she corrected herself. 'You ask me again – next month. No, next week. How is that?'

Perhaps it was better than Jonny expected. Silver and I went into our room for a while, leaving them to work this out alone. Liv told me the next day that Jonny had said that when she came she could bring the £2,000 as her contribution to 'household expenses'. It sounded more as if he was planning to set up some sort of suburban establishment rather than the more sinister arrangement I had imagined. She told him the money was gone, the mugger took it when he hit her father and fractured his skull. Jonny, who knew more than she guessed, said her father hadn't been carrying the money and where was it? Liv denied any knowledge of it, said she was resigned now to its loss. She thought Jonny would 'try to fuck me' but he didn't. She used the word, as many of our contemporaries did, in its correct sense and as part of ordinary conversation, but with her it carried no force, no self-consciousness or weight of associations, so that it sounded almost shocking coming out in that accent from those pretty pink lips.

He and she finished the wine and had a couple of whiskies each. This sent Liv back to sleep. Jonny was gone by the time we came out of our room. He never worried about driving when about ten times over the limit. He'd told Liv before he left that he was going to begin 'house-hunting'. Silver phoned Morna and asked if we could come over. There was something we'd like to discuss with her.

She shared a flat with three other girls in a Whitechapel back street. I had never been there before. The flat wasn't in one of the tiny terraced houses, now preserved and, for all I know, listed, but in a faceless sixties red-brick block, of which there were many in the area. I don't know if it belonged to a college or if they rented it privately. I was more concerned about the means of getting there. Silver, knowing the way I was – how could he forget, he said, considering the way we met on the best day of his life? – had already planned the three buses we must take. So it would take a long time? We had all the time in the world until Exodus Day One.

Morna insisted we have supper. It was a rich vegetable-laden beef stew and the first red meat, almost the first *meat*, I'd eaten since I'd

343

last gone out to dinner with Guy in March. Two of Morna's flatmates were out and the other was in her room among her biochemistry books. She said she'd willingly drive Silver and Jason to Heathrow, and if she couldn't borrow her mother's car she'd hire one. That was something we had never thought of, hiring a car. But she had a better idea.

'Why don't I take him to Sydney?'

We just looked at her. 'You'll have to get a visa.'

'They'll take less notice of a woman than a man. I can say I'm his aunt. Look at me, I might be his aunt.'

Morna was dark-haired and dark-eyed and her skin was sallow with no red flush on the cheeks, she was tall and big and voluptuous, her neck and arms deeply tanned, but somehow just the same she looked like what she was, a Celt born of Irish parents in Dublin. No sensitive person would have taken her for Asian but perhaps passport-control people weren't very sensitive. Still, her offer was too good to turn down. She was a better bet than a young blond man.

We said Andrew and Alison would be very grateful, though we weren't really sure they would be.

'If they've any qualms, tell them I was the first to see Andrew Lane. I spotted him when no one knew where he was. But hadn't I better come and see them myself first?'

We agreed and said we'd take her there. The most important thing was for her to meet Jason and, if possible, get him to like her and want to go with her. Morna agreed to Friday, produced for our pudding course a large apple crumble, and began on a long involved tale about how she had seen Lauren Bacall in Fortnum's, but it couldn't have been her because she'd seen a photograph of her at some Hollywood première the very same night.

'Maybe she can be in two places at once,' Silver said. 'There's a priest called Padre Pio that can. I read about him in the paper.'

I kept my diary quite meticulously from that day forward, noting the weather and the temperature and the comings and goings of visitors to the flat. Somehow I knew this time would be important and should be recorded. Of course, I didn't know it would be important in a quite different way from what I had expected. The day Morna offered to go to Australia in Silver's place was Thursday 16 September. On the 17th I was up early because I had to take our washing to the launderette – the first time either of us had gone since Silver's discovery of Guy's letter – and then go to work at the Houghtons'. I had just made tea when Wim came out of Liv's bedroom. He'd already been down and brought up the newspapers.

'I'll take her in a cup,' he said, astonishing me.

I'd never before heard him offer to do anything for her, still less wait on her. I handed him a mug of the milkless tea she preferred and he surprised me again by showing he knew her tastes and tipping into it two spoonfuls of sugar. This made me long to ask him if he meant to find somewhere for them both and take her away. Neither Silver nor I knew if he had a room to live in like Jonny or if he'd given it up when he began regularly spending nights with Liv. I longed to ask. Something about Wim, his remoteness, his seeming lack of ordinary human impulses, fears, needs, hopes, as usual held me back. So I made the tea and took a mug to Silver with one of the newspapers and hoped, when I came out of the bedroom again, that Wim would confide in me. He didn't. He ate bread and marmalade, three or four slices of it, and hunted around the uninhabited rooms in the flat for two bars of chocolate he said he'd put in a safe place the night before. I read the other newspaper, the one Silver hadn't got. Still unable to find his chocolate, Wim departed through the window.

It was a cool morning with a sharp wind blowing. Clouds like the froth on soapy water scurried across the sky. I watched Wim climb the mansard swiftly and gracefully. It was the last time I was ever to see him go up on the roof.

I closed the window, keeping the cold out.

Mr and Mrs Houghton had gone away on holiday. Before they left Mrs Houghton gave me a key to the house. 'To keep an eye on things' and, ironically, to perform the very tasks we'd used as an excuse for being in another elderly couple's home, watering the houseplants.

I had had the key since the previous Monday and nearly mentioned it to Wim that morning. The houses in Randolph Avenue at this particular point in the terraces were exceptionally tall. I wondered if Wim would like me to take him into the house and let him climb out of one of the top-floor windows. Would it be a betrayal of trust? Neither Mr nor Mrs Houghton had asked me not to take anyone into their house. Probably they took it for granted I'd invite my boyfriend in. They had met him and liked him. Wim would do no damage, would steal nothing, would want to take no advantage beyond climbing out of a bedroom window and perhaps climbing back again. I couldn't decide. I'd ask Silver.

Inside the house it was like old Mrs Fisherton's, full of furniture old-fashioned even when the Houghtons were young. There was a smell of old fabrics never washed or cleaned, of stuffiness and of substances used to keep away moths. If you're an untidy housekeeper in London, if you don't clear up crumbs and put away food at night, mice will come. They had come to Mrs Houghton's kitchen. I recognized their traces from the signs left behind by Liv's mice. One, or several, of them, having eaten the crumbs, had gone to work chewing up a cookbook. I watered the already dry and drooping ivy and cissus and maidenhair fern, and then I went outside to treat the lawn with hormone broad-leaf weedkiller and grass seed.

Silver came for me at four. I asked him about Wim and the Houghtons' roof.

'I don't know. I suppose you have to apply the Golden Rule.'

'What's the Golden Rule?'

'Do as you would be done by. You ask yourself: if you owned a house, would you mind your gardener taking a friend in to get out of your window and climb on your roof. *You* wouldn't and I wouldn't, but would you if you were seventy and scared of burglars and whatever?'

'You mean, better not?'

'Better not,' he said. 'I feel I'm growing old when I say that –' and almost petulantly – 'I'm sick of people making me an oracle on morals. What do I know?'

The way he spoke did a lot to restore my faith in him. I took his advice. But just the same my belief that everything he said came from some fount of integrity and wisdom was shaken. He had read my letter. I realized that if I had been asked by someone who didn't know him for a sketch of his character I'd have described him as being as unlikely to read someone's private correspondence as to steal their wallet. And, though this is the melodramatic way of putting things Silver so disliked, the poison seeped into other areas of our life. Up till then I had believed entirely in the rightness of what we were doing for the people in 4E. But that day, as we walked home to Russia Road, the doubts began. I didn't voice them. I told no one. But I set them down in my diary.

Suppose Sean Francis was right and Andrew and Alison were not the suitable parents for Jason they thought they were? Was it possible that the social services knew best? I'd read what the newspapers said. Andrew and Alison were rejected because Jason was of mixed race and they weren't. But there could be other reasons for that rejection, additional reasons. You wouldn't have called theirs a loving relationship, for instance. Perhaps it had been once but by now all the love seemed on Alison's side. Andrew was impatient with her, rude and bad-tempered, and, although he had almost got what he apparently wanted, discontented. The fact couldn't be got away from that they had abducted Jason. For all I knew, that might be a crime, it was certainly a serious offence. Silver had felt he was growing old when he warned me off inviting Wim into the Houghtons' house, and now, feeling the pull of prudence, I too seemed to be moving into an unwelcome maturity.

I thrust it away. Roll on September 22nd, it couldn't come soon enough for me.

We went to the cinema. We went to the pub afterwards. Now we had time to kill we had started behaving like other people. On the way home we made a diversion to check that the scaffolding between the end of the terrace in Torrington Gardens and Peterborough Avenue was still there, though it no longer mattered very much whether it was there or not. We mostly entered by the front door and the stairs. All the lights in 4E were out, and not only those. The whole house was in darkness. We were walking slowly along Torrington Gardens towards the burnt houses when the sound of a taxi's diesel engine made us turn round. It had drawn up outside No. 4. Two people got out of it, we could see them quite clearly in the lamp-light. The man paid the driver and he too got out to help them with their luggage, some of which was piled on the seat beside him. The woman ran up the steps and opened the front door.

We looked at each other. These must be the Nylands. I tried to remember who had told us they were an elderly couple. Was it Andrew? Had he ever seen them? When you're our age you think everyone over forty is old but Andrew *was* forty. I'm bad at ages and no doubt was worse then, but these two were younger than my parents. They seemed smartly dressed, though it was hard to tell from that distance. They were thin, strong and light on their feet. She had been carrying a case in each hand when she ran up those steps. We said to each other simultaneously, the same thought coming to each of us, that we were glad the scaffolding was still there. For safety's sake we might have to use it.

At Silver's all the lights were out too. This was unusual. It never seemed to happen that the last to leave or go to bed put out the lights. Darkness and silence make you feel you have to creep about. Someone had left one of the windows open and a wintry breeze was blowing in. I shut the window and we went to bed.

I've never suffered from insomnia but that night I couldn't get to sleep. First of all, I lay spoons-fashion close beside Silver, his arm round my waist. Then, restless and uncomfortable, I turned over and gently pushed him over, this time embracing him. That didn't work either and at last I got up and walked about, searching my mind for what was keeping me awake and finally deciding it must be those doubts I had had earlier. Those doubts and the return of the Nylands, such different people from what we had expected. I told myself what Silver would have told me, that worrying was useless and destructive. If one was doing what one knew was right, there was nothing to worry about. But was it right?

I went to our bedroom window, opened it, for the room was stuffy, and leant out. The night air was fresh and cool but not cold. A little breeze made the plane leaves rustle and their thread-like branches sway. Down in the street, up against the kerb on our side, an unmarked white van was parked. As far as I could tell no one was inside it. Was it Jonny's? How would one know? The registration number was obscured by darkness but it would have been useless if I had seen it. I had never noticed the number of Jonny's van.

Silver stirred when I went back to bed, turned over and put both arms round me. The arm that was underneath me dug into my breasts and the arm on top seemed set to crush my ribs, but I felt that this was part of his complete return to me and I soon fell asleep – to be awakened after what seemed a moment only, a second or two, by a scream loud enough and terrible enough to be heard on Maida Hill. I jumped out of bed. Silver's arm was numb from my lying on it. He staggered up, rubbing the cramped muscles. The screaming went on, then died to a dreadful low keening. It wasn't Liv's voice but a man's.

Someone was in the living room. The lights were still off. Still shaking his benumbed arm, Silver was heading for the switch when someone pushed past him. The front door came open and whoever it was crashed down the stairs. Silver put the light on. I gasped. There was blood on the carpet, not spilt blood but stains and smears as if someone had wiped it off his shoes. Liv's bedroom door was shut. From behind it came whimpers and sobs.

Silver, his hand on the doorknob, said, 'Don't come in.'

'I thought he'd killed her,' I said. 'But that's her, isn't it? Those noises?'

This time I didn't take his advice. I followed him into the room. I put the light on and saw blood all over the bed and the walls and the floor. Not Liv but Wim had been attacked. He had passed out but came back to consciousness as we approached the bed. I thought I wasn't squeamish but when I saw his right leg I had to go out of there, ashamed of myself as I was, and vomit into the bathroom sink.

It took a tremendous effort of will to go back. Wim lay still, moaning, half on his side, half on his front, blood pumping from the back of his leg. He had been struck with something sharp and heavy some six inches above the heel where the Achilles tendon passes.

'It was Jonny,' Liv sobbed. 'We were sleeping. He came in and pulled off the sheet and the blanket and hit Wim's leg with a – a –'

'An axe by the look of it,' said Silver.

30

I dialled 999, my hand shaking. When the woman's voice answered and asked me which service I wanted, I said an ambulance. Perhaps I should have said the police. Silver, sitting on that bloodied bed, was trying to staunch the flow. He had made a tourniquet with a pair of tights and at last it seemed as if that awful pumping was restricted. Liv had collapsed. She lay spread out on her back, stark naked, her arms wide and her hands open, her whole body splashed with Wim's blood. I did my best to control a fresh need to retch. Wim was speechless by now, silent, even the moaning had stopped. He lay open-mouthed, his neck stretched and his head back, the shaven crown almost touching his spine. He was pale as the sheet and looked as if he had died. In all my life I had only ever seen one dead person and that was Daniel lying at the foot of the pylon. I thought Wim was dead.

The ambulance came in exactly five minutes. I went down to let the men in with their stretcher. They didn't complain about having to climb four flights at three in the morning. One of them, the senior one I suppose, went up to Wim, asked him his name and how this had happened. He didn't answer so we gave them his name and told them someone had burst into the room and attacked him.

'Not a someone,' Liv said, opening her eyes. 'Jonny.'

Silver went with Wim in the ambulance. They took him to St Mary's Hospital, Paddington. Alone with Liv, I got her into the living room, wrapped a blanket round her and made her hot sweet tea. I'd read somewhere that this is what you're supposed to do. Then I stripped off all the bloodstained bedclothes and stuffed them into a rubbish bag. The idea of taking them to the launderette made me feel sick again. They could go out for the bin collection on Friday.

I lit two cigarettes, one for me and one for Liv. I noticed that one of the windows I had shut was wide open. A pane was missing on the left, the side nearest to the catch. Barefoot, I nearly trod on the pieces of glass which must have fallen on to the carpet. He had come across the roofs, removed the pane with a glass cutter and lifted the window latch.

Liv lay on the sofa, her mouth hanging open. I could see the gap where Jonny had knocked out her tooth. Wim's blood had splashed her shoulders, her breasts, her neck. It was in her hair. She drank some of the tea and a trail of it dribbled down her chin. Suddenly I felt very cold, I was shivering. A draught was coming in through the hole in the window. I drew curtains that hadn't been drawn for months, maybe years, and went to get sweaters for her and me.

Liv said, speaking slowly in a gasping voice, 'He got in – I am hearing nothing – till – till he is coming into the room – not then – no, he is quiet coming in, looking, looking, for something – all over the room – I am hearing a drawer open and then I am awaking – but I am dumb, Clodagh – I cannot – could not – speak.'

'What was he looking for?' I knew without asking.

She didn't answer. 'Wim is sleeping. Then – Jonny – then he come to the bed – he has a *thing* in his hand – a – I don't know –'

'An axe.'

'Yes, a axe. He is bringing it with him – I shout out – but too late – he is – is –'

She began to sob. It wasn't possible for her to go on. I said for her, 'Wim was lying face-down. Jonny pulled off the covers and hit him on the back of his leg with the axe.'

She stretched towards me, in almost a yearning way, as if she were pleading for something. 'Yes, oh yes. And the blood – oh, the awful blood. It is done, I know why it is done. Like that – there!'

I too knew why it was done there. It might have been better – almost – if Jonny had killed him. Later on, a psychiatrist who talked to Wim and encouraged him, in vain, to talk to her, said that Jonny's act had been a symbolic castration. We knew better.

It seemed likely to me that Liv would never want to go back into that room. But I never really understood her, I constantly under-estimated her. When she had finished her tea and her second cigarette she got off the sofa and went into the bedroom. I followed. The bed was stripped, the sheets were gone, but blood had seeped through to the mattress, the walls were splashed with it. There was blood on the rugs and drops of it on the bedside cabinet and Wim's chocolate bars and cigarette packet he'd left there. Liv pulled on a pair of jeans and pushed her feet into trainers. Blood was still all over her, under her clothes. She ran her fingers through her hair.

For the first time I noticed that the room had been ransacked. The cupboard door was open, drawers had been pulled out and one lay overturned on the floor. Liv knelt down and rummaged through its spilt contents to find a pair of nail scissors. Her tears had stopped, colour had come back into her face. She looked up and gave me what in any other circumstances I'd have taken for a smile of triumph.

'Now I will show you,' she said.

Like most of the curtains in the flat, those at Liv's window were never drawn. A blind kept out the daylight. The curtains were made of some blue linen-like material and had a very deep hem, something like four inches deep, presumably made that way in case they shrank in the wash. Not that they'd ever been washed. Their dark colour was more due to dirt than the original dye. Liv took the scissors in her hand and began unpicking the hem on the left-hand side. Instead of allowing the notes to fall out, she picked them out one by one as the hem came undone. I watched her, fascinated. When she had built a small stack of notes on the windowsill she began on the other side. Her expression was concentrated but quite calm and, unbelievable though this was, cheerful. Both hems let down, she took the £50 notes in her hand and held them out to me, to see, to touch perhaps but not to hold. She kept a firm grip on them. Then she counted them. Curiously – or perhaps not curiously at all – she counted them in Swedish.

'*En, tva, tre, fyra, fem, sex, sju* –'

Of course there were forty notes. 'What was in the packet you gave your dad?'

'Pages of the newspapers I cut into pieces with these –' she thought about it – 'shears.'

'Scissors. Why didn't you tell him? He got hit over the head for a bunch of bits of newspaper.'

'It was *mine*. It is my money. Why am I giving it to anyone?'

We'd been through it all before. I shrugged. 'But you let us all think . . .' There was no point in finishing the sentence. It was then that it occurred to me Niall must have slept through it all or else he hadn't come home the night before. I opened the door to his dining room very quietly. It was empty.

'You could have the rest of the night in Niall's bed,' I said. 'If you like.'

'I am staying here. I have things to do.'

What, I couldn't imagine. I went back into our room and sat up in bed trying to read one of Silver's books until he came back just before seven. He'd had a taxi from Paddington Green. He looked exhausted.

'Wim lost so much blood,' he said. 'I've forgotten how much but he's had to have a transfusion. They're operating on his leg now.'

'It was Jonny.'

'I know. It had to be. I didn't see him but I smelt him, that smell that's part sweat and part scent – cologne, I suppose.'

'Could you *swear* in a court it was Jonny?'

He hesitated, shook his head, said, 'Could you?'

I was so afraid he meant to do nothing, tell no one, keep silent, not worry, that I could hardly speak. I just about managed, 'The police?'

'I've already told them.'

'Ah,' I said.

'I went to them after I was sure Wim was being looked after. I told them what Jonny had done and about the mugging too. And I had to tell them I hadn't seen him. Not for sure.'

He took off his clothes and got into bed and I put my arms round him. He felt cold and stiff, less relaxed than I had ever known him.

It was after eleven when I woke up. The other half of the bed was empty. I found Silver in the living room drinking tea with Niall who'd come home an hour before.

'Liv's gone,' Silver said.

What did he mean, gone?

'See for yourself. Have a look in there.'

The bloodstains were still there. Silver said he hadn't touched them because the police might want to see them. The room had a bare look. Every ornament, the clock, the radio, the video recorder, all were gone. The blind had been raised and the curtains had a forlorn look, hanging there with ragged hems. Silver had left clothes of his in one of the drawers, swimming trunks, a sweatshirt, two pairs of socks, and these too had disappeared along with three large suitcases which had had their temporary home on top of the wardrobe. Truly, we had underrated Liv.

I told Silver about the money. He, who the night before had looked as if he'd never smile again, managed a laugh when I told him about hiding the notes in the curtain hems. He said Liv had missed her vocation, she'd have made a great spy.

'Maybe there's still time,' I said. 'She's never had a vocation yet.'

We tried to imagine what had happened in the night. Presumably she had begun by packing all the stuff she had taken from the room into the suitcases along with her clothes. I wondered if she had left wearing nothing but my sweater and a pair of jeans. I wondered if she had washed off the blood. She couldn't have called a taxi because the phone was in our room. We pictured her lugging those three heavy cases down four flights of stairs, staggering out of the front door and forcing herself to go into the street. Her agoraphobia had been real enough, her terror of seeing James and Claudia, but she had conquered both. She must have dragged those cases along the street, perhaps to the Edgware Road, perhaps only to Sutherland Avenue, and picked up a taxi there.

And gone where?

Not to Sweden. She would never have left for Kiruna without collecting her air fare, which was in Silver's bank account. I remembered her mother's friend in Elstree. Or had she simply gone to an hotel, perhaps the very one where her father had stayed?

We never found out. Neither of us ever saw her again until I went to her house in Hampstead and she was Mrs Clarkson with two small children and the molar Jonny had knocked out hanging on a chain round her neck. Why? For what sentimental or agonizing reason? That was eleven years later. When we heard nothing from her, Silver sent her air-fare money back to Håkan Almquist.

Now I wonder what she passed through in her transition from homelessness in a foreign country (though with £2,000) to marriage to a rich man, a beautiful house, a glamorous appearance. Who was the Lavinia she had implied she'd worked for, whose PA she had been? And what was this college she mentioned? How had she done it? Had she ever seen Jonny again or, come to that, Wim? I wondered too if she had ever seriously thought she might get money she had never lost out of an insurance company to which she had never paid a premium. Why had she worried and harried her parents about a sum of money she knew her father had never had? Solely for the better concealment of the money? I learnt the answers to none of these questions.

The police came. They looked at the room and asked where Liv was. We had to tell them we didn't know, that she had gone without warning. After they had left we did our best to wash the walls and get the blood off the mattress but unsuccessfully. Beryl, who never gave notice of her coming but popped in when the fancy took her, arrived in the early afternoon.

We told her what had happened. We couldn't think of a substitute story. She would of course pass it all on to the Clarks, the Asian couple and, possibly, to Max and Caroline Bodmer. Not much harm would be done as it would all be in the papers anyway.

'He's the one that's in *The King and I*, isn't he?'

'He *looks* like the one that's in *The King and I*.'

'There's too much of this sleeping with all and sundry,' she said, unusually severe. 'More trouble's caused in this world by that than wars. Look at the Professor.'

She scrubbed the walls and took the rugs away, saying that she'd wash them herself at home. But when she had sniffed the sheets in the bag, she agreed that putting them out with the rubbish was the only thing.

'Been worse if it had been his neck,' she said.

Would it? We went to the hospital to see Wim that evening.

He was barely conscious but perhaps this was only sleep, for he stirred after we had been sitting by his bed for a while, put out a hand and touched mine, feeling for it as if he were blind and then clutching it in a surprisingly strong grip. He wasn't blind but he kept his eyes closed on that visit. Silver said afterwards it may have been because he feared to see what had been done to him, didn't even want to see the outline of the cradle that kept the bedclothes from touching his leg. No one would tell us anything. We weren't relatives. I wished I had said I was his sister but it was too late for that. A staff nurse wanted to know where his next of kin were. Had he a wife? Had he parents? We knew so little, though Wim's having a wife seemed most unlikely.

The events of the night before, that terrible night and what had happened to Wim – not to mention Liv's disappearance – almost drove the inhabitants of 4E Torrington Gardens from our minds. They didn't need us, they were well supplied with provisions, and all was in place for the Exodus. I believe we had entirely forgotten about the Nylands, that couple who lived in the middle of the house and who had turned out to be so much younger than we had expected. Our heads were full of Wim and Jonny and, to a lesser extent, Liv. We spent a long time when we got back from the hospital speculating as to what the relations between those three had really been. Liv had seemed passionately in love with Wim, but could she have loved him and not even gone to see him when he lay ill and so fearfully injured? Had he come to love her? Or was there no more between them than an obsessive lust? Jonny's act must have been motivated by jealousy. Because he loved Liv? Or had he only felt that he owned her, that she was his possession no one else might touch? And was he envious of Wim because, apart from Liv's preference for him, he was tall and graceful and handsome and, in his own odd way, charming?

Silver said he would never rest until he had found Jonny. For some reason, in the cause of being absolutely straightforward and above-board, I suppose, he felt that, having told the police what had happened, he was duty-bound to tell Jonny he had done so. It was quite late at night when we made our way to Holloway. I insisted on going with him. But Jonny wasn't there and his van wasn't parked outside. A woman who came out of one of the rooms and spoke to us as we were going down the stairs said he had told her two days before that he was leaving. We walked up the street, turned left and walked down the next street, looking in vain for the white van. It seemed that Jonny really had gone. I said I hoped that didn't mean the police wouldn't find him. Silver looked miserable.

'You know how people always say finding a murderer won't bring the dead person back? I feel a bit like that about Jonny. Finding him and sending him to jail won't mend Wim's leg and I don't suppose it will stop him mugging someone next time or bashing him with an axe, do you?'

'No,' I said, 'but I want him caught.'

'He wanted revenge and now you do. Revenge doesn't help.'

'Doesn't it? Knowing Jonny's being punished may help Wim a bit when he realizes he'll never go on the roofs again, when he knows

Jonny did that to him to take away the great passion of his life.'

Silver shrugged. 'He knows already. When I hear that expression "a fate worse than death" – well, you don't hear it any more but you read it in books – I've always thought it was a bit of a joke. I mean, what's worse than death? Now I'm not so sure.'

Andrew and Alison came back into my mind and I was on the verge of voicing my doubts about the rightness of what we were doing. I had the words ready to utter. 'Are you certain we're doing the right thing, getting them to Australia? Making sure they keep Jason? Because if there's a doubt . . .' But even in my mind I left the sentence unfinished. I suppose I felt Silver and I were disagreeing too much. I was afraid of reopening a gulf between us. Besides, we were tired, Silver looked tired out, having had only about three hours' sleep the night before.

Niall had found himself a girlfriend and was spending the night at her place, was thinking of moving in with her. For the first time since I came to 15 Russia Road, Silver and I were alone. There had been times when I had longed for this, when it had seemed something to dream of, and that if it ever happened all would be bliss, all would be a kind of everlasting honeymoon. But now I felt afraid. I even wondered how we'd be together with no one else to talk to or escape from or complain about. But I was very tired, which perhaps accounted for it, and we had had a bad shock, been through a dreadful time, though not so dreadful as poor Wim had.

The next day Silver and I were both wanted at the police station. No one said so but it was plain Jonny hadn't yet been found. A policeman, who I think was a detective inspector, was perfectly polite but I could tell he didn't believe a lot of the things we said, though we told the strict truth. He had special difficulties with Liv's living in the flat while Jonny lived elsewhere and was openly incredulous when we said that she had left the house within hours of the attack on Wim. Nor did he seem to believe us when we said we had no idea where she was. We had given him the Almquists' address and phone number in Kiruna. I told him about her mother's friend who lived somewhere on the northern fringes of London. Silver told him about the Elgin Avenue hotel. Whether the police ever followed any of this up we never found out.

357

We went off on a routine visit to 4E and had a surprise. Two days before, the scaffolding between the end of the terrace and Peterborough Avenue was still there. This evening it was gone. No trace of it remained but a couple of rusty clamps and a plastic bag full of the builders' cigarette ends lying under the ilexes among the grass and weeds. Its removal seemed unimportant, we had long ceased to get into the flat by that means.

We had bought food on the way back from the police station, rather a lot of food because we hoped it might be the last we'd ever have to take up to 4E. We were each carrying two Sainsbury's bags. Our heads were so full of Wim and the police distrust of us, of Jonny and the mystery of where Liv might have gone, that we had forgotten the existence of the Nylands and came up the stairs talking to each other. The bags were heavy and, used to these staircases as we were, we couldn't run up as we might have done if empty-handed.

We had scarcely reached the first floor when the Nylands' door opened and Mrs Nyland came out. She looked older than she had appeared to be in the midnight street but young enough and with the physique, a kind of high-toned stringiness, of a woman who has been an athlete or a dancer. She wore a voluminous T-shirt and shorts which showed long dark-brown well-muscled legs.

'Oh, excuse me!' There's a certain kind of middle-aged woman, the county sort of whom I had seen plenty in Suffolk, who never say 'excuse me' without prefacing it with 'Oh'. The tone is authoritative and the last word rises to a high interrogatory note. 'Oh, excuse me!' Here was a perfect exponent of the art of it. 'But where exactly do you think you're going?'

It had all happened very quickly. We had never thought of any excuse or reason for going up to Flat E, though we should have done after bumping into Sean Francis. Silver came out with the truth. There was really no choice.

'Some friends of ours live on the top floor.'

'Are you quite sure of that?'

The door behind her had swung wide open. The hall was unlike anywhere else in the building and quite unlike 15 Russia Road. The carpet was black and the furniture white. A huge black and white abstract in a stainless-steel frame hung on the wall facing us. Silently, walking on sandalled feet, the man we had seen get out of the taxi came out into the hall and stood in front of it. The woman turned her head and spoke to him in a rather softer tone.

'Darling, I caught these people going to the top floor. They say friends of theirs live up there. Rather odd, don't you think?'

Nyland came nearer. 'Not squatters, are you?'

'Look,' Silver said, 'let us just get this stuff up there, will you? Then you can come up and check.'

He told me later he was expecting to have called their bluff. If he invited them up to Flat 4E, in the nature of things they wouldn't come, they'd be satisfied. But they weren't. Nyland, who was a very tall skinny man, the Clint Eastwood type, looked even more suspicious than his wife. He said he'd follow us up *now*.

Those were a nerve-racking forty-five seconds. With me going first and Silver behind me and Nyland behind him, I thought we had a chance. Luckily, Andrew happened to be just behind the door when I rang our code. I mouthed, 'Hide Jason.'

When you're on the run, when you're in hiding, you develop a new sense and one that makes you react quickly, Andrew simply called out to us to come in before retreating. We came into the hall one after another, leaving the door open behind us. Alison was nowhere to be seen. Jason, I suppose, had been taken into his bedroom. A radio was on in one of the rooms and chamber music was playing. It was greatly reassuring and gave to the whole set-up a respectable air, so that when Andrew re-emerged, absolutely calm, even smiling, I inwardly congratulated him. Afterwards he told us his manner was the tranquillity born of despair. He thought Nyland was a policeman.

Nyland, in much the same tone as his wife used, said, 'I'm so sorry to bother you but actually I'd no idea at all anyone was living up here.'

'My wife and I have been here for three weeks,' Andrew said.

'Ah, that accounts for it. We went away a month ago.' Nyland's suspicions weren't entirely quietened. 'Would you mind telling me who exactly let the flat to you?'

'Mr Robinson himself. He's a friend of my wife's.'

This was a mistake, or seemed to be to me, but Nyland was satisfied. He said again, 'I'm so sorry to bother you, but the times we live in, you know . . .' He looked at the Sainsbury's bags which we'd let drop on to the floor. You could see what was going through his mind.

Were these people invalids or agoraphobes (like Liv) that they couldn't do their own shopping? 'Well, I'll say good night, then, and maybe we'll see you around.'

The door closed behind him and we heard his feet on the marble stairs.

'Why the hell did you bring that guy in here?' Andrew's mood had changed from calm to rage. Relief had released fury. 'You could at least have warned us. Jason's frightened out of his wits.'

'We'd have warned you if we could,' I said. 'He just came out as we were going upstairs, or his wife did.'

I'd never heard Silver so aggressive. 'Come to that, why the hell did *you* tell *us* they were old? An elderly couple is what you said. We expected a pair of pensioners. Then out leaps this woman who looks like an Olympic gold medallist. Who said they were old?'

'Louis Robinson.'

Alison had appeared, holding Jason by the hand. He broke away from her and ran to me. I bent down and he threw his arms round my neck, pressing his cheek to mine. He was almost too heavy for me to lift but I managed it and hugged him, falling down into a chair with him on top of me.

'That's right, isn't it, Ally? Louis told you those Nylands were old?'

She looked ill, by now so thin as to be emaciated. Her eyes, which had never looked particularly large in her photographs or when we first met, were huge; frightened, threatened eyes of a faded blue in dark wrinkled nests. 'Louis told my mother that years ago. It can't have been long before she died. He told her they were an old couple. I think this may be the son. I think that was the daughter-in-law you saw.'

'A pity you didn't say so before,' Andrew snapped. 'Diana's been dead for years.'

'Let's not quarrel. Any of us.' She sounded tired to death. She had nothing to do and she never went out but she was exhausted. 'Shall we have a drink? I see you've brought the wine.'

Now everyone had calmed down we had a lot to tell them. Principally, that Morna not Silver would be taking Jason to Sydney. Our idea of introducing her to them had been lost in the awful events of two nights before. Now Alison insisted on meeting her. I'd never known her so firm, so single-minded.

'I can't entrust my son to someone I've never met.'

'My son' – I hadn't heard her refer to Jason like that before. 'Can't you look on her as just a courier?'

'If it was myself, yes. Not when it's Jason.'

Silver said he'd see if Morna would come with us the next day, the Saturday. We discussed the Nylands a little longer. Were they satisfied that Andrew was a bona fide tenant? Would they do anything?

'Like what?' Alison said. 'All they could do is get in touch with Louis. He'll tell them he was a friend of my mother's.'

Andrew voiced the fear Silver and I felt. 'I'm wondering if there's ever been anything in the papers about people like Louis. I mean, interviews with friends and acquaintances of ours, or even just a mention of their names as people known to us, people who might help us. Because if there has, that ass Nyland might make the connection.' He turned on Silver again. 'Why the hell didn't you tell him your mother lived up here or something?'

'You think that would have stopped him coming up? Let's not go into that again anyway. The important thing is you've only got four more days here and Jason's only got three. You say Louis Robinson lives in France and he's hard to get in touch with. By the time Nyland does, if he does, you'll all be out of here. We'll bring Morna to meet you tomorrow.'

But Morna couldn't manage the next day. She had a date with a new man. In the circumstances, we couldn't ask her to break it, she was doing enough for us already, or for Andrew and Alison, whose fates in a curious way seemed so bound up with our own. Especially with Silver's. Whatever happened to 'don't worry'? I asked him. What happened to the way he was when first we met?

'I'd nothing to worry about then,' he said.

Wim never mentioned Liv's name. He seemed to have forgotten her existence. Jonny was of no importance to him either, neither as himself nor as the perpetrator of his terrible injury. He was like someone who faces death, who has become used to the inevitability of death, and considers everything in the light of this. Yet there was no question of his dying. The only risk was of a thrombosis occurring in his right leg. The doctors had told him they feared at first his foot would have to be amputated but that was no longer a threat. He would walk again, they said. With time, and if the stretching of the ruptured tendon went according to plan, he'd be walking within months. You'll never win the long jump, a kindly registrar had told him, thinking this a restriction no reasonable man of nearly thirty would care about, you'll never run in the Marathon.

For Wim was nearly thirty. He'd been twenty-nine at his last birthday, a year or so older than we had thought. He told us so as we sat by his bed and the arrangement of pulleys and strings that held his leg up. His story, which we'd never expected to hear, he told us also, his right hand in mine and his left hand in Silver's.

His father was a Dutchman who'd been in a circus that travelled across northern France and Belgium, a tightrope walker. A *funambule*, Wim called him. It was when the circus made a stop in Wimereux that he met Wim's mother Catherine. She had driven in from the countryside with a crowd of girlfriends to watch him walk the tight-rope, which was suspended from one high building to another, right across the town's main square. It may have been from a church tower to the *mairie*, Wim didn't know, but it spanned the square and there was no safety net. Maurits, which was Wim's father's name, never used a net. A net would have removed the danger and spoilt the crowd's awed pleasure. Catherine went out for a drink, then a meal, with Maurits that night and left her girlfriends to go home alone.

She stayed with him for two months, travelling with the circus up into Belgium, to Liège, to Mons. In a town up there whose name Wim was never told, there were two churches, one on either side of the main square, each with spires about ninety feet tall. The tightrope was suspended from one to the other and Maurits commenced his walk by stepping out of the belfry of the Sacred Heart and heading for the belfry of the Queen of Heaven. No one knew why it happened. Catherine told her cousin he lost his equilibrium because he was so excited at the news she had given him that morning – news which excited her not at all – that she was pregnant. Perhaps he was tired. They had been travelling for most of the day and only reached the place in the early evening. Whatever caused it, he lost his balance halfway across and fell. The crowd screamed, people rushed forward to try and catch him, a vain effort. He died instantly, smashed on the cobblestones of the square.

Catherine went home to her parents. She was only eighteen. It was 1958, a time when pregnancy outside marriage was still a disgrace. But her parents looked after her. Her father was a wealthy manufacturer, there was plenty of money. They sent her to her aunt in Utrecht and there Wim was born in a small and very select nursing home. Catherine had had months in which to recount her experiences to her cousins, girls whose ages were very near her own, and it was one of them who passed what she knew on to Wim. For Catherine didn't stay long. One night when everyone was asleep, including the three-week-old baby, she went, leaving the baby behind. It was his prolonged howls which brought one of the cousins to the room and found her gone.

'No one wanted me,' Wim said, 'but they thought it their duty to keep me. I stayed a few months with Aunt Marie, during which she had me baptized in a name of her choosing, then a few more with my grandparents, then back to Marie. One of my cousins got married, so it was time for her to take her turn. I was with her for a year and then she had a child of her own, so it was back to my grandparents. They didn't mind how much they paid to have me looked after. It was just that they found it a bore doing it themselves. I was a nuisance, no one made a secret of that. They used to say so, sighing and smiling. 'He's a nuisance, poor little thing, but what can we do?' My father's mother turned up when I was eight. I spent two years with her. I think my other grandparents gave her a lump sum.'

He told all this in his deadpan way, saying nothing of his emotions, criticizing no one. A faint flush mounted into his face but that may have been caused by the exertion of talking so much – an unheard-of amount for him.

'My paternal grandparents sent me to boarding school. It was OK. My cousin Renée told me about my parents when I was about fourteen, the story of the tightrope fall among others. Nobody had heard from my mother since I was three weeks old. Then she turned up. I was a student, I was at the University of Utrecht. She waited for me in the street one Friday evening as I was going home to Marie's. She was in a nice car and was wearing a fine fur coat. No one minded about wearing fur then. She said she wanted to talk to me with a view to my coming to live with her in Amsterdam. Her husband knew about me, would welcome me, and so would the three children she'd had by him.'

'What did you do?' Silver asked.

'Nothing. I just walked on. She called after me but I took no notice. The funny thing was it was on the edge of the red-light district and passers-by must have thought she was a whore, a rich whore or one with a rich pimp. She called after me, she got out of the car and ran after me. People laughed. Someone said, "What's wrong with you, boy? I should be so lucky." She was very pretty, you see, and only about thirty-seven.

'She came to Marie's. She begged me to go to Amsterdam with her. At any rate, for the long vacation. I couldn't speak to her. I suppose it was wrong of me. But I kept remembering how she'd abandoned me when I was three weeks old.'

Wim said he had a law degree but he had never been able to hold down a job. He had had several but he couldn't stand the constraints, the routine, the regular hours. Being an artisan, doing labouring work, he thought might be the answer. He had to work. Once he had graduated Marie and her daughters no longer wanted to know him.

'They would have if I'd stuck to the law and got to be a judge. My grandparents were all dead. I worked on a building site, then doing odd building jobs. One of them was with a roofer. It was in Liège. There were these houses, a terrace, and the person who owned them wanted the leads taken off and tiles laid. I was happy up there. I suppose I was happy for the first time in my life.'

'Why did you come here?'

'First of all, I came on a trip, a tour. Very cheap, just four days. I'd never been to The Hague. I'd not even been to Brussels. The buildings in London were the highest I'd ever seen, that is, seen so many of them. And the roofs were mostly flat. I thought of climbing the Houses of Parliament, I thought of Westminster Abbey. I came here four years ago. I've never been able to get building work here, it's always been in kitchens. But that was good enough.'

He looked at his suspended leg and, covered though it was in plaster, he shivered. Neither of us said anything. We all thought the same thing, I'm sure of that. What would become of him? What do you do when the great thing in your life, the only thing, is taken away? I thought of Jonny too and the awful life he had had as a child. Was it any worse than Wim's, the same, better? It was impossible to judge. Had Wim inherited his passion for the heights, for walking in the sky, from his father? Or was that ridiculous, imagining there could be such an inherited tendency? It was more likely that he had wanted to follow his father's example. Perhaps Maurits had been his hero, a figure to worship. He didn't say. One thing seemed certain, his father was the only one of his relatives who hadn't abandoned him, let him down or cold-shouldered him. He had died instead.

Jonny's had been a brilliant revenge, a stroke of genius. The same day as when Wim told us his story, the police picked him up. Where or how they found him I don't know. Later we discovered he had appeared in the magistrates' court, been charged with causing grievous bodily harm to Wim. Just as we never again saw Liv, so Jonny passed out of our lives. But not entirely, not for ever.

I've seen him twice since then, the first time to talk to. The second time was last year, a few days before I got married. Knowing me now, you won't be surprised when I say I didn't wear a wedding dress on the day, but nor did I intend to go to the altar in jeans and a pea coat. I was coming out of a shop in Sloane Street with the blue dress and jacket I had just bought in a golden carrier more grand than my outfit, when I saw him sitting at the wheel of a huge cream-coloured Bentley parked round the corner in a side street. He was wearing a suit, a white shirt and a very sleek silver-grey tie, smoking a cigarette and dropping the ash out of the window. There's a point in Sloane Street where the pavement gets very wide, facing the gardens of Sloane

Square. I sat down on a wall and watched him. Did he see me? I don't know. If he had I doubt if he'd have acknowledged me. If he thought about me at all, he was probably happily anticipating what I was going to witness in a moment.

I thought he was someone's driver. That would account for his dropping his ash out of the window rather than sully the interior of the car. He lit another cigarette from the stub of the last. A woman of about twenty-five came out of the shoe shop on the corner, laden with shoe boxes in bags as smart as mine. She might have been a clone of Liv as she now was. Perhaps her hair was a brighter blonde, her make-up heavier, her legs an inch or two longer. I knew Jonny wasn't her employee when he didn't get out to open the car door for her. She threw the bags into the back, got in beside him, kissed him on the cheek. She took the cigarette out of his mouth, drew on it and handed it back. I saw him make a playful swipe at her, not something I'd like him to do to me, playful or otherwise, put one hand to the wheel and move out into the traffic stream.

Another success story. Silver had forecast it or something very like it as we walked along the canal bank on our way to Torrington Gardens. Jonny was irrepressible, he said, nothing would get him down for long. He'd end up a rich man, a big-time crook.

'Won't he get years and years in prison for what he's done to Wim? It's not the first time. Remember the Gilmore Hotel. And what about what he did to Liv's dad?'

'They'll never prove that,' Silver said. 'He may not even be convicted. It will only be Wim's word against his. We didn't see him. Liv won't go to court, she's disappeared.'

We were passing the spot where the woman who lived on the boat had been murdered in April. They'd never found the murderer. Had it been Jonny? As far as we knew he had never actually killed anyone, though he had come close to it. Still, if a miss is as good as a mile in any circumstances, it's never so true as between killing someone and nearly doing so. The trees that border the canal here had crowns of dense faded leaves, the water was flat, rocking a little like liquid in a shallow plate, the same dark green as the leaves. Someone had planted a garden near the towpath, bright and variegated as a florist's shop. I said suddenly how unpleasant it would be if it was some act of Jonny's which had brought Silver and me together. It was bad enough recalling that it was the violent death of someone which had done so, for if that woman hadn't been murdered down here and the police cordoned off the towpath, I'd never have hazarded the underpass or been saved from my terrors by Silver.

'It doesn't matter what it was,' he said, 'so long as it happened.' And looking into my anxious face, 'Don't worry,' which made us both laugh, though the voice he had used was like a ghost of the confidence he had once had.

Wim's fate overshadowed us. But it drew us together again as we clung to each other for support. Silver kissed me and a man coming out of the Prince Alfred whistled. We waved at him as we crossed the street into Torrington Gardens. For a moment I was filled with joy, exhilarated beyond words, at this, Silver's first spontaneous sign of love for a long time.

The street lights were almost lost in the heavy dark foliage of the plane trees. Where the scaffolding had stood shrubs crushed by the uprights and putlocks were uncurling and spreading upwards, released from their confinement. In the half-dark a squirrel ran through the long grass and leapt for the trunk of an ash tree. Its eyes glittered. I smiled at it, I was smiling at all the world. We used our key, came into the hall. There we took off our shoes and carried them, so as to pass the Nylands' door as silently as we could.

Lights suddenly came on above and below us. We were flooded with light, caught ascending a staircase with our shoes in our hands, clearly intent on performing some act by stealth. The people on the landing above us, the first we saw, we had never seen previously. It was apparent they had been the Nylands' guests for the evening. The Nylands were just inside their front door, with a black and white abstract for a backdrop, saying good night. We hadn't realized how late it was. People of our age never do realize how late it is. I doubt if either of us was wearing a watch. A clock inside the flat ominously struck eleven as Mrs Nyland came out on to the landing and asked us once more what we thought we were doing, this time not prefacing her question with an 'Oh, excuse me!'

'Visiting our friends.' Silver's voice was very abrupt. I wondered if he had gone too far when he said, 'If you don't like it, I suggest you call Mr Robinson in the south of France. He'll vouch for them and us.'

'What I don't like is your tone –' Mrs Nyland began but she was cut short by her husband's sharp utterance of her name.

'Vivien!'

'You can put your shoes on now. We know you're here. You needn't creep about like cat burglars.'

'Vivien, that's enough!'

The departing guests were embarrassed. I sensed a full-scale row breaking out between the Nylands after the rest of us had gone and their door was shut. No one said any more. We advanced up the next flight, still carrying our shoes, feeling foolish. The lights went out as suddenly as they had come on and I nearly fell over backwards down the stairs. I clutched to Silver and whispered that maybe we were too late and they'd have gone to bed but he said to go on, they'd rather get up to open the door than not see us at all.

Perhaps he was right but there was very little sign of it in Andrew's manner. He was fully dressed, though complaining he had been just about to go to bed. Alison, he said, was asleep and so was Jason. I was sure this was true of Jason but doubted if Alison ever slept much these nights, and the thought had barely taken form in my mind when she came out of their bedroom in a dressing gown whose sash tied her waist so tightly that it looked as narrow as my thigh.

We sat in the living room. Silver said we'd be bringing Morna to meet them the next day. Then he asked Andrew for the money they owed him. It was nearly £5,000, not including the cost of Morna's return ticket. Andrew again came up with his excuse that the money was in Jason's room.

'Could you see that it isn't in his room when we come tomorrow, please?'

Andrew raised his eyebrows. 'Are you insinuating I don't intend to pay you?'

'Look, you can think what you like,' Silver said, and while he talked his eyes had gone to the little china birds, a greenfinch, a thrush, a wren, clustered on the bookshelf. 'You can think what you like, but I'll just ask you one thing. Don't you understand that with anyone else of our sort of age, you'd have to have given them the money for all this *first*, not expect them to fund you and you owe it to them? Don't you?'

'Why are you looking at those birds?' Alison said as if he hadn't spoken.

'I don't know. I think I've seen them before but I don't know.'

Andrew said, 'How much is it? How much do I owe you?'

Silver seemed in a dream. From the birds he had moved his gaze to Alison. He was staring at her as if he had never seen her before. Women of her age, when their faces are free of make-up, can look surprisingly young. The only light in the room came from a low-wattage table-lamp. He looked at her and seemed to have difficulty wrenching his gaze away. 'It's £5,000 but I don't expect you to pay Morna's fare.'

'I should think not,' Andrew said, though why he should think not was a mystery, since she was going to Australia in his service as courier to the child he regarded as his.

'The bill comes to £3,890. I've a receipt but I haven't got it with me. I'll show you the cheque-stub if you like.'

A conman could write anything he liked on a cheque-stub, was what was going through Andrew's mind. And then I could see – for the first time – that in their eyes we might not be the creatures of probity we were in our own. It was true we had procured passports for them and Silver had the airline tickets in his hand but they had no guarantee these were genuine. Experienced forgers could produce airline tickets with ease. They had our promise but only our promise to take Jason to Australia and get them safely out to Heathrow a day later. Only a promise from people they knew nothing about . . .

Silver pulled his chequebook out of his pocket. It had been folded in half and looked rather shabby and disreputable. He had forgotten and I had forgotten we had told them, weeks ago, that we were both called Brown. We live in a society in which surnames have less importance than they have had since perhaps the Middle Ages. To them we were Silver and Clodagh. Andrew looked at the cheque-stub and looked at the next, unused, cheque in the book.

'Who's this M. R. Silverman?' he said.

'Me, of course.'

Silver realized then. He was going to explain, would have done so, but for the gasp that came from Alison. She stood up. I thought she was going to fall and I jumped up myself, to seize her by the arm. She stood as still as a statue, looking at Silver, and he, as he had been doing a few moments before, looked at her.

'You have seen the birds before,' she said in a thin, remote voice, quite unlike her usual rich tone. 'And you've seen me before. Oh, *Michael*, don't you remember?'

32

We went home at last, forgetful of Vivien Nyland. No doubt she was asleep. It was two in the morning. The lamps were out, no one was in the streets and all was as silent as the countryside but for the hum from the arterial roads. Silver looked very pale in the light of our hall, even paler than usual. His hands were icy to the touch.

'How long have you known?' I asked him.

'I don't know. Not to say *known*. I had a feeling sometimes, a kind of *déjà vu*. When you took the broken bits of the little bird out of your jeans pocket, I was really upset. I had that sort of sensation of the sun going in, do you know what I mean?'

'Of course.'

'Jeans pockets have got a lot to answer for.'

We went upstairs and straight into our bedroom. We lay on the bed. 'And then when Andrew talked about Diana, said that Alison's mother was called Diana, I was nearly sure. I didn't want to be. I suppose I realized then that I didn't want to know who'd abducted me.'

'The ship in the bottle?' I said.

'I told you I had this memory of a boat. Because it was on the coast, it was the seaside, everyone thought that meant I'd been taken somewhere in a boat. Small children talk about boats, not ships, but what I remembered was that ship in a bottle.'

The china birds, Alison said, they had brought with them from their home because they *were* home to her. It upset her a lot when one of them was broken. The ship in the bottle she hadn't seen for years until she saw it again here, in 4E, on a shelf in the bedroom that was to be Jason's. She liked to believe Louis Robinson had put it in there for Jason, but probably that was only wishful thinking. Her mother had given it to Louis's late wife Helen on one of her visits to London because Helen had admired it on one of *her* visits to Cornwall. It was here that Andrew had interrupted. I realized then that he hadn't known, that Alison had never told him. Had she thought he wouldn't understand?

Frowning, he said, 'Are you saying your mother abducted a three-year-old? Just snatched him and took him away?'

'Like we abducted Jason.' She nodded. 'Snatched him and took him away.'

'That's quite different and you know it.'

'Is it? As I see it, it's the same woman desperate for a child.' She gave a deep sigh. 'Not my mother, Andrew, me. I abducted Michael. That was what he told me he was called, Michael.'

He looked at her and his face underwent a radical, dreadful change. He aged years in a moment. 'I don't believe it. You're mad. This place has driven you mad.'

I saw that an abyss had opened between those two, and though I longed to know the rest of the story, the why and the how, I was afraid of the explosion that might ensue if any more at all was said. Yet more had to be said. Silver sat silently, leaning forward, his head bent and his elbows on his knees. The lamp-light gleamed on his thatch of pale hair. I noticed he had clenched his fists. To stop himself trembling? I had seldom before seen my calm and steady Silver so affected. Alison saw it too and a great tenderness came into her face. It was the way she sometimes looked at Jason.

Outside, down in the street, an ambulance siren began to howl. Andrew went to the window and shut it with a slam. The room shook. 'I don't understand.' His voice was cold. 'I'd like you to explain.'

'I knew I'd have to one day,' Alison said. 'I knew there'd be a day of reckoning. Well, it's a night, isn't it? This is *the* night.'

Silver looked up. The way he spoke was quite unlike his usual light and pleasant tone. 'Go on, please. I want to know.'

She glanced at me, I don't know why, perhaps because I was the only other woman there. She got up and sat in one of the straight-backed chairs at the table. Perhaps she needed to sit upright while she told us. 'You said I was mad. I suppose I was – then. I was twenty-three. I was only eighteen when I got married. Charles Barrie was fifteen years older than me, but that didn't make him so very old. He left me after four years, he said he couldn't stand me always going on about wanting a baby. He said I didn't talk about anything else. Even our love-making, he said, I only wanted so that I could have a baby.'

Andrew made a sound of disgust. She shrugged her thin shoulders at him. 'They told me the abortion had damaged me, it had been done by some woman who'd been a nurse, I'd very likely never have children. That was after Charles had gone. I was living alone in our house in Falmouth and one day I drove over to see my mother. She'd not been well, it was summer flu or something. I stopped outside a shop, a sort of village general stores, and bought her some milk and a bottle of aspirins and the morning paper. Isn't it strange how you remember these things? Every detail? I went back to the car and saw this little boy standing on the edge of the wood. Well, it wasn't really a wood, more a strip of trees between the road and the field on top of the cliff. He looked at me and said, "I want my mummy."'

Silver made an inarticulate sound of pain or memory. I couldn't tell which. Alison looked as if she wanted to touch him. If she did, I thought, if she just laid a hand on his arm, he'd strike her. It was a mad idea, he'd never do that, never, not Silver. She sat quite still, her hands on the table.

'Do you know what I thought? Suppose he was saying that about me? Suppose it was me he was missing and wanted? And I said to myself, I'll make it me. I'll make him want *me*. I said to him, "I'll take you to your mummy," and I picked him up and put him in the car.' She turned to Silver. 'I should say, I picked you up and put you in the car.' He gave no sign he noticed what she had said. He was in the same position, sitting quite still. 'I didn't go to my mother's. I never got the milk and aspirins and paper to her. I turned round and drove home. You told me your name was Michael. When I got you home and your mother wasn't there you started crying.'

Silver spoke then. 'I can do without the details.'

She seemed genuinely surprised. 'I'm sorry. I didn't imagine it would – well, hurt you. Not after so long.'

'Your imagination was at fault.'

Andrew seemed to approve what he had said. He nodded to himself. And suddenly everyone was ranged against Alison, I among them. I tried not to show how I felt because I was sorry for her too.

'I kept you three days. I looked after you, I gave you everything you wanted. I loved you. You had all the sweets and chocolate you wanted. I got toys for you.' Alison was crying by then. Her face wasn't contorted but the tears ran down her cheeks. 'My mother came over unexpectedly. She was terribly angry, not a bit understanding. I hadn't seen any newspapers, I hadn't watched television or listened to the radio. I'd just concentrated on you, Michael. I didn't know there'd been all that hue and cry. My mother said I either let her take you back or she'd go straight to the police.' She wiped her eyes with her fingers.

'It was all right for her. She'd had three children. She took you back. I thought I'd die, I was distraught, I was really mad then. I couldn't bear to look at that ship in a bottle because you'd loved it, you'd played with it, put it by your bed at night. I asked my mother to take it away, get it out of my sight.'

Andrew got up and walked out of the room. He slammed the door just as he had slammed the window. Alison was sobbing now, her head down on the table. Her body shook. Silver stood over her. Just as I'd thought she was going to touch him ten minutes before, so I fancied he was about to touch her. He didn't.

'Stop crying, Alison.'

His use of her first name helped. He said it again.

'Stop crying, Alison. Stop it now.'

She lifted her head. Her face was red and swollen, a wet terrain of puffs and pouches. Even her hair was damp. She ran the fingers of one hand through it. 'I suppose you won't want to do anything for us now. You won't want to help us.'

'Don't be silly,' he said. 'It makes no difference.'

But it made an enormous difference. As we lay on our bed side by side later on that night, I sensed for both of us that our whole attitude towards them had changed. Andrew we had always distrusted and, while making allowances for his situation and the plight he found himself in, rather disliked. But Alison had been a perfect woman, self-denying, maternal, enormously patient and kind. If we had lately seen Andrew as a less suitable father than we had thought at first, Alison had remained the ideal parent, so that the social services' bias against her, for any reason, seemed groundless and cruel. Now she emerged as a woman who would have had a criminal record if her mother hadn't intervened. We both wondered how many other attempts at securing a baby there had been, for we couldn't believe she had been content with childlessness for the sixteen years between the abduction of Silver and fostering of Jason.

I asked Silver what the connection between Diana Lomax and the Robinsons had been. He reminded me of his father's gratitude to her and her (now explained) embarrassment at his effusiveness.

'Dad knew Diana had friends somewhere in Maida Vale. He wanted to know who they were and where they lived, he wanted to ask them all to dinner while Diana was staying with them. I remember she wouldn't tell him. I remember her one visit to this house when she came on very strong. She actually said she'd done nothing, she didn't want gratitude and he forced her to say that she thought it was best to leave things as they were. She meant not to get to know each other any better. She asked him not to write to her and not to phone her. I remember that because the atmosphere got quite nasty. I was about eleven.'

'What was she afraid of?'

'Oh, principally, I think, that if the families grew close, which was what Dad wanted, I might see Alison and recognize her. Or I might see something I recognized from that house. Diana had moved in to share with Alison then.

'Mum was completely in agreement. She didn't want us to keep on knowing Diana, she said she and Dad had nothing in common with her, and it was time Dad realized after eight years that Diana had only done her duty, it was what anyone would have done. As for Diana, I can see it was natural for her to be embarrassed. After all, it was her daughter who was at fault. She hadn't found me and brought me back out of duty or public-spiritedness or whatever but to save her daughter's skin. All she wanted was to put a lot of time and space between her family and us Silvermans. She only succeeded by dying. Dad had gone on pursuing her with letters and phone calls. I don't think he could bear the idea of someone not wanting to be friends with him. He was a bit like a stalker, only he didn't actually stalk. When I was older I wondered if he'd been attracted by her and that accounted for it, but I don't think it was that.'

'Does Alison look like her?'

'She does a bit. I saw that too when we first met them but I didn't know it. I think it's what drew me to them, a kind of familiarity. Not that Alison reminded me of the woman who had taken me away but that she looked like Diana Lomax. I was saying my dad wasn't attracted by her. For one thing, I'm sure he's strictly monogamous, he adores Mum, and for another, Diana – I don't like saying this about a woman, it reminds me of Jonny – but she was quite plain. I expect she'd been prettier a long while ago but she was very wrinkled by then and very thin and sort of scrawny.'

'I'm thin,' I said.

'You're young. Oh Clodagh, hug me, hold me. Let's go to sleep.'

Morna came with us to see Wim. She was excited about her new man and the long night they had spent together. Her face was radiant, her eyes brilliant, and I wondered if I too had been given something approaching beauty when I was first with Silver. Wim barely seemed to know who she was. He had a drip going into his arm, suspended from a kind of hat-stand affair, and was on anti-coagulants because a blood clot had formed in the injured leg. He turned his face away from us. Our hands were not to be held that day.

After a while he found a voice. The police had been with him most of the morning. Jonny had been charged but they wanted more information. Where had the axe come from that Jonny used? How did he get into the flat? What did he mean, across the roofs? They had questioned the Asians, Dr and Mrs Clark and even Max and Caroline Bodmer, so convinced were they that Jonny must have come out of the window of another house in the terrace.

We had brought Wim several half-pound bars of fruit and nut chocolate. He let them lie on the bedside cabinet, barely looking at them. Five minutes before we left he pulled himself up a little and said, without preamble, with nothing to preface such a declaration, 'When I get out of here I shall kill myself.'

What does one say? 'You'll feel differently when you get home' or 'You mustn't talk like that'? Where, anyway, was home? What do you do when your true home is no longer accessible to you?

We kissed him, Morna and I on the lips, Silver on his forehead. I felt near to tears as we walked down the hospital stairs. I had seen evil and its results and it was the first time I had seen it. What I had thought of as evil before was just ignorance and folly and failing to understand. That day before my wedding, when I saw Jonny at the wheel of that luscious car, I remembered the evil he had done and the tendency I had to smile at his success and inwardly congratulate him on pulling that flashy blonde, all that vanished in the smoke of his cigarette.

★

If the prisoners of 4E were satisfied with Morna as a courier and temporary guardian of Jason, they gave no sign of it. They shook hands with her, they thanked her in a perfunctory kind of way and, of course, offered her a glass of the wine we were all having. She was ebullient, full of enthusiasm for the task ahead, rapidly making friends with Jason, who took her by the hand to show her his room, his possessions, the ship in a bottle. Alison and Andrew were subdued. The atmosphere of a quarrel not long past was almost palpable in that room. Andrew was the kind of man who harbours a grudge. I thought he might hold what Alison had done against her for ever. While Morna was out of the room she began talking once more about Diana Lomax, speaking in a low voice.

'My mother thought it a terrible misfortune that your father wouldn't – well, let her go, Michael. She was afraid he'd somehow find Louis and Helen Robinson and get to know them and, through them, try to get closer to her. She'd been at school with Helen, they'd been friends for ever, but after that day when your father wouldn't be discouraged she said she'd never go and stay with the Robinsons again. She got paranoid about it, she thought she might meet him by chance in the street or meet him and your mother while she was out with Helen and Louis. I know your father meant well, Michael, but she saw it as persecution.'

'Would you mind calling me Silver, please? Everyone does.'

'Oh, yes. Yes, of course.' After that she went back to doing what she had done before, calling him nothing. I had seen him wince every time she had used his first name. 'The Robinsons still came down to stay with us. Well, with her. I was in Plymouth by then, doing a Business Studies degree.' That nearly made me laugh, remembering as I did GUP, but laughing was inappropriate. 'They were in Falmouth when my mother was dying. She was in hospital and she died while they were there.

'We kept in touch. Helen was my godmother. Things changed a bit later on. I was living in the north and Andrew didn't much care for them, did you, darling?'

'I hope I appreciated the great kindness Louis Robinson did us in letting us live here.' Andrew spoke very stiffly. 'My liking them is neither here nor there.'

Morna came back, Jason pulling her by the hand. I saw I had been supplanted in his affections and that was all to the good. She kissed him goodbye and said it wouldn't be long before she saw him again. They were going to the opposite end of the world together.

'Where the water goes down the plughole the other way round,' Jason shouted.

'That's right. Absolutely. See you on Wednesday.'

He wanted to go out on the balcony to wave to her as she passed along the street. Andrew opened the window for him and he climbed out. We watched him waving vigorously, going on much too long as children do. Morna must have turned her head to look back at him many times. Alison continued on as if she had never been interrupted.

'When Helen died I wrote to Louis. I managed to get down to London for the funeral but Andrew couldn't make it. Louis went to live in their house in France after that. They'd always gone there for quite extended visits. My mother had stayed there with them and I'd been as well. But Louis decided to settle there. This place, this house, was pretty much the way it is now. From living in the lower half of it while owning the whole, Louis and Helen had just kept the third-floor flat for themselves. The lower two were sold and the top and basement flats left empty. I think Louis thought that if he decided to make France his permanent home he'd sell off the third and fourth floors as a duplex.'

Andrew had been growing more and more impatient. 'Do we have to have this schedule? You sound like a bloody estate agent.'

'I'm sorry. When the trouble over Jason started we didn't get in touch with Louis, he got in touch with us. He took the English papers and kept reading about us. He offered us this place as a bolt-hole if things got desperate, and after the caravan and the hotel and the B and B, they did. I knew the Silvermans lived round here somewhere, but what did that matter? We would never go out. Besides, it was my mother they'd known, not me, and –' she looked almost fearfully at Silver – 'the little boy would be grown up.'

'It's a strange coincidence,' I said.

Andrew shook his head. 'It's not a coincidence at all. The only parallel circumstances are that the mother of the *criminal* who snatched a child happened to have friends living within half a mile of that child's parents.'

It was true. But it wasn't so much the truth of Andrew's statement that struck me as its savage coldness, which told me that his marriage with Alison was doomed, was perhaps over. It had been secure while they lived in affluence, had a nice house and car, jobs, money in the bank, but not strong enough to withstand being cooped up together in this flat, prisoners, fearful, desperate. They were no support to each other. They each loved Jason, I could see that, but they loved him *separately*, as individuals. It wouldn't be long before each was asking him to take sides, to back one of them against the other. I was watching them, thinking about all this, again doubting if we were doing the right thing, when Silver asked very politely if he might remind Andrew that he owed him £3,890. Perhaps he'd see to it now, before Jason went to bed, since it was apparently kept in his room.

'You're not going to like this,' Andrew said, 'but just the same, if you don't mind, I'll wait to pay you until I've seen Jason on his way.'

'In that case, I shall hold on to your tickets.'

'That's your decision.'

In some strange way the discoveries of the past twenty-four hours had hardened Andrew against Silver. Instead of sympathy he felt resentment. It was almost as if Silver had been a party to Alison's weight of distress, or perhaps Andrew simply saw him as the cause of it. Or it was a case of simple jealousy, the kind that endures even after love is gone.

'It would be better,' Silver said, 'if we didn't quarrel.'

'I'm not quarrelling. I'm simply looking after my own.'

But who was his own? Certainly not Jason, who, if he was anyone's, might be said to be the local authority's. A painful thought. Not Alison, who was his wife but, I suspected, hadn't been his lover for some time. Her eyes went to him when he uttered those words but his own refused to meet them.

'It's Jason's bedtime,' she said. 'Say good night, Jason.'

He made no protest. He came up to us, kissed me, held out his hand to Silver, and in that gesture became a little old man, grave and courteous. We didn't wait for Alison to come back but left, giving Andrew a curt goodbye. I expected him to slam the front door behind us. Instead he left us to see ourselves out.

Silver was angry, with a cold silent anger. Our shoes in our hands, we tiptoed past the Nylands' door. He whispered to me that if it hadn't been for Jason, if he hadn't been convinced being with these imperfect parents was far better than with none at all, he'd have given up the whole enterprise.

'You hate her,' I said.

'Let's say I'm trying very hard not to. At least I know now I wasn't abandoned on a beach with the tide coming in.'

The first instalment of Nelima Patel's life story had appeared in the Sunday paper. She might have had a strong personality, an interesting character, but whatever she had, none of it came through. It had clearly been written for her by a journalist who specialized in clichés and well-worn metaphors. I took the page out and kept it folded up inside my diary. I'm looking at it now. What use I thought it would be I don't know. True, it told me a lot of things about a young girl who had been born in Bradford of parents born in Varanasi, but nothing very personal and nothing about Jason at all. He was not to exist until the next instalment.

Eleven years turn newsprint yellow and bring out the smell of printer's ink. The blurred photograph, a much enlarged snap, shows Nelima with her parents, her three sisters and her brother in a tiny, cramped, untended garden against a backdrop of chain-link fences and the rears of small terraced houses. The clear photograph is a glamour shot of a good-looking if heavy-cheeked young woman with satiny black hair, a pendant hanging over her forehead and a jewel stud in her nose. The headline reads: 'Why Did I Ever Give Up My Son?'

'I hope I never have a child,' Silver said.

He was thinking of what people do to children. Give birth to them without thought or care, bandy them about, abandon them, transfer them, fight over them, above all, steal them. It took him a long time to get over knowing that it was Alison who had taken him away on his lost weekend. That morning, after we had read 'Nelima's Story', he spent hours trying to recreate details of those days, believing as he did for a while that what she had told us would open windows in his memory. It didn't. All it had established was what the nature of the boat was and what the birds were. Playing with Alison, eating the food she gave him, sleeping in a bed with the ship in a bottle beside him, none of that came back. There was no enlightenment.

'I wish she'd at least admit she did wrong,' he said.

'She doesn't see it as wrong. She thinks a woman who wants a child is justified in anything she does to get one.'

'You don't feel like that, do you?'

I said I hoped I'd have a child one day but not like Nelima did or as Alison was doing now, but in the natural course of things and with someone I loved. He looked at me abstractedly.

'Maybe with me?'

'You don't want children.'

'Come back all I said. Isn't that a funny expression? My grandmother, the one that left me the money, she used to say it. Only you can't call back what you've said.'

'*You* can,' I said. 'I'll let you.'

So you can see that we were nearly restored to our former happiness. Set to be together for ever and ever. As far as 'ever and ever' means anything when you're twenty. Apart from the faint anxiety of a great sympathy with Silver and an understanding of his disturbed feelings, I felt happy. I saw our future plain and clear. It never once occurred to me – why would it? – that I had once seen my own just as brightly, Daniel and Oxford and science in academia, before the pylon.

Wim was sitting up in a chair, though the drip was still there and the pulleys and weights on his leg. He looked very uncomfortable. Silver told him that as soon as he came out of there he was to return to the flat. It would be his home as long as he wanted. Poor Silver hadn't seen, though he soon did, that Russia Road would be the last place on earth Wim would want to be in. I won't say 'set foot in', for anything of that nature seemed a long way off. Looking back, reading the diary, I can see that Silver and I never really understood Wim's feelings, we never gauged the full dreadfulness of what had been done to him. We knew and discussed the magnitude of Jonny's intent, but Wim as a suffering being, a strong carefree man disabled and broken, that never really came home to us. Silver once said he was like Samson, blinded, put to the mill with slaves, but I see now that this was just a metaphor, all right to give you an idea, not much when it comes to real agony, real loss of all that makes life worth living.

We meant well. I can see now that meaning well, which is supposed to pave hell, ruled us. It paved our lives, covering shifting sands.

I sometimes saw policemen walking in pairs along the streets of Maida Vale but I had seldom seen a police car parked with a driver at the wheel and another man sitting beside him. In this case it was a woman officer at the wheel and a man next to her. The car was parked a little way down Torrington Gardens, on the same side as the burnt houses. We passed it, coming back from the hospital. It was quite unimportant, nothing to get alarmed about. Beryl had told me a few days earlier that there had been looting in those houses and had given a graphic description of some of the horrors vandals had left behind. That would account for the presence of the police car.

Judy had told us Sean's filming schedule had been changed. It had been put forward a week and was now over. We were meeting them both for lunch at Crocker's Folly across the Edgware Road in St John's Wood. This was policy as well as pleasure, an occasion to remind Sean of all the arrangements. Now there was something we wanted him to do and this would mean his coming out from his passive role. Would he go upstairs and call on Vivien Nyland just before we were due to go downstairs with Andrew and Alison? Distract her so that we could pass down the stairs unimpeded?

Sean was half-asleep. He had been through a gruelling week of filming which hadn't ended until quite late the previous night. His relationship with Judy seemed to be getting serious. She had been down to Lyme Regis to stay with him in his hotel, even though she had seen very little of him between six in the morning and eight at night. I wondered if Silver would say anything to Judy about his discovery. My jealousy of her was past but I knew they had been lovers for a year when they were both nineteen – it had ended quite amicably long before Silver and I met – and I was sure he must have told her about his abduction. But we had all been together no more than five minutes when I saw that he was going to tell her no more. He might even be regretting those earlier revelations. The outcome had affected him very powerfully and his only recourse was silence.

The others must have noticed he was subdued. Or perhaps they were too wrapped up in one another to see anything much outside the bell jar of mutual attraction that enclosed them. Seeing that Silver didn't speak, I asked Sean if he'd take care of the distraction of Vivien Nyland. He protested that he didn't know her, had never spoken to her beyond saying hello.

'That doesn't matter. You can ask to borrow something or complain about the noise from her TV or – and this is better – say you've workmen coming in and you hope they won't object to the hammering.'

Surprisingly, it was Judy who objected on his behalf. 'And if you and those people are caught, the police will come and get Sean too. For conspiracy or something.'

'That's a bit far-fetched, isn't it?'

'Not really. It's been bad enough me taking the photos. They could find that out too.'

Sean put an end to this rather sharp exchange by saying he'd think about it. He'd think about it and let us know.

'You'll remember you've got less than forty-eight hours to let us know in, won't you?' Silver had broken his silence. 'Morna will be coming to pick up Jason at ten tomorrow morning.'

We were nearly there. We both felt that once Jason was safely gone, our troubles were over. Without him, Andrew and Alison would be the ordinary not-worth-a-second-glance Mr and Mrs Rogers on their way to spend a long holiday with a relative in Sydney.

'I wish I hadn't come to dislike them,' Silver said. 'It makes things much harder.'

For me, what made things harder was the awareness that if the social services had known in the first place what we knew, they'd never have so much as allowed Alison to foster Jason, let alone adopt him. It's very disquieting to find out that the objects of your good deed may be unworthy of it. But we both agreed it was far too late to back out. Much earlier than was usual with us, at about six, we walked round to Torrington Gardens to make the final arrangements.

I had read in the paper that day about a woman who had been sent to prison for three years for travelling with a man who had a false passport. The charge was something to do with trafficking in human beings. I decided to say nothing about it to Silver.

33

It was twilight. The evenings had begun to draw in and the nights to lengthen. It was dry but cold, a wind blowing in short sharp gusts. There would be a time of calm and then a rush of wind, enough to hold you still if not blow you off your feet. The tarpaulin on the roof of the burnt houses moved up and down with a melancholy flapping sound. We stopped for a moment to look at the now derelict façade, top windows boarded up, water streaks staining the plaster like black tears.

The police car was no longer there. We let ourselves into 4 Torrington Gardens, closing the door as quietly as we could behind us. Putting my ear to the keyhole, I could hear Sean's television, most likely a video of one of his films he had put on for Judy's entertainment. He had never let us know what he had decided to do about distracting Vivien Nyland. We had been trying to get in touch with him but he must have unplugged his phone. The voices from above we heard as we began to climb the first flight of stairs, Vivien talking to a man. The voice wasn't her husband's. We went back down. The hall, from which Sean's front door opened, bent round at a right angle at the end where a cupboard held electricity and gas meters. Hidden in this small lobby, we couldn't see the man come downstairs but we saw him step across the wide area of hall and head for the front door. He was just a man. Young middle-aged, going bald, wearing grey flannel trousers and leather shoes and a green anorak. Silver said only policemen dressed like that, a remark I thought a wild exaggeration.

We went very carefully upstairs, shoes in hand once more. There were a thousand reasons why a police officer, if police officer he was, might have called on the Nylands. I remember Liv's panic when one had called on us. Their car might have been broken into. They might have had their car stolen and the policeman come to say it had been found. Or they had had a burglary, or Vivien had lost her purse in the supermarket. A thousand reasons. The last thing the policeman had been thinking about was who lived upstairs and if Vivien had ever seen them. If he was a policeman. Very likely he was her brother-in-law or the man next door or someone from the Maida Vale Society.

Her door was shut. We went on up, relieved to be out of her range. Silver dreaded seeing Alison. He was in a curious relationship with her, an embarrassing, intensely awkward kind of closeness. There was something sexual about it which he hated. She had bathed him and fed him and, no doubt, cuddled and kissed him, yet his attitude towards her couldn't be what it might have been to someone who had been his nanny or baby minder, for Alison's brief presence in his life was illicit. He said it made him feel the way he imagined you would if you had been seduced into a one-night stand when drunk by someone years older than yourself, someone you wouldn't normally have looked at and whose character and personality and manner of speech were repugnant in the cold light of day.

'I'm making a fuss, I know,' he said. 'Ignore me. I'll shut up.'

We gave them our signal on the bell and Jason came. He wanted to know why we hadn't brought Morna. His face registered bleak disappointment. Why do we mind so much when children who have been fond of us suddenly prefer someone else? It might be natural if it was our own child or a child we've been caring for for years, but we feel it when it's a stranger's child, any child. I wouldn't have cared a bit if Andrew or Alison had liked Morna better than me or if Wim or Niall had. It must be because we know children's emotions are genuine and can't be disguised. They haven't yet learnt dissembling and subterfuge. I couldn't show my feelings, of course, so I pretended not to miss the kiss I usually got. In the circumstances, it was good for him to like Morna best.

They had been packing. You could tell by the state of the suitcases, the things already in and the things discarded, that they were having to make agonizing choices. Alison, with what I thought amazing insensitivity, said, 'I'd give you the ship in a bottle, Michael, only it's not mine, it's Louis'.'

'Silver,' said Silver. 'Not Michael.'

'Would you like one of the birds? You're welcome if you would.'

'No, thanks. Have you all got your passports? If Jason's wearing a jacket his should be in his jacket pocket by now.'

They showed us the passports. It reminded me of going on a school trip abroad, something I'd done once or twice, and the passport inspection that went on in the history room the day before we left.

'And your money,' Silver said. 'How are you carrying that?'

'I don't know. I hadn't thought about it.'

'Would you like me to change it into £50 notes for you tomorrow? It would be less bulky. I'm sorry, I should have thought of that before.'

Andrew gave an unpleasant laugh. 'You wouldn't have thought of getting your hands on it, I don't suppose?'

Silver went bright red, the way only people with transparent white skins can. But what he'd have said I never knew. There came a sound I hadn't heard before in that flat. It was like the unmusical twittering of a flock of birds, the kind that chatter not sing.

'What's that?'

'The front-door bell,' Alison said.

Andrew looked at her, then at Silver. 'No one ever rings that bell. Well, they do. On a weekday morning maybe, the gas-meter man or whatever. We don't answer. We have to send the bills to Louis. No one ever has called in the evening.'

He went to the window. The twittering began again. Insistent, prolonged, as if the little birds were anticipating a shower of crumbs. Andrew went to raise the sash.

'Don't!' Alison shouted. 'Don't put your head out!'

'There are two police cars down there. The two officers who've been at the door are going back to their car. They're talking to someone inside. A chap's getting out. He's a guy about my own age, going bald, in a green jacket.'

Silver said, 'The only thing for you to do is to go. Now. Get the money and your passports. Leave everything else.'

Down there, entering Torrington Gardens from the Peterborough Avenue end, a siren began to wail. It was a familiar noise but it sounded different, menacing, powerful, a real threat and therefore frightening. We couldn't hear ourselves speak for the noise. As the wail died away on a series of short sharp cries, Andrew said, 'Go where? Down into the street? Into the lion's mouth, that would be.'

'We'll go over the roofs,' Silver said.

Three minutes was about what we had. That was the time we calculated it would take them to summon Vivien Nyland to open the front door, come in and climb the eight flights of stairs. Andrew complied with Silver's order but he argued all the time. The money he insisted on carrying himself. If he was caught he was afraid of being found with a false passport on him.

'I'll carry all your passports,' I said, and no one disagreed. That's how I happen to have them now, the three of them with their photographs and their false identities.

'Change your shoes,' Silver said to Alison. 'Quick. Now.'

Jason was wearing the new trousers we had bought him. We had never noticed before that Alison always wore shoes with heels, most of them high. She had no flat shoes, no trainers, no walking shoes. I couldn't imagine her on that mansard in pumps with two-inch heels. Both she and Andrew grabbed a coat. I pulled a sweater over Jason's head. He was excited, full of enthusiasm at the idea of escaping his pursuers by a rooftop flight.

'We'll go out of a back window,' Silver said. 'If we try the front on to the balcony they'll see us. This way we'll be quite safe.'

Alison reached for one of the china birds, the greenfinch I think it was.

'Leave the bloody bird,' said Silver in a voice I'd never heard him use before. He went to the front door, opened it. A ghost of the twittering we had heard was coming from the flat below. Then, soon, came the clatter of Vivien Nyland's shoes on the marble treads. Silver closed the door and shot both bolts. It would take additional minutes to break it down.

Andrew had a small bag with him. It was the kind of thing that has replaced the satchel schoolchildren carry, a canvas backpack. As soon as Jason saw it he wanted to carry it himself. It was his. I was surprised when Andrew said no. He and Alison were usually indulgent parents. We climbed out of the window in their bedroom, it faced the rear and there was no mansard. Jason was better at it than they were, showing promise of being as skilled as once poor Wim had been. He shinned up over the stone ridge at the top of the architrave and began to shout that he had done it, he was on the roof. Silver, close behind him, told him to be quiet and laid a finger on his own lips. I gave Alison a hand, took her shoes from her and threw them up on to the leads. She scrambled up, cutting her hands and scraping her shin. Andrew needed a lot of help from Silver but finally we were there, all five of us, safe on the flat roof of Torrington Gardens, the long wide empty road. Then Silver had to go back.

We dared not leave the window open. Silver reminded me that the police knew the man who had attacked Wim had come across the roofs and entered by the window. They might remember that. He slipped down, stood on the ledge made by the architrave of the window below, and pulled down the sash. What he couldn't do was fasten the catch on the inside. We banked on their not noticing. The open suitcases might deceive them into believing the family was still living there. They'd conclude they had gone out for the evening and maybe they'd wait outside for their return. Long before that we'd have them safe in 15 Russia Road and Exodus could as easily take place from there as from Louis Robinson's. More easily, whispered Silver, climbing back up, because there'd be no Vivien Nyland living in the middle of the house and no Sean Francis to keep everyone dangling while he made up his mind.

'We should have done it before. We should have moved them out earlier.'

'We didn't know,' I said. 'How were we to know?'

For a while we lingered, trying to hear if anyone was attempting to enter the flat. We were as much concerned with their hearing our footfalls as with our hearing movement from them. A heavy silence had fallen. No more sirens, no police conversation, no bird-like bells twittering. The only sound was the wind. Alison retrieved her shoes, sat down on the parapet and put them on. The whole roof area was scattered with the green leaves of the plane trees, blown off by the high wind. A gust caught us now, sweeping the leaves along with a rattling sound, nearly making Alison topple backwards.

'Be careful,' Silver said.

We had had no chance to say anything about this rooftop journey to each other. It had begun without warning, it had seemed the inevitable, the only, course to take. But I knew we were both thinking of the climb down the nailhead steps on the end gable, the climb up the other side, the trek across the uneven roofs of the single house, the ascent on to the last terrace in Russia Road. Were any of them afraid of heights? Andrew shook his head, Alison shrugged. It was Jason who shouted an unqualified 'No!' and jumped up and down, waving his arms, until Silver hushed him.

Into the silence and the wind came, all of a sudden, a heavy reverberating crash from immediately below us. The roof shook as the room had shaken when Andrew had slammed the window. This was more like an explosion, as if a bomb had been detonated to smoke the family out.

'They've broken the door down,' Silver said. 'They've broken the bolts. Let's get moving.'

It was at this point that the wind rose. From a sharp but sporadic gustiness, it blew up into a gale, fierce, violent, ripping leaves from the trees. A sudden swirl of torn leaves descended, almost hiding us from each other. As it died and before the next blast came, we started across the roof, keeping close to the rear where no one in the street stood a chance of seeing us. By then it was dusk, it must have been close on seven, and below us the street-lamps were coming on. We could see them in Sutherland Avenue and Delaware Road. The gale tore at a bunch of papers stuck on someone's windscreen and flimsily held in place by the wipers. They struggled against its onslaught like living things until at last it tore them free and tossed them into the air so that they separated and floated high, borne up by the wind. We came round the back of first one chimney stack, then another, we alone, we two making a guess at what we would see. In front of us was the tarpaulin. It was still, just about, covering the burnt roof timbers but the wind had stripped half of it away so that you could see the black depths underneath.

A couple of times we had stepped across it ourselves and not felt we were in much danger. Now, because of the gale, the materials used to cover that gaping hole and protect the top floors from the weather had almost ceased to perform their function. Another few gusts like the one that struck us now, almost toppling Alison over on her high heels, and the tarpaulin would be ripped off. I've often wondered since how differently things would have turned out if it had been a quiet evening, the sky sleek and cloudless, the air still.

Silver told Alison to take off her shoes. Her feet were bare, she wore neither stockings nor tights. They looked vulnerable, white and tender. Her shin was bleeding where she had grazed it climbing out of the window. Andrew's leather shoes were less than ideal for the crossing ahead of us but at least they were flat lace-ups. Jason was proud of his new trainers, stopping to stare at them and once retying the laces. At a lull in the wind, when the storm seemed to pause and catch its breath, I knelt down and tried to restore the tarpaulin to its former position across the exposed timbers. Andrew helped me, but we had no tools, nothing but our bare hands, and though we pulled the rough heavy stuff under the battens which had once held it firm, a sudden sharp flurry of wind tugged away a corner and hurled it high into the air.

'I can't cross that,' Alison said. 'I'll fall, I could break my leg.'

Andrew was leaning over the parapet. 'We could go along the balcony.'

'The roof is safer,' Silver said.

'How do you know? Are you a civil engineer?'

Silver didn't answer. He too was eyeing the balcony, the broad irregular crack which divided it into two sections. How could fire nearly split a stone and concrete structure in two? I didn't ask. No one would have known. They were all looking at the ruined balcony now. It was about fifteen feet long and less than three feet wide, intended as an ornament to the façade, not for use. Railings of painted iron lacework ran around its edge but these had been bent and twisted, not by the fire but probably during measures taken to put the fire out.

Between us and the balcony came first the parapet, then a step or shelf of stone, decorated in the 'running dog' pattern of repeated scrolls, then the row of windows, for there was no mansard in this section of the terrace. If we were to use the balcony, Silver was saying, it would be essential to hold on to the step. By gripping this three- or four-inch wide projection, it should be possible to swing along hand over hand, arms and hands taking the weight and feet on tiptoe, just touching the balcony floor.

'We'll be seen from below,' I said.

'Not if we're quick. They're too busy inside the house. Ransacking the place, I expect.'

What made me hide the passports instead of carrying them with me? Perhaps just the fact that I didn't want to carry *anything*, not even three lightweight booklets. Or perhaps because, in the event of the police catching up with us, it seemed best not to add the possession of false passports to our list of crimes. I remembered too that story about the woman who had got three years in prison for 'trafficking in human beings'. At the base of the nearest chimney stack was a hole in the brickwork, quite a deep cavity. I put the passports inside, reasoning that I'd be able to come back and fetch them the following day.

The wind blew my long hair so that it streamed out horizontally. I felt suddenly strong and powerful, full of energy, my hands empty, my feet properly shod. Silver came over to me. The noisy wind cut off his words from the others.

'Why did the police come this evening? What happened to bring them here now?'

'I don't know,' I said. 'I suppose they've been checking leads or whatever they call it. Maybe they've found the Louis Robinson connection.'

'Not Sean, surely? Not *Liv*.' Silver shook his head, then took my hand and squeezed it. 'Let's go.'

Before Alison could protest, he told Jason to run across the damaged roof area, keeping close to the parapet. Jason was light and quick. He alone of us could do it safely. And he did it, as swift and light-footed and unafraid on the flapping tarpaulin in the gathering dark as if he were running across a lawn in the sunshine.

'Good boy,' Silver said. 'Now you take the balcony, Andrew.'

I didn't expect him to obey but he did. He climbed rather clumsily over the parapet and dropped on to the balcony, scraping the soles of his shoes against the brickwork. He landed much more heavily than a fit person would have done and the walkway shuddered and groaned as its broken back felt his weight.

'Hold on to the step,' said Silver.

Andrew clung on, raised himself on to the tips of his toes, or as near to the tips as he could get in those hard leather shoes. He must have weighed fourteen stone. His hands went red and his knuckles white with the strain. The worst bit to cross was the crack. I fancied it had got wider since he dropped so heavily. But he did cross it with painful slowness and managed a few yards more, the school bag swinging from his shoulder, his feet dragging along the floor. Then there was the business, difficult for those not experienced in roof-climbing, of hauling himself up on to the leads again. Swinging yourself upwards so that your bent legs are on a level with your head and upper body is something all children can do. Grown-ups soon lack the strength for it. The muscles of their upper arms and backs grow flaccid.

And so it was with Andrew. He tried, he made the effort, but his muscles lacked the necessary power. There was a window ahead, a window behind which people lived, but he had to take the risk of being seen and climb the architrave. He made it, hooking one leg, then the other, over the parapet and dropping on to the leads, gasping with the effort, his hands grazed and bleeding. Jason was waiting for him, laughing with delight. He threw himself on Andrew, the way children do when showing pleasure and love, and Andrew took him in his arms, giving him a smothering hug.

All this time I had been keeping an eye on the activity, or lack of it, in front of No. 4. Vivien Nyland had come down into the street and was talking to someone at the wheel of a police car. A man came out of the house, possibly her husband, but it was too dark to see clearly. Then two policemen came down the steps and four more went up them and into the house. And suddenly it was dark no longer. Car headlights came on, brilliant beams, an explosion of light almost blinding me. I shouted to everyone to keep down but Alison, with Silver to help her, had already descended on to the balcony. The beams flooded it like searchlights. The trees offered the two of them some protection, but the lights penetrated the flailing, twisting, leaf-burdened branches, in scattered rays. A beam of light struck Silver's bright blond head and made a spot of dazzlement. Afraid the end might be near, I went back to the chimney stack and pushed the passports right to the back of the cavity.

I had to reach a decision: whether to follow Silver and Alison on to the balcony or attempt a crossing of the tarpaulin. I couldn't make up my mind. If we were going to be caught, I wanted to be with Silver. Suppose we weren't? Suppose they failed to reach us before we had crossed the remaining roofs to safety? In that case I ought to get to the end of the terrace and be there to help the others down the nailhead steps on to the house that stood alone.

The searchlight had moved away. Darkness came down like a curtain until my eyes accustomed themselves to it. What I saw on the balcony frightened me. Alison was frozen where she stood, unable to move, her hands not gripping the stone ridge but flat against the brickwork. I said she was frozen but just the same I thought I saw her body shaking, a continuous tremor thrilling through it. Silver had hauled himself up on to a window frame. The room inside, part of one of the fire-damaged flats, was of course empty. I could hear him whispering quite coolly and calmly to Alison to put one of her hands on the step and give him the other, he'd hold her, he'd guide her across the crack. Slowly, after much more urging, she drew her hands from the bricks and stood, holding on to nothing, looking wildly around her.

'Take it easy,' Silver was saying. 'Take it slowly. Give me your right hand. Give me your hand now, Alison. I'll put both of your hands on the step and all the while I'll hold you under your arms. You're quite safe.'

She took not the least notice of what he said. He slid down the architrave on to the windowsill, put down one foot on to the balcony floor, then, gingerly, the other.

'No, Silver,' I said to him in a loud whisper. 'No. Don't.'

They were both on the balcony, on one side of the widening crack. I don't know what possessed Alison, I shall never know. She looked down. She and Andrew had denied that any of them was afraid of heights but she was. It takes one to know one, and I could always recognize a phobic. She looked down over the sagging iron balustrade, down through the swinging thready branches and the shuddering leaves, to the paving and the grass plots forty feet below. Pools of light lay down there and blocks of shadow. She looked down and then she ran. As Jason had run but at twice Jason's weight. One of her feet caught in the crack, and as she stumbled and pulled it free, the stone walkway began to split. It seemed to happen very slowly, to take a lifetime, as the two sides parted with a grinding crunching sound, the fissure between them gradually widening. Then the half furthest from Silver separated itself, appeared for a moment to hover in the air, and fell away. A lifetime, it seemed, it was probably about thirty seconds, just as the time it took to fall was no more than half that. The silence was broken by the sound it made landing on the paving below, a splintering and an echoing roar.

Alison's feet slid from under her and she fell backwards, her body on the intact half of the balcony floor, her legs hanging over the fractured edge. It looked like a miracle that she hadn't gone down with the mass of masonry. Beryl told me afterwards that the crash its falling made brought crowds pouring out into Torrington Gardens. Flats and houses emptied. Meanwhile, the police cars' headlights flared and the cars moved faster than I'd have thought possible, turning, snaking in and out, tearing up the street. Somewhere another siren blared. On the far side of the tarpaulin Andrew had been squatting. He got up and with Jason behind him, came to the parapet and looked down.

Children have a completely different idea of danger from ours. They think themselves and everyone close to them immortal. If they have confidence in the grown-ups in whose care they are, they trust them to take care of them and themselves. So I suppose it was with Jason. With absolute reliance on Andrew to be in control of the situation, he was getting bored with it. He wanted something else to do. The bag Andrew was carrying was *his* bag, so without bothering to look down, with no interest whatever in what was going on in the street or on the broken balcony, he undid the buckle on the bag to take a look inside, at the same time easing the strap off Andrew's shoulder. A huge gust of wind blew the freed flap back and banknotes spiralled into the air.

Andrew shouted out. He spun round, making hopeless grabs for the money as it flew. The wind was too high for him to stand a chance. I saw a purple note, a £20 note, brilliant in the searchlight, fly airily and come to rest in tree branches. But I didn't stay to see any more. I climbed over the parapet myself, put one foot on the curved top of the nearest architrave, let the other drop on to the window ledge. I turned, my back to the façade now, spreadeagling myself against the broken blackened window. Silver was edging along what remained of the balcony to where Alison seemed to be sliding towards the brink. Repeatedly, he shouted at her to hold on. She took no notice. She was lying on her back, her hands beside her, palms upwards, her legs dangling over the chasm.

Utterly silent, she was staring up at the glowing grey sky, across which the wind drove paler clouds scurrying. Crawling on all-fours now, Silver reached her. He squatted and stretched out his hands to take hold of her under her armpits. She might have been saved. Silver and I between us could have lifted her over the parapet and back on to the leads. I was watching and I'm sure I saw her edge a fraction away from him. I've never told anyone but Silver but that is what I saw. She turned her hands over, put them palms downwards on the balcony floor and pushed herself, the way when on a slide beside a swimming pool you give yourself a small shove to start the downward progress. I shall always believe her action was purposeful. She wanted to die. Her love for Andrew and his for her were over, and Jason would now, inevitably, be taken away from her. She had tried to find herself a child, she had tried too many times, and it was all for nothing. Now to put an end to it. She lay staring at the sky as if she was praying to it or making some final despairing statement. Then she moved her hands, placed them on the stone floor beneath her to get a purchase, and slid forward. With sudden swifter momentum she slipped over the edge, still silent, giving herself to the force of gravity. A swirl of banknotes accompanied her, dancing round her falling body, drifting down.

Silver had fallen on his knees. He knelt there, quite still, his eyes shut. Down in the street an ambulance had come, a fire engine had come. The men were bringing out ladders. I said, 'Stay where you are. Wait.'

He gave no sign of having heard. 'They'll get you down,' I said.

He opened his eyes then and looked at me. 'This thing is rocking like a boat on the sea.' A ship in a bottle? 'I've got to get off it.' Then he said, 'Is she dead? She must be.'

I turned my body, faced into the window again and kicked in the broken glass and the half-burnt sash. I raised the remaining sash, making a cavity in which to seat myself. 'I don't know.' I seemed to keep on saying I didn't know. 'If you won't wait for them, can you reach me? If I lean forward, can you take hold of my hands?'

'I'll try.'

He got very carefully and gradually to his feet. He was facing me. I saw him sink. I saw the remains of the balcony dip, give a final shudder like an earth tremor and tear itself away from the wall. It made a crumbling roar as it fell. Silver leapt for the window and I caught his hands. Below him was a void, a great wound in the wall where the balcony had been He made no sound but hung there, suspended from my hands. It was the pylon all over again, I and my lover on the heights, high above the abyss.

I knew I couldn't hold him. It was even harder than with Daniel. Him, at least, I had held round the waist, I had held on to his clothes, and would have saved him if help had come sooner. Now all I had was my hands and Silver's. I slid backwards into the opening where the window had been. I put his right hand on the lower frame, though I knew I'd lacerate it in the process on the chips of glass. I bent as far forward as I could, reaching for his underarm. By the time the other hand was on the frame and he was wincing, his face contorted from the pain of the the glass splinters, I had both my hands under his arms. He began pulling himself up, careless of his cut hands. Strength comes at these times, though from where you don't know. There's a final spurt that seems to stem from absolute, ultimate need. Thin though I was and three-quarters of his weight, I made my gargantuan effort and lifted him till his upper body was lying across the sill. His poor hands hung bleeding inside the black and filthy wall.

The first ladder was put up against the brickwork as he brought one leg and then the other over the sill and down on to the floor of the room. I kissed him and I kissed his bleeding hands.

'You saved my life.'

'It was time I saved a life,' I said. 'It's good it was yours.'

A fireman's head appeared in the window opening. 'My God,' he said. 'A couple of kids.'

34

I'm expecting him home within two hours, just time enough to finish this. To put the diaries away, because I made no more entries for a year, and write from memory. Perhaps to get some of the time scale wrong and put events in the wrong sequence. To remember and do my best. Even if I get things in the wrong order, the facts will be as they were.

After we had been brought down by the firemen, after we had been arrested and Alison's body taken away, more and more people flocked into Torrington Gardens. They were after Andrew's money and they went on coming for days. £20 and £10 notes littered the pavement and stuck in the trees and drifted under the wheels of cars. Some sandwiched themselves between the little leafy twigs of privet hedges, some caught under windscreen wipers. And they were always on the move because the wind kept up all night.

It was Beryl who told me this, making a story out of it that would become a legend in Maida Vale. 'They was mostly deadbeats as came. Bagwomen and dossers. Like bundles of rags, some of them was. There was one old bugger as broke his wrist trying to get a tenner out of a drain, they had to take him to St Mary's. Mind you, there was tens of thousands, hundreds of thousands, down there, untold thousands. I picked up fifty meself.'

How much money did Andrew have in that school bag? More than we guessed, far more than he had led us to believe. But still nothing like the vast fortune that was rumoured.

All that was much later. We were taken to Paddington Green police station and spent the night there. In the morning, the day Morna was to call for Jason and take him to Heathrow and thence Sydney, we appeared in court, Silver's hands white bundles of bandages. We had forgotten all about Morna, which wasn't perhaps surprising. She went round to 4 Torrington Gardens at the appointed time, found no one in Flat E and finally got the facts out of a furious Vivien Nyland, or the facts as she knew them.

They threw the book at us. I think that's the expression for when the police find as many charges as they can to level at you. Some of them were absurd, some justifiable enough. I suppose we were guilty of conspiracy, we did aid and abet an abduction and false imprisonment and we did resist arrest. A manslaughter charge against Silver was mooted and dropped. It all came to nothing much in the end. In the Crown Court we were given conditional discharges, which meant we were free but would have a criminal record for ever. Before that, we got bail.

Much the same thing happened in Andrew's case. I think everyone, even the Crown Prosecution Service, was sorry for him because of what had happened to Alison, but he wasn't allowed to keep Jason. I read in the paper recently that he had married a woman who already had two children, had sold his father's house and used the money to set himself up in a PR business. He is a tireless campaigner (as they say) for a change in the laws covering adoption. Journalists always follow up these stories, probably pursuing the protagonists until they die of old age. But no one pursued Jason. I don't know what happened to him or where he is now. I hope he was adopted, or at least fostered, by people he could love as plainly as he loved Andrew and Alison and that he got a better chance than looked likely.

Silver and I were separated, that is, our parents separated us. I went home for a while to Suffolk. Things were different from what they had been after the pylon, for then everyone accused me of corrupting my boyfriend and leading him astray. This time Silver and I were accused of corrupting each other. I was a bad influence on him and he on me. Otherwise life in Suffolk was as bad as last time. My mother decided I was a lost soul, or almost lost, only to be redeemed by getting engaged to, working for, and ultimately marrying, Guy Wharton.

For he had reappeared, still faithful, still wanting me. Mum adored him. I felt quite sorry for her, so set on something she could never have, so absolutely doomed to disappointment. Dad wasn't so keen. I once heard him describe Guy as 'any port in a storm'. Silver phoned me, he wrote to me. I wasn't told about the calls and I never got the letters. Mum used to go up our drive just before the time the one post a day came and collect the letters from the postman. Because we had no answering machine Silver couldn't leave a message. The Silvermans were so determined no letter of mine should reach Silver that they had a redirection notice put on 15 Russia Road, forwarding all letters for him to their home in St Albans where he never went. Last year Jack told me, laughing, that he had had no compunction about forging Silver's signature to get that notice. And by then I could laugh too.

I went to London to look for him. Jack and Erica had changed the lock on the front door and my key no longer worked. What no one knew or had forgotten was that I still had a key to No. 19. It was February, just before my twenty-first birthday. Eleven in the morning seemed a good time to effect an entry, as the police say. They said it several times to us while we awaited our first court appearance. I went stealthily down the iron staircase and let myself into old Mrs Fisherton's. There were no longer any signs of Caroline's occupancy. No doubt she had moved upstairs with Max months before. It seemed darker, mustier and drearier than ever. As I had guessed, no one was in. The house was empty. I climbed out of Max's study window on to the roof.

It was bad being alone up there. A pang seemed to pierce me, a thrust of pain and longing for what had been and for Silver. How could he have abandoned me? How could we have been so quickly and easily parted? The only explanation seemed to be that he no longer cared for me, yet his look had been full of love, our old early love, when he said I had saved his life.

I hung down over the parapet, Wim-wise, to look in at the window we had always used. It was shut. All the windows were shut, it was a cold raw day. It gave me a shock, what I saw inside, for someone else appeared to be living there. The old furniture was gone, the leather sofa, the scuffed chairs and the gateleg table, the old stained threadbare carpet. The walls had been painted duck-egg blue, the same colour as the covers on the three-piece suite, only these had pink and yellow flowers on the blue chintz. I could see a calendar of Venetian scenes and a bookcase containing the *Encyclopaedia Britannica*. It was enough. This was no place for Silver.

I walked to the end of the terrace, dropped over the edge on to the house that stood alone, climbed up the nailhead steps and on to the roofs of Torrington Gardens. The tarpaulin was gone, the burnt area replaced and the leads back. I looked down over the parapet, saw a builder's truck parked below and a pile of builder's rubbish in the front garden where Alison had fallen to her death. Remembering made me wince and I felt the pain again.

The broken-off piece of balcony hadn't yet been restored. I suppose they had put the roof on first to make the place weather-tight for the winter. Here Andrew had leant over and seen Alison fall and Jason, in his innocence, had undone the strap on the school bag and released the money. I put my hand into the cavity at the base of the chimney stack. The passports were still there.

They went into the pocket of the pea-jacket I was wearing. Back in Max's house I left the key to old Mrs Fisherton's on the hall table and let myself out of the front door. It brought me a small flicker of amusement to think of Max or Caroline finding that key and wondering where it came from. Then I had a piece of luck. I met Beryl coming in. One of the great things, the many great things, about Beryl is that she is never shocked and never much surprised by anything. To use her own phrase she 'takes things as they come'.

'Made it up with the Professor, have you?' she said. 'That'll be her doing. She's done wonders for his nasty temper, he's a changed man.'

I assured her I hadn't seen the Professor but had got in with a key I had no business to have. And then, with my heart in my mouth, I asked her about Silver. She could tell, she knew how I had felt, but there was no way she could soften the blow.

'I only know what his mum says, love, and as you're well aware, she's not a frequent visitor to these parts. He's gone to one of those places in Africa as starts with a M. I said to her, I just hope he's taken enough of that sunscreen, that's all, him with his colouring.'

If she saw how this affected me, she gave no sign of it. She said a young couple were renting the top flat, she was the daughter of a friend of Erica's, they were 'yuppies' and worked 'all the hours God gave'. Then she told me about the money and the people coming to pick up the notes, adding inevitably that this was all she knew and it was no good my asking because I now knew as much as she did. On an impulse I asked her if she had heard of anyone with a room to let.

'There's me,' she said.

I went home first. To get my things and the £50 I had saved from my gardener's pay and hung on to. After that was gone I'd get a job or go on the dole.

'But what are you going to *do?*' my mother wailed.

'With your life?' said Dad. 'You're nearly twenty-one years old,' as if I was already far over the hill.

I told them. I'd like to be able to say I chose the trade I did because of the pylon, because if I hadn't been so ignorant I'd never have climbed it and brought about Daniel's death. A kind of redress or compensation. But that wasn't the reason. I said the first thing that came into my head, put there by the fact that this was what Beryl's son did, the one who had moved out of the room I was going to rent.

'I'm going to be an electrician,' I said.

My parents exploded. Dad reminded me this was his own father's trade and asked me if I was returning to the working class out of spite. Mum said a woman couldn't be an electrician. No one would employ her. All this made me begin to like the idea. From coming out with something wild, a mere association of ideas, I was getting quite keen. I'd do it properly, I thought, I'd get a degree in it or the nearest thing, I'd get as highly qualified as I could. And I did. I went to college – well, two colleges – for a total of four years, and worked in the students' canteen for the last one because my grant ran out. I said none of this and predicted none of it but answered them that being an electrician was a useful trade.

September was when I began, just a year after our ill-fated Exodus. Up till then I had been living with Beryl, right on the top of one of the highest tower blocks in west London. That suited me fine. I kept off the dole and took odd jobs, helped along by the wonderful and varied references she wrote for me, and studying basic electrics from a library book on wiring and lighting. Unwise, as it happened, because I had to relearn all I had picked up.

Silver I had never heard from. I had long ago stopped writing to Russia Road and hardened my heart, as you do in this sort of situation, telling yourself that if he doesn't want you, you certainly don't want him. And so forth. I even found myself another boyfriend, an Indian called Romesh. Just before I went off to my college in the north of England, Beryl told me Silver was back from Africa but never came to Russia Road. His mother said he was due to return to university to read, in Beryl's own words, 'social services'. I thought that meant Queen Mary College. Hearing about him brought me such a pang, in spite of Romesh and my well-planned future, that I wrote to him there but got no answer.

I had done three years and gained my membership of the Institute of Electrical Engineers when I came back to London to see my friends: Beryl first, Lucy, who had got married to Tom and had a flat in Tufnell Park, then Niall and his girlfriend, who were living together in a house they had bought in a not-yet-fashionable part of Islington, and Guy and his wife. He had married his father's secretary, a very beautiful girl who had taken the job once intended for me.

I've never completely got over my fear of underground places, though I'm much better than I used to be. But I don't believe in causing oneself unnecessary suffering, so I went to Tufnell Park on the bus. It was while I was walking along Dalmeny Avenue that I met Jonny. The first I saw of him was an unmarked white van parked at the kerb.

It could have been anybody's. It's very unlikely it was the same one Jonny had before he went to prison. But women don't look into the cabs of vans. If by chance they catch the driver's eye, he'll take it as a come-on. I walked past with my eyes averted and suddenly Jonny was in my path. He had jumped out and stood there blocking my way.

'Long time no see.'

'I thought you were in jail,' I said.

He grinned. 'Fancy a cuppa or something stronger?'

'Not with you.'

I probably only dared talk to him like that because there were a lot of people on the street. He took it with an amiability strange to him. Or new. 'Don't be like that. Give me a nice smile. No? OK, *do* be like that. I've got questions for you I'd like answered and I bet you've got plenty for me.'

I sat down on the wall of someone's front garden. 'What do you want to know?'

'That Liv, the one I used to go about with, what's with her? Where did she go? And there was a big dark girl –' he sketched in the air a grotesquely curved female shape – 'I don't recall her name. I wouldn't have half minded getting in there.'

'Liv disappeared.' Judy had told me Morna had got a university post in Japan but I resisted passing that on. 'I don't know any of those people any more.' I thought of Wim, wondering about him as I so often did. 'I haven't plenty of questions for you. I haven't any.'

The amiability was all gone, the pseudo-friendliness. He stood in front of me, bending towards me, his hands on his hips. 'You've got *one.*'

'Have I?' I started to get up.

'You sit down. I won't keep you. Don't you want to know how the bill knew where those three were, the two of them and the kid? Of course you do.' He paused, smiling, keeping me in suspense, for by then it was suspense. 'I told them.' He said it triumphantly. 'Silv, he was banking on me never saying a word to the police. Nor I would've but they'd got me in custody. I told them in the hopes I'd get a lighter sentence.'

Through him Alison had lost her life, Jason his happy childhood, Andrew his life savings, and I'd lost Silver and he me. 'And did you?'

He shrugged. 'I got off. They hadn't got nothing on me. No one to identify me, see?'

'So something good came of it,' I said, though knowing he wouldn't appreciate irony, and I got up and walked off without saying good-bye.

And that's nearly all.

I had another year to do at college. By then I was having a half-hearted relationship with a fellow-IEE. And I thought of Silver every day. I was living at Beryl's again, for my college was in London, and her place felt more like home than anywhere I had ever lived apart from Silver's flat in Russia Road. One day I ran into Judy by chance. It was near Lisson Green. I had just walked through the passage above the canal that leads through from Aberdeen Place to Lisson Grove and there she was, coming down from the Grove End Road direction. We hugged each other, there in the street, we were both so pleased.

She and Sean were living in Violet Hill and had been for two years. It was one of those unhappy *non*-coincidences that we hadn't met a dozen times before. My heart in my mouth, I asked her if she had ever heard from Silver.

'We see him sometimes,' she said. 'He got his degree. I think it's some charity he's working for, but it's here in London. He asks about you all the time but we didn't know where you were.'

I was so flooded with joy and bliss I wanted to shout aloud and dance. Judy said I had gone dark red and my eyes as bright as live coals. 'Tell me where you live and I'll pass it on.'

I wrote my address down on the back of a bus ticket, adding that the bit of the Harrow Road where Beryl's block stood was opposite the turning into Cirencester Street. After that I waited to hear from him. It was quite a long time before I found out Judy had lost the bus ticket. She tried to remember Beryl's address but somehow got it into her head I was living in Cirencester.

One evening I saw in Beryl's *Evening Standard* that a George Rathbone, of Blaker Street, Brighton, had been found drowned. His fully clothed body had been washed up on the beach. There was nothing to show whether it was murder, suicide or an accident. Jonny's father had been called George Rathbone and Jonny had told Silver he intended to kill him as soon as he had enough money. On the other hand, this man was eighty, younger than Jonny's father would have been, I had never heard he lived in Brighton, and I couldn't see why you needed to be rich to drown someone.

It must have been a week or so after that, perhaps a fortnight, that the electrics in Beryl's tower block failed. A couple of men were working on it when I got home. I went over to talk to them about it and at first they didn't take me seriously but once I had convinced them I knew what I was talking about, they were quite pleased and forthcoming. (The story of my life as an electrician, incidentally.) Still, unless I was prepared to wait down there for an hour or two, I'd have to walk up.

'Go round the corner for a pint, why don't you?' one of the men said, hugely amused by his own wit in treating me like the man they thought I ought to be or wanted to be.

I walked up. Beryl's block is twenty storeys high and there are two flights to every storey. It's a long haul, forty flights of stairs. And it's not as if there's anything to look at on the way, only grey concrete and graffiti. If I had known what was waiting for me at the top, I'd have done my best to run. I didn't know and I toiled up, once pausing to give myself a Polo Mint out of a packet in my bag, the second time to blow my nose. A woman came out on to the seventeenth landing and said it was a disgrace, all councils were a disgrace, she had lived in seven blocks like this one all over London and the lifts were always breaking down. She seemed somewhat cheered when I told her work on the lifts was progressing satisfactorily.

At the seventeenth floor I wished I had taken the men's advice and gone down to the pub. At the nineteenth, for variety, I ran up the first stairs two at a time and turned on to the final flight. Silver was sitting on the top step, looking down at me and smiling. He put out his arms and I ran up and threw myself into them, toppling him over backwards and me with him.

Shall I resist the trap Silver says so many women writers of fiction fall into and, quoting *Jane Eyre*, write: Reader, I married him? Anyway, this isn't fiction. It's an account of things, as much for him when he comes home as anyone. So: Reader, I married *you?*

I suppose it was easy to guess the identity of the husband I've been referring to. There was no one else for me really, and no one else for him. He had found me (after scouring Gloucestershire) by studying a London guide, spotting a Cirencester Street off the Harrow Road where he knew Beryl lived, and putting two and two together. It was fitting that we who loved heights were reunited in a high place, at the top of a long hard climb. The next day I moved in with him, into the flat he had near Morna's in the East End. He had got rid of three-quarters of his grandmother's money but kept enough to put down a deposit on this place.

'Is that allowed?' he said, laughing.

'It's allowed.'

We had grown up. Or perhaps, as our parents had said, we had corrupted each other. They came round very quickly – in both senses. We were forgiven and occasionally visited. I finished at college in the summer, went to work for a firm of electrical engineers with a good reputation and planned setting up my own company. When I said I'd be a Stoic and learn to bear it if he had to be out of the country for months at a time, Silver changed his job and moved to Famaid. All the time we searched for Wim.

The trouble is, we hardly knew where to begin. There were a lot of 'if onlys' at that time. If only we had found out where he had that room 'in south-west London but north of the river', where he worked in the sandwich bar, even the name of his mother's family or some other relatives. If only we had asked him when he told us his story.

Sometimes we had fantasies about going on the roofs again and dreams that if we did we'd meet him up there, scaling the heights, restored to his old agility and grace. But we had done with the roofs, they held unhappy memories that spoilt them for us. We looked up at them less than once we had and we turned our backs on Maida Vale. That's why, when we married, we chose Highgate.

Both of us remembered, all too well, Wim's last words to us when he said he'd kill himself. But his leg *might* have got better, *might* have been completely mended, strong again and supple. Liv (or so we thought then) might have found him or he her. Silver set himself the task of searching for Smiths or Van de Smiths in London electoral registers, but the former were legion and the latter non-existent.

We tell ourselves that someday we'll find him. We refuse to believe in his death. Perhaps, if he sees my advertisements or reads Silver's name in a Famaid story, he'll find us. But I'll have no news of him for Silver when his taxi arrives, any minute now, and he comes up to me in the lift.

I'm looking down now from my roof garden. The taxi has just turned in. Before he pays the driver or starts to get his bags out, he looks up straight into the sun to wave to me. And I wave back and run to open the front door.